THE KIN

Duncan Williamson was born in 1928 to a travelling family originally from Argyllshire. Leaving school at the age of thirteen Duncan became an apprentice stonemason and worked steadily, gaining expertise as a cattleman and horse dealer, living under canvas close to the animal kingdom on the shores of Loch Fyne and later in Perthshire, Aberdeenshire and Fife. A powerful singer of the ancient ballads and skilled in playing the mouth organ, the tin whistle and the Jew's harp, in later life he has become particularly well known for the telling of traditional stories. Many of these tales have been recorded for the School of Scottish Studies Sound Archive; written and edited by his partner Linda, they have been published by Canongate in several well-received and influential collections

Linda Williamson was born in 1949 and comes from Madison in the American Midwest. Her early studies were in classical keyboard music and she took a Master of Music degree at the University of Edinburgh in 1974. She met Duncan Williamson while on field trips collecting Scottish songs and ballads and together they realised a critical enthusiasm for the expressive, affirmative and educative power of traditional stories and storytelling. Married in 1977, the couple brought this art to a much wider audience, and scholars, folklorists and traditional performers from around the world visited the Williamsons' tented home in the late 1970s. The Williamsons have played a key part in the phenomenal revival of interest in oral narrative which has come about in the last two decades. Linda received a doctorate in Scottish Studies from the University of Edinburgh in 1985 while Duncan has become a professional storyteller and a revered *seannachie*.

Duncan Williamson and
Linda Williamson

The King and the Lamp

Scottish Traveller Tales

*

Introduced by
Barbara McDermitt

CANONGATE
CLASSICS
96

This edition first published as a Canongate Classic in 2000 by Canongate Books Ltd, 14 High Street, Edinburgh EH1 1TE.

The publishers gratefully acknowledge general subsidy from the Scottish Arts Council towards the publication of the Canongate Classics series and a specific grant towards the publication of this volume.

Set in 10pt Plantin by Hewer Text Ltd, Edinburgh. Printed and bound by Omnia Books Ltd, Glasgow.

10 9 8 7 6 5 4 3 2 1

British Library Cataloguing-in-Publication Data
A catalogue record for this book is available on request from the British Library

ISBN 1 84195 063 7

www.canongate.net

To Granny Bella Macdonald

NOTE ON LANGUAGE

Readers should approach these stories with their ears up front. Because they are written from the oral tradition, the best way to understand them is to let your inner voice, analogous to the mind's eye, speak them. The words should ring true. As a painter would approach his canvas, I have equipped myself with a complete pallete of colour, including tints. Thus, you will find variations of common words, different 'shades' of pronunciations. And, with a selection of brushes, I have responded, realising the incantatory storytelling genius of the teller's own voice.

I heard all these stories
from the story-teller.
I loved them
with a musician's ear.
If the reader gives me
his voice and inner ear
the page will never
be silent.

Linda Williamson

Contents

Introduction

TRAVELLER STORYTELLING: A LEGACY

It was 1979 on a still, starry autumn night near the shore of Lochgilphead. Inside the Williamsons' tent Duncan's famous pancakes had been enthusiastically devoured accompanied by much laughter and noisy talk. Now, already past ten o'clock, it was time to settle down for stories. A fire gently crackled in an old tin drum, a pipe going up and out a hole in the roof emitted smoke skyward. Baby Betsy, curled up in her mother's lap, was already fast asleep. My own daughter Heather, age nine, sat cross-legged at Duncan's feet. She loved Duncan's magic tales and was determined not to miss a one. Thus began another wonderful night when I was privileged to hear a true master storyteller share the stories of his people – the Scottish travellers.

Scotland, and for that matter, the whole English speaking world owe a special debt to the travelling people and most especially to the master storytellers among them such as Duncan Williamson. At one point in the past all Scots/English speaking peoples had access to the same rich well of oral stories and legends, including a wealth of international wonder tales. But it was the travellers who preserved those oral traditions, the birthright of all Scottish people, long after mainstream society relegated traditional fare to fairy tale books for children. Live storytelling as a central part of cultural, community and family life died out first in the urban areas in the early nineteenth century. Improvements in education, better access to books, and the spread of roads and transportation meant such simple entertainment was no longer needed or wanted. However, modern ways were slower to reach far-flung and out-of-the-way areas in the country. This meant storytelling around the hearth continued to have its central place in some isolated crofts and farms throughout the 1800s.

A great nineteenth-century collector of Highland Gaelic oral tradition was John Francis Campbell of the island of Islay. He realised he had to work fast if the oral traditions of his people were going to be preserved. Gaelic storytelling had a stronger hold on the Highlands and Islands than did Scots/English tradition in the Lowlands. Even so, the art was already showing signs of disappearing in Campbell's day. With the help of local Gaelic speakers whom he trained as assistants, Campbell managed the amazing feat of collecting a total of 791 stories, many of which he published in four volumes called *Popular Tales of the West Highlands*. In the introduction to his collections, he sets out to explain the gradual erosion of storytelling. First, he says, the minister and then the schoolmaster stifled the old storytellers. Then came modern civilisation in the form of roads, railways, newspapers, tourists, book sellers. Tradition is out of fashion and books are in, was how he summed up the demise of Gaelic oral traditions.

The same could be said of the Lowland Scots traditions which had started to pass even earlier. Nineteenth century collectors of tales in the English and Scots tongues were too late to match the rich Gaelic pickings of Campbell. Sir Walter Scott in the Borders, Robert Chambers in the Lothians and Peter Buchan in the Northeast, three of the most important early collectors, were only able to record a smattering of international wonder tales along with the songs, simple legends, children's lore and rhymes that were accessible at the time. It is interesting to note what Robert Chambers said about this in the introduction to his chapter on Fireside Nursery Stories in the 1841 edition of his *Popular Rhymes of Scotland*:

> What man of middle age, or above it, does not remember the tales of drollery and wonder which used to be told by the fireside, in cottage and in nursery, by the old women, time out of mind the vehicles for such traditions? These stories were in general of a simple kind, befitting the minds which they were to regale; they derived an inexpressible charm from a certain antique air which they had brought down with them from the world of their birth, a world still more primitive, and rude, and romantic, than that in which they were told, old as it now appears to us.

This shows that Chambers, as was true with other collectors in the nineteenth century, viewed Scottish storytelling as already a relic of the past rather than a living tradition. What they didn't know was that all this time storytelling was very much alive, certainly in Scotland, both among the Gaelic and the Scots travellers. Why was it that the travelling people carried on this tradition when the rest of Scotland was decisively moving away from it?

A BRIEF HISTORY OF THE TRAVELLING PEOPLE

The Scottish travelling people are an ancient race (as they describe themselves). Though much conjecture has been made as to who they are and where they came from, their true origins have never been substantiated. It is clear they should not be confused with gypsies who arrived in Britain from Europe and the Middle East in the fifteenth and sixteenth centuries. In the case of travellers, it is generally accepted that most of their ancestors were indigenous to Britain, and probably had distant links with the itinerant families of early Ireland. As far back as pre-Christian Pictish days, they roamed Scotland as free-spirited wanderers from place to place living in caves or tents. In fact right up to living memory the life style of travellers was nomadic. They moved from site to site as mood and necessity dictated. They were once known as 'tinkers,' referring to their skill as tinsmiths. Unfortunately this term took on a derogatory connotation when in more modern times city dwellers scorned these outsiders. For this reason the tinkers renamed themselves equally appropriately as the travelling people.

Though the origin of the travellers is uncertain, much more is known about their history since the 1700s. Their itinerant life style has always been at odds with the settled community, especially in urban areas where prejudice ran rife against them and, sadly, still does to some degree. Townspeople only saw the travellers as lazy and good-for-nothing. But back in the eighteenth and nineteenth centuries travellers managed to play an important role in the smooth running of country life. Before major roadways opened up and modern communications changed the face of Scotland, the then tinkers were welcomed as news-bringers to isolated hamlets. They were basket weavers, hawkers, beggars, pearl fishermen, fortune tellers, tool and clock menders, and of course tinsmiths. They could turn their hand to any task and farmers counted on them for many jobs like harvesting the hay, berry picking and lifting the neaps and tatties. But these early travellers also had another function – entertainment. They were welcomed by the rich landowners who hired them for their fine pipers, fiddlers, storytellers, singers and fortune tellers. It must be remembered at this time that the travellers and the country hantle (the travellers' name for country folk) shared similar oral traditions and much the same superstitions, most particularly a belief in otherworldly creatures and the supernatural. Though the two groups kept socially distinct, they readily swapped songs, pipe tunes, ghost stories, fairy and selkie legends and international wonder tales or *Märchen.* In this way the travellers continually augmented their repertoires, and in passing-on their newly acquired tales and songs to other travellers as they moved from campsite to campsite, they made the stories their own. And it must be remembered that even after the country hantle no longer told stories or held to the old superstitions, the travellers continued to do so. Besides the shared wonder tales, travellers would also tell their family experiences, memorates and legends. A memorate is a 'true' story told about a family member no longer living. Somewhere between personal experience and legend, it comes closer to legend but is specific to that person. Such stories constituted a main form of entertainment, but at the same time they also richly reflect and uphold the travellers' beliefs and superstitions, thus ensuring the preservation and perpetuation of their own shared heritage.

Always among the travellers would be the recognised master storytellers. These men were honoured for their ability to tell the big *Märchen*, often about a hero named Jack. Even after such storytellers were long dead, they continued to be honoured by their families who would pass on their stories in their name. The great storytellers who performed publicly at community gatherings were almost always men. The women, often equally skilled, reserved their performances mainly for the family and most especially the children.

The close-knit traveller life as it once existed throughout Scotland began to crumble with the onset of the Great War when travellers were called up to serve in the armed services. But the irreversible damage to their culture only began at the end of the Second World War when many forms of modernisation resulted in the growth of cities and the ultimate shrinking of the countryside. Already the government had long passed a strict law that traveller children had to attend school a minimum of 120 days a year. Now local councils and landowners openly closed down their traditional camp-grounds, forcing travellers, against their will, to move into dismal city council flats. All this was done in an effort to destroy the unpopular traveller solidarity and to get travellers to conform with and integrate into mainstream life.

The travellers did not succumb readily to the pressures of mainstream conformity. Their lifestyle, living close to nature and by nature's rules, tough as it was, suited their strong spiritual and moral instincts. They saw the settled community as immoral, where people cared more about money and the accumulation of possessions than things of the spirit. Materially travellers were poor, just barely eking out an existence. On the other hand they were rich in the love of close family relationships and in the traditions so necessary for their very survival. So when they were forced to send their children to schools and their camp-grounds were closed to them, they fought back with the weapons that had always served their solidarity, now become even more precious to them. Thus it was that in the face of fierce adversity they doggedly maintained their own customs, superstitions and oral traditions – most especially story-telling.

THE FUNCTIONS OF STORYTELLING FOR THE TRAVELLERS UP TO THE NEAR PRESENT TIME

One of the key functions of storytelling was as a cultural bonding mechanism to save a treasured way of life against the onslaught of outside influences. Traveller stories (some, like the Jack tales known among all the traveller families, and others, like the family memorates and legends, personal and specific to a given family) mirrored the many aspects of their culture and gave them pride in belonging to their ancient roots. Also, the actual act of travellers performing their stories served to validate their culture, and to justify the rituals and belief systems implicit in the stories themselves.

A second function of storytelling was its pleasure factor as entertainment for children and adults alike. Communal entertainment was mostly associated with summers when different families would meet up at favourite camping grounds. Every night around the fire there was music and singing, and most men had a story to tell. It might be a personal experience, a ghost story, a strange happening on the road, or a joke tale. The telling of the long complex *Märchen*, mostly Jack tales, was a showcase reserved for the best narrators. Each teller would try and outdo the others in winning the approval of the audience. This kind of friendly competition was popular and caused much delight to the listeners. Storytelling as family entertainment occurred in winter as well as summer, and was especially important for the children. Be the narrators mothers or fathers, or grannies and granddads, children heard stories, rhymes and songs from the time they were babies. It was a way of life.

Which brings us to the third important function of traveller storytelling – the role it played in the education of the children. Many parents could see the value of their children learning to read and write and do their sums, but beyond that, the travellers strongly disapproved of schooling. They were horrified to see their children taught in school to measure success by how much money a person earned, or by his or her position on the social scale. These were regarded as destructive values that ran counter to traveller mores. Parents felt the need to counteract such teachings and stories were their teaching tool. So traveller stories served not only to entertain, but they served to pass on the strongly held values of the parents to the young. In fact it was through the ritual of storytelling that traveller boys and girls learned the wisdom of their ancestors – a wisdom both practical and spiritual that prepared them for life within their closed society as well as outside it. Stories offered rich symbolic material steeped in essential truths. Plots revealed the inevitable dualities in nature and human beings: good and evil, love and hate, weakness and strength, cruelty and gentleness, pain and joy – universal opposites intrinsic in society at large but also displayed, often in extreme measure, among the travellers themselves.

The heroes and heroines of the stories were their role models, most especially Jack, the number one traveller hero. Jack had to battle the evils of the devil and his warlocks and witches. In doing so, he exhibited traits such as respect for the old and wise, courage, faith, generosity, kindness, cleverness, self-reliance, humour and a will to survive against all odds – all very essential for a traveller's hard life. Parents wanted their children to grow up like Jack, strong and able. He is always the underdog in the stories, but he comes out the winner in the end. Young travellers were quick to grasp the lessons of Jack and the innate truths the Jack tales revealed, because they had a direct bearing on their own lives. Parents knew that if children didn't learn these truths when young, as adults it would be too late. Such lessons bound travellers into a sense of group loyalty starting at a very early age.

Other stories the parents told their children were tales about the Burkers from the days of the infamous Burke and Hare. Many a family memorate was told of a relative's near escape from the Burkers who, it was believed, murdered unsuspecting travellers in lonely camps at night in order to sell their still-warm bodies to the medical schools. Besides providing a lesson in how to face danger and outwit an enemy, such tales were used by parents to deter children from wandering away from camp or having anything to do with strangers.

So it was that stories were the teaching tools of the parents. It was no wonder that children learned more at home than ever they did at school where, more often than not, they were badly treated and made to feel like outcasts by both the teachers and the other pupils.

Now there was a fourth function related to the first one. Keeping traditional stories alive was one way to ensure the preservation of the traveller culture and especially its sense of family and history. The stories and their remembered narrators kept travellers in touch with their roots. Duncan, for example, when he is telling stories publicly, always credits past storytellers from whom the stories were passed down. This process of giving recognition and honour to those of a bygone era, of deliberately linking with the past, helps to bind travellers of the present with the spirits of those who have gone before and ensure a living, unbroken heritage.

So it came about that after the demise of storytelling in mainstream society, it was the travellers who continued telling the old stories, quietly and practically unknown to the settled community. They became the custodians of a tradition which has been honoured again in Scotland only in recent years. How did this resurgence happen?

THE SCHOOL OF SCOTTISH STUDIES

In the early 1950s, collectors of oral tradition working in The School of Scottish Studies, among them Dr Hamish Henderson, were busy in the field trying to record the remaining fragments of traditional Gaelic and Scots lore, including ballads and bothy songs, local legends and pipe and fiddle tunes. As far as the long wonder tales were concerned, folklorists believed they were no longer to be found among Scots/English speakers in Scotland. Even among Highland Gaelic speakers, collectors considered themselves fortunate to find the occasional remembered mythic legend as passed down originally from Ireland, or a recognised wonder tale as once recorded by John Campbell. Then it happened that on a ballad hunt in the North-east and in Aberdeen itself in 1953, Hamish Henderson was led to the late Jeannie Robertson, possibly the greatest traditional ballad singer Scotland has ever produced. Hamish was immediately struck by her fabulous natural voice and equally impressed with her incredible repertoire of songs. It wasn't until months later in the summer of 1954 that it occurred to him to ask her for stories. Without hesitation she told him a version of the international wonder tale known as 'The Dragon Slayer' (AT 300).

As Hamish put it: he knew then that he was standing at the edge of a newly opened subterranean treasure house.

And so the doors, later to become flood gates, of the guarded mine of traveller stories were at last opened. Next came the discovery by Maurice Flemming, also from the School, of the amazing Stewart family of Blairgowrie – Belle, her husband Alec, his sister Bella Higgins, his brother John and their cousin Willie MacPhee– all travellers with stories to tell. In the following years others such as Betsy Whyte and her husband Bryce, and Jeannie Robertson's nephew Stanley, added their stories to the growing archive of the School. But one master storyteller in particular was to provide the greatest repertoire of them all.

IN CONVERSATION WITH DUNCAN WILLIAMSON, COLLECTOR AND MASTER STORYTELLER

Duncan Williamson was born to storytelling. When he was a young boy in the 1920s he was one of a family of 16 (three children died) and lived in a big tent in the great woods of Furnace owned by the Duke of Argyll. He learned most of his earliest stories from his parents and his mother's mother Bella McDonald. Duncan remembers his wee granny as keeping enticing things for children in her apron pocket and always smoking her clay pipe. But best of all she was a wonderful storyteller and told tales she heard from her mother when she was a young child. (She was past 80 when he remembers her telling him stories.)

Duncan, like all his brothers and sisters, went to the local village school. They were obliged by law to attend 240 half-day sessions each year. As a pupil he did well, though for him his important learning did not come from school.

> We used tae work with my faither on the farms and I learned my education there. And when I left home I

got wee jobs with the farmers and slept in the barns. Or the hay shed. Or the aul bothy. It wis the auld farmer's wife and the farmers gave me my education. All the teachers at school taught me was my A,B,Cs and tae write. But as far as my education it was my family, the stories, the songs, and the music and the ballads that came from my people from my granny and grand-faither, and stories I learned from the local people.

Duncan especially liked the Jack tales he heard from his father and other travellers. Jack tales were popular with his people, and one or two could be found in practically every family repertoire.

Jack was the great man. They looked up tae him. And naturally that's why if they wanted tae tell a story, even if the chap in the story's name wasnae Jack, then it became Jack tae the travellers, because it was their man, their hero, they visualized themsels as Jack, the only way they could compete and be superior to the settled community, tae the landowners and farmers, wis be somebody. So in their beliefs they were Jack. That's why there's so many Jack tales.

According to Duncan the most important gift traveller parents can give their children is not material possessions, easily lost and quickly forgotten, but stories and songs. These are true treasures that help keep alive the memory of parents and grandparents, and bind living travellers with their rooted past.

They gave (their children) tales and songs that they had heard from their forebearers. They would say, I remember my auld faither tolt me this. It's always the remembrance of the auld folk. As long as they are there in their stories, they're alive. We can bring them back. And with me telling you a story I can visualise in my

> mind my faither sittin there. I remember his pipe, putting a coal tae his pipe. And my mother sittin there. I'm building up a picture and memory. I can remember my granny sittin there, a wee bone comb, there's nae but three teeth in it. She's sittin and telling me stories. You think when a person's gone, he's gone. But travellers are never gone. They may be done in body, but they're still here in spirit. Because naebody dies in traveller tradition. They're always here.

Duncan started telling stories when he was still a child. He remembers well the time he told his first one. He was seven and his teacher asked him to look after the infants for the afternoon.

> My first story ever was the fox and the crow up the tree wi a bit o cheese. And the children was so quiet listenin tae me telling that story that the teacher slipped in tae see why they was so quiet. I says, I'm telling a story, I says, they're enjoyin it. And I tolt them another story – the stories my faither and mother and my granny tolt me. So I took an interest in stories ever after that.

Throughout his childhood Duncan was learning and squirreling away stories in his mind, not only stories from his family and other travellers, but from neighbours and people he met when his father would take the family camping at Loch Fyne while he worked at odd jobs on the farms.

When Duncan was thirteen he left school and began to work for Neil MacCallum, a skilled stonemason and drystone dyker. During the three years of their association, Neil passed on all his Gaelic stories (in English) to Duncan. This was the start of Duncan's serious collecting which led him through Argyll, Perthshire, Inverness-shire, Fife and Ayrshire, the Northeast and even across to the Hebrides.

> I've been collecting stories for about 60 years. I collected stories from travellers and the local fishermen. I travelled to the Hebrides and collected stories there. Went to the *ceilidhs*. Told one story and left with two, and left with three.

Now his repertoire, unmatched by any traditional storyteller today, runs to over 700 tales and among his collection there are more than 100 international tale types. Looking back to the 1950s, when the early collectors from the School of Scottish Studies identified less than 30 tale types existing in the English language, you can understand what a rich contribution the travelling people and most especially Duncan Williamson have made to the preservation and perpetuation of Scottish traditional culture and what a great debt we owe them.

Barbara McDermitt

FIRESIDE TALES OF THE TRAVELLER CHILDREN

The Cockerel and the Fox

I remember my daddy telling me this wee story. Och, the cracks and tales they used to tell round the camp-fires long ago, there were hundreds and thousands of them. Parents would take turns, you see, telling stories, and we children used to sit and listen curled up to the fire.

ON this farm there was a big cockerel. And this cockerel had a wife an about half a dozen o' wee chickens. They were picking round about the farm all day. But in these days farmers didna keep nae hen-houses or nothing. And the cockerel was ay telling the hen, 'Look, you'd better keep an eye to these wee weans! Keep an eye to them because you ken the foxes an things comin down from the hill would snap you awa in a minute. An eagles! I cannae be guarding you all the time, ye ken,' he said to the hen. 'I've got to scrape an look for my bit livin the same as you.'

She said, 'I'm doing my best. How about you watching them for a wee while?'

'Aye,' he said, 'I'm doing my best too. Well, I'll tell ye, they're beginning to grow now and we'd better draw them all round about us an tell them this wee story.'

So the cockerel sat down on this wee branch and the hen sat aside him. And he gathered all the wee chickens round about him. He said, 'Look, weans, come here! I want to tell you a wee story. When I was wee wi my father years and years ago I stayed on this farm too. And like me, my father was here wi my mother too. There were eight o' us. And me being a wee bit bigger than the rest, I was a wee bit flyer than the rest o' them.' Now all the wee chickens were sitting listening on top of the branch, and the hen was sitting. 'My father tellt me to watch for foxes,' said the cockerel. 'But we didna ken what foxes was in them days when I was young.' And all the wee chickens were curled up aside their mother, ye ken? And they were listening to their father telling the story.

The cockerel said, 'So my father didna care very much, he didna watch us very much. We were runnin about the stockyard pickin here an pickin there, an he never looked after us at night-time or a haet.[1] My poor old mother, she looked after us better than him. But anyway, down cam a fox yin night – snapped ane o' my brothers awa. Now there were only seven o' us left. My mother went into an awful state, but my father didna bother so much. Man, my father was a fool! But on the farm where we stayed was a big spruce tree, and every night we used to climb up on a branch an sit on a branch so that nae beast could get us, me an my brothers and sisters.

'But yin night we were just going to hop on a branch when down came the fox and nicked awa another brother belongin to me! Now there were only six o' us left. And I was the only laddie. But I was a wee bit older than the rest. But my father was a fool! We all hopped up on the branch at night. My mother gathered us all together and took us up on this branch, here we were sittin. We looked down just on this moonlit night – here's a fox comin. And he came right in below the tree where we were all sittin. He stopped. He cracked to my father.

'He said to my father, "What are ye doin sittin up there? Come on down, man, and hae a wee bit crack! I'll tell ye where I was, and you can tell me what you've been doin all day."

'But my father being kind o' soft-wittit, he hopped down on another lower branch, an he's cracking away to the fox. An him an the fox got to be good pals.

'Fox said, "Man, I keep stretchin my neck to tell ye a wee

1 a haet – nothing at all

story. Can ye no come down a wee bit closer so's I'll no need to reach up to crack to ye?"

'My father hopped down to another branch. So him an the fox cracked away again for another long while. But the fox sat that way, an he coaxed an he coaxed an he coaxed till he got my father down, right down to the last low branch. And he says to my father, "Listen, I'll tell ye another wee story."

'My father got interested an he hopped down aside him. That's the last time I ever saw my father! The fox went away wi him. Now my mother was left wi the wee weans and she had to rear us all up her ainsel. My sisters were sellt. But I was the only brother and I was kept.

'Now,' says the cockerel, 'I'll no be so silly as what my father was! Come on, it's gettin kind o' gloamin. Come on, we'll go to the tree.'

He hops up the tree. He's sitting in the tree . . . first thing comes down is a fox! He says to the hen, 'Look, look comin down there – a fox! Get the weans hopped onto the next branch. I'm no as soft as my father was,' this big cockerel said.

In comes the fox, stops below the tree. 'Aye,' he says, 'it's a fine night.'

'Aye,' says the cockerel, 'it's a fine night.'

Fox said, 'Eh, what's about comin down for a wee crack?'

'Na, no me,' Cockerel said, 'I'm no comin down for nae crack. It's too cold down there more the night. The moon's too bright, you never ken who's knockin about . . . dangerous folk.'

'Dangerous folk!' he said. 'There's naebody here to speak to[1] ye, man. It's only me, a wee fox who wouldna speak to ye – I wouldna touch ye!'

'Aye,' he said, 'ye never ken who would touch ye – you could be as bad as the rest.'

'Na, na,' Fox said, 'I wouldna touch ye. Come on down!

1 speak to – trouble

I'll tell ye a wee story, where I've been and where I've no been, and who I've seen, how many folk I've seen.'

Cockerel said, 'Did ye see yin body passin here a minute ago?'

'No,' he said, 'I never seen nae— who was it?'

He says, 'A man wi a gun an two dogs passed there just now, passed by this tree a wee minute ago. I dinna ken what he was lookin for.'

'Ah,' Fox said, 'he might be lookin for me! It's a good job you didna come down. If I'd hae got ye down here, you would hae never hae got back!' And that's the last o' the wee story.

The Fox and the Goat

An old uncle of mine, Sandy Reid, told me this old tale on the shores of Loch Fyne when I was only about five years old. He was a great story-teller who travelled every summer to Argyll.

IT was a fine summer's morning and the old fox wakened in his den. He stretched himself. He'd had a great supper the night before in the rocks, and where he had his den was warm and hot. He felt thirsty, so he said, 'I must get up and go and have a drink in the first little brook that I come to because I am very thirsty this morning.'

He came out and stretched himself again. It was the middle of June and already the rocks were hot with the sun. So he went to look for a drink in the first stream that he came to, but all the streams were dry. The sun had dried them all up, and the fox wandered for nearly half a day but couldnae find a drink. He got more thirsty; the further he went the thirstier he got. So he said, 'I must find a drink some place!' But no. He searched as far as he could – all the water was dried up – no drink. So he sat down and his tongue was hanging out dry.

He thought and he thought, where was the nearest pool or lake or stream that he could get to without being seen? He said, 'There is only one place . . . that is down at the farm. And down at the farm there lives my enemy, the farmer. If he sees me he will shoot me because farmers do not like foxes running about their farms. They are afraid of us killing their hens.' But finally the thirst got the better of him and he made his way down to the farm.

Now in those bygone days the farmers didnae have any

water inside the houses. They had these wells outside the farm. And on the wells they had what you call a 'windlass' with a rope and two buckets: this rope lowered one bucket down and you pulled it up; then you reversed it and lowered the other bucket down, and pulled it up. As one bucket went down the other one came up.

The fox crawled his way down to the farm hiding himself as much as possible. Finally he made his way to the well thinking that the farmer would have left a wee drop water in the bucket. When he landed there the two buckets were dry. One was down in the well and the other bucket was up at the top. He looked down into the well, he saw the beautiful clear crystal water. He longed for one taste of that water. He was not hungry, he was thirsty.

And he thought and he thought, 'How can I get a drink? Because I can't do what the farmer does, wind the handle and call up the bucket, wind it up. Probably if I jumped in the bucket it would take me down into the well, then I could drink until my heart's content.' At last he decided the only way he was going to get a drink was to jump in the bucket.

So he jumped in, and the weight of him took the bucket right into the well, which was about ten feet down from the ground. The bucket landed right side up in the well. And the fox leaned over and he licked, he licked and he licked – all this beautiful clear water – until he was finally contented. He lay in the bucket fully contented . . . then it dawned on him. He looked up, he could see the sun shining above him in the well.

'Now,' he says, 'I am a silly old fox. I was so dry and thirsty that I never gave it a thought: I foolishly jumped in the bucket, and now I am down in the well how am I going to get up? How am I going to get out of this bucket? There is no way I'm going to climb up there! And the first person that is going to come along will be the farmer, he is going to wind up the bucket for water. And sure enough if he gets me in his bucket he is going to shoot me! Because farmers do not like foxes very much, we are farmers' enemies.' Now he begins to get worried. He sits and he sits, he sits in the bucket; the day passes by. He knows from past experience that the farmer always comes late in the evening for two buckets of water.

But unknown to him an old goat belonging to the farmer was having the same trouble: he was thirsty with the sunshine and he too wanted a drink. He knew that the farmer always drew water from the well, and after having searched all round the farm he thought, 'There is only one place I'll get a drink – that is at the well. Because the farmer always leaves a little water in his bucket.' So the old goat made his way to the well. (This was an old goat the farmer had had for years, a pet for his children. And it just wandered around the farm doing what it pleased.)

When he landed at the well, one bucket was up and the other was down. He looked in the bucket and there was nothing – it was dry. Then he looked into the well: what he saw was old Mr Fox sitting in the bucket.

Now the fox was sitting looking up and the goat was at the top looking down. Now the fox and the goat were good friends, because all animals really are; they never really hurt each other unless they want something to eat. That is the only time they kill, when they need something to eat.

So the old goat looked down and said, 'Hello, Mr Fox!' in the best voice he could put on.

And the fox looked up surprised, because he thought it was the farmer at first. He said, 'Hello, Mr Goat!' Then he thought, 'I will have to work something here, I'll have to work up a fast plan.'

The goat said, 'What are you doing down there, Mr Fox?'

And the fox said, 'Oh, Mr Goat, you have no idea how lovely it is down here in this beautiful well beside this lovely clear water.' The old goat's tongue is hanging out for a drink – he's really thirsty. 'You have no idea how the shade is so cool,' said the fox; 'there is no sunshine. The well is so lovely and the water so cool, I just want to stay here for ever and ever and ever!'

The goat said, 'I'm so thirsty, Mr Fox. I wonder how could I get a drink?'

And the fox said, 'I cannae give you a drink because I am enjoying myself too much. I cannae give you a drink!'

'Well,' the goat said, 'Mr Fox, please try to help me – I'm thirsty! I can hardly stand it any more.'

'Well,' the fox said, 'seeing you are a great friend of mine and you and I have never been enemies, why don't you join me? Then both of us can sit in the well and we can talk, have a nice good crack and have a good drink!'

'How can we do that?' said the goat.

'Well,' said the fox, 'there is no problem. All you need to do is jump in the bucket and come down beside me!'

So the goat said, 'Do you think I could manage it?'

'Och, that is no trouble! If I can do it you can do it – you are bigger than me and heavier than me, Mr Goat. And if I can jump in the bucket . . .' (because they were large wooden buckets, ye know, and they held about four or five gallons of water).

So the goat climbs into the bucket. It is just poised above the well, and with the weight of the goat – down goes the bucket into the well. When the goat's bucket goes into the well, up goes the fox's because the fox is lighter than the goat. And the goat's bucket splashes in the top of the water. The goat is no worrying – he is leaning over and licking up, drinking up this beautiful water.

Now, when the fox's bucket goes up the fox is so glad he jumps out when it reaches the top. He stands for a wee while; he looks down at the goat. The goat is busy drinking away. Until the goat has drunk enough the fox waits, because he knows fine he is free and has plenty time to spend. He is not even hungry. He looks down . . . and he never felt sorry for the goat because he knew the farmer would not touch[1] the goat when he got him in the well in the bucket. So he said, 'Are you enjoying yourself, Mr Goat?'

'Oh,' he said, 'Mr Fox, I am enjoying myself! The water is so cool. But why did you not wait beside me? You promised you would wait beside me and we could talk about things, have a nice long talk!'

'Well,' said the fox, 'I am really sorry. But you see, your weight was the cause of the trouble, because when you went in the bucket you were so heavy that you pulled me up. And I have no way of getting down to ye: even if I jumped back in the bucket I still couldnae come down beside ye.'

And the goat said, 'That is all right for you – you are up out of the well now. I've had my drink, now I would like to get up and get something to eat.'

'Well,' the fox said, 'Mr Goat, I will have to get on my way. I can't tarry any longer, because you know what happens to me if the farmer comes and finds me here – he will shoot me!'

And then the goat said, 'What about me, Mr Fox? I am your friend. You are not going off to leave me here all by myself in this well?'

The fox said, 'There is not much I can do about it.'

'Please, please tell me – what can I do?' pleaded the goat.

So the fox looked down. He said, 'Well, Mr Goat, there is only one thing I can tell you . . .'

'Tell me, please!' said the goat. 'Tell me please!'

The fox said, 'Just sit in the bucket and wait till a *silly old goat* comes along and jumps in the other bucket! Then you will probably get up here where I am right now!' At that the fox strutted off home to his den in the rocks. And that is the last of my story.

1 touch – harm

Lion and the Four Bulls

Now the next story I'm going to tell ye is a very old story. There's a lot o' folk tell it in different ways, ye know. But I heard this one from my father, who told it to me a long time ago.

NOW there was this lion. And he was out hunting in the forest when he spied four bulls grazing peacefully together in a corner of this little field in the middle o' the wood. So him being an old lion, things were very bad wi him and he couldna catch any younger animals. He knew fine that he wouldna be able to tackle the four bulls by himself. He just sat down and said to himself, 'Well, I'll have to be cunning here, I'll have to plan . . .' And like any other animal lions can be cunning if they really try. So he raiked his brains. 'There's only one thing for it,' he said, 'I'll just have to wait till I get one bull away from the others a wee bit, get a wee talk to him and see what I can do. If I can get them separated from each other, I can manage them one by one. But I'll never manage them all together.'

So he kept guard on the four bulls, an they kept grazing beside each other. They were the best o' pals these four bulls, kept good company, slept beside each other at night and grazed beside each other every day. They were good friends these four bulls.

But anyway, the lion comes down this one morning as usual and he spies three bulls, just the three. He says to himself, 'Now's my chance. I wonder where the other one is?' So by sheer good luck for the lion, bad luck for the bull, it had wandered a wee bit away from the rest. Up goes the lion to the bull.

And the bull saw the lion coming, he just stood. He didna worry, he wasna afraid o' him.

'Good morning,' says the lion to the bull.

'Good morning,' says the bull. 'Ye're far off yer hunting grounds this morning.'

'I am,' he said. 'In fact, I wouldna hae been here if I hadna come to see you!'

'See me?' says the bull. 'Why should ye come an see me? Ye know, lions an bulls have always been enemies, down through the centuries.'

'Maybe so,' says the lion, 'maybe so. But anyway, I hate what's going on around here.'

'And what may that be?' says the bull.

'Well, the likes o' me,' he says, 'a lion being king o' the forest and all these things . . . I hear many things.'

'Ah, I believe that, says the bull, 'ye hear many things.'

'But,' he says, 'things I don't like are when folk speak at other folk's back!' (As you naturally know, in these days the beasts, animals, could all speak to each other.)

'Like what?' says the bull.

'Like you an yer pals there,' he says.

'Oh,' he says, 'ye mean my mates, the other three bulls?'

'Aye.'

'Oh,' he says, 'I dinna see why they should hae much to say about anybody. We graze peacefully here, we never bother anybody.'

'Ah, but that's no the thing,' the lion says. 'Ye maybe dinna bother anybody, but what about yersels?'

'Oh,' says the bull, 'we get on fine, we, we're the best o' pals.'

'Maybe,' says the lion, 'to you, but no to other folk an the other beasts o' the jungle.'

The bull begins to think, ye see! 'Like what, Lion?' he says.

'Och well,' he says, 'a lion like me who wanders about hears a few stories here and there, and there may be nae truth into them or bits an that.'

'Well,' he says, 'What did ye hear like?'

'Well, I heard,' he said, 'the other three there, I overheard the other three the other night. And they were discussing you!'

'Me?' says the bull.

'Aye.'

He said, 'You're the oldest o' the three or the four?'

'Oh,' he says, 'I am.'

'Well,' he said, 'they were just saying a lot o' things about ye I didna like, so I thought ye would hear them!'

'Oh?' Now the bull begins to pay attention, ye see. 'What were they saying about me?' he says.

'Well, they said they were just planning, the other three,' he says, 'it will soon be coming near the summer-time, an it's time youse is all splitting up. And they were thinking that you were getting too old, you couldna keep up wi the herd, an they were thinking about turning ye out, they said, an the three o' them was planning to do ye in. They said you were no more use, an ye would never manage to go out to the spring pastures an keep up wi the rest an everything. In fact, for making calves they said you were past yer prime!'

And this made the bull very very angry. 'Well,' he said, 'I'm no very fond o' hearing the likes o' that said about me! It's no so bad if it's tellt to my face, but when it's tellt at my back . . . it's just like the three o' them, them being a wee bit younger than me. But we'll soon see about that when I go back!'

'Well,' said the lion, 'I'll be on my way. But eh, I just thought ye ought to know.'

'Well, thanks,' said the bull, 'for telling me. And eh, you being the king o' the animals I know you wouldna tell me a lie!'

'No,' says the lion. 'Well, I'll be bidding you good-day!' The lion waited till the bull walked away and he gave a wee laugh to himself. 'Now,' he says, 'the fun will start, an I'll get what I want.'

Very well, back goes the bull. The other bulls were

pleased to see him, they talked to him. But he wasna very friendly to them. So he starts to the three o' them right away, and he gets on to[1] them.

'Us?' says the three bulls. 'We never said a word about ye. In fact, we were just thinking how, even how old ye are how good a fighter ye are, an what the battles ye've took us through an everything ye led. Ye led us through many's a battle against wolves and everything. We thought ye're the finest bull, ye ought to still be wir leader!'

'I don't believe ye,' says the bull, 'not one single word yese are saying! The lion wouldna tell me a lie.' And in a huff he walks away. He says, 'It'll be a while before I bother youse any more. I'll keep to mysel after this, and nobody needs to speak about me!' So he wanders away to the far-away corner o' the forest and stays by himself.

The next morning early when the other three bulls are grazing by themselves down comes Mr Lion. When the bull's back was turned to him, he jumps on the bull and kills it. He has a good feast and leaves the rest to the jackals. So anyway the day passes by . . . he keeps his eye on the other three till he gets one o' them away from the herd. And he tells the other one the same story, the same story.

Back goes the other bull to the other two, and he gets on to the two. And the same thing happens: he splits up, he goes away, an naturally the lion kills him just the same. Now there are only two bulls left. Now these two bulls are grazing by themselves in the field.

One says to the other, 'What do ye think happened to the other two?'

'Well,' he says, 'it's up to them. They ought to know better, that we, you and I, werena talking about them or nothing.'

'Oh well,' he says, 'maybe they're better off by theirsel, but I'll tell ye one thing, we were a great team the four o' us. And I miss them.'

1 gets on to – attacks with words, accuses

'Well,' says the other ane, 'I dinna ken. But eh, I'm feeling dry and I think I'll go for a drink.'

'But anyway,' he says, 'me and you hae been good pals for a long while, an I don't think anyone will ever split us up.'

'I hope so,' says the other bull, an away he goes for a drink. So he wanders down to the shallows for a drink, and the first thing – out from the bushes pops the lion.

'Well,' says the lion, 'it's a fine morning!'

'Aye,' says the bull, 'it's no a bad morning at all.'

'I see ye're down for a drink.'

'Aye.'

He said, 'Eh, what happened to the rest o' yer pals that used to be up wi' ye? I see there's only twa o' youse there now.'

'Oh aye,' he says. 'Och, stories an tales wandering through the forest, somebody's been telling clypes an tales. And the other two thought they'd be better if they went on their own.'

'Oh, I believe that,' says the lion. 'But, ye ken, stories and tales have a way o' spreading – they can be true sometimes.'

'Ah, I believe that!' says the bull.

'Anyway,' he says, 'you were just the one I was wanting to see.'

'Me?' says the bull.

'Aye,' he says, 'it's you I was wanting to see. Eh, I was just wanting to tell ye something I think ye ought to hear.'

'Like what?' says the bull.

'Well, I just overheard yer mate,' he says, 'the other day saying an awfae[1] things about ye.'

'Me?' says the bull.

'Aye,' he says, 'you – just saying how—'

'Like what?' says the bull.

'Well,' the lion said, 'he said you were too young, you werena able to keep up wi them and you were a poor

1 an awfae – a great many

fighter. And when any fights took place against wolves or animals ye always made sure that ye were away behind the rest and ye were never touched. And ye havenae got a scratch nor nothing to show for it – in all yer years!'

This made the bull very very angry and he said, 'He did say that about me?'

'That's what he said,' the lion said, 'an me being the king o' the forest I dinna like to hear naebody spoken about! So I thought ye ought to ken.'

'Well,' says the bull, 'we'll see about that, if I'm feart or no!' So back he goes. And he challenges the other bull to a fight.

The other bull said, 'I never said a word about ye, I never spoke about ye! Somebody's been telling ye clypes an tales.'

But he was so angry that he says, 'Look, I think it's the best thing that me and you should part company. I still believe the lion – the lion wouldna tell me any tales!'

'Well,' says the bull, 'if that's what ye think ye can be on yer way! I've nae more need for yer company!' So away he goes. And the next day the lion kills him. Till there's only one bull left. And he's wandering around grazing by himself, when out pops the lion and kills him.

So after this was finished the lion says, 'Well, that's my job done! I got the four o' them an I enjoyed myself wi these four. But they listened to me, but one thing they should have known: there's always safety in numbers.' And that's the last o' the story!

Boy and the Snake

There are many beautiful stories on the West Coast of Scotland, but the most beautiful, the most wonderful story of all I think is kind of sad. This story was told to me by an old crofting man who had it told to him when he was a child by his grandfather. I hope you will like it.

AWAY back in the West Coast where I come from there's an old derelict farm building, and it's out on the hillside. It is ruins now and has been for many years, for over a hundred and fifty years. It all started with a shepherd and his family, his wife and his little boy. This shepherd had a little sheep farm on the hillside and he had many sheep. And he had a little boy called Iain. Because Iain was so young, just about five years old, and because it was so far to the village, Iain couldn't go to school. His daddy said, 'When you get a little older I will buy you a pony. Then you can ride the five miles to school. But in the meantime you must stay with your mother, help your mother around the house with her work while I tend my sheep.' Iain was a very happy little boy. There was no one more beautiful and happier than him. And he played around the farm all day. He had plenty pets – dogs, cats, geese, hens – but he paid no attention to them.

But one summer's morning his father was out hunting the sheep as usual, when he fell over a rock and he hurt his leg. He barely managed to walk home. Now he could not tend his sheep.

So Iain would always come downstairs in the morning to the kitchen table, and his mother would give him a plate of porridge and milk for breakfast. Then he would take the plate and walk out the door, walk away up the hillside, among the heather . . . there Iain came to a large rock on the hillside. He took the spoon and he halft the porridge down the centre, put one half to that side o' the plate and the other half to the other side of the plate. Then he 'tap, tap, tapped' on the rock with his spoon. And from out behind the rock came a large adder, a poisonous snake – there are many on the hills in the West Coast. The snake came to his plate. It started to eat the porridge off the one side of the plate, and Iain ate from the other side. If the snake dared cross to his side of the plate he tapped it with his spoon, and it pulled its head back. 'Stay on your own side, Grey Pet!' Iain would say. Every morning he would go out and do this.

But this one morning the father said to his wife, 'Why does Iain go outside with his porridge? Why doesn't he take it at the table?'

She said, 'Husband, he's not doing any harm. He's a bright little boy an he just goes out . . . he likes to eat it by himself.'

So his daddy having a sore leg said, 'Well, why doesn't he stay here with us? I like my son to have his breakfast with me. Where does he go anyhow with his porridge?'

And his wife said, 'He just goes out an eats it out on the hillside, he loves doing it outside.'

'Well, why doesn't he stay and have it at the table? I want my boy to stay and eat porridge with me at the table!'

But the next morning, as usual, Iain comes downstairs, gets his plate of porridge and walks outside with it. And his daddy's leg is beginning to get a little better by this time. He takes a walking stick from behind the door and he hobbles after Iain keeping a little distance behind him, among the heather. He watches Iain going to the rock. He watches Iain taking the spoon and halving the porridge in two; and he watches him 'tap, tap, tapping' on the rock with his spoon. He watches the snake coming out . . . he is terrified. He has seen so many snakes on the hill in his time hunting sheep, but he has never seen one as large as this! This one is over four feet long. Iain's father is terrified. It comes up to the plate, it starts to eat the porridge. And when it finishes its side it tries to cross the plate, an Iain hits it with the spoon – it pulls its head back!

He quickly hobbled back home to his wife and he said, 'Do you know what your son is doing? He's out there, in the hillside, an he's eating with a snake, a poisonous adder! And to make matters worse he hits it with his spoon! If that snake bites him he shall die!'

'Well,' she said, 'husband, he's been doing that all summer long, and if that snake was going to bite him it would have done so a long time ago. I think ye should leave him alone.'

'I'm not having my son eating with a snake, I'm not having my son eating with a snake! That terrible adder,' he said, 'that's a poisonous adder. Tomorrow morning when he comes downstairs for his breakfast you send him up to tidy up his bedroom, an I'll take the porridge to the snake!'

So sure enough, next morning Iain comes downstairs and he says, 'Could I have my breakfast, Mummy?'

She says, 'After you tidy up your room. It's in a terrible mess, your bedroom. Collect your toys and tidy up for your mummy!'

While he was gone his daddy took the empty plate and spoon, and he hobbled out of the kitchen. He took his gun from behind the door and he walked . . . to the stone. He tap-tapped on the rock with his spoon. Out came the snake, and he shot the snake. He carried it back to the house. He buried it in the garden. Iain knew nothing of this. He was busy working in his room. His father came in and sat down at the table.

Sure enough, soon Iain comes downstairs once more. He says, 'Mummy, can I have my breakfast, please?' And his mother gives him a plate of porridge and milk and his spoon. He hurriedly – happy little boy – walks away through his little path through the heather.

His father turns round to his wife and says, 'He's in for a big surprise when he goes back. I shot the snake.'

'Well,' she said, 'I don't think you should have done that.'

Iain goes to the rock once more with his spoon, and he halves the porridge in two as usual – one side to that side, one side to the other side o' the plate – then 'tap, tap, tap' on the rock. And he waits.

No answer.

He taps again with his spoon.

No answer.

Three times he taps. No snake. He says, 'Well, my pet, you seem to not be hungry this morning.' And he lifts the plate, porridge and all, he walks back with it. He puts it on the table.

His mummy says, 'What's the trouble, Iain? Are ye not having yer breakfast this morning?'

He says, 'I don't feel very hungry.' He walks up to his bedroom.

The next morning he went with his porridge to the stone. The same thing happened. He went with it for three times. Nothing happened. On the fourth day Iain did not come downstairs.

By this time his daddy's leg is better. He says, 'What's the trouble? Where is Iain this morning?' He goes up to get Iain.

Iain is just lying in bed staring at the ceiling. He would not talk to his father in any way. Nor he would not talk to his mother in any way. He just lay there. He completely lost the will to live, in any way. He lay there for nearly a week without food or drink.

His father said, 'This cannot go on.' So he took his pony, he rode down to the little village and brought back the doctor.

The doctor came in and asked the trouble. They told

him, but they never mentioned the snake. The doctor went up to Iain's bedroom, he examined him in every way. He could find nothing wrong with him. But Iain wouldn't even talk to the doctor, he just lay staring into space. Then the doctor came down and he said to Iain's mother and father, 'I can't seem to see anything wrong with yer son. He just seems to have lost the will to live. Has anything happened to upset him in any way?'

And it was Iain's mother who said, 'Prob'ly it was the snake.'

The doctor said, 'Snake? What snake? Tell me about it.' Iain's father told the doctor about the snake he had shot.

The doctor was very upset. He said, 'Ye know, children are very queer sometimes, and they love to choose their own pets in their own time.' And he said, 'I'm sorry, ye should not have touched the snake. I don't think it would ever have touched him in any way. How long had he been feeding this snake?'

She said, 'He'd been doing this since the beginning of summer, an the summer before that when he was only four. I never knew anything about the snake. But he was a quite happy child, an I just let him take his breakfast outside every morning,' said his mother.

'Well,' the doctor said, 'I think you've made a grave mistake. I'll come back and see him again, but I don't think there's very much I can do for yer son. He'll have to come out of it himself.'

But Iain lay in bed and he just pined away. He finally died. And his mother and father were so upset, they sold the farm and moved off to another part of the country. The funny thing was, no one seemed to want the farm after the story spread from the doctor.

The farm stood there till it became a ruin. But Iain's daddy never forgave himself for shooting the queerest pet that any child could have – a poisonous snake. And that, children, is a true story that happened a long time ago on the West Coast of Scotland. If you were there with me today I could lead you to the same place, to the ruins of the farmhouse; I've passed it many times on my travels through the West Coast.

The Dog and the Peacock

When I was young we were very very poor and we never got anything for Christmas, nothing at all. Probably my mother was just around the doors begging a little bit of supper for us at night-time; and that was our first meal, the only meal of the day. To us Christmas was just another day . . . glad my mother was home, her feet were wet and she dried them at the fire. My mother would dry her shoes by the fire and hang up her stockings for the next day. Probably she'd been away among the snow.

And Daddy would say, 'Well, children, thank God it's Christmas. We havenae got very much tae give ye for Christmas, but I'll tell ye what, I'll give ye something that'll be a lot better tae ye than a present – I'll give ye a nice wee story for Christmas.' And we sat round his feet by the fireside. The thing about our fire was it was right in the middle of the tent, and everybody could sit round about it.

THE old collie dog was tired. He'd wandered around the village all day seeking little pieces of meat to eat from anyone who would help him. He'd wandered the village in fact for years. No one owned him, he was just to the village folk 'the old collie'. He was an old dog, disregarded, forgotten by his owner. But he was loved and respected in the village. Whenever anyone had a tidbit to spare, it was always the old collie who would get something to eat. He slept here and slept there, he was a friend to the children, a friend to everybody. All the cats, dogs, everyone in the village knew him. He never touched no one.

But one particular evening the old collie got up from his

sheltering place where he lay and it was cold. He thought to himself, 'I'll wander down the village and see if my old human friends will give me something to eat.' He wandered round the village and round the village two or three times, but lo and behold he never met a soul because everyone was indoors. The evening was getting darker and everyone had their Christmas trees up, their Christmas lamps going. And the old collie thought to himself, 'It must be Christmas, people are all in celebrating their Christmas Eve.' He said, 'I think I'll go down and have a talk to my old friend the peacock. Maybe he has something lying in his dish that'll help me.'

So he wandered down the street to a large bungalow owned by a merchant, and this merchant had two peacocks, a hen and a cock. The old dog went through the hedge, came round the back of the bungalow and there sitting on a post was the peacock. The old dog spoke, he said, 'Hello, Peacock!'

'Oh,' he said, 'it's yourself, old Collie.'

He said, 'It is.'

He said, 'You're on your wander tonight again.'

'Yes I am,' he said, 'I am on my wander tonight again. But there's not many people around.'

'No,' said the peacock, 'there's not many people around. My master and his wife and children are busy celebrating the Christmas Eve. And my old wife is sitting on an egg in there in the shed. She's sat there all summer on it and I don't think she's going to make much of it with the way I see it! And I'm just sitting here watching the moon and stars coming up.'

The collie says, 'It's a funny evening, all these people celebrating their Christmas and the coming of Our Blessed Saviour among us.'

'True,' says the peacock, 'true. But there must be some other people who are not as well-off as some of them.'

'That's true,' says the collie, 'very true – in particular one good friend I have, my old friend the old widow-woman who lives in the last cottage at the end of the village. I passed by an hour ago and her light was out.'

'Sad,' says the peacock, 'sad – why some people have so much and other people have so little.'

'I feel sorry for her,' says the collie. 'She's good to me and she shares anything she has with me whenever I go around, though little she's got to spare. But,' he says, 'I wish there was something I could do for her. She probably won't have a fire, she'll probably have no light, she'll probably have no food and probably no one will give her a thought.'

'It's sad,' says the peacock, 'very sad.'

Says the collie, 'I wish there was something I could do.'

'Well,' says the peacock, 'between us we probably could think of something. I'm doing nothing here all night just sitting on this perch. And I mightn't go in and talk to my old wife, she's too busy sitting on that egg.'

The collie says, 'Look, are those peats you have there?'

'That's my master's peats,' says the peacock.

'Man,' he says, 'if the old widow had a couple of these, it would really give her a good fire for Christmas Eve!'

'Sure enough,' says the peacock. 'And I don't think my master would miss any if a couple went amissing.'

They were sitting talking, discussing the problem, when who should come down but the village tomcat. He too was owned by nobody; he was just a large black tom, a friendly tom who walked the village and was everyone's pet. 'Well, you two,' he said, 'you are busy chatting away again?'

'Yah,' says the collie, 'we're just here chatting away and discussing this evening.'

'Well, let me into the discussion,' says the cat. 'What's the problem?'

'Well, our main problem,' says the collie, 'is the old widow-woman at the end of the village.'

'A-ha-ha,' says the cat, 'her I know well! I just passed her house barely half an hour ago. It looks dark, there's no light and seemingly no fire on in it.'

'That's what we're discussing, that's our problem,' says

the collie. 'The peacock and I have made up a plan here. Peacock thinks that he could manage to get a couple of peats, take a couple up to the old widow-woman's house and give her a wee fire for Christmas Eve even though she has nothing else.'

'Well,' the cat says, 'she's good to me, she treats me very well: whenever she's got a wee drop milk or a bone to spare or anything she has for eating, she always shares it with me. And I would like to help.'

'But,' the peacock says, 'what good is a fire to her when she has nothing to eat?'

The collie says, 'Wait . . . all the shops are closed for the evening. But I know a way into the back of the butcher's, a secret passage where I go in and help myself to some bones. And I could help myself to much more than bones if I needed to, but I always just take the bones he leaves in a bucket. That's enough for me. But there's sausages and meat of all description! And I'm sure the butcher wouldn't miss a string of sausages!'

'Fair enough,' says the peacock, 'you do that!'

'But wait a minute,' says the cat, 'how about me? You know I too have my secrets, though I'm a cat! I know a secret way into the back of the fish shop. And the fishman always leaves heads and tails in a bucket and I go in and help myself. But there are many more things than that – there's fish and kippers and herring and everything in the fish shop. If the old widow-woman could have a pair of kippers it would make a lovely supper for her tonight. And,' he says, 'I'll go for a pair of kippers!'

'And I'll go,' says the collie, 'for a string of sausages, a large string of sausages.'

'I'll be waiting here at the gate,' says the peacock, 'and I'll have a peat under each wing. And we'll all go, we'll visit the old widow and spend our Christmas with her!'

Sure enough, their plan was made! Away goes the old collie, he isn't long gone when back he comes with a big string of sausages in his mouth. And he's keeping them high so's they'll no touch the road. Within minutes back comes the tomcat. Oh, he is a great big black cat, and across his mouth he has a pair of large kippers, carrying them nice and tender in his mouth in case they touch the ground! And there stands the peacock, a peat under each wing. 'Are you ready, gentlemen?' he says. 'Let's go!' And away go the peacock, the collie and the cat marching up the street.

Everybody was inside behind their doors watching their Christmas trees and having their Christmas Eve lunches. Nobody paid attention to the peacock, the collie and the cat on their way up the street. They hadn't far to go to the end of the village.

Now the old widow's house sat by itself and round it was a large hedge and a gate going into her garden. When up came the peacock, the collie and the cat. The gate was open. But sitting on the gate was an owl, a large tawny owl. The old cat and the old collie knew the owl well because he was another old fellow who flew around the village. He said, 'To-hoo, to-hoo!'

'Hello, Owl,' says the dog, taking care that the sausages shouldn't drop out of his mouth. 'We are bound for the widow's house.'

And the owl says, 'The widow is very poorly tonight. She's very hungry and she hasn't thrown me any scraps for two days, and she has no fire.'

'Well,' says the peacock, 'we are on our way to give her her Christmas. The collie has got some sausages and the cat has got some kippers and I've got two peats.'

'I'll come too, I'll come too,' says the owl, 'I'll come too!' And he hopped off the gate on his two feet behind them. And they all marched – the peacock, the dog, the cat and the owl – all walked up the path. And they came to the door.

'Scratch-scratch, scratch-scratch,' went the dog with his foot on the door. No answer. 'Scratch-scratch-scratch,' again went the dog.

And they heard footsteps. And lo and behold the door opened and this was the old widow-woman. The dog could see right into the room and the fire was burning very low – there was very little on her fire.

'Oh,' she said, 'it's yourself, old Collie Dog,' she said. 'It's Christmas, and I'm sorry I've little to give you.'

But the dog never said a word. He just walked in – followed by the peacock, followed by the cat, followed by the owl. And they all came up in front of the fire. The old widow-woman closed the door, she came in behind them and she looked and she saw: the dog left down the sausages, the cat left down the kippers and the peacock left down the two peats.

'Oh, my children, my children!' she said. 'You've brought me my Christmas.' She took the two peats, gathered all the coals together and put the peats on the top of the fire. 'Sit there children,' she said. 'And you've brought me sausages and you've brought me kippers. Oh how wonderful, we're going to have a Christmas feast!' She picked up the sausages, picked up the kippers, went back into the kitchen. And the dog, the cat and the owl and the peacock sat before the fire.

The peats began to kindle up. The shadows began to leave the walls, the room began to come cosy with the brightness of the fire. When lo and behold the peacock said, 'It's a lonely old house this, for a lonely old woman – without a Christmas tree!'

'Well,' says the old dog, 'we can't find a Christmas tree.'

The peacock says, 'We can't find a Christmas tree? Of course we can – we'll find the nicest Christmas tree of all for the widow-woman – I have a Christmas tree!'

'You,' says the collie, 'have a Christmas tree?'

He says, 'I have the nicest Christmas tree of all.' He says to the owl, 'You didn't bring a present, but your eyes are bright! You sit by the side of the fire, Owl!' And he says to the cat, 'You sit by the other side of the fire, Cat!' And the cat sits at one side, the owl sits at the other. The peacock turns his back to the fire and spreads up his tail – it covers the whole fire-place. He hears the old woman humming away to herself in the kitchen.

And lo and behold the next thing she walks through with a plate of kippers and a plate of sausages, one in each hand. And when she comes through she sees the light from the cat's eyes, the light from the owl's eyes, the peacock's tail spread across the fire reflecting light. 'Oh my children,' she says, 'you've brought me a Christmas tree, the most beautiful Christmas tree of all!' And she cried and wiped her eyes with her apron, she was so happy. She said, 'My children, you are the greatest little friends anyone could ever have. And now we're going to sit down, we're going to enjoy our Christmas Eve lunch.'

And the old widow sat down with the peacock and the dog and the cat and the owl. They ate up the kippers and they ate up the sausages. And the old woman sat and told them stories, talked to them till she got tired. Then she said, 'Children, it's time for me to go to bed. But till the day I die, I'll never forget how my wonderful little friends gave me such a wonderful Christmas Evening.'

So the old woman opened the door, and the dog went out and the cat went out and the owl went out and the peacock went out, and they bade the old woman 'good-bye'. And down in the village everyone was happy enjoying their Christmas Eve. No one ever gave the old widow-woman a thought, but the peacock, the dog, the cat and the owl. And they had the most wonderful Christmas of all, and that's the end of my wee story.

Tatties from Chuckie-stanes

Mammies and daddies and grandmothers used to tell these wonderful tales of Christmas around the camp-fires to their children, to give them comfort. Some of the stories were sad, every one was good. It was just the parents showing you that having a lot of things at Christmas wasn't really necessary. Having a belief and the understanding of Christmas was far better.

ONCE upon a time there was a poor lady that lived beside the forest. She had an awful lot of children, an sometimes it was pretty hard fir her because she didna have a husband. She scraped an scratched as much as she could, she used tae take in washin and sewin and things fir tae keep the children alive – she had aboot seven or eight o' them, all wee steps an stairs, ye know!

An it cam roon about Christmas time. She had nothing tae give them, not a thing in the house, but she had nae idea whar tae get anything. They start't asking fir something tae eat. So tae keep them quiet she start't tellin them stories, but the stories wisnae fillin their stomachs. They said, 'Mammy, we want somethin tae eat, boil us some potates!'

So tae brighten their hearts up a wee bit, she goes out tae the front o' the house. There used tae be a wee brook runnin past the house many years ago, an durin the summer when times wis better wi her she'd gathered all the bonnie wee white stanes, we call em 'chuckie-stanes', an pit them round her garden path. So she took her pot an filled it full o' stanes, put water on em, shaken some salt on em an put them on the fire. It was one o' thon old-fashion't fires wi the big old-fashion't arm that comes oot the side – she hung the pot on.

All her kids gather't round. 'What are ye doin, Mammy?' says the little one.

She says, 'Youse asked fir potates an I'm going tae boil ye some. I hope youse enjoy them because they'll take a long while tae boil' – thinkin in her own mind, 'be the time thae "potates" wis supposed tae be boiled the hunger would leave them and they would all faa asleep.'

But she didnae know . . . who had restit on the wind-aesole but a woodland fairy! It had landit an heard what wis goin on. An the fairy felt very sad – the mother wi all the children should have nothing but everybody else in the village had plenty – specially comin nearer Christmas. So the fairy cast a spell on the pot.

The pot begun tae boil and the children wis saying, 'Mammy, lift the pot off now, lift the pot off an see – the potates is boiled!' Mammy liftit it off, poured the water off; it was only stones she had put in the pot. All the wee children gather't round. But when she lifted the lid off there wis the most beautiful potates ye ever saw in yir life, dry as anything, jist burstin up like flowers!

An the lady was surprised – she felt that God . . . 'At least,' she says, 'I've got potates – but hoo in the world?' She says tae hersel, 'It must ha' been a fairy.' So she liftit all the potates oot an pit them on a nice plate on the table. She gave them all round tae all the bairns, and there were nothing left fir hersel. So she looked in the bottom o' the pot. All the wee scrapins o' tatties that wis left – she took a spoon an says tae hersel, 'This'll have tae be enough fir me.' She scraped the bottom an put them on a plate, but when she turned up the spoon it was full o' gold sovereigns! An she scraped the pot clean till she had a full plate o' gold sovereigns. She stood an scratched her head, 'I wonder,' she says, 'whar that could come fae? Because they werenae in the pot when I put them stones in fir the bairns tae boil. Some lucky fairy must ha' been thinkin o' me the night when she done that fir me.'

So she washed all the potates off the gold sovereigns, took the money an told the oldest one, 'You look after the wee ones ti I come back, an I'll no be long.' She run doon tae the village, intae the shops and she bought everything she could think of: decorations fir the house, yon big Christmas bells, oranges an apples, all the fruit, nuts an everything, presents fir every one o' them, ti she wis loaded an couldnae carry no more. An she still had gold sovereigns left cause the fairy had gien her plenty. She gev her children the best Christmas they ever had in their life; they were happy blowin on things an puttin paper hats on their heads. They didnae know it wis a wee woodland fairy that had given them that lovely Christmas, and that's the last o' ma wee story.

The Dog and the Manger

The travelling folk are religious in their own way. Mostly their religion comes from all the animals; animals can teach you because they know and are intelligent towards things that humans never regard or respect. The donkey or 'cuddy' is sacred to the Scottish travellers, they'll not ill-treat this animal, overload or be bad to it in any way . . . This is the story, so sit down and listen! Then you'll be able to tell it to your children when you grow up.

THE old collie dog was tired as he lay beside his master on the hillside that lovely moonlit night. His master was a shepherd who watched the sheep all night through to take care of them, because in these days long long ago there were many wolves and foxes. The shepherd had two young dogs he'd reared up and kept along with the old collie, but he loved and respected his old collie most because he'd had it for many many years. So they sat on the hillside and the moon rose higher; it was beautiful and the stars were shining.

The shepherd turned round and said to the collie, 'Old fellow, you must be tired. You ran a lot this morning, more than you should have, and you know you're getting old now. I'm sure there's no use the four of us sitting here. Why don't you go home and go in the byre, sleep among the hay for the night? It'll make you fresh for tomorrow. Me and your young offspring here will take care of the sheep.'

The old collie sat up, his tongue hanging out, and he looked at his master. He wondered why his master didn't want him. He understood the language all right, but some things his master said he didn't really understand. When the master said 'go home old friend' he knew the meaning perfectly. He thought to himself, 'My master doesn't need me this night so I'll go home.' He really was tired.

So the old dog trotted back to the small steadings and the farm where he lived. He curled up in the byre among the hay and straw that had been placed in the stalls. And his old friend the donkey came in from the cold; he was a free agent who wandered around the farm to his heart's content. And the collie couldn't remember when he'd ever seen the place without the donkey. The donkey walked into one of the stalls and started chewing on the hay or straw or whatever was left out. The collie curled up to go to sleep. He heard his friend the donkey chewing, chewing, chewing, on and on and on.

Then a little later he heard voices coming through the doorway. He wondered, 'Is that my master coming home?' And he looked out. It was still dark, but the moon was shining clear, he thought to himself, 'It can't be my master, it's not his time yet. He always comes home by daylight when the sheep'll be safe, because no predators or any kind of wild animal will disturb them during the day.' So he was wide awake and sitting in the stall one down from the donkey, when lo and behold who should walk to the stall beside him but a woman! A young beautiful woman and a man with a beard. The collie had never seen these people before and he wondered who they were. He said to himself, 'They must be strangers seeking their lodging for the night.'

So the dog curled back, he never said a yelp, never said a bark. He watched them; the man took his wife by the hand and led her into the empty stall that had little straw in it. And there was a manger above them for holding the hay for feeding the cattle but there were no cattle in the byre this night. The dog sat and he listened, he heard the man talking and he knew well what they were saying.

The man said, 'This is where we'll stay, we shall find shelter here for the night.' He looked around, 'It's only a dog and a donkey and I'm sure they won't disturb us.' He said, 'Are you all right, my dear?'

'Well,' she says, 'I don't feel very well.'

And the man rakes up the hay, he places it, makes a little bed. He says, 'I'm sure . . . will it happen tonight?'

She says, 'I think it'll happen in moments.'

The collie dog he's sitting there. The donkey stops chewing his hay and all is quiet. And then lo and behold the man says, 'Are you needing any help?'

'No,' she says, 'I'll manage myself. Just you stand there at the stall entrance and see that I have a little privacy for a few moments.'

And the man stands there . . . he walks back and forward. And the dog lies, he never says a word but he hears everything that is going on. Lo and behold the next thing the dog hears is the crying of a little baby . . . a little baby cried.

And the dog said, 'This woman, this being, this human being must be giving birth to a baby right here beside us in the stall! I have never seen this before.' And he crawled slowly round a wee bit closer, he keeked round the stall. Lo and behold the woman was holding up the most beautiful little baby that you ever saw! It had long dark golden hair. It was wet. And the husband ran in.

He pulled off his covering of cloth, his cloak, he told her, 'Use this!' And his wife wrapped the baby in it.

She said, 'He's a wonderful child.'

Then the husband said, 'We need some place to put him for a wee while.'

And she said, 'Put some straw in the manger just above where I lie, and put him there for a few moments.'

The husband shook the straw along the manger and he took this little baby wrapped in his own cloth, he stood naked to the waist, and he put him up in the manger. And the old collie dog, he was keeking round the stall, he saw the most beautiful thing he ever saw in his life: he saw a star shining through the window. The star seemed to come closer and closer and closer – till it shone right above the window. The dog had never seen this before and he wondered why such a star had come so close . . . his thoughts were on his master in the hillside. He wondered if his master would be disturbed by this same shining star. But then his thoughts changed, he heard the man and the woman talking.

He said, 'Look, we must stay here for the night. But we must find better shelter for our child tomorrow. I'm sure he will be all right, though, nothing's going to happen to him. He's a lovely child.'

The old dog sat and listened to all they said. And the child never said one word. Finally the talking stopped and the dog fell asleep. But he wakened early in the morning when he heard a disturbance next to the stall where he lay. This was the man and his wife getting up and taking the child from the manger where he lay during the night.

And the man says, 'I must go to the village to find some help for you. There must be someone there who'll give you help.'

She says, 'I feel well, husband, I feel fine, lovely.'

He says, 'I know you feel lovely but I must find some help for you and the child.'

She says, 'Husband, it's a long way to the village. We passed it through and they wouldn't give us any shelter and that's why we ended up here.'

He says, 'We'll go back with the baby, and when they see the baby they'll probably give us shelter.'

'But,' she says, 'husband, I'm too weak, I can't walk.'

'Oh,' he says, 'don't worry, my dear, don't worry. You'll no need to walk. There's a little donkey here and I'm sure the farmer won't mind if I borrow it for a few hours to take you to the village.' So the man walked in and took a rope, a halter from the wall. He put it on the donkey's head, but no saddle or bridle or anything. He lifted his wife up and placed her on the donkey's back. He went to the manger and picked out the wee child, put him in her arms.

And the old collie's sitting watching this. He wonders and he wonders, wonders . . . if his master knew about this . . . what a story he could tell if only he could speak to him! Then daylight came and the man with the beard, with not a stitch on his body because his cloak was wrapped round the Baby, walked out the doorway leading the donkey with the woman and the child. And he walked away. The collie had never seen anything like this before in his life. He wondered, 'Would he ever see his old friend the donkey again?' But he loved that little child and he wished he had seen him closer. He crawled up in the straw and fell asleep.

The next thing he heard was a whistle – his master was back from the hills with the two young dogs. He came before them with a large tray of food and he put the dogs in the byre. Then the shepherd walked to his little cottage beside the farmhouse to have his own breakfast. But the old dog didn't feel like eating. He didn't feel like anything. He just wanted one thing in his life that he'd never had – to look at the baby because he had never seen his face. After the young dogs had fed themselves, they curled up and went to sleep, and the old collie dog went to sleep.

How long he slept he doesn't know, but the next thing he hears is 'hoof hoof' beats on the floor. In comes the old donkey, just by himself. And instead of going to his own stall, he walks into the stall where the old dog lay. The old collie looks up, says, 'Hello, old friend, you're back.'

And the donkey speaks to the dog, 'Yes, I'm back. I had such a wonderful experience. I walked to the village and I carried this beautiful young woman and her child. But,' he says, 'I feel queer and funny now.'

'And did you see the baby?' says the collie dog.

'Yes,' says the donkey, 'I saw the baby, the most beautiful baby in this world.'

And the old collie says, 'I wish I had seen the baby.'

'You will,' says the donkey, 'some day you will see him. He will come again. He will come again and everyone will understand. But not talking about him or talking about you,' says the donkey, 'do you see something strange about me?'

'No,' says the collie, 'I don't see anything strange about you. You're just a donkey to me and I'm just a dog to you.'

'Look again,' says the donkey. 'Look once more. See if there's something about me that you've never seen before.'

And the collie looks and says, 'You've four legs like me and you've got a tail, you've got a head and ears like what I've got. You've got a mane and hair – just like me.'

'No,' says the donkey, 'there's something else you must see. And I hope in the future many people will see it, for when they see it they'll probably understand!'

'Understand what?' says the collie dog. 'Tell me what you mean!'

'Look on my shoulders,' says the donkey, 'and tell me what you see.'

The collie stood up, he put his front paws up against the wall and he looked. The donkey wasn't very high. He looked on the donkey's back, and lo and behold for the first time in his life – across the donkey's shoulders was *the cross* in black. 'What is that?' said the collie who had never seen this before.

'That,' said the donkey, 'is the mark of the child who was born this night. It was given to me and will remain with me for eternity, until some day he comes and shows his face to everyone.'

'Then maybe I'll see him,' said the dog, 'maybe I will see him again?'

'You'll see him,' said the donkey, you'll see him again; maybe not in this world, but maybe in another one when we leave this place.' And that is the end of my story.

I Love You More Than Salt

This is a most popular story with children, especially in my school sessions. I remember my sisters were very fond of this one. Old Willie Williamson, my father's cousin, told this story to us when we went for sticks for him, in the summer when he visited us in Argyll.

MANY years ago there once lived a king and his queen and they had three beautiful daughters. The king and queen loved these daughters from their heart, but lo and behold the queen took sick, very very sick. She pined away and she died. The king was so upset to lose his beautiful queen, and his daughters were very sad to lose their mother.

But the king drew his daughters together, he told them, 'Look, children, your mother has gone to another world an some day I hope we'll meet her again. But the main thing is you must be happy an take it for grantit ye have me to take care of you. And some day when I'm gone one of youse will be queen of all this country.'

So years passed by and the three little princesses grew up. The king enjoyed his hunting and his shooting, he enjoyed everything; he was a good king, his people, subjects of the country, loved him. But one particular night the king thought to himself, 'I'm getting older as the years pass by an I don't have a son to come after me to be king. One o' my daughters will surely make a good queen. But who? Which one would be the best? I know they are carin an they're lovin, they're very nice. But I'll have tae put them to the test – see which one is fit to be queen tae rule after me.'

So the king being a busy king attending to all his subjects

and things in his country, he didn't have a lot of time to spend with his princesses. He saw them from day to day and dined with them and talked to them, but he had never had a serious discussion with them. So one evening he told his couriers and all the people in the palace he wanted to be left alone because he was going to spend this evening with his daughters. After their meal he called the three princesses together, and they came and sat round beside him.

'Now,' he said, 'young ladies, I want tae talk to youse. You know that it's been a long while since your mother died. And I've tried my best, everyone around the palace has tried their best, to bring you up an teach you, make you what we want you to be – young princesses of this kingdom. I've not really had a serious talk to youse before, but tonight I want to find out which of youse will be queen after I'm gone!'

And the princesses were upset. They said, 'Daddy, we don't want tae be queen, we would just want you to be here forever!'

And he said, 'No way can I be here forever, children. Some day I will have to be gone from this world. I'll join your mother in a faraway place and youse'll be left alone by yourselves. I don't want any arguin, disputin an fallin out among the three of youse – if there was only one it'd be different! So,' he said, 'to love me is to love my people. I'm gaunna put youse a task this evening: I want youse to tell me how much youse really love me.' So he spoke to the oldest daughter first.

And she says, 'Father, I love you more than diamonds an pearls an all the jewels in this world.'

'Very well,' he says, 'that's nice.' So he spoke to the second daughter, 'How much do you really love me?'

She says, 'I love you more than all the gold in the earth, I love you more than all the money in this land.'

He says, 'That is very nice, that is very good.' So to the youngest daughter of all, who was lovely and beautiful and only fifteen at that time, 'Now,' he says, 'little one, how much do you love me?'

'Well, Daddy,' she says, 'I love you more than salt.'

'You love me more than salt?' he says.

'Yes, Daddy,' she says, 'I love you more than salt.'

And the king was upset, very upset! He said, 'Your sister loves me more than diamonds an jewels, an your other sister loves me more than gold, all the gold in this world. And you – you love me more than salt! Well, if that's the way you feel, I don't love you! And tomorrow morning you shall go on your way, you are banned from me, I never want tae see you again! You have disgraced me – the lowest thing on earth is salt!'

The king ordered her the next morning to be on her way, find her own way in the world and never show her face again back at his palace. He was so upset. So the poor little princess felt sad and broken-hearted. She gathered a few possessions together . . . and her sisters laughed and giggled. She was sent on her way for disgracing her father.

The princess wandered, she travelled on, she had nowhere to go. She travelled on and on. But she came to a great forest and she found a wee path. She followed the path and said, 'Pro'bly it'll lead to a little village or a little hamlet where I can find some place to shelter.'

But the path led right into the middle of the forest many many miles from the palace. There lo and behold she came to a little cottage. And the princess thought to herself, 'Pro'bly I'll find shelter here.' She came up to the cottage and knocked on the door.

And the door opened, out came an old woman with long grey hair and a ragged dress on her. She said, 'What are you doing here, dearie?'

And the princess said, 'Well, it's a long story. I'm seekin shelter fir the night.'

'But where in the world are ye bound for?' said the old woman.

And the princess said, 'I'm bound fir nowhere, I'm on my way . . . I've been ordered away from my father.'

'Your father?' said the old woman.

'Yes,' she said, 'my father the king!'

'Your father the king,' she says, 'has ordered you on your way? You'd better come in an tell me the story.'

So the old woman brought the young princess into the little cottage in the forest and gave her something to eat. She sat her down by the fire. There sitting by the fire was a large black cat. And the big black cat came over, it put its head on the top of the lassie's knee. She petted it. It purred as if it was a kitten. And the old woman when she saw this was amazed, said, 'You know, there's never been anyone, though my visitors are few an far between, has ever come here and been friendly with my cat. Because it knows good from bad . . . you are good! Tell me yir story.'

So the princess told her story about her mother dying, she was reared up with her father and she spent all her life in the palace, then her daddy had called her before them. She told the whole story I've told you before.

And the old woman said, 'Such a sad event. *Your daddy is needing tae be taught a lesson.*'

'But,' she said, 'I cannae go back, I am banned from the palace, my daddy never wants to see my face again.'

And the old woman said, 'Well, mebbe some day he will be glad tae see ye!'

Now back in the palace the king lived with his two daughters, the third little daughter was gone. And naturally the king used to get all his meals brought into him. They brought him beef and roast and mutton, and the king loved his meat with salt. But lo and behold when one meal was placed before the king one day, he tasted it, 'Bring me some salt!' he told the chef and the cook. 'Bring me salt!'

And they came in shaking in fright, 'Master, we have no salt,' they said.

Said the king, 'I need salt for my food!'

'Master,' the cook said, 'we've searched the town, we've searched all around and there's not one single grain of salt to be found anywhere!'

The king said, 'Take it away, I can't eat it without salt! Bring me something else!'

So they brought him sweetmeats to eat. And they brought him sweetmeats the next day, and the next and the next. But by this time the king was getting sick of all this. He said, 'Bring me some beef, bring me some roast, some pork, something I can eat! Bring me food, some sensible food!'

The cooks and chefs brought him sensible food, but there was no salt. The king sent couriers, he sent soldiers, he sent everybody around the country . . . It was all right for the princesses, they could eat sweetmeats which they loved. But their father the king couldn't get one grain of salt in the whole kingdom.

In the little cottage in the forest the princess stayed with the old woman and they became the greatest of friends. She cooked and she cleaned for the old woman, and the cat was her dearest friend. The old woman loved the young princess like she never loved anything in this life. But one day the old woman came back from the forest with a basket of herbs – which she spent most of her time in the forest gathering.

She said to the princess, 'Ye know, I'm gaunna be sad tomorrow.'

And the princess said, 'Why, grandmother, are you sad tomorrow?'

'Because you must leave me.'

'But,' she said, 'grandmother, I don't want tae leave ye, I've nowhere to go.'

She says, 'You must go back to yir father!'

Princess says, 'I can't make my way back tae the palace, because my father has banned me.'

'Not this time,' she said. 'Luik, give me yir dress!' And the young princess took her dress off. The old woman went into the back room, she was gone for minutes. But when she came back the dress was full of patches and tatters, in rags. 'Now,' she said to the princess, 'take off your shoes.'

The princess took off her shoes. And then the old woman took a pair of scissors and she cut the princess's hair. Next she went to the fire and gathered a handful of soot. She rubbed it on the princess's face, 'Now,' she said, 'you make yir way back to your father!'

'I'm banned, I'm not – I can't go back to the palace!'

'You must,' said the old woman, 'because *you* are going to be the next queen!'

'Me,' said the princess, 'the next queen? One of my sisters is gaunna be the next queen: they love my daddy like gold, they love my daddy like diamonds.'

'But,' she says, '*you love your daddy more than salt*!' And she goes into the kitchen, takes a wee canvas bag and fills it full of salt. 'Now,' she says, 'you take this and make yir way back to the palace – I'm sure you'll be welcome.'

So, the princess knew the old woman was telling the truth, she knew the old woman had been good to her. She says, 'Remember, I'll be back!'

'Come back,' says the old woman, 'when you're queen! Make yir way back tae your father's palace the way you came!'

So she bade the old woman 'good-bye'.

Now unknown to the princess this old woman was a witch. And she had destroyed every particle of salt in the country because the princess had told her the story . . . And even if somebody had brought some within a certain distance of the palace, the salt just disappeared, because the old witch had a spell on the palace – no salt would ever be near it.

And by this time the king is going out of his mind, he can't eat, he can't taste anything – he'd give his kingdom for one particle of salt. Then lo and behold two days later when he's calling up for salt and says he's going to die for the want of it . . . there comes a bare-footed beggar maid to the palace. And the guard stops her, asks her what she wants.

She says, 'I want to see the king.'

'And why do you want tae see the king?' he said.

'Well,' she said, 'I've brought the king a present.'

'What could a bare-footed beggar maid bring the king?'

She says, 'I have brought him a bag o' salt.'

And when he heard this she was rushed – they couldn't take time to get a hold of her – they just rushed her before the king. And the guard said, 'Yir Majesty, we have brought someone tae see ye.' She was there before the king, hair cut short, face blackened with soot, bare feet, ragged dress. And in her hand she carried a little bag.

The king said, 'Who is this you've brought before me, this ragged beggar maid?'

And the guards, the cooks and everyone were so excited, they said, 'You don't know what this beggar maid has brought . . . she has brought something special!'

'What could she bring tae me?' said the king. 'Nothing in the world I desire: I have gold, I have diamonds, I have everything.' He said, 'If only I had a little salt.'

He said, 'Yir Majesty, the beggar maid has brought you a bag of salt.'

'Oh, oh,' said the king, 'she's brought me – she . . . bring it to me!'

And she walked up and said, 'Here you are . . .'

The king looked in. He put his finger in and he tasted it. 'At last,' he said, 'sal-l-t, the most wonderful thing in this world! It is better to me than diamonds or pearls or gold or anything in my kingdom! At last I can have food, I can have something to eat. And he turned round to the beggar maid, he said, 'What would you desire? You have brought me the one thing in this world that I need . . . What do you want? What kind o' reward do you want?'

She turned round and she said, 'Daddy, I want nothing!'

And the king said, 'What?'

She says to him, 'Daddy, I want nothing. Because *I love you more than salt*!'

And then the king knew, this maid was his youngest daughter. He put his arms round her and he kissed her, he made her more than welcome. He had found the truth – salt was more important to him than anything in the world. And she was made welcome by everyone in the palace. When the old king died she became queen and reigned over the country for many years, and she never forgot her friend the old woman in the forest. And that's the last of my story.

The Hunchback and the Swan

This is an old old story, told to me many many years ago by an old uncle of mine, Duncan Townsley, who really was a great story-teller. He wandered all over Scotland by himself for years and years. He was a piper and played his bagpipes for a living. In the winter-time he would have settled in some traveller community, played his bagpipes to them, spent his time with them and picked up all their stories. He travelled in the summer-time but as he had been born and reared in Argyllshire, he often returned there and spent the winter with his sister who was my mother. On the winter nights in my time there was no television or wireless, and my uncle, to keep us quiet, would tell us a story.

MANY years ago there lived an old hunchback, and he was mute, he could hear but he couldn't utter a word. He lived in the forest by himself and he had nobody, no friends or relations. And he used to make his living by gathering sticks in the forest, cutting them up into firewood, taking them into the village and selling them to the local inhabitants. Everybody liked to buy the sticks from the hunchback, but they really hated him because he was so ugly – he had a hump on his back, his face was long and his chin was long, and he had so ugly an appearance – just to look at him kind of frightened you! And when he went to the village to sell his sticks the children used to shout and call him names. It made him so sad. And he couldn't get his sticks sold fast enough, so he could get back home to his little hut he had built in the forest.

But unknown to the local inhabitants, he had more friends than anybody could every ask for: he had friends in the forest, the birds, the mice, rats, squirrels, rabbits, all the little people of the forest. The squirrels would come, they would sit on his knee and take things out of his hand. Dormice, rats and rabbits, they loved him dearly and he loved them.

Many's the day he used to walk into the middle of the forest where a wee lake was, and on this lake there lived one swan, a mute swan. And unlike the whooper swan, it was there all summer and winter as well. But good as the hunchback was to all these little animals, one he could never get to come near him was the swan. And he loved and adored it. Once he had sold all his sticks, had come back and fed all his little animals, after they had all come round about him, he would take up a wee bit sandwich or a piece and make his way to the lake in the forest. He would sit by the lakeside, sit and admire the swan. Time passed by.

It came summer again. The hunchback made his way back to the lake and he took some of his pieces and some food with him and cast all these bits of bread into the water. But the swan wouldn't come near him. Day out and day in the robin would come and sit on his shoulder, the squirrel would come and sit on his knee, the dormouse, the rabbits and the rats, even the deer, would gather round him. And he would pet them, give them his time. But in his heart he only lived for one thing – he admired this most beautiful swan, its long graceful neck and its wings and its feet as it sailed round the lake – but it would never come near him. Day out and day in he pined . . . threw pieces in the water, cast them as far as he could, see if he could entice it near him . . . and he had the power upon all animals! But he had no power upon the swan. It seemed to ignore him completely.

But this didn't stop him: day out and day in he cut his sticks, went to the village, sold his sticks to the people, and they gave him just enough money so he could buy whatever he needed in the shop, just enough to keep him alive. Then back he would come, home again, set sail[1] and try, sit by the

1 set sail – set off on the walk

lakeside and cast his bread upon the water, see if he could feed the swan – but no. In vain. Could he entice the swan? No way could he entice it to come near him. Till day passed and day passed and the summer was beginning to end.

Now the summer passed away and October came in. The cold bite of the winter wind began to blow through the forest and all the little animals began to think the winter was coming in. The dormouse started to build up his little bit of stores and the robins began to choose their bits of territory where they were going to spend the winter, the hedgehog looked for a place to curl up and the deer began to grow their coats of long hair. All the animals began to see that winter was coming.

But the hunchback still went to the lake. And the swan still sailed round. Not a sound came from the swan because it was mute. And as the summer faded, the days grew shorter, the more the hunchback became in love with the swan. Till one morning.

The people in the village were waiting on their sticks – the hunchback never turned up. Now these people depended on the hunchback every day. But for a second day the hunchback never turned up, and for a third. The people in the village, who really hated him, and even the children who used to shout names at him, call 'Hunchback!', began to miss him. But he wasn't missed as much in the village (the people only missed him because they had nothing for their fire) as he was in the forest.

The robin and the sparrow and the shelfie and the blackbird, and the deer and the rabbits, and the vole and the hedgehog – all began to wonder what had happened to their wee friend. He never put in an appearance and he had always used to, every day. Even the swan, who evaded him so much, began to turn round in the lake in circles and wonder – she had spied him many times and she *wanted* to come, but something kept her back, something kept her apart because she was a mute swan. Till the third day passed and all the animals in the forest began to wonder why their little friend didn't come and feed them and play with them, come and see them!

And the squirrel went to the robin and the robin went to the blackbird and the blackbird went to the mavis and the mavis went to the shelfie and they all gathered together. They were a-chirping and a-singing and a-singing and a-chirping in the forest, wondering what had happened to their friend the hunchback. They were going to have a meeting to see what was wrong. So, the robin – he was the master of the lot because he is the master of winter – gathered them round. There were the deer, the rabbits, there were the hares, there was the hedgehog, the squirrel, and even the pine marten was there! The rats and every little creature in the forest gathered into a circle. Everyone was worried.

And the robin spoke up, 'Ladies and gentlemen,' he said, 'I know we're gathered here today in the forest and it's a sad thing we have to talk about. Our little friend who comes and visits us and who's been so good to us every day, there's something wrong because he's never put in an appearance for three days. We must find out what's wrong!'

So the little squirrel, he was very clever, he says, 'Well, Robin, you've chosen youself to be spokesman for the crowd, what do you think we should do?'

And the robin said, 'Well, there's only one thing we can do, we must find out what is wrong with the hunchback!'

'But how,' Squirrel said, 'are we going to find out what's wrong with him? His house is shut, the windows are closed, the door is locked there's no smoke coming from his chimney, and we can't go into his place. What can we do? We know there's something wrong.'

'Well,' said the robin, 'there's only one thing we can do, we'll go and see Mr Owl and he'll tell us what's wrong.' So all the wee animals forgot about being bad to each other, they all went together to the old hollow oak tree. There sitting in the tree was Mr Owl. So they told him their story.

And the owl said, 'Yes, I believe it,' and he listened to

what they had to say. 'Well,' Mr Owl said, 'ladies and gentlemen and friends, I know we are here today, and we're all enemies and we're all friends. But the dearest friend we have is ill. And there's something we must do about it.'

So the robin said, 'Mr Owl, tell us what we've got to do! We know we miss him and we love him dearly. We know he's not missed in the village, they'll only miss his firewood. But we can't live without him! What can we do?'

'Well,' says the owl, 'you, Mr Robin, being spokesman for the crowd, the only thing you can go and do – we must get a message to Our Lady, send a message to Our Lady and tell her! I have seen him and he comes every day, he sits by the lakeside and tries his best to encourage Our Lady to come and see him! But she never pays any attention to him. I've watched him from my tree up here, watched him coming day out and day in trying to entice her with pieces and everything you could ask for. He is in love with Our Lady of the Lake and she doesn't want anything to do with him!'

So all the little creatures gathered round together and they hummed and hawed and talked about it to each other. They said, 'Well, Mr Owl, what is it we can do?'

'Well,' the owl said, 'the only thing we can do is send a message and tell her that she is hurting us and disturbing us by being unkind to our little friend! Can she come and see him, so he will know that everything's all right? Probably it will make him well again.'

'But,' the robin said, 'I can't go out into the lake, fly out there and tell her!'

'Aha,' said the owl, 'that's no trouble! Call on our friend Mr Swallow. He is the man that can deliver any message, all over the world he can deliver messages!'

So they called on the swallow. He came in and they told him the story. 'Swallow,' they said, 'would you be kind enough to go out to The Lady in the Lake, Our Dearest Lady whom we all love and admire, and tell her the story we're going to tell you: our little friend, the hunchback, whom we love and admire and adore, is ill in his little cabin in the forest, is ill and sick! And there's nothing we can do, that she is the only one who can come and help him!'

'Gladly!' said the swallow. 'I'll gladly do that because he also is good to me. I enjoy his company. Many's the time he sits in the forest – not that I eat the food that he gives me – but I like the company he has around him.' And just like that away goes the swallow.

The swallow flies out into the middle of the lake and he hovers above the swan. Now all the little creatures of the forest were sitting on the bank of the wee lake and they were waiting to see what happens. So the swallow stops, and while he circles he tells her the story. Then the swallow circles round and comes back. They all wait and wait and wait . . . and the swan turns. She begins to swim towards the bank. When all the other creatures see the swan swimming towards the bank they begin to feel happy! They know now that the swan has received the message and she's going to do something about it.

So the swan comes in, steps up onto the shore and makes her way up the wee path to the forest. Step by step goes the swan, step by step right to the hunchback's cabin, pushes the door with her beak and the door opens. And all the little creatures of the forest gather round! There's some trying to keek through the windows.

Inside the hunchback is lying on his back quiet and still, not a movement from him lying still on his bed. As ugly as sin. And the robin goes to the window – he's the only one that can fly up to the window – and all the other little creatures are sitting on the ground. And they're shouting up to him, 'What is she doing now?'

And the robin's flying up and flapping at the window (he couldn't stop, you see), he's shouting back to them, 'She's coming through the door!'

'What else, Robin?'

'She's walking up to his bed,' he says, broadcasting what the swan's doing back to all the other creatures. Now the squirrel, the hedgehog, the rabbit, they're all gathered round the wee cabin.

So the swan walks up to the bed and she looks. There's the hunchback lying on his back, pale as could be, ugly as sin. Sick as could be. And the swan looks and the swan feels sad. She thinks back, 'How often I've seen him sitting on the bank casting the bits of pieces on the water for me to get. He could never hurt me,' she said to herself, 'he never meant to hurt me in any way. Why is it that I thought so often he would do me an injury?'

And the swan goes up. She reaches her neck across his neck – her long slender neck that the hunchback loved so much – and she lays her neck across the hunchback's. The minute she did that the hunchback opened his eyes and he looked – he saw the swan. And he put his hands around the swan's neck.

The robin says, 'The swan has finally accepted him! And he's cuddling the swan,' passing the words back to the wee animals all around the cabin.

And they say, 'He cuddles the swan, he cuddles the swan, the swan is accepting him! Our Lady, Our Lady's accepting him! Now perhaps he will be well!'

After the hunchback opens his eyes, sees the swan and pets her neck, he sits up in bed and says to himself, 'It feels so good . . .'

But all in a minute the swan turns round her beak and picks a feather from her wing and holds it up . . . she takes it and pierces it into the hunchback's chest. And an amazing thing happens – the hunchback's ugliness begins to disappear, his body stretches . . . and he turns into a swan!

And the robin's watching at the window and all the wee animals said, 'What's happening now, what happened? Tell us what's happening now, tell us what's happened!'

The robin's breast was so full that a lump came in his throat. The robin couldn't speak because he was so happy. He couldn't say a word but only twittered. And he sat down. And all the animals asked him to speak up and tell them what was going on, but the robin couldn't speak or say another word, he was so full.

Then, all the animals gathered round the front door and the next thing they saw was *two swans* walking out the cabin door, one after the other. The one followed the other to the lake. And in the lake they went sailing away. All the animals gathered round, they said, 'At last our little friend is happy.' But the robin couldn't speak. From that day on to this day the robin only repeated himself; he's never said another thing.

So the two swans dwelt in the lake and the animals said, 'Our Lady has finally found a friend.' And from that day to this, the swan utters nothing. That is the story of the mute swan, the way it was told to me is the way I'm telling you. And that's the last of my wee story.

The Goat that Told Lies

My daddy used to tell us this one; aye, he told us dozens of times. This was a most fantastic story among the travellers and it has passed through the travellers by word of mouth, as far as I know, for some four hundred years, maybe more – from when the travellers began. When travelling people gathered around the camp-fire and the children were a wee bit annoying to their mothers and fathers, one of the fathers would say, 'Come on, I'll tell you a story!' to keep the children quiet. The children would gather round and he would say, 'What will I tell you?' And they would say, 'Daddy, tell us about the goat, the goat that told lies.'

MANY years ago, long before your day and mine, there lived a woodcutter in the forest and he had three sons. He and his wife depended on what little money they could make from cutting the trees in the forest but they had a contract with the laird that they wouldn't cut any green trees, only what was blown down with the wind, or dead wood. This old man and his sons used to go into the forest every morning and cut all this wood and they didn't have a pony to take the wood from the forest, they hurled it with a hand-cart. It was a long way into the forest but the sons, Willie, Jack, and Thomas, loved their father and mother dearly and helped them every way they could.

From where they stayed it was about a ten-mile hike to the village. The old man used to take the hand-cart and hurl all the sticks he had cut and sell them in the village for money. And once a month they used to go to the village for their rations, the groceries they needed to keep themselves, to survive in the forest.

The story really begins one morning, before the old man and his three sons went into the forest. The old man got up and had his breakfast, and he said to his old wife, 'Well, Maggie, we'll have to go again today and I think we'll be gone for a while.'

'Well,' she said, 'you know it's lonely for me being here by myself all day. I wish I had something to keep me in company, a dog or a cat, anything, something to talk to.'

'Och,' he said, 'don't worry. You'll be all right. If we get a quick load we'll be back early.'

But the father and the three sons went on their way to the forest. They had a good distance to walk and when they landed at their work place in the forest the father said, 'The best thing we can do is split up: Willie, you go that way; Tommy, you go that way; and Jack, you go this way. And if you come to any dead trees, just knock them down, put them in a heap and we'll collect them later.'

So the boys said, 'All right!' to their father and away they went into the forest.

But the old man had chosen a part of the forest he had never been in before and he walked forward. He saw some dead trees and he said, 'Probably I'll get a better one farther on,' and he walked farther in and farther in. He came to this large tree – it was dead right to the top. And he had his axe with him, he was ready to cut it, when right at the foot of the tree he saw this thing. It was a baby goat, a young kid. And the old man stopped, he looked.

'Well,' he said, 'upon my soul! Where in the name of God do you come from, little creature – where did you come from?'

'He-eh,' the goat said, 'ha-a-haah, where did I come from – that's a long story.'

And the old man looked all around as if there was somebody else there. But he saw there was nobody. He felt kind of funny. He said, 'Did that animal speak or am I hearing things?' He rubbed his ears.

The goat said, 'Look, Johnnie,' (he called the old man

'Johnnie') 'you mightnae rub your ears or look for anybody else here in the forest – there's nobody here but me!'

He says, 'Goat, do you speak?'

And the goat said, 'Aye, I speak. But I only speak to folk that I like! And I know about you and your wife and your three sons, and I know how you come to the forest every day.'

The old man was mesmerised, he didn't know what to do. He said, 'Never in my life did I hear a goat speaking!'

'But,' the goat said, 'dinnae think I'm going to speak to your three sons! What kind of a woman is your wife?'

'O-oh,' Johnnie said, 'my wife is the nicest old cratur – I've been married to her for sixty years and she's the nicest old woman that God ever put on this earth.'

'Ah,' the goat said, 'that's good! I like that.'

'Well,' he said, 'I can't leave you here. I think I'll take you back with me. My old wife needs somebody like you to keep her in company.'

'Well . . .' the goat says, 'but I'll tell you something, old man, before you go any further, I know about your three sons – Willie, Jack and Tommy – they're out there in the forest not far from here cutting trees. But don't think I'm going to speak to[1] them because I'm not! I'll speak to you and I'll speak to your old wife, whatever kind of woman she is – I'll make my mind up what kind of person she is when I get there.'

The old man says, 'You're a funny goat. But I like you, I like you a lot.'

'And I like you too,' the goat said, 'I like you a lot. I think I'll just go with you.'

So instead of cutting any sticks the old man picked the goat up under his arm and walked back through the forest. He landed in a clearing in the forest and he met his three sons, and they had all these heaps of sticks packed up.

Willie said, 'Daddy, did you get any sticks?'

1 speak to – attend to

'Oh, stop speaking about sticks, son!' he said. 'I got something better than sticks. I've got something for your mother.'

The boys said, 'What is it?'

He said, 'A goat!'

'A goat, Father?' they said.

He says, 'A baby goat.' But the old man never said it could speak! 'I got a baby goat,' he said, 'this is the thing your mother's been wanting for years, something to keep her in company. She can feed it and pet it and do what she likes with it while we're out working in the forest.'

So Willie came over. He looked at the goat, and the goat gave him the eye. Jack came over and he looked at the goat, and the goat gave him the eye. And Thomas, the youngest one, came over and he looked at the goat, and the goat didn't look very pleased at him.

'So I'll tell you what we'll do,' the father said, 'you each take some sticks and carry them home on your backs and I'll carry the goat. We'll go home more the day[1] to your mother.'

So the three young men carried a load of sticks on their backs and the old man carried the goat. And back home they went. But the old man couldn't wait to get into the house, and while the sons were putting down the sticks he ran round and opened the door.

He said, 'Maggie, Maggie!'

She says, 'What is it, did you cut yourself or something?'

'No,' he said, 'come here! Look what I got for you!' And old Maggie looked. He said, 'I got you a goat.'

She says, 'What?'

He says, 'I've got you a goat.'

'But where, in the name of the world,' she said, 'did you get a goat?'

He says, 'Wheesht – don't say a word, don't tell the boys! This is not the kind of goat that you find about any place.

1 more the day – for the rest of the day

Maggie, this is a different kind of goat – this goat can speak!'

'Away!' she said, 'Johnnie, a goat can't speak. A goat can't speak!'

And the goat up and said, 'Aye, Maggie, I can speak. Take me in and give me a wee heat at the fire, I'm kind o' cold.'

Oh, old Maggie's eyes popped out of her head. She says, 'Give me the wee cratur!'

Old Maggie got the goat, took it in her bosom and put it in beside the fire. She gave it a heat and the goat sat down beside the fire. She had the boys' supper made, the boys came in and had their supper. They were tired. The old man and his wife had their bed downstairs and up the small stair to the floor above the three young men had their beds. So the three young men went away to their bed. Now, old Maggie was sitting at one side of the fire, Johnnie was sitting at the other side, and the goat was sitting in the middle.

'You know, Maggie,' he said, 'it's a funny thing . . . I wonder where that wee creature came from?' The goat was sitting, its ears hanging down, not saying a word.

'Well,' she said, 'you could ask where it came from – ask it!'

He said, 'Maggie, it'll no speak – it'll speak to you, it'll speak to me – but it'll no speak to the laddies. It doesn't want the laddies to know it can speak, and it'll no say a word!'

'Oh well,' she said, 'but Johnnie, what are we going to do with it? I can't leave it in here by the fire all night because sparks might land on it, and it needs to go outside sometimes.'

He said, 'Maggie, I'll go out and make a nice wee place in the shed for it.'

So he went out to an old shed that he used to keep for his hens (he had no more hens because they ate them all when they had no more food), and he filled it full of straw and hay and he got a nice pail of water and he made a nice wee bed for the goat. And he put her down. 'Now,' he said, 'you sleep there, wee cratur, and we'll take good care of you.'

'Thank you, Johnnie, you're awfae kind,' the goat said. 'And tell old Maggie I'll see her in the mornin.'

So the old man went in. She said, 'Did you take care of the goat?'

'Oh,' he said, 'I took care of the goat, and it thanked me awful much.'

'What did it say to you?'

'It said, "Thank you, Johnnie, thank you very much for being so good to me, and tell old Maggie I'll see her in the morning." '

'All right,' said old Maggie, 'I'll see it in the morning all right!' So the old couple went away to their bed. But old Maggie couldn't rest thinking about this goat. She spoke about this goat, she said, 'Johnnie, it's just the thing I need here all day with me – it'll keep me in company, I can take it into the house with me and I can feed it and I can look after it and I can brush it and take care of it. While you're away – I'll no miss you away in the forest all day now – I have somebody to speak to!'

So the next day old John and his three sons go away to the forest and Maggie spends her time with the goat. She and the goat become the greatest of friends. She cuddles it, kisses it, does everything with it. 'Wee cratur,' she said, 'I'll be good to you.' And she called it 'Nellie'. 'Nellie, I'll look after you.'

'Well, old wife,' she says, 'I'll love my life here with you and old Johnnie, but I'm no so keen on those laddies. I doubt[1] they would be bad to me if they got a chance. They don't look at me very pleasantly. I don't like the looks of them, I don't—'

'Oh,' she said, 'my laddies are all right. They wouldn't hurt a hair on your body – it wouldn't pay them either to

1 doubt – believe

hurt a hair on your body – if I got them lifting a hand to you, it'd be the cause of their death!'

So from that day on Maggie and the goat became the greatest friends in the world. She loved it from her heart, and because she loved it and old John loved her, he loved the goat as much as he loved old Maggie. And every night when the boys went to their beds he carried Nellie in to the fire, where he put her down. Nellie sat and she cracked to them, she told them stories and tales, she told them everything – but she never said where she came from – not a word did she tell them about where she came from.

But, to make a long story short, it came time when somebody had to go to the village for messages. By this time Nellie had begun to grow, and she was a good-sized, half-grown goat. The father called all his sons together that night after the hard day's work was finished.

He said, 'Boys, we're kind of short of food. And I need tobacco and your mother needs some things from the village. Tomorrow I want one of you to go to the village and bring back some messages, whatever your mother needs.'

And old Maggie said, 'Aye, and you'll take wee Nellie with you to the village for a walk because she's been tied up here all day at home with me while you've been away. I've made a belt for her and a nice collar – you'll take her with you for a walk to the town! And upon my soul, be good to her! Don't walk her feet on the hard road, keep her on the grass and stop along the way and give her a good drink. Treat her like you would treat your own mother!'

So Willie said, 'Mother, I wouldn't hurt your wee goat, I know you love it, though I don't like it!' Now the goat hated these boys – jealous of them! It didn't like them at all. The next morning came.

Willie got up, got his breakfast, got money from his mother and he got a bag. He went into the shed, took the goat by the rope and led the goat into the village. He walked it on the grass and he stopped along the way, he gave it a drink of water and he fed it and he took his time with it, bought it apples from the shop and he treated it like a queen, all the way to the village and all the way back! After he came home, before he even took the messages into his mother, he took the goat into the shed, tied it up, made it a bed of soft straw, got a nice pail of water and put it down beside the goat. Then he went in for his supper, gave his mother his messages and his father his tobacco. They sat and talked for a while, they asked him about the village and he said that everything was okay there. And Willie went away upstairs to his bed. So the old mother and father sat and talked for a wee while.

'Johnnie,' she says, 'I think you should go and bring wee Nellie in for a while. I'm wearying to see her, I haven't seen her all day. And put her down by the fire where I can see her!' The boys were upstairs in their beds. It was about twelve o'clock at night and the old man was sitting smoking his pipe at the fire and old Maggie was sitting in her chair.

'Well, I will go out and bring wee Nellie in,' he said, 'she must be feeling kind o' cold out there! I'll bring her in for a wee heat.' So out he went and brought in the goat. They had a sheepskin rug at the front of the fire. He put the goat at the front of the fire.

She said, 'How are you feeling the night, Nellie?'

'Oh woman, dinnae speak to me,' she said, 'dinnae speak to me!'

'What's wrong with you?'

'Oh-oh,' she says, 'what's wrong wi me? You've nae idea what's wrong wi me – that laddie o' yours—'

'What's wrong with that laddie,' she says, 'what did he do?'

'Do to me?' she said. 'Oh, you've no idea what he's done to me – he kicked me and he battered me and I never had a bite today – and he pulled me on the rope as hard as he could and my poor feet are that sore I can hardly stand up! And when he got to the village he tied me up to a wall where I couldn't get a bite and he put wee weans on my back for pennies, and gave them a hurl. And my poor back's that sore I can't even move!'

The old man said, 'Nellie, are you telling the truth?'

The goat said, 'I'm telling the God's honest truth, why would I tell you a lie, to you people who are so good to me? That's what your son has done to me, that laddie! That son you've got – he's a beast, he's an animal!'

'Well,' the old man said, 'it'll never happen again in this house. Tomorrow morning, when he comes down that stair, I'm going to make him so that he'll never again be cruel to his mother's wee pet!'

True to his word, the old man got up the first thing in the morning, and before he got breakfast – never even tied his boots – when his son came down the stair (Willie always came down first because he was the oldest one), he took a walking stick from behind the door and gave Willie the biggest beating he ever had in his life. He laid into him for an hour.

'Now,' he said, 'go on your way and never show your face back here about this house as long as you live! Don't ever come back! You cruel boy who was cruel to your mother's wee pet – the only thing she has to keep her in company! Willie was sent on his way never to be seen again.

So the two brothers were kind of sad at losing their brother because they liked to be together. Now, there was more animosity towards the goat – they hated the goat worse for this! But they didn't know what happened because their mother and father never told them. They worked hard with their father just the same and a month passed by and it was once again time to go to the shop for their messages.

Now it was Jack's turn, the next brother. And he did the same thing. But if Willie was good to the goat, Jack was ten times better. He half-carried it to the town and half-carried it back! He bought cookies and he bought scones for it and he fed it on flowers along the way and gave it a drink of water, and did everything he could possibly do for the goat

– but no, it was no good. He gave his mother the messages, gave his father his tobacco, sat and had his supper and went upstairs to bed.

She said, 'Johnnie, I don't know – that laddie, he might have been bad to that wee goat today – you'd better go and bring her in and see what she's got to say the night!'

Old Jock goes out for the goat, brings it in, puts it down by the fire. The goat, she's stretched out.

'How are you feeling the night, Nellie?'

'O-oh,' she says, 'don't speak to me, woman, I can't talk, I can't talk to you – I'm too sore. That laddie o' yours took revenge on me and he kicked me the whole way to the town and he kicked me the whole way back. I'm so sick I can't even move, so dinnae speak nae mair tae me. I just want to lie doon. And please! Don't put me back in that shed the night – can you let me lie by the fire?'

The old man said, 'God bless us, that's terrible! You poor wee beast! But wait, upon my soul, he's no getting off with it – tomorrow morning when he comes down that stair – I'm going to make him so that he'll never treat you badly again, Nellie! Don't worry, you'll no need to worry about him.'

So the next morning, true to his word, the old man – before he even got breakfast – when Jack came down the stair he laid into Jack with the walking stick. And if he gave Willie a beating he gave Jack a bigger beating. And he said, 'Look, *you* follow your brother and never show your face about my house as long as you live! You *cruel* laddie, what you did to your mother's wee beast!' So Jack was sent on his way, the same as his brother.

Now there were only the father and Tommy left. Tommy was kind of fed up and he hated the goat worse by this time because he knew there was something wrong. He said, 'My brothers couldn't be bad to that goat. My brothers never hurt anybody, and how did they know anyway – the goat can't speak – the goat can't tell them anything.' This is what Tommy said to himself, 'Well, I'll tell you one thing, if it comes my chance to take it to the town, I'm not going to be bad to it! I don't want to leave my father and mother and I have no place to go.' And he worried about this, you see.

But another month passed by and it came to Tommy's turn, and the same thing happened to him. If the two brothers were good to the goat, Tommy was ten times better. He treated it even more like a queen! He picked wee soft flowers and put them on the grass and patted wee Nellie. 'Now you be a good wee goat and come with me, and I'll look after you, and don't worry,' said Tommy. He did all the things he could for the goat on the way to the village and on the way back, bought it sweeties and he fed it sweeties. He came back, put her in the shed, filled a nice pail of water and made a nice wee bed for her. 'Lie down there and keep yourself warm, wee Nellie,' he said. He went in, had his supper and went to his bed.

The old mother and father, old Johnnie and old Maggie, were sitting at the fireside. She said, 'Johnnie, I wonder how wee Nellie's getting on, I'd like to see her before I go to bed,' because this old woman loved the goat from her heart!

'Oh well, I'll bring her in for a wee while,' he said, 'it's getting kind o' cold, it's getting near the winter-time now and probably she'd be better to sleep by the fire tonight.'

He brought the goat in and put it down by the fire. And the goat just lay down, stretched its legs out – couldn't move.

And old Maggie said, 'How are you feeling the night, wee Nellie?'

'O-o-oh, dear-dear woman,' she said, 'I can't speak to you, I can't speak! Don't ask me questions – I'm just about finished – I don't think I'll see the night out, I think I'm finished for good!'

'What's wrong with you?'

'Oh, that laddie of yours,' she said, 'he killed me, he finally finished me. What his two brothers didn't do, he finally did it. I'm just about finished, I'll never see daylight, I'll never see the morning!'

And the old woman started to greet. And when the old woman started to greet, the old man felt so sad. 'I'm no waiting till morning,' he said, 'I'm going to get him right now!' So he goes up the stair and pulls young Thomas out of bed and gives him the biggest beating he ever got in his life and sends him – in the darkness – off! Never to show his face again.

The goat heard this and the goat said to itself 'Haa! That's the last of them. Thank God, that's the last of them gone. Now it's just me and old Johnnie and Maggie and I'll enjoy my life here with them two.' It sprung up to its feet and sat right at the front of the fire. It sat and it joked and it told cracks and stories to the old man and the old woman till the old man and woman felt sleepy.

And old Maggie says, 'Nellie, my doll, I'll have to go to bed more the night. I've enjoyed this night, this is the best night that ever I had in my life! Will you be all right Nellie?'

'A-aye,' she said, 'old woman, I'll be all right.'

'How are you feeling, is your body still sore?'

'Ach, I'm no so bad noo,' she said, 'since I had a wee crack to youse and I'm feeling a wee bit better, I'll probably be all right by the morning.'

So the old man and the old woman kissed the goat, cuddled it and bade it 'good night'. 'You'll stay by the fire the night, Nellie?'

'I'll stay by the fire, old wife,' she said, 'and I'll be all right.'

So the old man and woman went away to bed. And she said, 'Johnnie, I can never thank you, never thank you enough for what you've done for me getting me that wee goat. I love my wee goat!'

'Old wife,' he said, 'look, I love you. And anybody who'd be bad to your wee goat, I wouldn't have any time for them – even my own sons. But I'll tell you something, I'm going to miss the laddies. But they'll have to learn to go their own way. If they'd been good to your wee goat, they wouldn't have got what they got. And, it's me and you and Nellie from now on. I'll manage by cutting sticks, I'll manage myself to get as much as will keep me and you alive. As long as you've got wee Nellie to keep you in company.' So, the goat was happy. The old man was happy, and the old woman was happy, but they missed the laddies.

But the old man was true to his word, he worked hard and he worked away for a month. And the goat was in with old Maggie every day in the week and she and the goat spent a fantastic time! She loved the goat so much she just couldn't bear to have it out of her sight. But things began to get short, they had no food and it came the time that somebody had to go to the village.

And the old man said, 'Well, you can't go, old Maggie. I'll go to the village and I'll take wee Nellie with me! I'll no be bad to her. Whatever's going in the town, she gets half of it, everything I buy she gets half.'

So, true to his word, the next morning the old man got up bright and early, and before he got breakfast he went out and brought the goat in. 'Come on now, Nellie, sit by the fire and have a wee heat,' he said, 'and have a wee crack to the old wife there because me and you are going to the town today, and I'll get you something bonnie. What do you like?'

'Oh well,' she said, 'I'm fond of sweeties and I like pancakes and I like scones and anything that's kind of sweet.'

'I'll get you plenty of sweet things, Nellie, don't worry,' he said. 'I'm not like these laddies, I'll no be bad to you.' So he said to the old woman, 'Give me some extra money to get something for Nellie. She and I will go to town.'

So the old man got Nellie by the rope and a bag on his back, and away he went. And if the three boys were good to Nellie, the old man was ten times better. He treated her like a baby, all the way to the town and on the way back he treated her the same! When he came back, he put her into the shed – before he even had a bite to eat himself – made a nice wee bed of straw for her, got her a nice pail of clean water. And he said, 'Nellie, you lie down there and keep yourself warm. When I get a bite to eat I'll bring you in to the fire to see the old wife.' And the goat lay down. Now the goat never said anything. It wasn't very happy.

So he came in, he gave his old wife all the messages, she made a nice supper for the old man and he lay back, lighted his pipe, untied his boots. And she said, 'Johnnie, before you take your boots off, would you bring wee Nellie in?'

'Aye,' he said, 'I'll go and get Nellie now! She'll tell you how good I was to her. I'm no like your sons, I'm no bad-hearted.' He goes, carries in the goat, and puts it down in the front of the fire.

'Well, Nellie,' old Maggie said, 'how are you feeling the night?'

'Oh woman, don't speak to me, how am I feeling – you shouldn't ask these things of me!' she said. 'How could you manage to stay all these years with that animal of a man you've got? That's a beast, that's worse than every son you ever had. The laddies were bad, but God bless us, that man was worse!' And the old man was sitting at the fire. 'He kicked me and he battered me and he blamed me for his sons. When he got me away from your house a wee bit, he put all his ill will on me because his sons weren't there to help him, and he nearly killed me dead! And I'm no able to move. I cannae talk to you – let me lie doon by your fire!'

'Ah,' said the old man, 'so that's the way it is, is it! Well, Nellie, I brought you to this house for the sake of my old wife to keep her in company, but you ruined my sons' lives. I never hurt you in any way but I'm going to hurt you now!' And he caught the goat and he pulled it outside and he got a walking stick. He beat it and he beat it and he beat it, till the goat couldn't move. 'Now,' he said to the goat, 'get on your way and never show your face back about my house again as long as you live! You unsanctified *jeejament* animal!' he said. 'My poor wee laddies treated you the way I treated you and that's the thanks we get.'

So the goat makes off. And the goat goes, travels on and travels on.

And he went back in, 'Woman!'

She said, 'What did you do to wee Nellie?'

He says, 'I did to Nellie what Nellie needed. Woman, that's an evil beast! All that time when me and you were thinking the world of it . . . I never hurt it, I never touched it on the way to the village!' And the old woman believed him, she believed her old man because she knew he was telling the truth. She kent him through and through.

He said, 'I treated it like a baby and you heard what it said to me. I bet you a pound to a penny the laddies did the same thing, and I gave my wee sons a beating and sent them off – God knows where they are now – for nothing, over the head of that beast, *that animal*, that unsanctified goat!' He said, 'Nothing good will come out of it!'

And the old woman said, 'Johnnie, I believe you, I believe you because there's no goat could speak anyway – unless it was evil. God knows where my wee laddies are . . .' the old woman started to greet.

The old man said, 'Never mind, maybe we'll come across your laddies sometime.'

But we'll leave the old people now and we'll go with the goat.

The goat travels on, it travels on, travels on all night, right through the forest till it comes to the sea. And the heavy waves were lashing against the shore, and it's looking for a place to sleep. A goat's a good climber, and it climbs up the face of this cliff and comes to a nice wee cave in the cliff-face. It goes in, it lies down in the cave. And oh, it's sore, its body is sore with the beating the old man gave it. And its feet are sore with walking so far.

It's saying, 'O-oh-dear-o-dear-o-dear, I'm sore! Ooh my feet, my feet, my body. O-oh dear, what did I do this for? Was I no better back with my old woman, lying among straw and getting petted by the fire? What in the name of God was I thinking about, why have I been so stupid and so foolish?' And the goat's talking away to itself and it's moaning with the pain.

But unknown to the goat a fox had its den in this cave and it had two wee cubs at the very back, and they were lying among a wee puckle straw that the fox had brought in. Now this mother fox had been away hunting all night for something for the cubs to eat. She had caught a rabbit. And by the time she had got back it was daylight. It was the summer-time and the sun was shining. When she came back to the cave she heard this noise from within.

'O-oh-dear-o-dear-o-dear, I'm sore! O-o-o-oh-o-oh-o-oh me-me, what did I do this for?'

The vixen was afraid to go in. She said, 'It must be the devil in there! I can't go in there, and my two wee babies are going to die with the hunger – I can't go in to them!' And she's sitting greeting with the wee rabbit in front of her, sitting in front of the cave.

And the goat's still carrying on and moaning away with the pain, when who comes by but a bumble-bee. And he goes 'bvizzzzz', hunting for flowers. And the bumble-bee was well acquainted with the fox, so he buzzes around two or three times, 'bvizzzzzzzzz', and lands beside the fox. The bumble-bee says, 'What's wrong, Fox?'

'O-oh wheesht!' the fox said, 'In there – the devil – in that cave! My two babies are in there and I've got a wee bite here for them, a wee rabbit I managed to catch. I've been all night looking for it and I can't go in! Listen,' she said to the bumble-bee, 'listen! The devil – it's in there!'

And the goat's lying, 'O-o-oh-me-o-o-o-oh, I'm sore-I'm sore, I'll never see daylight, I'll never see the morning! Oh my poor legs and my poor feet, o-oh, curse upon that old man and curse upon his sons, curse upon his old woman – they've done this to me!'

The bumble-bee went in, flew round about, and he saw the goat lying on its side. He came back out. He said to the fox, 'Don't worry, I'll help you. Just hang on, just sit there! I'll no be long till I'm back.'

And away the bumble-bee goes, 'hmmmmmmmmm', two hundred miles an hour! Away he goes back to the hive, he lands in the hive and says to all his friends, 'Look, you've been hanging about this hive all day! You've never done very much, now come with me, I've got a job for you! Come with me,' said the bumble-bee, 'I need you very quickly, sharpen your stings!'

And all the bumble-bees say, 'Right, we'll go with you!'

So they all landed back at the cave, about seventeen hundred bumble-bees, nearly two thousand! And they stopped. The fox was still sitting.

'Now,' says the bumble-bee, 'in there! And where you hear a noise, moaning and groaning going on, sting to your hearts' content! Sting hard and sting strong.'

So in go the bumble-bees, and one after the other they stung the goat. They stung the goat, every part of it. And the goat got such a fright – it went straight out of the cave – with the pain of the stings! And when it came out it forgot it was on a cliff, and went right out, into the sea and was drowned. It never was heard of again, never heard of!

And the fox went in to its wee babies, gave them the rabbit; and the bees went back to the hive. And that's the end of the goat, and that's the end of my story!

The King and the Lamp

Now, I want to tell you a good story, and I hope you're going to like it. This story's been in our family for hundreds of years and is one my daddy used to tell me when I was wee. Because I was very fond of a story and I used to say to him, 'Tell us some stories, Daddy!' See, when we were carrying on and being wild Daddy used to say, 'Come on and I'll tell you a story!' So you be quiet, listen. And some day when you're big and have wee babies, you can tell them the same story that I'm telling you!

MANY many years ago there was an old tinkerman. And he wandered round the country making tin, because in these days everything that we needed was made from tin. And everything he used to make his tin he carried on his back. Some of the tools of his trade were shears for cutting the tin and a soldering bolt for soldering it, and he went from place to place mending pots and kettles, ladles, toasters and all these kinds of things. But unlike any other old traveller, he was only by himself. He met other travellers along the way and they wondered why, but this old man had never got married.

So, one summer he would be in one place, the next summer he would be in another place and the next summer he would be in another, in villages and towns. But there was one particular town he liked better than any other and he always used to come back, every year, because he got a lot of work there. And the funny thing was, something always drew him back – whether it was the town or whether it was because it was close to the king's palace – nobody will ever know. But one day he landed back.

Not far from the town was the palace, it sat up on a great big hill, and in the palace lived the king and the queen. The old man carried his tent on his back as well as his working things, his tools for making tin. He was quite happy when he landed back near the village. It wasn't very big but he loved this village. That night he sat up and he worked late, and he made kettles, pots, ladles, spoons, everything that he thought he could make.

And the next morning he packed them all on his back and walked into the village. He met a lot of people along the way, people that he had known before and had done some jobs for, he asked them, 'Have you got anything to mend?'

And they said, 'Yes, we've got things to mend but we just can't afford it.'

'Do you want to buy something then – can I sell you a pot, can I sell you a ladle, can I sell you a toaster?' the tinkerman asked. But he met the same problem all the way, wherever he went. And the old man began to think, 'Times must be really hard. Nobody seems to want my tinware any more.'

So at last he landed at the end of the village. An old woman lived there and he had known her for years. He said to her, 'Are your kettles and pots needing mended, my old friend?'

She said, 'Yes, old tinkerman, my kettles and pots need mending.'

'Well,' he said, 'let me do them for you!'

'Well,' she said, 'you can do them for me, but I'm sorry I can't pay you.'

'Oh! Why can you no pay me? I'm sure I don't charge you very much for your kettles and pots,' he said. 'Pennies is all, I think.'[1]

She said, 'I couldn't pay you a penny. Old man, I couldn't even pay you a penny.'

'Well,' he said, 'how about a new pan?'

1 I think – I expect

She said, 'My pans are burned through.' (Because tin pans in these days didn't last very long, they were only made of thin tin.) 'We'd love to . . . but everyone here in the whole . . . Old man, you'll no sell much here this time.'

He said, 'It's been a year since I've been here!'

'But,' she said, 'last year was different from this year.'

'But why?' he said. 'Why was last year so different?'

'Well, our taxes have been raised since last year,' she said. 'Our king doesn't give us much chance. And the same thing happens in all the country and all the villages around. The king has made new laws and raised all our taxes. The farmers can't pay them, neither can the villagers pay their taxes to the landlords. And we're so poor that if things don't change, soon everybody'll have to be like you, old traveller man. We'll have to pack up and go on the road, because we can't afford it.'

'Well,' said the old tinker, 'bad business for you is bad business for me. Why doesn't somebody do something about it?'

'What can we do?' she said. 'We can't go to the king and tell him so stop raising our taxes. He takes three-quarters of the corn from the farmers, three-quarters of everything they grow, if they don't have any money to pay his taxes. Then the landlord who we work for does the same with us, and we're so poor we're hardly able to survive.'

'Well,' said the old traveller man, 'there must be something done about this.'

'Well,' she said, 'there's nobody who can do anything about it. Because we don't want to lose our homes, we don't want to lose our village, we don't want to lose our land – there's nothing we can do.'

So the old traveller man had tried his best but he never made one single penny that day. He walked home very sad to his own little tent which he had camped outside the village. And he kept in his mind the thought that something had to be done, Nobody was going to do it, 'So,' he said, 'it's up to me. I'll have to do it. Because it's in my interest to do it in the first place.'

Then he lay all night in his bed, his little bed of straw on the ground in his tent. And he thought and he thought and he thought of a plan to try and help the villagers and the small farmers around the district who were so good to him . . . and then he came up with the answer: the king must be made to understand, and he – a poor tinker, a traveller tinsmith, he was the very person – the one who was going to make the king understand about the predicament in the village!

The very next morning he got up bright and early, had a little breakfast – which was very meagre at this time – because he had made no money in the village. He packed his camp on his back, and his tools and made his way through the village to the king's palace. But he didn't go straight to the palace. On the way from the village there was a road that led up through a forest and then there was a large driveway that led up to a hill, on the hill was the king's palace.

The story I'm telling you goes back nearly seven to eight hundred years. In these days there were lots of trees, hundreds of trees! The whole country was overrun with them. There was more wood than anything else, and the old tinker had little trouble finding a place to put up his tent and sticks for his fire. So where did he choose to put his tent? On the drive going to the king's palace! It was nothing like the drives you have today – it was just a track right through the wood, beautiful and better made than any in the village. In the village they had no roads. But going to the king's palace they had a road made especially for the king's horses and carriages to pass along. The old tinkerman chose a piece of land as close to the palace, as close to the road as he could find, because that's what he wanted to do!

Then he put up his tent and kindled his fire and started to work on his tinware. But he hadn't been working very long, when who came along but the king's caretaker. And he saw the old traveller man on the pathway.

'Get out of here!' he said, 'Old man, who are you? And what are you doing here?'

The old traveller man said, 'I'm doing nothing. I am at my work and at my job.'

'But, you can't, man,' he said. 'You can't work and kindle a fire here – this is the king's, the driveway to the king's palace!'

'Well,' the old man said, 'I don't care, the driveway to the king's palace or not. I've pitched my tent here and I'm making my tin here, I've got to make my livelihood.'

So the caretaker who was guarding the palace tried his best to get rid of the old man. But no way, the old man wouldn't move. 'Well,' he said, 'I'll soon find somebody that'll shift you.' So up the driveway he goes and he sees some of the king's guards. (Now, there were no police in the land in these days, and any soldiers that were available belonged to the king, and the king could command these soldiers to do anything that he wanted.) And the first person that the caretaker of the king's land met was the captain of the king's soldiers.

He said to the caretaker, who was out of breath by this time for he had run nearly a mile and a half, 'Stop, man, what's the trouble?'

He said, 'The trouble' (panting) 'the trouble is there's an old tinkerman on the driveway leading to the palace. And he's got his fire kindled! He's got his tent there, and he's busy making tinware. And the king is due to go to the village in a very short time!'

'But,' said the king's guard, 'that's no problem. We'll soon square it up.' He called to five of his troop. They jumped on their horses and rode down the drive. They arrived and the old tinkerman was busy – he had his fire going – working at his tinware. So the king's officer jumped off his horse along with his soldiers, and commanded the old man to get moving away from the place because the king was due to pass down this way in a very little time.

But the old man said, 'No. I too am a subject of the king.

He's my king as well as yours. I don't own any land, I don't have any land, but any land that belongs to the king belongs to me. Because he's my king! And if he's my king and I'm one of his subjects, I'm entitled to park my tent on his land and make my living as well as the next person.' As he was an old man, the guards did not want to be rough or man-handle him, so they tried to argue with him.

They argued and tried to get rid of him when who should appear right at that very moment, but the king in his carriage! Ahead of the coach rode two or three couriers. When the king came to the six horses and his officers standing in the road, he ordered the driver to pull up. He opened the door of his coach, he said, 'What is the hold-up here?' And then he saw the fire, he saw the smoke and he saw the tent of the old man. 'What's going on here?' said the king. They lowered the steps from the coach and the king stepped down. And he walked out onto the driveway.

The captain of the king's officers bowed to the king and said, 'Your Majesty, we don't want you to see this.'

'Why not?' said the king. 'Why shouldn't I see? What-wha-what's going on? What's the trouble here? I am late as it is to make an appearance in the village.'

'Well, Sir,' he said, 'I've a little explaining to do. It's one of your subjects.'

'One of my subjects?' said the king. 'What is the trouble then?'

He said, 'Sir, it's an old tinkerman.'

'An old tinkerman? Well,' he said, 'I'm sure you are a troop of soldiers – I don't think you need to be afraid of an old tinkerman.'

'But, Sir,' he said, 'he's got his fire kindled and he's got his tent up and he's making, he's making his livelihood on your driveway!'

'Oh well,' said the king (chuckling), 'that I would love to see! Move – step back!' And the king walked forward.

Sure enough, there was the old tinkerman making things

he would need to sell. But the thing he was specially making was a lamp – the most beautiful lamp – and he was just about finished with it, when the king stepped forward. And the king was amazed: he saw the common fire, he saw the common tent and he saw a piece of leather laid out, and all the working tools that the old traveller man had used. The king had never in his life ever seen anything like this! The king had seen lamps and seen kettles, but he had never had an idea where they came from.

So the king was mesmerised and so happy to see this that he told everyone, 'Stay back for a moment, please, just stay back for a moment!' And everyone had to obey the king. The captain of the guards couldn't do anything. They stood back and held the horses.

And the king sat down on his hunkers beside the old man. He watched the old man. The old man paid no attention to the king, never letting on that he knew this was anybody other than a spectator, till he finished the lamp. Then he polished it.

And the old man looked up, he said, 'Your Majesty, will you forgive me?'

The king said, 'Certainly, my old man, I forgive you. But forgive you for what?'

'Well,' he said, 'last night I was in the village and things were not too good. I had a little money and I went into an ale tavern and I got kind of drunk.' (The old man told him this story.) And he said, 'Eh, with my possessions on my back I wandered here and I wandered there and I didn't know where I was going to find a place to pitch my tent. The only place I could find was here. And I hope you will forgive me, my lord, my king. I didn't know this was the road going to your palace.'

'Oh, come-come, old man,' he said, 'why not? Why not? I'm enjoying this! What is it you're making?'

He said, 'Your Majesty, I am making a lamp. A special lamp.' The king looked and it really was a special lamp. This old man was a really good tinsmith. He made this lamp and unto his mind he'd made it specially for the king. And no one could make a better lamp!

The king looked, 'Is it finished?'

And the old man said, 'Yes, my lord, it's finished.'

'Well, you know,' he said, 'my lamps in my palace are not very good and I think that's a better lamp than any I've ever seen. How much would you take for that lamp from me?' said the king.

'Oh,' he said, 'Your Majesty – I would never take anything from you! I would never take anything from you – I just want you not to be angry with me for staying on your ground!'

'Oh no,' said the king, 'I shall not be angry with you, I'm willing to pay you for your lamp. You need to be paid for your lamp! I get paid for everything that I do – why should you not be paid?' And the king put his hand into his own pocket and took out four gold crowns and put them in the old man's hand. 'Now,' he said, 'I'm giving you these four gold crowns for your lamp because I want it for myself, for my own room. And I hope that it works. But to be fair on you, if it doesn't work the way I want it to, you're going to be in trouble! So that I can find you again, you stay where you are and don't move! You've got my permission to stay here.' The king took his lamp in his hand and he walked to his coach, and bade all his soldiers and everybody to go about their business.

The king told his footman, 'Drive me on!' He put his lamp in his coach with him. 'That,' he said, 'I'm taking back,' and he waved to the old man through the coach window.

The old tinkerman was quite happy. 'Now,' he said, 'my task is half done.' So the tinkerman stayed there all that day.

The king went about his business, visited the village and did all that he wanted to do, met all the people he wanted to see in the village. And the moment that he returned to his palace in his coach, the first thing he took out with him was his lamp.

Into the palace he went, met his queen who was happy to see him returned, and she said, 'You're home, my lord!'

'Yes,' he said, 'my darling, I'm home.'

'But,' she said, 'what is that you have in your hand?'

'Oh, this is something special,' he said, 'my dear. This is a lamp!'

'Oh,' she said, 'I would love to see it working.'

The king said, 'Well, it will be in our bedroom tonight. We will have the most beautiful light that anybody ever had!' Now, the lamps in these days weren't very popular because you couldn't afford lamps, not the way the old tinker could make them. You had to be very rich to be able to buy a good lamp. So late that afternoon the king called for the headman in the castle and told him to fill his lamp and have it ready, that he and his queen would have their lamp while they had their evening meal.

Now the old tinkerman was in his tent and he kindled his fire, made a little meal to himself, and he just sat back and waited. And he waited. He knew what he was waiting for.

Back in the palace it was evening and all this beautiful food was brought forward to the king and the queen, and placed before them for their supper. But evening in the olden times came very quickly because these old palaces were all built of solid rock and stone, and windows were just barred. So the king and queen were dining and they had a few lights going. The king said, 'Bring more light! Bring me my lamp, my special lamp that I got this morning as a present from my old friend, the tinkerman. Bring my lamp! And put it beside my meal where I can see what I'm eating!'

Oh, in these days they filled the lamps with tallow, common oil made from melted down animal fat. And they placed what you call 'rushie wicks' in the lamps made from rushes, the insides of rushes plaited together. They didn't have cotton because cotton wasn't invented at that time, so they took the natural wild rushes and split them, took the centres from the rushes and wove them together to make wicks. To make a large flame you would use maybe five, to make a small flame for a night light, maybe one. Or, if you wanted a brighter light you used two. So they had special people to make these rushie wicks; not anybody could make one. It could have been a turn for a butler or maybe the cook who made rushie wicks for the lamp. And to make a bright light for their king, the head butler or the head cook had plaited five rushie centres together to make a large wick, and placed it in the king's lamp. And lit it.

The lamp was placed before the king, right beside his supper. The king was delighted because it was blazing and he could see all around him! Shadows had been climbing up the walls; then they disappeared as everything was lit up inside the palace chamber. The king said to himself, 'That is a beautiful lamp. I underpaid the old man who made the lamp for me.'

But as he was eating his supper the funniest thing happened: the tallow in the lamp began to leak out and spread across the table. The king was halfway through his meal when he looked and saw the tallow leaking from the lamp, floating right out over the table. And the light of the flame began to get lower and lower as the tallow escaped – the king looked – the lamp went out.

The king was angry, more than angry, because he had told everyone about his special lamp, then it went out! He was so angry he couldn't eat his supper. And he got so wild he began to shout and walk round the inside of the palace chamber. 'Go!' he said to the captain of the guard, 'and bring me that old tinkerman here at once. Bring him before me! I'll have his head. I'll have his head for this!'

So naturally, the old tinkerman was waiting. He saw the guards coming. And he knew what was up. They arrested him immediately and fetched him before the king. And he hung his head before the king, right in the king's chamber.

By this time the king's anger had subsided a wee bit. The king was up; he'd only half finished his supper. The queen had retired to her chamber. 'You call yourself a tinsmith?' he said to the old tinker.

'Yes, my lord,' he said, 'my king, I call myself a tinsmith.'

'And,' he said, 'you made the lamp?'

'Yes, my lord,' he said, 'I made the lamp.'

'And you told me that it was the best lamp that you ever made?'

'Yes, my lord,' he said, 'it was the best lamp I ever made. I never made a lamp before like it.'

'And you promised me that it would give me light – better light than any other lamp that you'd ever made?'

'Yes, my lord,' he said, 'I said it would give you better light than any lamp I'd ever made.'

'Well,' said the king, 'look at my table! And I never finished my meal because of your lamp leaking! It destroyed the table, the oil from the lamp destroyed the table and upset me – I never even finished my meal! And you call yourself a tinsmith!'

'Well, Your Majesty, my dear lord, my king,' he said, 'have I your permission to speak in my own way?'

'Yes,' said His Majesty the King, 'you can speak in your own way. And tell me why that lamp is not fit for me!'

'Well,' Your Majesty,' he said, 'I work hard, and I made sure that the lamp was fit for you, but it's not my fault.

'It's not your fault?' said the king. 'Why is it not your fault – you made it!'

He said, 'Your Majesty, my king, my lord, I made it. But I couldn't make it any better than I made it. Because if there's anyone to blame, it's not me. It's the man who gives me the tin to make my lamp that's at fault, not me. If he'd given me good tin to make a good lamp for you, my lord, I would have made a good lamp.'

'Well,' the king said, 'there could be something in that. Go find the village tinsmith,' he told the captain of the guards, 'and bring him before me this moment!'

Naturally the captain of the guards wasn't long going to the village and he brought back this tinsmith. And the tinsmith stood before the king, and he bowed.

The king said, 'You are the tinsmith of the village?'

He said, 'Yes I am. I am the tinsmith of the village.'

'Did you sell this old tinsmith,' he said, 'some tin today?'

'Yes,' he said, my lord, I sold him some tin.'

'Well,' he said, 'he made me a lamp and the lamp is hopeless because your tin is hopeless.'

'Well, my lord,' he said, 'if my tin is hopeless it's not my fault.'

'Why is it not your fault?' he said. 'You are the man who sells the tin to people who make these things that everyone needs, and you turn around and tell me that it's not your fault?'

'No, my lord,' he said, 'it's not my fault.'

'Well,' he said 'whose fault is it?'

He said, 'It's the man from the foundry who produces my tin that's at fault, not me.'

So the king sent two guards to the smelter in the small iron foundry who made tin. The man was arrested and brought to the palace. Now the old tinker and the tinsmith were sitting there, and then the man from the foundry who made the tin was called. He was taken before the king and questioned.

His Majesty said, 'Did you sell some tin to the tin dealer who sold this tin to the tinkerman who made my lamp?'

'Yes, my lord,' he said, 'I did. I supply all his tin.'

He said, 'Why is your tin not fit to make a lamp for me?'

'Well, my lord,' he said, 'if the tin's not fit enough, it's not me to blame.'

'Well,' he said, 'who is to blame? Someone has to stand accused for the mistake that was made for me!'

'Well,' my lord, it's not my fault,' he said.

'Whose fault is it?' said the king.

He said, 'The fault must lie with the man who makes my bellows to blow my fire to make my heat to make my tin!'

'Well,' said the king, 'fetch him! Bring him here.'

So naturally, off went the king's guards again and brought back the bellows-maker who made the bellows for pumping the air into the fire foundry to melt the ore to make the tin. And he was brought before the king.

The king said, 'Step before me! Bellows-maker, you're charged with . . .' and he told him the whole story as I'm telling you.

The bellows-maker said, 'My lord and my king, you must forgive me! Because—'

'Why should I forgive you?' he said. 'You're the cause of all my trouble, and the trouble of these other men who stand before me – they're condemned! They're going to suffer.'

And the bellows-maker said, 'Well, my lord, my king, it's not my fault.'

'Well,' he said, 'whose fault is it?'

'My lord,' he said, 'it's the man in the tannery's fault, who sells me my skins to make my bellows.' (Now all these bellows that pumped the fire with air were made from skins.)

The king said, 'Get the man here from the tannery at this moment! I want to get to the end of this. Bring him here before me!'

Naturally, the man from the tannery was sent for, who had tanned all the skins and made the leather that was used in the bellows to blow the fire to melt the ore to make the tin for the old tinkerman. And they were all before the king. So the man from the tannery was brought forward, before the king.

The king accused him straightaway and said, 'Look . . .' and he told him the story I'm telling you. 'You are a man of the tannery?'

'Yes, my lord, I am from the tannery,' he said.

He said, 'You make the skins and tan the skins that makes this man's bellows that this man uses to melt this ore to make tin to sell to the tinsmith who sold it to the tinker who made my lamp – and my lamp leaks on my table and upsets my supper?'

'Yes,' says the tanner, 'it's true. But, my lord, it's not my fault.'

'Then, who's at fault?' says the king. 'Someone stands condemned for this thing that's really happened!'

And the man from the tannery said, 'My lord, it's not me. My lord, it's the farmer who sends me the animals, who I get the skins from.'

'Well,' said the king, 'bring the farmer to me! Immediately. I must get to the end of this, to the bottom of this thing tonight!'

So naturally, the farmer was sent for. And he stood before the king. And the king told him the story I'm telling you.

'You are the farmer,' he said, 'who supplies the skins to the tannery?'

'Yes,' he said, 'my lord, my king, I am.'

'And,' he said, 'the tanner supplies them to the bellows-maker and he sells bellows to the man who melts the ore and the man who melts the ore makes tin to supply tin to the tinsmith and the tinsmith supplies it to this old tinker who made my lamp that destroyed my evening meal?'

'Yes, my lord, that's true.'

'Well,' he said, 'why is it that your skins are not good enough?'

'My lord, and my king,' he said, 'I hope you will forgive me.'

'Forgive you for what?' he said. 'I know I shan't forgive you!' said the king.

He said, 'My lord, there is no one at fault, if I must tell the truth before my king,' and he bowed. 'Your Majesty, if the skins don't work to make the bellows and the bellows don't work to heat iron and if the iron doesn't work to make the tin and the tin doesn't work well enough to supply the tinsmith who sells it to the old tinkerman to make your lamp, then, my lord, you're at fault!'

'Me,' said the king, 'I am at fault?'

Yes, my king and my lord,' he said, 'you probably will have my head for this, but I have to tell you – you are at fault.'

'And why,' said the king, 'am I at fault? You mean to tell me I'm at fault for the lamp that I never saw before that spills oil on my table and destroys my evening meal, I'm at fault?'

'Yes, my king,' he said, 'you're at fault.'

'Well, tell me,' he said, 'truthfully, why am I at fault?'

'Well, my lord,' he said, 'to begin with, I grow little grain and three-quarters of that goes to you. With what I've got left I'm not able to feed my animals through the winter. Their skins are so poor that they're not even fit to make a bellows to blow a fire to heat some ore and make some tin to sell to a tinsmith to make a lamp for yourself.'

And the king said, 'Is that the truth?'

'Yes,' he said, 'that's the truth.'

And the king sat back and thought. And he thought for a while. He turned round and he said, 'Gentlemen, come, gather round, and sit there beside me. You have taught me something that I didn't know. Bring forth the wine!' said the king. And they brought forth a flagon of wine and he gave every single man a drink.

'Drink to me – but a special drink,' he said, 'I want you to give to the old tinkerman.' And he took his own golden cup, he handed it to the old tinkerman. And the old tinkerman drank half and the king drank the other half.

He said to the old tinkerman, 'You are the one who taught me to be a real king! From now on, no more taxes on the farmers! What they grow they can keep it to themselves, for what good use is it being a king to rule over people who can't even make something for me that I need, because of my own fault!'

And from that day on to this day, the king laid no more taxes on the farmers, and they produced grain and they produced animals and produced skins for the bellows-makers. And the farmers produced the greatest of skins and these great skins were given to the bellows-maker and the bellows-maker made bellows past the common, and these were used in the foundries to blow air into the furnaces to melt iron and the iron was made into beautiful sheets of tin and the beautiful sheets of tin were sold to the tinsmiths, and the tinsmiths made the most beautiful things. And for evermore everyone was happy, except the king – he was left with his lamp that leaked from the old tinkerman! And that is the last of my story.

The Boy and the Boots

The travellers believed that there were people who lived in this world long before your time and mine who used to steal people away and take their bodies, kill them and cut them up, and use them for research in colleges for the education of doctors. The tinkers and travellers called them 'burkers' – body-snatchers. And they still believe that there are plenty of body-snatchers alive at this present moment, though the demand for bodies is no as much as it was in the olden days.

This was our favourite story that Daddy used to tell us; it was one of his favourites too – he told it to us as children often. We used to say, 'Daddy, tell us a wee story when you were near burkit with[1] the body-snatchers.'

Daddy turned around and said, 'Well, I'll tell you a wee burker story that happened to me a long time ago when I was very young.'

ME and my mother and father and the rest of the children were in this town. We had travelled all over the country and we were in a new town every day, and this was a strange town to us because we had never been here before. I was about fourteen at the time. We landed in the town and my mother was selling some baskets, my daddy was making and selling some tin. We always used to go and sit on the village green. My daddy would maybe go and have a wee drink and my mother would make us some tea. We could play ourselves in the village green but we didn't interfere with the rest of the children that inhabited the village, we kept to ourselves.

1 near burkit with – almost secretly killed by

But I got very curious, because I had never got much room to be on my own for a wee while. I said to myself I would have a wander through the town, see all the beautiful things that I had never seen. Because naturally, travelling people like us never had much chance to come to the town unless it was the week-end, when my daddy had something to sell. So I wandered through the town.

There were shops full of clothing, beautiful clothes that I would love to own but had no way of getting, and there were shops full of toys and shops full of food, butcher shops full of meat – it just made my mouth water! And I passed my time in the town for a long long while. But time had passed so fast for me I never realised that, looking at all these things in the town, hours had passed, and I had to go back. I made my way to the green where my mummy and daddy were supposed to be waiting for me. But when I landed back my mummy and daddy were gone! They had packed their little hand-cart with the tent – they went and left me.

I'm left in the middle of the town, and I never knew in a million years what direction my father went! He could have gone south, he could have gone east, he could have gone west, he could have gone in any direction. So I said to myself, 'Now, I'll have to find my mother and father,' because I was only fourteen and I'd never been left by myself before and I'd never spent a night away from my father and mother in my life. And my father had told me all the stories about evil people who were burkers with coaches who would take my body and sell it to the doctors for money – I was terrified.

But anyway, I thought I'd take the main road out of the village because I thought, 'That's the road my mummy and daddy would take.' And I travelled on and travelled on, by the time I got to the end of the town it was getting dark. And I said to myself, 'I'll never catch my mummy and daddy tonight, what am I going to do? I can't stay by myself,' because I was afraid.

So I travelled on and I travelled on and I travelled on, and the farther I travelled the darker it got, because it was the winter months and it got darker by the minute. It was very very dark when I came to a long straight piece of road between two forests with not a house in sight. Then I listened! And I heard coming behind me – the patter of horses' feet – the thought dawned in my head, the stories my daddy had told me, the burkers' coach! I said, 'This is bound to be a burkers' coach!'

And I got in the ditch among the long grass, I hid down in the ditch. Then I heard the horses' coach coming, the patter of horses' feet . . . they passed me by. There were two horses on the coach and the coach was all in black except for one light on the roof. I waited and waited and waited, till the coach got well on before me. I said, to myself, 'As sure as God in heaven, my daddy told me, that is a burkers' coach out looking for bodies tonight. Well, they're not going to get me!'

So I travelled on, I travelled on, I travelled on, and I came to this piece of road going up a wee piece of hill, and lying in the road was a pair of boots – the most beautiful boots I had ever seen in my life – long brown leather boots! And they were tied together with a pair of laces. I picked up the boots and said, 'This'll do me,' because all my life I had wanted to own a pair of boots like this. And I put them across my shoulder. I travelled on for about ten yards.

And I looked: there was a gate. The moon began to come up. I looked in the gate and I saw all these things standing up, all these white things standing up. But I wan't afraid! The moon got brighter – and I saw that it was a graveyard, and the gates were open. Now my daddy had always told me, 'You're safe enough passing a graveyard if you don't pass it by between twelve and one.' I knew that I had left the village when it was only getting dark, that now it could only be about nine or ten o'clock. It couldn't be evil time in the graveyard. So I naturally walked past the gates of the graveyard, about ten yards from where I had found the boots – they were on my back. I travelled on, I travelled on, this long weary road.

I looked at all the places at the roadside to see if I could see a light of a camp-fire or something – but no, there was no light or camp-fire. But now the hoolits began, 'cahoo-cahoo-cahoo'. It was night-time, the road was long and dreary, I got kind of afraid. I said, 'I just can't stay out tonight, I can't sleep under a hedge or something,' because I had never done it before. And I travelled on, there wasn't a house in sight.

Then, above the road a wee bit, I saw a light. And this road led up to it. Now my daddy had always said to me, 'If you're down and out, look for a light well back from the road,' because coaches and burkers didn't go off the road – it was too much of a pull for the horses. So I see this light up on a hillside and there was an old rough road going up the way.

I said, 'Probably it's an old farmer and his wife, probably I can sleep in the shed for the night and nobody'll know I'm there till the morning. And I'll jump out and be gone before they ever see me.' So I walked up, slowly up the road, but my feet were making terrible noises on the coarse stones going up it.

I walked up and walked up and walked up, I just landed at the end of the road when out comes a man with a lantern. He had one of these old-fashioned lights in his hand, a paraffin lamp. And he sees me before I had a chance to get into the shed and lie down – he sees me. He says, 'Come here, you!' So naturally I was a wee bit afraid, and he came forward. He held the light up and shined it in my face – he looked at me. 'And, hey,' he said, 'who are you and where do you come from?'

'Oh,' I said, 'sir, I'm sorry – I must have taken the wrong road – I'm looking for my daddy and my mummy and the children, my wee brothers and sisters.'

He said, 'Say that again?'

I said, 'I'm looking for my mummy and my daddy and my wee brothers and sisters.'

He said, 'Who are you?' And he shined the light on me, saw I was ragged and torn and my clothes weren't very— 'Are you one of the tinker people?'

'Oh,' I said, 'yes, sir, I'm one of the tinker people – I'm the oldest of the family and I was in the town today back there with my mummy and daddy and I lost them – and I didn't know what road to take. And I, I–I'm looking for them.'

He said, 'Come with me.' He took me past the house right to the door, opened the door of the big shed, a barn. He said, 'Get in there! You can sleep in there for the night, you'll be all right!' He closed the door and he locked it. I heard the key going 'click'.

I walked forward through the barn and it was heaped with straw. And then I looked – there was a stall in the one corner, in the stall was a cow and the cow was chewing hay. I looked up, there were some couples[1] up above the cow's head and on the roof there was a skylight – I could see the moon shining through it. I tried the door but the door wouldn't open; there was no other way out.

I said to myself, 'I don't like this very much. I can't stay here. I don't like this man very much.' But anyway, I sat down among some straw and then I heard the key turning in the door. The door opened. And the light shone on me.

He said, 'Are you there?'

I said, 'Yes, I'm here – what is it?'

'Come awa, come out a minute!'

I came out. And this man who had the lantern was about six feet tall, red-haired, with brown eyes, a red face. He said, 'Eh, I suppose you'll be hungry?'

'Well, sir,' I said, 'I've had nothing to eat all day.'

'Well,' he said, 'come with me!' And he led me into the house.

1 couples – pairs of rafters

In the house was a big old-fashioned fire and a bare table, nothing on the table, some chairs. And there was this woman, about the same size as the man, with red hair, and freckles on her face. And I looked at the other side of the table – there was a young man who must have been his son, and on the other chair sitting was his daughter – she was red-haired! And my daddy had told me, 'Beware of red-headed people, especially farmers or land-owners who are red-haired and have brown eyes!' He told me they were bad people, 'Never to be sure of red-haired people or brown-eyed folk, keep away from them.' And me – I was as blond as a baby, fair curls down the back of my neck and blue eyes.

And the farmer's wife said, 'Isn't he a pretty little boy – it's a pity . . .'

When she said 'it's a pity', didn't I think – 'it was a pity that I had lost my daddy and my mummy'! I didn't know!

She said, 'Isn't it a pity, isn't he a beautiful boy! Where do these travelling tinker people get all the good looks and the beautiful hair and blue eyes?' But I didn't pay much attention. I heard her saying this but it didn't dawn on me then what she was meaning.

She said, 'Are you hungry?'

I said, 'Yes, ma'am, I'm hungry.' So she brought me a big bowl of porridge and milk.

She said, 'Eat that up!' So I sat there and I was really hungry and I ate this big bowl of porridge and milk.

Then the man took the lantern and he said, 'You sure you're all right now – had you enough to eat?' I didn't like him very much because he had a big high Roman nose, hooked nose, curly red hair and evil-looking brown eyes.

'Come on,' he said, 'I'll take you to your bed!' And he took me back into the same place. 'You can find a place to sleep among the straw.' And the cow was busy chewing away on the hay, chewing away.

So I lay down but I couldn't sleep among the straw, I couldn't sleep. I said to myself, 'I remember all the things that my daddy and mummy told me about red-haired people – they swore that they were burkers!' And they had a reason to believe that, because they had known from past experience these people really would sell someone's body for money. And I was terrified.

Now I had left my boots in the shed when the farmer took me in to give me some supper. And I picked my boots up, put them around my neck, and I said, 'I'll have to find a way to escape.' But the door was locked, I couldn't escape. There was no way out. 'I'll have to escape!' And then the moon came up again, it shined through the skylight and I said to myself, 'That's the way out for me!' Me being a tinker, I knew how to get out. I said, 'I'll climb up that wall and I'll get through that skylight window.' But the thing was, the skylight was directly above the cow and the cow was tied right at the bottom. The cow wouldn't bother me. Now there were two long wooden beams to the left of the cow's head that went straight up to the roof. I said, 'I'll climb that beam and get up there, open that window, go out on the roof and escape – get going! But,' I said again, 'probably I'm just exaggerating a wee bit. Probably if I stay here the people'll not bother me.'

Then I lay for a wee while, not asleep, when I heard a horse and coach coming in to the front of the farm, with lights on it. It stopped! And the farmer came out with a lamp in his hand and he said, 'Okay, come in and have a wee drink! I've got something for you tonight, I have something for you.'

And the man who stepped down from the coach had this long coat on him, a swallow-tail coat and a tile hat. Three of them stepped from the coach, three men. And I could see by the light – with their long coats and their hats – they were the evil people my father had told me about. I could see the horse, a black horse, and a black coach parked right in front of the farm. I said to myself, 'They're here for me! But they're no going to get me!'

'Come in and have a drink,' he said, 'you can pick him up

later!' That was me they were talking about – they were going to pick me up later! They were going to burk me, take me and kill me and sell my body to the doctors.

I said, 'No-o-o-o, they're no going to get me!' So I picked the boots up, put them around my neck and started to climb the pole above the cow's head – right to the skylight. And I climbed and I climbed. I got up and I put my arms right up, and as I reached up my arms the boots fell off my neck. But as the boots fell, I looked – o-oh, I nearly fell off too – there were legs in the boots cut from below the knee! Raw bloody legs, and they fell right at the cow's nose! I managed to reach the skylight window and lifted it – it was open. I lifted it up slowly, crawled out through the hole, got out on the roof, ran along the roof. And I looked all around, it was kind of dark, and I jumped. I said, 'I'm no caring suppose I break both my legs, I'll crawl on the grass before I get taken with these people!'

And then I landed, in the dung heap in the back of the place. It was lucky for me that the farmer had packed all the dung at the back of the shed. I landed right to the waist in the heap; I never even hurt a bone in my body. And I crawled out and ran away for my life, down through the moor and on to the main road. I said, 'I'll make my way back to the town as fast as I can!' Now I don't know what happened behind me, but this is what I believe happened.

After they had something to drink, the farmer said to the three men, 'I've something for you tonight, a nice young man for you. I've got him locked up in the byre with the cow. And he's a good specimen. You can have him tonight!' And they paid the farmer a lot of money – for me – for my body! The farmer said, 'He can't escape, I've got him locked up. Just grab him when you go in!'

They opened the door and they looked all around with their lights. But they couldn't find me, I was gone! They searched every place in the byre. They couldn't get me.

And then somebody said, 'Maybe he's hiding behind the cow.' They took a light up beside the cow and the cow was chewing away at the grass. 'Maybe he's hiding under the cow's head, at the front of it.' And they looked. 'Oh,' somebody said, 'oh look! There's his boots – grab him!' And they grabbed the boots and they pulled them out and looked . . . nothing in the boots but the legs.

The farmer said, 'That's him, that's his boots – I remember his boots.' (He never noticed the boots had been on my back.) He said, 'I never knew – a cow ate him, the cow has eaten him!' And the poor simple cow was standing chewing away at its cud. It had saved my life, chewing away, chewing its cud. And they believed the cow had eaten me! Because the boots that I had found at the gate of the graveyard had legs in them, and they believed *that* was me.

And I made my way back the next morning. I hid in the wood till the sun came up, then made my way back to the town. I wandered round the town and the first body I found was my mother, who was in tears looking for me.

She said, 'Where have you been?'

'Oh,' I said, 'Mother, where have you been, where have I been? Look, Mummy . . .' and I started to cry. I said, 'I can't tell ye the noo but I'll tell you the night when you take me home to my daddy!'

She said, 'I'm in here looking for you – your daddy's only along the shore a wee bit. We've got our camp just at the end of the town. I'm only in for to get some messages to make something for the bairns to eat. We're frantic looking for you all night. We're near off our heads looking for you!'

I said, 'Mummy, take me back.' So my mummy took me back.

My daddy said, 'Where have you been?'

I said, 'Daddy, listen, and I'll tell you where I've been . . .' and I told my daddy the story that I told you. And that is the God's honest truth – that really happened. That was me when I was near burkit many many years ago!

THE BROONIE, SELKIES AND FAIRIES

The Broonie on Carra

This is a wee story that was told to me by a friend of mine way back in Argyll many many years ago, and he told me that this story was true. The country folk's[1] *beliefs in the Broonie are just as strong as any traveller's, in fact maybe a wee bit stronger. Old Duncan McVicar, the Gaelic-speaking farmer I used to work for at Auchinagoul, he wouldn't mention his name at all – just called him 'the wee fella'. It was the same as the travellers' belief in God; they won't say his name either – it's 'the Good Man' they call him, the same name for Jesus.*

DOWN near Campbeltown in Argyll there's a wee island called Carra, and the local villagers believe that that is the home of the Broonie, he stays on Carra. The island is small and there's only one house on it. There's water on Carra – I once walked down the steps cut out of stone to the Broonie's well – where he's supposed to drink his wee drop o' water. But otherwise Carra is uninhabited.

Now many years ago this minister, who was a great believer in the Broonie, bought the wee house on Carra and he and his wife moved out to the island. They lived very happily on Carra, they took a cow across with them to supply them with milk. The minister loved the island, he set lobster pots and he fished, did everything – he was quite happy and content. He had no family, just him and his wife.

So this minister had a boat and he used to travel across to Bellochantuy when he needed to go to Campbeltown for his messages. But in these days there were no cars on the

1 country folk's – non-travellers'

road, it was only a track to Campbeltown, just a horse-track, it was all done by pony and trap. Once a week he had to go across to the mainland to give a service in Campbeltown. He drove by pony and trap and always took his wife with him when he went. They would row their boat across from Carra, tie it up, borrow a pony and trap from a local farmer and drive to Campbeltown, do his service in the church and drive back, leave the pony and trap at the farm, and row across to Carra to his house.

But one morning, it was a beautiful Sunday morning, his cow was about to calf. So he said to his wife, 'I think we'll take the cow out.' Now next to his house was a wee shed where he kept a wee byre for holding the cow. He took the cow out and said, 'Poor sowl, you're better walkin aboot – it'll help ye when ye're gaunae have a calf, ye can walk aboot, for you seem very sick.' He let the cow go.

He and his wife went down, took the boat, rowed it across, tied the boat up, borrowed the pony and trap from the farmer and drove to Campbeltown, which is about fifteen miles. (It's not far for a horse, a horse'll do it in an hour and a half.) He did his service in the church, came out of the church, talked to his friends, yoked the horse and left Campbeltown. But there came a storm, a terrible time of rain and wind.

He said to his wife, 'Come storm or hail or rain, we'll have to get home tonight tae Carrie.' But the weather got worse. He drove back the fifteen miles to Bellochantuy, then on to Muasdale. When he came to Muasdale the weather was still worse, you could hardly see – the rain was battering, the waves were lashing!

And his wife turned round to him, 'Husband, we'll never get home tonight to Carrie, there's no way in the world that we're gaunnae get across, take our own boat across tae Carrie tonight!'

He says, 'Wife, we'll hev tae! What about wir cow? What's about the wee cow – it's out there itself – wanderin on the island the night among this rain and sleet!' They drove the horse back to the farm, drove up to the house.

The old farmer came out and met them. After the horse had been tied up and its harness taken off, the minister came in and had a cup of tea or a dram. The waves were lashing and the boom was coming across from Carra. So the old farmer said to the minister, 'Look, there's no way in the world you're gaunnae cross that sea tonight! For the peril o' your wife's life . . .'

But the minister says, 'What about my wee cow!'

He said, 'Does the cow mean more to ye than your wife, or your own life?'

The minister said, 'Look, the cow's wanderin the night – I let her loose before I left.'

The farmer finally persuaded the minister that there's no way in the world he was going to take a boat across that night to Carra. It was impossible! Now the cow was on its own. The island is desolate, it's not very big, only about three acres, practically all rock. Not a soul is on the island, just the house, the byre, and the cow – no dogs, no cats, nothing. The minister was very unhappy but he stayed in the farm, the old farmer put him and his wife up for the night. He passed a terrible sleepless night because he was thinking on his wee cow, in the island on its own, wandering alone with the cold and the wind, and it was going to calf.

But anyway, morning came, which it alway does. And the minister was up bright and early, it was a beautiful day. The sea was calm, the wind was gone, the rain was gone, and there was hardly a wave to be seen. And he called his wife, he couldn't hurry quickly enough. They had a wee bit breakfast from the farmer and bade him 'good-bye', left the pony and trap for the farmer to take care of (the minister probably owned the trap), and hurried down across the road, about four hundred yards from the farm, through a wee field down to the boat. The minister got in the boat and his wife got in the back. They were just a young couple, in their thirties, no children.

He got into the oars and pulled the boat across as fast as he could. And och, the sea was as calm as the palm of your hand – not a wave, nothing. The sun was shining. He rowed across to Carra. And right where you land the boat is a wee place in the rocks, there's a few steps which go down to the Broonie's well – and water comes out of this rockface. The minster pulls in the boat, and there's a bolt in the wall and a ring to tie up your boat. He tied the boat to the ring, couldn't hurry fast enough, helped his wife out of the boat, and the two of them hurried up the wee shingle path to the house. But before the minister went near the house he searched all around as far as he could see, looking for the cow. Cow was gone. He said to his wife, 'She's prob'ly been blown over the rocks and carried away in the tide!' Into the house the minister went.

The wife made a cup of tea and he was sitting down in his chair, completely sad and broken-hearted because he loved this wee cow dearly . . . it was the only thing gave them milk on the wee island. They loved the solitude and peace and quietness of this island, that's why they went there in the first place, because he could think about God and his sermons – he was a good man, a really good man. He said to his wife, 'I'm really sorry . . . look what happened. Well, I'll take a wee walk and walk aroond the shoreside, see if I can find the carcass o' her, she was prob'ly carried away wi the tide.' But as he went outside he thought he'd have a last look in the byre where he used to tie the wee cow up at night-time. He said, 'If I only had left her tied in the byre, she'd be safe.'

Now he used to always fill a pail of water for the cow and carry it in. And before he had gone away, when he'd left the cow out on the grass, he'd carried the pail and left it outside – he remembered this – that he'd left the pail of water outside, because there was no running water inside the wee byre. When he walked out the door of the house, he looked at the door of the byre – the pail was gone! He said, 'I remember I took the pail oot, and left the pail at the door when I let the coo oot!'

There was nothing to do – he walked to the byre, opened the door and walked into the byre – there was the wee cow standing, a pail of water at her head, a beautiful heap of hay in the wee heck at her nose and the bonniest wee calf you ever saw standing at her feet! And the chain was round her neck, she was tied up, tied up to the stall where he had tied her before. The minister stood and he looked, he was aghast. He ran into the house, called his wife and told her, 'Come oot,' he said, 'I want to show you something!'

'What is it?' she said.

'Come here, come here. I want to show you something! Look!' he said to his wife. He opened the door of the byre and he showed her – there was the cow and there was the bonnie wee calf standing at her feet – there was the pail of water and there was the hay in her wee heck at her nose and the cow was as healthy as could be and so was the calf! He turned round and told his wife, 'Look, there's only one explanation,' he said, 'there's only one explanation and you know as well as me . . . there was nobody on this island when me and you left.'

'I know,' she said to him, 'Angus, there was nobody here when we left.'

He said, 'There's only one person responsible for this.'

She says, 'I know.'

He says, '*That was the Broonie.*'

And that man spent all his days on that island, till he became an old man when he retired to Campbeltown. He believed, and he was a man of the cloth, nobody in the world could convince him otherwise, that it couldn't have been anybody but the Broonie who tied up his wee cow that night on the island of Carra. And that's the last of my wee story!

The Broonie's Farewell

The Broonie can take any form if he wants to. But he doesn't come to deceive people, rather to test them, so he comes in the form of the lonely old tramp with a ragged coat, the lowest form of life, who is thought of as nothing. It's like God coming in another form. As a tramp he will get the person's true personality, the person's true feelings towards the lowest type of person you could ask for.

People were very privileged to be visited by the Broonie. And if he ever visited any place at any particular time, his visit was never forgotten. Word of it always passed down, from generation to generation, and this is where 'The Broonie's Farewell' really came from. An old traveller man told me this story a long time ago when I was very young. He said it really happened, he was supposed to have been at the farm, away back in the highlands of Argyllshire near Rannoch Moor. I don't know the name of the farmer in the story, but the Broonie didn't care for anybody without a 'Mac' in their name. The Broonie was the patron spirit of the Macdonalds.

MANY many years ago there lived a small farmer on a hill farm in the West Highlands of Scotland. He and his wife had this wee farm between them. They were very poor off, they didn't have very much to start with. But as years went by he became a rich man, and when he was middle-aged he had a wee son. The mother and father loved this wee boy dearly. And his mother was such a kindly woman, she couldn't see anything going wrong with him; they gave up everything in the world they really needed for the sake of their son. And the son returned it every way possible, he was really good to his mother and father, helped in every way he could. If ever there was a job needing to be done about the place he would always say, 'Daddy, I'll do it.'

His mother would say, 'No, son, just dinna hurry yourself, take your time and jist help your daddy whenever possible.' So it came a Saturday afternoon. By this time the laddie was about eleven years old. The old woman was sitting in the kitchen and she said, 'Can youse two men no find a job fir yoursels? Because I'm gaun to bake.'

And the father said, 'Come on,' to the laddie, 'that's a sign that me and you are no wantit!'

So they walked out of the house and he said, 'Daddy, what are we gaunnae do?'

'Well, son, I'll tell you what we're gaunnae do,' he said. 'We've got everything done, hay's all cut, so we'll need to go in and clean up the barn because it's gettin kind o' tottery. I'm beginnin to fa' ower things in the mornin when I go in there.'

'All right,' said the wee laddie, 'I'll go and get a wheelbarra, Daddy, and we'll clean out the barn.'

So the wee laddie got a wheelbarrow, hurled it into the barn. And the man's picking up old bags and all kinds of stuff, he's putting it in the barrow. But hanging behind the door of the barn inside was a coat and a pair of breeches and a pair of hose. They were covered in cobwebs. The wee laddie reached up. 'Okay, Daddy,' he says, 'here's some old clothes.'

'Oh no, son,' he says, 'no, don't touch that!'

'Why, Daddy,' he says, 'it's only old rags.'

'No, son,' he says, 'it's no rags. While your mother's bakin we'll keep oot o' her way . . . and we hevnae much tae dae in here, we're nearly finished . . . sit doon there and I'll tell ye a wee story.' So the farmer took a pitchfork and raked up a bunch of hay, he made a seat. 'Now,' he said to the wee boy, 'sit doon here, son, and I'll tell you aboot that coat, breeches and the hose. . . .

'Many years ago, long before you were born, when me

and yir mother cam here, this place was pretty run doon and we didna have very much money. I got it at a very cheap rent. We cam up here and we workit away hard, both your mother and me, and tried tae make this place intae a kind o' decent fairm. Well, we hadna been here for over a year and things was really tough.

'And one night late, about the month o' October, yir mother and I were sittin doon tae a wee meal, an we didna hae very much at that time, when a knock cam to the door. And your mother said, "Go and see who that is at this time o' night."

'So naturally I went oot, and there standin at the door was an auld man.'

'What kind o' man, Daddy?' the wee boy said. 'What kind o' man was he?'

'Well,' he said, 'he was just an ordinary auld man, but he wisna very big and he had a white beard. But he had the two bluest eyes that ever I saw in my life. So I asked him what he wanted.

'He said, "I'm just an auld man and I thought you mebbe have some work, or cuid gie me shelter for the night."

'So your mother shouted tae me, "Who is it, John?"

'It's an auld man luikin for shelter.'

' "Well," she said, "bring him intae the kitchen!"

'So I said, "Ye better—"

' "No, no, no," he said, "I can't come intae the kitchen."

'The old man wadna come into the kitchen even though yir mother cam to the door. An she coaxed him, but he wadnae come, in any way. So wi yir mother being a kind-herted sowl, she asked him, "Are ye hungry, auld man?"

' "Oh," he said, "I'm hungry, yes, I'm hungry."

' "Wad ye like something tae eat?"

' "Oh, I would love something tae eat. Cuid ye give me a bowl o' porridge an milk?" And naturally, that's what me an yir mother wis haein that night – porridge and milk.

'So yir mother filled a big bowl and I carriet it oot tae him and gied it tae him in his two hands. And I tuik him intae the barn, I said tae him, "There auld man, ye can find shelter fir the night-time."

'Well,' the farmer said, 'I put him in the barn, an believe it or not what I'm gaunnae tell ye, that auld man stayed wi me fir six months and I never saw a harder worker in my life! I had practic'ly nothing tae dae round the place. He was up, first thing in the mornin he startit tae work, tae the last thing at night he was still workin. He had everything about this place prosperin like it never prospered before. I never lost an animal of any kind, I had the greatest crops that ever I cuid ask for and I cam in an offered him wages, but he wouldnae have any. Or he wouldnae come intae the house, all he wanted tae do was sleep in the barn.

'Well, after workin fir about six months yir mother took pity on him. And one night she sat down special hersel and made him a pair o' breeches cut doon fae mine and she knittit him a pair o' hose. And one mornin when she cam oot wi his bowl o' porridge, she brought them and placed them beside his bowl. Later in the morning when I cam oot, the coat, the breeches, and the hose wis gone, an the bowl was empty – his auld breeches and his coat wis hung behind the door. And there they've been hung, son, fir over eleven year. And remember: someday this farm will pass on tae you but promise me, as long as you own this place, ye'll never part with these breeches, or that coat or thae hose!'[1]

1 The breeches the Broonie left in the barn were short, just came below the knee, the hose was pulled up to meet them. They laced down the side of the leg and were made of corduroy. They hung at the back of that door for years and years, and were never allowed to pass away from that place. You're not to pay the Broonie, you see. You can thank him, but the minute you pay him, you're finished. He wouldn't take any money, and when the farmer's wife left the clothes down beside his bowl, he thought, 'That's your payment – we've nae mair use for you' . . . he was gone! So that's why the old man told the laddie to hang on to the coat, he thought maybe the Broonie might come back.

'No, Daddy,' he said, 'I never will.'

And when the man passed on and the young laddie got the farm, the breeches and the coat and the hose hung behind the door till it passed on to his son. And that's the last of my wee story.

Selkie Painter

There are many tales and legends told about the seal-folk or selkies, as they are called by some people in the Western Isles. It is their belief that seals have the power to turn themselves into human beings for a certain length of time. Seal-folk are supposed to help you, do good things for you. They've never been known to do anyone any evil! So the story I'm going to tell you is about an old woman and a seal.

MANY years ago on the West Coast there lived an old fisherman and his wife. They had this wee cottage by the shoreside. The fisherman used to set his nets, and what fish he and the old woman couldn't use he took along to the village and sold. The old woman kept a couple of goats and some hens; she used to sell eggs and goats' milk in the village. In the small village where they stayed there was only one post office, a hotel and a small police station, and everybody knew everybody else. But they never had any family – the old folk lived pretty well by themselves. The old man only had one enemy, the seals. He hated the seals because they used to tear his nets and eat the fish. He couldn't stand seals in any way.

And he was always getting on to the old woman and telling her, 'That's another seal Mary,' he would say, 'that's another good fish destroyed by these seals again, these animals! They're making a terrible mess of my nets. I wish to God they would clear out and never come back. I hate these terrible beasties!'

But the old woman, she was a kindly old cratur. She said, 'Well, John, you know they have to live just the same as everybody else.'

In her spare time the old woman used to gather seaweed, the dulse that comes in with the tide – these big thick stems of seaweed that break away with the heavy storms, with the working of the sea. And the old woman used to collect these big thick tangles and stack them up to dry. When they were dry a man used to come and buy them from her. He sent them away to the towns to get made into perfume or whatever.

One day the old woman was down on the beach. She was as usual gathering seaweed and putting it out on the beach to dry, when she came over behind this rock. The first thing she saw was a wee baby seal, a new-born, two or three days she thought it to be. So she bent over to pick it up and said, 'Poor little thing.' She looked all around her to see if its mother or any other seals were about before picking it up, but she never saw another seal. So she thought to herself, 'I think maybe I'd better leave it.' She just left it and walked away a wee bit . . . then she took another thought. And she walked back, picked it up. She had one of those rubber aprons for keeping her legs dry for picking up the seaweed, so she lifted up the apron and put the baby seal in it, held it in front of her and walked home.

By the time she walked home to the wee cottage at the shoreside, her old man had pulled up the boat. He was back and in a rage again: the seals had been at his nets, made holes in them and ate most of his good fish. The old woman came walking up, 'Well,' he said, 'Mary, you're back again.'

'Aye, John, I'm back.' She said, 'You look terrible. What's wrong?'

'Och,' he said, 'it's these seals! I'll have to get a gun and shoot them.'

'You know, John,' she said, 'I don't like you shooting seals.'

'Well,' he said, 'what else can I do? They're making a terrible mess of my nets – we'll have to do something about them.'

'Well,' she said, 'come on in anyway and we'll have a cup of tea.' So they walked in. She had her apron rolled up in front of her.

He looks. 'Mary, what's that you've got there?'

She says, 'John, it's a baby seal.'

He said, 'What! Have you got a baby seal? You mean to tell me you've brought back a baby seal, here to this house, to me, when you know I don't like these animals!'

She says, 'John, it's lost its mother.'

'Well,' he said, 'woman, you keep it away from me or it'll lose more than its mother. Because you know I hate these things. What are you going to do with it anyway?'

'Well,' she said, 'John, I thought, seeing it lost its mother, that I would try to rear it up for a wee bit till it gets strong enough and then put it back in the sea.'

'Of course,' he said, 'but you'd be better to take a walking-stick and hit it at the back of the neck! If you make it strong enough and big enough, it'll just go back to the sea and be one more to eat the fish in my nets.'

'Oh well,' old Mary said, she was a kindly soul, 'if that happens, it happens. But I'm not going to do anything to the baby seal.' Away she went and got an old creel and she put some straw in it. She put the baby seal down by the fire and went round by the back of the shed where she milked a goat. She had a teat and bottle for feeding young goats; she filled it full of goats' milk and fed it to the baby seal. The baby seal sucked the bottle of milk and lay contented by the fire.

So the old man, he's sitting and he's watching the seal; and old Mary's sitting at the other side of the fire. 'Now, woman, you know that I don't like these animals,' he said, 'and I just can't have you having it here!'

'Well, John, what am I going to do with it?' she said. 'You know fine I want to keep it warm.'

'Ach,' he said, 'keep it warm – put it out in the shed beside the goats!'

'No,' she said, 'I'm not putting it out in the shed

beside the goats. It's staying by the fire; it's only a little baby.'

But anyway she won her way; the old woman kept her seal. Old John carried on as usual and old Mary carried on as usual, doing her jobs; and time passed by. But within three or four months the seal grew and it began to follow the old woman every place, every place the old woman went. It followed her to the shore and followed her back, just like a dog. It loved the old woman dearly. But the old man – he couldn't stand this seal, he hated it! He couldn't look at it.

Time passed by and in came the spring of the year. Now the seal was nearly full grown, and Mary loved this seal like she never loved anything else in her life. One evening they were both sitting at their supper when they heard a knock at the door.

Mary said, 'John, did I hear someone knocking at the door?'

'Yes,' he said, 'there's someone at the door; go and see who it is.'

So Mary goes to the door. She opened it and standing there was a young man in his twenties, a nice-looking young man in his twenties.

'Hello young man,' she says. What is it? What can I do for you?'

'Well, ma'm,' he said, 'to tell you the truth, I came up from the village and they told me . . . I'm looking for a, a room to rent . . . and they told me in the village that sometimes you and your husband rent a room to people for two or three weeks in the summer-time.'

'Yes,' she said, 'we do, we really do that. It's only both ourselves here, we stay, just me and my husband, we have no family of our own and we've got a large house; sometimes we do let a room. But don't let me have you standing in the doorway – come in!' So she took the young man in, to the kitchen fire.

She told old John, 'John, this is a young man here who

has walked up from the village and he's wondering if we could rent him a room for a few weeks.'

'Well,' John says, 'I'm sure the spare room is never used very much by you and me, and if the young man is needing a room for a few weeks I don't see any harm in letting him have it.'

'By the way,' the old woman says, 'what is your name?'

'My name is Iain,' 'he said, and I'm an artist. I've come to do some landscape painting and I would be very much obliged if you would let me have the room for a couple of weeks.'

'Fine,' the old man says.

She said, 'Would you like some supper?'

So the old woman told him how much she needed for the room, and the young man was quite pleased at what he had to pay, and she said, 'You can have your meals with us if you feel like it.'

'That'll do nicely,' the young man said. 'That'll just suit me fine. I won't be any trouble to you.'

But he never as much as glanced at the seal sitting in the basket by the fire! He never paid any attention to the seal; he just treated it as if it didn't exist. And the old woman thought this very queer. So while he was sitting down at the table having some supper with them the old woman looked at him, at the young man, and she thought she'd seen him some place before. When she looked at his eyes she thought she'd seen those eyes somewhere before. But she raiked her brains to think – who had she seen that he was like? He was like somebody she had seen before, but she couldn't remember. Anyway, with talking to him and the old man, the thought of his resemblance went out of her mind.

But the old man, old John, he and the young man got to talking and cracking, and they just made it off together like two peas. The old man started explaining to the young man, to young Iain, about his nets getting torn with the seals and how his fish were destroyed, how this affected his living and he's wishing that something would be done to get rid of the seals round the bay so's he could do more fishing.

And old Mary said, 'You're always getting down upon the poor seals. I'm sure they must have their time, too, they must live just the same as everybody else. But anyway,' the old woman says, 'come and I'll show you your room!'

So she took the young man upstairs and showed him the room. He thanked her very much. 'That's very nice; that'll just suit me fine.' But she noticed all he had was one small package under his arm. He didn't have any cases or anything . . . one package under his arm.

So they walked out on the landing and the young man said, 'I'll be bidding you both good-night.' She went down the stairs and they heard him shutting the door. Then all was quiet.

Now, while the young man was in the bedroom, the seal got up out of the basket and started going 'honk-honk-honk' round the floor. The old man says, 'What's wrong with that animal?'

'Och, he's a wee bit excited tonight,' she said. And the old woman sat and petted him, 'You're getting excited; I never saw you like that before.' But she managed to calm the seal and got him quietened. She and old John talked for a while and then went off to their bed.

The next morning they were at breakfast when the young man came down the stairs. He said to old John, 'You wouldn't mind if I were to go out with you, maybe sometime when you're – when I'm not painting – if it's too dull for painting, to watch you fishing?'

'O-oh, no,' he said, 'Iain, I'd be only too glad to have you along for company! In fact, did you ever row a boat before?'

'Well,' Iain said, 'I've never rowed a boat before, but I know how it's done. I believe I could learn quick enough.'

So, after breakfast the old man took him down; he showed him the boat and some of the spare nets he had hung up on the sticks along the beach to dry. And he showed him all the holes that the seals had caused and some of the carcasses of fish he had thrown away that the seals had left. But the young man never said a thing.

He stayed there for a week. He had his meals in the house and he walked away every morning; some days he was away all day and sometimes he came back late at night.

But one night the old man said, 'You know, Iain, tomorrow I'm going to shift my nets farther round the beach to a place I've never fished or set a net before. And I wonder if you would come and give me a wee help?'

'Oh, certainly,' he said, 'I'd be willing to help you. In fact, I don't think I'll be doing very much tomorrow, so I'll go with you, if you want me to.'

'I would like that very much,' the old man said.

To make a long story short, the next day after breakfast he said 'good-bye' to the old woman – Iain treated the old woman casually, just casually. But he loved old John, he loved the old man. He would do anything and go anywhere with the old man, and the old man was the same way with him: at night-time when the young man was in his room the old man used to sit and talk to the old woman, 'My, such a nice young man, that! I wish we had a son like him. What a young, strong powerful man. And you want to see him rowing a boat!' The good things he would say about this young man to the old woman!

That morning he and the old man got ready to go away in the boat. He put a net in the back and they rowed away out, farther than John had ever been before, out in the bay.

The old man looks up, 'I hope it doesn't come rain, or wind.' And it got kind of dark.

The young man says, 'Maybe it's a storm going to blow up.'

The old man said, 'I hope not, because I don't want to have to come back out here tomorrow in rough weather.' But no sooner were the words out of the old man's mouth than it started to rain, then the wind got up. And it came a storm!

They were a good mile and a half away from the beach.

The net was out. And it got so rough they could barely make their way back. So the old man said to the young man, 'You take one oar and I'll take the other and we'll row as fast as we can!' They rowed hard against the waves, but the waves got too rough and they were battling against the heavy waves when the boat overturned. The old man fell into the sea. And the young man fell into the sea.

He was shouting, 'Iain, Iain! This way, Iain, this way, Iain. Grab an oar, Iain, and try to keep yourself afloat, grab an oar and try to keep yourself afloat!' The old man got hold of one of the wooden oars and he got it under his arm; he was swimming with one hand. But he looked all around for Iain . . . Iain was gone.

And he swam on; he could see the land in the distance. He swam on and on till he was getting fairly exhuasted – he knew he was never going to make it – he lost the grip on the oar and was just about sinking into the water when he felt this thing coming up under him. He put his hands out. He thought it was a bit of floating stick – and he felt – it was a big furry seal! It came right up under him and he put his two arms round its neck and away the seal went as fast as it could go. Right to the beach, and the old man's clinging on to the seal, fairly exhausted, clinging on to the seal.

So it swam right in, on to the beach till it couldn't go any farther with the weight of the old man, and the old man sprachled on his hands and knees and crawled up on to the shingle on the shore where he flung himself down completely exhausted. The seal turned and went away.

By now the old woman's out, waiting and waiting and walking up and down the beach, looking to see, spying away out, looking to see if she could see the boat. But she couldn't see any boat. She never noticed the old man was lying on his fours on the shingle on the tidemark with his feet in the water. After she walked along the beach a ways, though, she saw him. She pulled him up and asked him what happened. Oh, he was in a terrible state!

'Oh,' he said, 'Iain is gone. The storm caught us and the

boat capsized and Iain is gone. We'll never see him again, he's gone!'

So the old woman oxtered him up to the house and made him take off his wet clothes and she put a blanket round him, put him sitting in the chair and gave him a drink of whisky. But all she could get out of his mouth was 'Iain is gone; we'll never see Iain again.' Finally, the old woman got him kind of settled down. She asked him what happened.

He told her the tale . . . 'I was finished, I was exhausted, completely gone – only for a seal.'

She said, 'A seal!'

He said, 'A seal,' he said, 'saved my life!'

'How did it save your life?'

He said, 'It came up below me and I put my arms round it – and would you believe it, Mary,' he said, 'after all the things that I've said about these animals – it saved my life!'

'Well,' she said, 'it's good that it did you a good turn; maybe now you'll change your mind about seals.'

He said, 'You know, from now on I'll never say another angry word against a seal, because it's thanks to the seal my life's been saved, been spared!'

After a while they went to bed. But the old man couldn't rest, he tossed and turned all night. 'Tomorrow morning, Mary,' he said, 'we'll have to go down to the village and notify the policeman, tell him what happened to the young man.'

So, true to his word, the next morning the old man went down to the local police station in the wee village and reported the young man to the policeman – one constable that stayed in the wee village. John walked over to the hotel and asked them in the hotel if Iain had been staying there. And nobody – there were only about a dozen houses in the village and the one hotel – nobody had ever heard tell of the young man! Nobody had ever seen him! He had never come to the village the whole time he'd been with John and Mary. Nobody ever saw him coming, nobody ever saw him going, nobody ever sent him up to the old man and woman in the first place! It was a complete mystery: nobody knew him.

So the old man walked home and he told the old woman. She says, 'Somebody must have seen him somewhere about the village when he came here first!'

'No,' he said, 'nobody saw him at all. It's a sheer mystery.'

Anyway, by the time the old man had got back and had sat down for a cup of tea, the policeman had arrived with his bicycle to have a talk to the old woman and the old man about this missing young man. So the old man explained to him what happened . . . they went out in the boat and the boat capsized and he swam to shore – but he never mentioned the seal, about the seal saving his life, to the policeman, never mentioned it.

Well, the policeman took all the particulars he could. 'Now,' he said, 'how long had he been here?'

'Well,' the old man said, 'he'd been here, he was with us for about ten days . . . such a nice boy, too, such a beautiful, a handsome young man. We got on so well together, he was just like a son to me. And I'm going to miss him terribly.'

The policeman looked – the seal was sitting in the basket. 'My, Mary,' he said, 'your seal is fairly growing!'

'Aye,' she said, 'it's fairly growing; he's getting a wee bit too big. It's about time he was going back to the sea.'

So, the policeman asked, 'Did he have any identification or anything about him – where did Iain stay?'

She said, 'He stayed up in the bedroom, the spare room up the stairs,' she said.

'Well, you don't mind,' the policeman said, 'if I go up and see, have a look through his papers and things? Maybe I'll get the address of his parents or his family or something. Then we'll know where he came from, for a report to his people that he's a-missing.'

'All right,' say the old man and woman.

So the old man and the woman and the policeman walked up the stairs, the old woman opened the bedroom door. And they walked in. They looked around – the bed was made the same way as the old woman had made it when she made it the first time – it never was slept on. There were no cases, there were no parcels, there was nothing! In the room – not one single thing – except over in the far corner next to the window was a picture-frame, a canvas picture framed. The back of it was turned to the old man and the old woman, the front facing the window. And the old man walked over.

He says, 'This is what he's been working on the whole time.' And he turned it round, he looked at it and stepped back – the old man gasped.

The policeman said, 'What is it, John?'

'Well,' he said, 'it's this picture . . . would you come here and see this, Mary?'

'What is it?' she said, 'What is, what has he been drawing? He said he was an artist.'

'Yes, he's an artist; he was an artist,' he said, 'poor boy, he was an artist all right, and a good one, too!'

They turned the picture round: there was the most beautiful picture you'd ever seen in your life. The picture of an old woman gathering dulse on the shore – old Mary the way she was, exactly as if you were looking at the old woman herself, picking up a baby seal from among the dulse – was the picture Iain had made. And the policeman was amazed but old Mary never said a word.

John said, 'Mary, how did he manage to paint that?'

'Och,' she said, 'I told him the story, he probably painted it from memory.'

So the policeman says, 'Well, there's little we can do about it.'

But time passed by and there never was another word about the man, young Iain's body never was found. About a week after that, the old man and woman carried the seal down to the shore, put it back in the tide and away the seal went. But there never was another word about Iain, and the old man never complained about seals. And whenever the old woman went down to gather her seaweed along the shore, she would look out and see the seals in the bay floating about; she would give a wee smile to herself and say, 'Well, Iain, you've finally proved your point!' She knew he'd been a selkie.[1]

1 That was a selkie that came to teach the old man a lesson for being so bad to the seals and cursing their life away. It was a story kept in his family and ours. The island folk believed in these things, and, after all, there must be something in it.

Neil McCallum, the old stonemason I was apprenticed to when I was fifteen at Auchindrain, told me this story and he believed that this really happened. It was a story kept in his family and ours. The Highlanders were a very close-knitted kind of folk and didn't go telling the whole world about their stories and tales and cracks because people would have thought they were crazy. But Neil maintained that his great-great granny told him this story, 'the old woman and the seal', because she had the picture in her house.

Mary and the Seal

This is a Gaelic tale from the Western Isles. It was told to me when I was only about fifteen years of age, doing the stone-dyking in Argyll at Auchindrain with Neil McCallum. He was from crofting stock; he was a crofter, his brother was a crofter. And, just to sit there listening . . . I can still hear his voice in my ears; you know, his voice is still there after, maybe, nearly forty years. And every little detail is imprinted in my memory. And when I tell you the story, I try to get as close as possible to the way that he spoke to me. Do you understand what I mean?

MANY years ago in a little isle off the West Coast of Scotland – it could be Mull, Tiree, or any island – there lived an old fisherman and his wife. And the old fisherman spent his entire life fishing in the sea and selling whatever fish he couldn't use himself to keep him and his wife and his little daughter alive. They lived in this little cottage by the sea and not far from where they stayed was the village, a very small village – a post office, a hall and some cottages. But everyone knew everyone else. And his cousin also had a house in the village.

This old man and woman had a daughter called Mary and they loved her dearly, she was such a nice child. She helped her father with the fishing and when she was finished helping her father, she always came and helped her mother to do housework and everything else. The father used to set his nets every day in the sea and he used to rise early every morning. Mary used to get up and help her father lift his nets and collect the fish. After that was done she used to help her mother, then went off to school.

Everybody was happy for Mary. And her father and mother were so proud of her because she was such a good worker. But she was such a quiet and tender little girl and didn't pay attention to anyone . . . she did her schoolwork in school. But the years passed by and Mary grew till she became a young teenager. This is where the story really begins, when Mary was about sixteen or seventeen.

She always used to borrow her father's boat, every evening in the summer-time, and go for a sail to a little island that lay about half a mile from where they stayed, a small island out in the middle of the sea-loch. And Mary used to go out and spend all her spare time on the island. Every time she'd finished her day's work with her father and helped her mother and had her supper, she would say, 'Father, can I borrow your boat? Even in the winter-time sometimes, when the sea wasn't too rough, she would go out there and spend her time. Her father and mother never paid any attention because Mary's spare time was her own time; when her work was finished she could do what she liked. Till one day.

Her mother used to walk down to the small village to the post office where they bought their small quantity of messages and did their shopping, it was the only place they could buy any supplies. She heard two old women nattering to each other. Mary's mother's back was turned at the time but she overheard the two old women. They were busy talking about Mary.

'Och,' one woman said, 'she's such a nice girl, but she's so quiet. She doesn't come to any of the dances and she doesn't even have a boyfriend. She doesn't do anything – we have our ceilidhs and we have our things and we never see her come, she never even pays us a visit. Such a nice quiet girl, all she wants to do, she tells me, is to take her boat over to the island spend all her time there on the island. Never even comes and has a wee timey – when our children have their shows and activities in school – she never puts in an appearance! And her mother and father are such decent people . . . even her Uncle Lachy gets upset!'

This was the first time her mother had heard these whispers so she paid little attention. She came home, and she was a wee bit upset. And the next time she went back to the village she heard the same whispers again – this began to get into her mind, she began to think. But otherwise Mary was just a natural girl: she helped her daddy and she asked her mummy if there was anything she could do, helped her to do everything in the house, and she was natural in every way. But she kept herself to herself.

One evening it was supper-time once more, and after supper Mary said, 'Daddy, can I borrow your boat?'

'Oh yes, Mary, my dear,' he said, 'you can borrow the boat. I'm sure I'm finished – we've finished our day's work. You can have the boat.' It wasn't far across to row the little boat, maybe several hundred yards to the wee island in the loch. And the old woman and the old man sat by the fire.

Once Mary had walked out the door and said 'good-bye' to her father and mother, the old woman turned round and said to her husband, 'There she goes again. That's her gone again.'

Mary's father turned round and he said, 'What do you mean? Margaret, what do you mean – you know Mary always goes off, an-and-and enjoys herself in the boat.'

She said, 'Angus, you don't know what I mean: it's not you that has got to go down to the village and listen to the whispers of the people, and the talk and the wagging tongues.'

He says, 'Woman, what are you talking about?'

She says, 'I'm talking about your daughter.'

Angus didn't know what to say . . . he said, 'What's wrong with my daughter? I'm sure she works hard and she deserves a little time by herself – what's the trouble, was there something that you needed done that she didn't do?'

'Not at all,' she said, 'that's not what I'm talking about.'

'Well,' he says, 'tell me what you're trying to say!'

She said, 'Angus, it's Mary – the people in the village are beginning to talk.'

'And what are they saying,' he said, 'about my daughter?' And he started to get angry.

'They're talking about Mary going off herself in her boat to the island and spending all her time there, she's done that now for close on five years. And they say she doesn't go to any dances, she doesn't go to any parties and she doesn't accept any invitations to go anywhere and she has no boyfriend! And the wagging tongues in the village are talking about this. It's getting through to me and I just don't like it.'

'Well,' he said, 'Mother, I'm sure there's nothing in the world that should upset you about that; I'm sure Mary's minding her own business! And if she's out there, she's no skylarking with some young man – would you rather have her skylarking around the village with some young man or something? And destroying herself and bringing back a baby or something to you – would you enjoy that better?'

'It's not that, Angus,' she said, 'it's just that Mary is so unsociable.' But anyway, they argued and bargued for about an hour and they couldn't get any further.

By the time they were finished Mary came in again. She was radiant and happy. She came over, kissed her mother and kissed her daddy, said, 'Daddy, I pulled the boat up on the beach, and everything's all right.'

He says, 'All right, Daughter, that's nice.'

'And,' she says, 'Daddy, the tide is coming in and some of the corks of the net are nearly sunk, so I think we'll have a good fishing in the morning. I'll be up bright and early to give you a hand.'

He said, 'Thank you, Mary, very much.'

And she kissed her mother and said, 'I'll just have a small something to eat and I'll go to bed.'

But anyway, the old woman was unsettled. 'There she goes again,' she says, 'that's all we get.'

'Well,' he says, 'what more do you expect? She's doing her best, Mother. She's enjoying herself.'

'What is she doing on that island? That's what I want to know.'

Said the old man to Margaret, 'Well, she's no doing any harm out there.'

So the next morning they were up bright and early, had their breakfast. And Mary went out with her father, collected the nets, collected the fish, and they graded the fish and kept some for themselves. Then they went into the village and sold the rest, came back home, had their supper. It was a beautiful day.

And Mary said, 'Is there anything you want me to do, Mother?'

'Well no, Mary,' she says, 'everything is properly done: the washing's finished and the cleaning's finished, and I was just making some jam; and I'm sure your father's going to sit down and have a rest because he's had a hard day.'

Mary turned round and she said, 'Father, could I borrow your boat?' once again.

'I'm sure, my dear,' he says, 'you can have the boat. Take the boat. Now be careful because there might be a rise of a storm.'

'I'll be all right, Father,' she said, 'I don't think it's going to – the sky looks so quiet and peaceful. I doubt if we'll have a storm the night.' And away she goes.

But as soon as she takes off in the boat, oh, her mother gets up. 'That's it, there she goes again,' she said. 'To put my mind at rest, would you do something for me?'

Angus says, 'What is it you want now, woman?'

'Look,' she said, 'would you relieve my mind for me: would you go down and borrow Lachy's boat, your cousin Lachy's boat, and row out to the island see what Mary does when she goes there? It'll put my mind at rest.'

'That's no reason for me to go out,' he said. 'Let the lassie enjoy herself if she wants to enjoy herself! There's no reason for me to go out – I'm sure there's no one within miles. Maybe she's wading on the beach and she sits there, an-and-and maybe she has some books with her, and she – she likes to be by herself.'

But no. She says, 'Look, do something for me, husband! Would you go out, Angus, and see what she does?'

So Angus said, 'Och, dash it, woman! To keep you happy, I'll go out and see what she's doing. It's only a waste of time anyway.' So he walks down; it was only about two hundred yards down to Lachy's cottage.

Lachy had the same kind of boat. He was sitting at the fire; he had never married; their fathers had been brothers. Lachy stayed in this cottage, he was an old retired seaman and he always liked to keep a boat. 'Well, it's yourself, Angus!' he said. 'Come away in. And come you, sit down and we'll have a wee dram.'

'No,' he said, 'Lachy, I'm not here for a dram.'

'Well,' he said, 'what sent you down? It's not often you come for a visit.'

'I was wondering,' he said, 'if you would let me borrow your boat for a few minutes?'

And Lachy said, 'Well, what's the trouble?'

'Ach, it's no trouble, really,' he said, 'I was just wanting to borrow your boat for maybe half an hour or so.'

'Well, what is wrong with your own boat?'

'Och,' he said, 'Mary's using it.'

And Lachy said, 'Och, that's Mary off on her gallivant to the island again. And you want to follow the lassie and see what she's doing. If I was you I would leave her alone. Come on, sit down and have a dram with me and forget about it.'

But old Angus was so persistent, 'I want to borrow your boat.'

'Well,' he said, 'take the dashit thing and away you go!'

He takes the boat and he rows across to the island and he lands on the small beach. There was Mary's boat beached. And he pulls his cousin Lachy's boat up beside Mary's, and beaches it. And he walks up a path – it was well worn because Mary had walked up this path many many times –

he follows the path up, goes over a little knowe. There are some rocks and a few trees, and down at the back of the island is a small kind of valley-shaped place that leads out to the sea. Then there's a beach, on the beach is a large rock. And beside the rock is a wee green patch. Old Angus came walking up, taking his time – looked all around and looked all around.

There were a few seagulls flying around and a few birds wading along the beach because the tide was on the ebb. And he heard the laughing coming on. Giggling and laughing – this was Mary, carrying on. And he came up over the knowe, he looked down – here was Mary with a large seal, a grey seal. And they were having the greatest fun you've ever seen: they were wrestling in the sand, carrying on and laughing, the seal was grunting and Mary was flinging her arms around the seal! So Angus stopped, he sat down and watched for a wee while.

He said, 'Ach, I'm sure she's doing no harm, it's only a seal. And her mother was so worried about it. She's enjoying herself; probably she's reared it up from a pup and she comes over to feed it, and I'm sure it won't do her any harm. She's better playing with a seal than carrying on with a young bachle as far as I'm concerned!' So, he takes his boat and he rows home, gives his cousin Lachy back the boat, lights his pipe and walks up to his own home. He comes in through the door and his old wife old Margaret is waiting on him.

She said, 'You're home, Angus.'

'Aye, I'm home,' he said, 'Margaret, I'm home. And thanks be praised to God I am home!'

She said, 'Did you see Mary?'

'Of course,' he said, 'I saw Mary. She's out on the island.'

'And what is she doing? Is she sitting – what is she doing?'

He said, 'She's enjoying herself.'

Old Margaret said, 'What way is she enjoying herself – is she wading on the beach or something?'

'No,' he said, 'she's not wading on the beach.'

'Is she reading?'

'No, she's not reading,' he said. 'She's playing herself with a seal.'

She said, 'What did you say?'

He said, 'She's playing herself – she has the best company in the world and she's enjoying herself – she's playing with a seal! A large grey seal. They're having great fun and I didn't interfere.'

She said, 'Angus, Mary's enchanted. It's one of the sea-people that's taken over. Your daughter is finished – ruined for evermore. I've heard stories from my grandmother how the sea-people take over a person and take them away for evermore, they're never seen again – she's enchanted. What kind of a seal was it?'

He said, 'It was a grey seal and they were having good fun so I didn't interfere.'

She said, 'If you want to protect your daughter and you want to have your daughter for any length of time, you'd better get rid of the seal!'

He says, 'Margaret, I couldn't interfere with them. It's Mary's pet.

'I don't care if it's Mary's pet or no,' she said, 'tomorrow morning you will take your gun and go out, instead of going to the fish you'll go out and you'll shoot that seal and destroy it for evermore!'

'But,' he said, 'it's Mary's pet – she probably reared it up unknown to us, she probably reared it up from a young pup, and it's not for me to destroy the seal, the thing she has to play with.'

'I'm sure she can find plenty of company in the village instead of going out there to the island!' But the argument went on, and they argued and argued and finally old Margaret won.

He lighted his pipe to have a smoke before going to bed. 'Well,' he said, 'in the morning I'll go out and see.'

Then Mary came home and she was so radiant and so

bright, so happy. She came in and kissed her daddy and kissed her mummy. She had a cup of tea and asked Mummy and Daddy if they needed anything or wanted anything done.

And they said, 'No, Mary.' The old woman was a wee bit kind of dubious. She wasn't just a wee bit too pleased.

And Mary saw this. She said, 'Is there something wrong, Mother?'

'No, Mary,' she said, 'there's nothing wrong.'

'Well, I'm going off to my bed.' Mary went to her bed. In these cottages in times long ago in the little crofts, the elderly people stayed down on the floor and there was a small ladder that led up to the garret in the roof. If you had any children they had their beds in the garret. Mary lived upstairs.

So the next morning Angus got up early. And before he even had any breakfast, he went ben the back of the house and took his gun. He loaded his gun and took his boat and he rowed out to the island, before Mary was up. And he walked up the path, the way Mary usually went, over the little hillock, down the little path to the little green part beside the bare rock – sure enough, sitting there sunning himself in the morning sun was the seal.

Angus crept up as close as he could – he fired the shot at the seal, hit the seal. And the seal just reared up – fell, and then crawled, made its way into the sea, hobbled its way into the water and disappeared. 'That's got you,' he said.

And then he felt queer. A funny sensation came over him. And he sat down, he felt so funny – as if he had shot his wife or his daughter. A sadness came over him. And he sat for a long while, then he left the gun down beside him and he looked at the gun . . . he felt that he had done something terrible. He felt so queer.

So he picked up the gun, walked back to his boat and he could barely walk, he felt so sick. He put the gun in the boat. He sat for a while before he could even take off in the boat and he had the queer sensation, a feeling of loss was within him, a terrible feeling of loss – that something he had done could never be undone . . . he could hardly row the boat. But he finally made his way back to the mainland, tied up his boat, picked up the gun and put it back in the cupboard. He walked in and old Margaret was sitting there.

She said, 'You're back, Angus.'

He said, 'Yes I'm back.'

She said, 'Did you do what I told you to do?'

'Yes, Mother,' he said, 'I did what you – what you told me to do.'

She said, 'Did you see the seal?'

'Yes,' he said, 'I saw the seal. And I shot the seal.'

She sat down. 'Are you wanting . . .'

'No, I don't want any breakfast,' he said.

She says, 'Are you feeling . . .'

'No, I'm not feeling very well. I'm not feeling very well at all.'

She says, 'What's wrong with you?'

'Well,' he says, 'I feel terrible, I feel queer and I feel so kind of sad . . . I've done something wrong and you forced me to it, I hope in the future that you'll be sorry for it.'

'Och,' she said, 'it's only a seal!' But they said no more. by this time Mary had come down.

She said, 'Good morning, Father; good morning, Mother,' and she sat down at the table as radiant as a flower and had some breakfast. 'Are you not eating, Daddy?'

'No,' he said, 'Daughter, I don't . . .'

She said, 'Are you not feeling very well?' And she came over and stroked her father's head. 'Are you not feeling very well, Father?'

'Oh,' he said, 'I'm feeling fine, Mary. I'm just not, just – what I should be.' And the mother tried to hide her face in case Mary could see something in her face that would – a giveaway in her face, you know.

'Well,' she says, 'Father, are you ready to go out to lift the net?'

'Well, Mary, to tell you the truth,' he said, 'I don't think the tide'll be on the – the out-going tide won't be for a while yet. No, I think I'll sit here and have a smoke.'

'Mother,' she says, 'are you needing anything done?'

'No, Mary,' she said, 'we don't need anything done.' Now they wanted to try and be as canny with her as possible. They didn't want to upset her in any way. And the mother said, 'No, Mary, I think everything's done. There's only a little cleaning to be done and I think I'll manage.'

Mary says, 'Well, after I milk the cow, Father, would it be all right if I take the boat?'

'Och, yes, Daughter, go ahead and help yourself to the boat,' he said, 'I'm sure you can have the boat any time. You don't need to ask me for the boat, just take it whenever you feel like it.'

So Mary milked the cow, brought in the milk and set the basins for the cream, and did everything that was needing to be done. She said, 'Good-bye, Mother, I'll see you in a while. I'm just going off for a while to be by myself – I'll be back before very long.'

Mother said, 'There she goes again! If you tell me it's true, she'll be home sadder and wiser.'

But old Angus never said a word. He just sat and smoked his pipe. And he still had this – as if a lump were in his heart. And he was under deep depression, just didn't want to get up, just wanted to sit. He had this great terrible feeling of loss.

So Mary rowed the boat over to the island. And he sat by the fire and he smoked and he smoked and he smoked. Maggie called him for dinner and the day passed by, but Mary never returned. Evening meal came, Mary never returned. Her mother began to get worried.

She came down and she said, 'Angus, has Mary come home? It'll soon be time for milking the cow again.'

'No,' he said, 'Mary has never come.'

'Perhaps,' she said, 'she – would you go down and see if

the boat's in? Has she tied up the boat? Maybe she walked down to the village.'

Angus went out and there was no sign of the boat. 'No,' he said, 'the boat—'

'Well, she's not home. If the boat's not home, she's not home,' she said. 'I doubt something's happened to her . . . I doubt something's happened to her – Angus, you'll have to go and see what, you'll have to go out to the island. Go down and get Lachy's boat and go out to the island and see.'

So Angus goes down, just walks down and takes Lachy's boat, never asks permission, just pulls the rope, unties the rope and jumps in the boat. He had the feeling that he doesn't even worry what happens, he's so upset. And he rows out to the island and there's Mary's boat. And he pulls the boat in because the beach was quite shallow. And he lays the boat beside Mary's boat, his own boat. And he walks up the path, over the little hillock, down by the big rock to the little bay and the green patch beside the big rock, and walks right down where he saw the seal. He looks. The side of the rock was splattered with the blood where he had shot the seal. And he walks round the whole island, which wasn't very big, walks the whole island round – all he saw was a few spots of blood. Nowhere did he find Mary. Mary had completely disappeared, there wasn't a sign of her, not even a footprint. And he walked round once, he walked round twice and he went round a third time; every tree, every bush, every rock he searched, but Mary was gone.

And he felt so sad, 'What could happen to Mary, my poor wee Mary, what happened to her?'

Then at the very last he came back once again to the rock where he had shot the seal – and he looked out to sea, the tide was on the ebb. And he stood, looked for a long long while. And he looked at the rock, saw the blood was drying in the sun. And he looked again, then – all in a moment up come two seals, two grey seals, and they come right out of the water – barely more than twenty-five yards from where he stood! And they look at him. They look directly at him – then disappear back down in the water. And he had this queer feeling that he was never going to see Mary any more.

So he took his boat and he rowed home, tied up his boat. Just the one boat, took his own boat, left Lachy's boat on the island. He sat down beside the fire. His wife Margaret came to him.

She said, 'Did you see Mary?'

'No,' he said, 'I never saw Mary. I never saw Mary, I searched the entire island for Mary and Mary is gone. And look, between you and me, she's gone for ever. We'll never see Mary again.'

And they waited and they waited, and they waited for the entire days of their lives, but Mary never returned. And that is the end of my tale.

The Tramp and the Boots

I heard this story a long time ago in Furnace when I was about twelve years old. I think I first heard it from a cousin of my father's, an old man called Willie Williamson whose brother stayed in Carradale.

THE old tramp was weary and tired, for he had walked all morning along the dusty highway, which in these days was just a track across the country. He had travelled for many days and come across very few places where he could find any food. All he'd had for the last two days was a rabbit he'd found by the roadside roasted over a fire.

He said to himself, 'If I don't find some habitation, a farm or a croft or somethin along the highway before nightfall, I'm sure I'm gaunnae be very hungry.' Because these old tramps begged whatever they could, whatever they needed to eat. It was only by the kindliness of the local people along the way that these tramps managed to survive. And he'd travelled for so many miles his feet were sore . . . the day was hot and the sun was shining. It was a beautiful summer day. Even suppose he was so hungry, tiredness began to overcome the hunger.

And then he came down by this little hill. Beside the roadside he looked across the moor and there was the most beautiful little hill he'd ever seen, covered in daisies and flowers! He said to himself, 'Wouldn't that be a nice place fir tae have a rest if I could afford tae rest.' The hunger pains in his stomach were bothering him, but the soreness of his feet overcame them. He walked over to the little hill and he sat down. He stretched himself out to rest and thought, 'In such a lovely place, if a person wasna so hungry. . . .'

He'd rested for a long while, three-quarters of an hour or so, when all in a moment he heard a little voice saying, 'Auld man, you'll hev to be gone from this place.'

And the tramp looked around, saying to himself, 'Am I hearin right? Is there someone talkin?' He looked all around, he could see nothing because the grass was high and the flowers were beautiful.

Then the voice spoke again, 'Old man, you'll hev tae leave here.'

And the tramp looked again . . . sure enough, there stood aside him a little man – not very big, maybe, say, twelve inches high, with a long white beard and a peakit cap and peakit shoes. The tramp was amazed because he had never seen anybody . . . he'd heard of people so small as that many many years before, but he'd never experienced meeting one. He couldn't hardly speak for a moment or two, he was so amazed. Then he found his voice. 'Little man,' he said, 'I am tired!'

And the little man said, 'Old man, look, you must move from this place immediately!'

And the old tramp man said, 'But who are you, little man? I have never seen anyone like you before.'

The little man said, 'Never mind who I am,' and he came up closer to the old tramp man.

When he came a little closer, the old tramp man had to bend over and look down. The old tramp had pulled up his knees to himself and the little man hardly came as high as his knee . . . there he stood with his long white beard and his wee cap and curled shoes. And the tramp thought in his mind, 'This is queer, this is very funny.' He was so tired and weary, but with the excitement of seeing this little creature the hunger in his belly was forgotten about.

And the little man said, 'Old man, you'll hev tae move.'

The old tramp said, 'Look, I am an auld tramp. I am weary. I have come a long long way and I am hungry. I have come here to rest.' Now in these days a long time ago there were no fences along the way, no hedges; there were no roads. A person could walk off the track and sit down, rest theirself anywhere. So this is what the old tramp had done. He said to the little man, 'Look, there's no reason why – that I can't rest here because this is a free place. I'm enjoyin myself on this little hill restin myself!'

And the little man said, 'You must go!'

The tramp said, 'Not tonight, I can't go another step!'

Then the little man saw he couldn't persuade him in any way. He said to the tramp, 'What would you take to move on? Is it food you want?'

And the tramp said, 'Not exactly food. My feet are sore, and food wouldn't make my feet any better.'

The wee man looked down and saw the poor old tramp's boots were worn right through to the soles, with his toes sticking out. And the little man said, 'I see yir feet really is in a sorry state.'

'Yes,' said the old tramp, 'my feet are in a sorry state and they're really sore.'

So the little man felt sorry for the tramp; he didn't argue or command him anymore. He asked, 'Auld man, what would you really take to move from here?

And the old tramp said, 'Why is it so important I should move from here at this very moment?'

But the little man did not answer. 'Well,' he said, 'what would you really take tae move from this hill?'

And the tramp said, 'Well, I am hungry, the pains are botherin my stomach at this moment, and I wad like to go on to the next village or the next house or farm where I could find something to eat. But my feet are so sore and my boots are so worn . . . the pain overcomes my hunger.'

So the little man said, 'If you had a nice pair o' boots that made your feet comfortable, would you move on?'

The tramp said, 'If I had some nice comfortable boots for my feet, I would surely be gone!'

The little man said, 'Just wait a minute – I will find you some boots!'

Now the old tramp in his hunger thought he was dreaming. He thought he had fallen asleep. He looked around and the little man was gone, completely disappeared. He rubbed his eyes with his hands and thought, 'I must have dozed over, I must hae been dreamin.' And he looked around the little hill: all the flowers were blooming so beautifully. He thought to himself, 'I'll jist spend the night here, relax and have a sleep.' Because these old tramps always slept out in the open. They had no home or no place to go.

But he hadn't waited more than three to four minutes, when back comes the little man. And over his back he had a pair of boots. The tramp looked, saw the little man with the boots, and said, 'I am not dreamin, I have not been asleep!'

And lo and behold, the little man came up beside his knee. But the boots were just small things. The little man said to the tramp, 'I have brought you some boots and I hope you will keep to your promise.'

But the tramp said, 'Little man, I don't know where you came from, but do you realise that these boots would never fit my feet in any way – they wouldn't even fit my little toe!'

And the little man said, 'Wait, jist wait and watch!' The little man looked at the tramp's feet, saw his old boots with holes in them and his toes sticking through. He measured the size that the old tramp's feet really were, and he placed the boots down on the ground. He waited.

And the tramp watched. The boots got bigger and bigger and bigger, till they came about the size that the tramp really needed, and then they stopped. The tramp looked – there before him were the most beautiful boots he had ever seen in his life. Many's the time the tramp had seen gentlemen and lairds and people of high degree with beautiful boots which he admired, but he had never owned a pair in his life. His one ambition in life was to own a beautiful pair of boots, because these tramps walked many many miles.

Then the tramp said, 'I just can't believe it! Are these fir me?'

And the little man said, 'Yes, they're for you! Old man, they're fir you! You can have them with good heart and good will,' he said, 'providin that you try them on yir feet and move on from this little hill immediately!'

The tramp bent down and took off his old boots, which were worn and dusty, no laces – a piece of lace tied across the centre – and his toes sticking out at the front, holes in the soles. He put them down. Then he stretched out his feet and picked up one boot that the little man had brought. He put it on his foot and it just fit perfectly! Then he picked up the other one, put it on, and it fit perfectly.

And the tramp stood up. When he stood up, the pain of his feet was gone. He wanted to be on his way, he felt so free! His hunger pains were gone, he just wanted to walk on. But he could not walk away – he bent down, as close as he could above the little man – and said, 'Little man, I am thankful fir what you've done for me.'

And the little man said, 'Does yir feet feel good now?'

He said, 'They feel wonderful. They feel wonderful!'

And the little man said, 'Cuid you walk now, auld man?'

He said, 'Walk? I cuid walk for miles! I'll be on my way and leave ye in peace.'

But the little man said, 'Stop!'

And the tramp said, 'Why?'

'Oh, don't go away right now,' said the little man. The tramp was a wee bit worried because he thought the little man was going to take the boots back from him. And the little man said, 'Before ye go, I want ye tae make me a promise!'

The tramp thought, 'Make ye a promise? I'll make ye a promise,' said the tramp, 'what is yir promise?'

The little man said, 'Listen very carefully because I'm gaunna tell you something.' And the tramp listened. The little man said, 'Now, you have got some boots!'

The tramp said, 'Yes, I have got some boots, some beautiful boots like I never had before in my life. I've seen people with boots but not nothing like this! And I've admired people's beautiful boots along the way but I never saw boots like this before in my life. And are they really mine?'

And the little man said, 'Yes, they're yours. But make me one promise! These boots will carry you on yir journey for evermore, till the end of yir life. They'll never need to be cleaned, they'll never wear, they'll never be worn out. You'll never have sore feet anymore – providin on one thing . . .'

'And what is that?' said the old tramp.

'That ye never tell a soul where you got them! Will you promise me that?'

The old tramp turned round to the little man and he said, 'I make ye my promise. . . .'

And the little man held out his hand. The tramp took the little man's hand – just a wee wee hand in his – and he shook hands with the little man.

'Now,' said the tramp, 'I'll be on my way. Can I go?'

'Well,' said the little man, 'you can go.'

And the old tramp walked on the road, never even looked back, left the little man on the little hill by himself. The tramp went on his way. He felt no pain in his feet and no hunger pains. He just wanted to walk on and on, for ever! He travelled on for miles and miles and he travelled for a year, he travelled for two years . . . And wherever the old tramp went, every night he took off his boots, and placed them beside his head when he went to sleep. And when he woke up in the morning his beautiful boots were there beside him as clean and polished like they had never ever walked a single step! And the tramp loved these boots like he had never loved anything in his life. Although he had walked many many miles, the tramp never felt tired. So one day the summer came again.

He came to this river. And the sun was shining, the day was so beautiful. The old tramp thought – he wasn't tired and his feet weren't sore – but he thought his boots were so beautiful, he was ashamed when he put his dirty feet in them. So he thought he'd walk down to the river and wash his feet – to fit his beautiful boots! He walked down to the river, took off his beautiful boots and placed them by his side.

He was washing his old feet in the river, cleaning his toenails so's he could put them back into his beautiful boots and feel no shame . . . when who should come walking up the river but a fisherman, who was fishing the river from pool to pool. He came to the pool where the old tramp was sitting. And the fisherman was amazed when he came up and saw the old tramp washing his feet. But he stopped and said, 'Hello, auld man!'

The old tramp looked round. There was the fisherman with his fishing bag on his back and his fishing rod. He said, 'Hello!'

'Ye're washin yir feet?' said the fisherman.

'Yes,' said the tramp, 'I'm washin my feet. Because the day is hot.'

And then the fisherman looked: beside the old tramp sitting was a pair of boots, the most beautiful boots that the fisherman had ever seen in his life! Then he looked at the tramp in rags, torn coat, long beard, straggly hair – and beside him sat the most beautiful boots he'd ever seen. 'Tell me,' said the fisherman, 'are you a tramp?'

'Well,' said the old man, 'people call me that. I have walked many many miles – I am a tramp.'

'I suppose,' said the fisherman, 'ye've been many places?'

'Yes,' said the old tramp, 'I've seen many sights.'

'But tell me truthfully,' said the fisherman, 'how in the world could an auld tramp like you own such beautiful boots?'

And the tramp turned round and smiled. 'These boots,' he said, 'they be mine!'

'But,' the fisherman said, 'you've after told me you're a tramp!'

'Yes,' said the old man, 'I'm a tramp.'

'But how,' said the fisherman, 'could a tramp own these boots, so beautiful like that – did you steal them?'

'No' said the tramp, 'I never stole them. They're mine!'

'Did you buy them?' said the fisherman.

'No,' he said, 'I never bought them. These were given tae me as a present.'

The fisherman said, 'Luik, I've never seen boots like that before. These boots are fit fir a king – never mind a tramp!'

Then the tramp said, 'They were made for a king; they were made for a king a long time ago. They were made fir the King o' the Fairies! And the fairies were so kind tae me because I landed on their little hill and they wanted me to move on, they gave me their boots.' (The tramp had broken his promise to the fairies!)

The fisherman said, 'The fairies, and the Fairy King! Ha-ha-ha!' And he picked up his rod and he walked on.

The tramp watched him while he walked up the river. Then the tramp turned round and he looked – his boots were gone . . . mysteriously disappeared. And then it dawned on him, he had broken his promise to the little man. He was so sad! His boots, the most beautiful boots that had carried him so many many miles, were gone. He sat and he sat for a long long time and he knew in his heart there was no solution to his problem. The fairies had gifted him the boots to move from the little hill because they were going to have a fairy party there.

So he had to get up and walk on his way in his bare feet, till some poor crofter or some poor farmer took pity on him and gave him a pair of old boots. But to the end of his days the old tramp never saw his boots again, because he had broken his promise to the little man who had given him the boots of the Fairy King. And that is the end of my story.[1]

1 According to legend and the travelling folk's idea about the Other World, all the different beings have their own places: witches, for instance, are connected to old houses in forests, kelpies are in waterfalls, the broonie in old mills and old buildings, and fairies have their fairy hills. The travellers say, in their cracks and tales and stories, that the fairies are shut up under the hills all winter, for nine months of the year. When it comes to the first of May, the King of the Fairies lets them loose, sets them free for three months to do as they please. And they do plenty, you believe me! Nobody ever sees any fairies, but the proof is there. They work among flowers and work among plants, helping Mother Nature. And at the end of July the fairies are gone. But they are so excited when they are set free at the beginning of summer, they have their party, their ceilidh; and lucky is the person who is in this very place on the first of May!

The Taen-Awa

This is what you would call an 'international tale' among the travelling folk; every traveller I have met in my travels across Scotland has this story. Some call it 'The Banshee', some 'Johnnie who Gret.' And the thing is, within the same family a brother and sister-in-law or two cousins may each have their own different way of telling the story. But this was my Granny Bella Macdonald's favourite. I hope you enjoy it. I'm going to tell 'The Taen-Awa' the way Granny told it to me way back in Furnace in 1935. That wasn't the first time I'd heard it because my daddy told it to me too, when I was younger – I was seven when I heard Granny telling it. But even my daddy enjoyed old Bella's version, it was different altogether from his. She was a good story-teller and came from a line of story-telling folk who went back many hundreds of years, because the Macdonalds were famed for their tales, they really were.

MANY years ago away on the West Coast in a wee hill farm there lived a farmer and his wife. His father had died and left him the farm and he was just newly married. He didn't remember his mother because she had died years before, but he'd loved his old father. Being left the farm and all alone, the first thing he had done was find himself a wife, this girl in the village whom he'd loved and respected. Alistair and Mary Maclean were their names. They had this farm in the glen and a little money that his father had left him and they lived happily together.

Now up on the hills on the West Coast of Scotland there's not much arable land. But Alistair liked to keep a few cattle and a few sheep, and for the cold winter months he just couldn't buy feed. So he tried to make a wee puckle hay, the best he could possibly make. Anything that looked like it was growing to be hay he would leave, keep the animals off it, and cut it with the scythe in the spring or at the beginning of summer.

But one day Mary said to him, 'Alistair, I think I've got to give you good news.'

'Oh well,' he said, 'after a hard day's work I would enjoy any good news – what is it you're gaunna tell me?'

'Alistair, I think, Alec,' she said, 'we're gaunna have a baby.'

'Oh,' he gasped, 'we're gaunna have a baby are we! Oh, it's the best news you've given me today,' he said, 'it'll make me work ten times harder this afternoon!' So he put his arms around his wee wife and kissed her. He sat down and they made up plans what they were going to do. 'But,' he said, 'are you sure?'

'I'm sure,' she said, 'as sure as can be.'

Now Alistair wanted to have a son as much as his father had wanted to have him. But to make a long story short . . . sure enough, they had a baby, a beautiful wee baby boy. And when Alistair came in and saw the wee boy born beside his wife, he said, 'Whit are you gaunna call him?'

'Well,' she said, 'what do you think I'm gaun to call him? I'm gaun to call him "Alistair" after you, because you're my husband and we live in this glen, on this farm cut off fra all other people – and two Alistairs in the family is not enough for me!'

But anyway, Alistair was so happy to have a baby son and so was his wife. Time passed by and the baby grew up naturally . . . three months, and by this time it was the end of April. And he was sitting up in the cradle. Now what did Alistair have in the house but an old-fashioned wooden cradle that had passed down through his family, from generation to generation of the Macleans for hundreds of years. The cradle had a hood and was made in one bit of solid oak with rockers, whereby the woman could sit and put her foot to it to rock the baby. This cradle was about four feet long with a hood to keep the sun or the light off the baby. And Alistair had always promised himself, someday he would have something to put in it – so finally he had!

But this day, April the thirtieth, he said to his wife, 'Mary, I'll have tae cut the wee puckle hay the day otherwise we'll no have nothing for the cows in the winter-time.' In the hills grass grows but you can't grow good hay. But they had a few cows they kept for milk and he said, 'Or mebbe for a stack or two, we'll try and get a stack or two – I'll hev to cut a wee bit o' hay.'

'But Alec,' she said, 'I'll come out and gie ye a wee bit help.'

'It's no cut yet.' He said, 'I'll cut it today – it's no very high, it's very thin, and I think by the day's sun, if it gets a day's sun, I'll be able tae turn it tomorrow.' (They turned it with these hand rakes: you walked along behind where the man had cut the hay, after it had a day's sun, and you turned it with a rake that had a long handle and about fourteen teeth on it.)

'Well,' she said, 'Alec, I'll come oot wi ye tomorra.'

'Okay, but,' he said, 'what about the baby?'

'Ach, it's nae problem, I'll take the cradle under my oxter and,' she said, 'I'll come oot. I'll put him beside me.'

'Okay,' he said, 'at'd help me a lot.'

So Alistair cut all day with the scythe. It was about two acres and it was a hard job cutting with a scythe, but he finished it. The sun was beating down from the sky and he was tired. He took his scythe and stuck it in an old roan pipe beside the barn; took his stone from his belt (he carried a sharpening stone), shoved it beside the scythe, and walked into the farm-house. His wife had his supper ready, so he sat down to eat. 'Mary, I've had a hard day.'

'I know,' she said, 'Alec, ye've had a hard day, but tomorra will be better for us.'

'But,' he said, 'ye know, Mary we need the wee puckle hay for the kye in the winter-time.'

'Of course,' she said, 'we need the puckle hay. It's all right, Alec, tomorra we'll take little Alec in the cradle, he'll be no bother tae me! And I'll turn it while you build it intae wee stacks fir the winter.'

But that year they'd cut the hay early in the hill because it was a good spring. He said, 'Mary, what is it, what's the date on the calendar?' It was an old fly-bitten calendar on the wall.

She said, 'Alec, I think tomorra is the first o' May.'

'Well, upon my soul,' he said, 'I have never even remembered as a child wi my father, ever bein able tae cut hay on the end of April, the first of May, for a long long time. I remember my father tellin me we've done it earlier but,' he said, 'this is early for me, and prob'ly by the time we get it raked up and gaithert mebbe the second crop'll be fine tae let out the goats on it, after we get it built up.'

'Alistair, I wouldna let it bother ye,' she said. 'If we get this little pick o' hay gaithert up before the rain comes and stacked up wi my help, I think we should manage tae keep the animals alive fir the winter.'

He said, 'Mary, thank you for all yir help.'

She said, 'Tomorra morning we'll go out both together.' Sure enough, the next morning they got up bright and early. The baby was lying in the cradle, bonnie young Alistair was lying giggling and kicking his bare feet in the cradle. They had their breakfast, porridge and milk and tea, scones, cheese, whatever they had. And the sun was shining, it was a beautiful day.

She said, 'Alec, I'm gaun with ye.'

He said, 'Ye're sure you can manage?'

'Yes,' she said, 'my dear, I'm sure I can.' So she picked up the cradle below her oxter.

He walked out, took the rake from the back of the barn, and said to Mary, 'Will ye manage the rake – and I'll take the scythe and gae round the borders, cut whatever's left – you turn what's ever there.' And wee baby Alistair was lying in the cradle giggling to himself after he'd had his bottle, after his meal.

Now in the middle of the field was a wee bit hill, nothing grew on it but flowers, daisies, but no hay. And Alistair had cut round it with his scythe – it was high up in the middle of the field, a hillock, or a knowe. So Mary came walking up with the cradle, she thought the best thing she could do was walk up the wee knowe and leave the cradle at the top. While she's turning the hay round the knowe she could look up and see him in the cradle – if anything happened to the baby she would hear it. So she carried the old-fashioned wooden cradle under her oxter and put it on top of the knowe. Baby was fast asleep; she placed it down.

And you know a man cuts bouts of hay with a scythe, lines in circles. Mary walked round and she's turning the hay. Round she goes and round, and round, right round the field for about two hours. But all in a moment she hears the baby screaming. She puts down the rake, runs up. There's the baby crying from its heart, greetin like it never gret before and Mary'd never had any trouble with the baby since it was born.

She said, 'Prob'ly it's wet . . . mebbe something's wrong with it, mebbe it's been stung with a bee or a wasp in its cradle.' She sat and she coaxed it. She did everything, checked it all over. But no way in the world – it just cried and cried and cried. It cried so much that Alistair, who was away with his scythe on the other side of the field, stuck the scythe in the ground and walked up.

'Mary, what's wrong?'

She said, 'It's Alistair – there's something happened tae him, something's wrong with him.'

'Well,' he said, 'mebbe it's wind, it's something . . . what's wrong wi him? What happened?'

'Well,' she said, 'I left him there and I was turning round . . . everything was peace and quiet. All in a minute he startit tae cry, he startit tae greet. And I cannae get him settlit, I've checked everything about him but there's nothing seems tae make him pleased in any way.'

'Is he hungry?'

'No,' she said, 'he's no hungry.' But baby Alistair cried so much the mother and father couldn't get any peace.

He said, 'We'll pack it up fir the day.' So Mary took the cradle under her oxter away with the baby in it, walked back to the cottage, checked him every way again.

But he still gret, and he swinged and gret and he swinged, gret and swinged![1] Alistair came in, washed his face, had his wee bit supper. But the baby still cried, And he rocked the cradle but it was no good. They rocked the cradle, it was no good – no way in this world. They tried their very best. But the swingein went on. It wasn't really crying! It was just 'aa-heyn, aa-heyn, au-in'. It gret and gret and gret – it wouldn't stop, went on and on and on, put the mother and father to their wits' ends!

They sat up all night, but finally about twelve o'clock when the moon was high, the crying stopped. When the full moon came up on the first of May – it went peaceful, quiet! Oh, they blessed each other and thanked God! They went to bed, fell asleep. But about six o'clock in the morning it started again, the greetin.

'God bless us,' he said, 'what's wrong wi that wean!'

'I don't know, Alistair, what's wrong,' she said, 'there's something terrible wrong wi him.'

'Well,' he said, 'we'll have tae get the doctor up.'

'Well—' she said.

'Luik,' he said, 'I cannae stick another night like this. I'm gaun for the doctor.' So he had a garron pony that he sometimes put in the shafts to pull his mowing machine. Alistair put his riding saddle on the horse and rode the three miles down the glen to the village, to the doctor's. The doctor had visited Mary after she'd had the baby.

'Oh, what's the trouble?' he asked.

Alistair told him the story I'm telling you: 'We were oot doin the hay, we took baby Alistair oot in his cradle and put

1 gret and swinged – cried and whined

him on the wee hill. My wife was busy turnin the hay, he startit tae cry. And frae then on, doctor, we have no peace – no pleasure in the world. He just greets and swinges and cairries on . . . he's breakin wir hearts! But the only thing was, twelve o'clock at night he stopped. But,' he said, 'it's terrible: that's only the first day, this morning it was worse. And I'm here, I don't know what tae do.'

Doctor said, 'I'll come up and see him.'

The next morning the doctor, with his satchel in his hand, yoked his gig, drove up the glen in his pony and trap, tied his pony to a tree – never unyoked it because doctors didn't unyoke their horses in these days, they just took the reins and tied them round a tree because they knew they weren't going to stay long. He went in. He looked at the baby, checked it, turned it over, stripped it, examined it, sounded it every way in the world. The baby was perfect. The doctor said, 'I cannae find no complaint with it, no way.'

She said, 'Doctor, is there no something you can—'

He said, 'No, there's nothing.' And it was still girnin, still greetin. Doctor said, 'Nope . . . I've skelped its bottom, checked its legs, checked its knees, did everything in the world with it. I can find no complaint with it in the world,' he said, 'it's perfect in every way.'

'But, doctor,' she said, 'luik, cuid ye no stop it, give it something tae stop it fae greetin?'

It wasn't really greetin, it was swingein, going, 'A-hung, eh-heng, a-hayn'. And this was more upsetting than really greetin. The mother gave it the pappy, she gave it the breast, she gave it the bottle, tried everything – but no way could she content it. It went on and on, for day out and day in.

Now, they didn't have much correspondence with the outside world being up on the wee hill farm, they didn't write many letters or get many visits from other people. But now and again, the old postman used to come up and tell them if there was a sale or a market on in the village. The postman used to cycle his old bicycle up the glen and come to Alistair's farm, have his tea there and a crack to Alistair and Mary, because he'd known them since they were children.

So this day, after a couple of weeks had passed by and Mary and Alistair were so very exhausted with their baby they didn't know what to do – they loved it dearly from their hearts – who should happen by? They're sitting down and the baby's sitting in the cradle, with Mary rocking him by the fire, when who had come up but the old postman! A knock came to the door. Alistair said, 'Who's at the door?'

'Och, it'll be the postman,' she said, 'it's just about his time.' So Mary went to the door and she brought the old postman in.

He sat down. And the natural thing was for Alistair to give him a dram, because they always kept a bottle of whisky for visitors. 'I cam up, Alistair, tae tell ye,' he said, 'there's a big market tomorra in the village and there's a lot o' sheep and cattle and goats and hens and everything gettin sellt. So I thought prob'ly that you would maybe be interested.'

'Och-och, you know fine, postie, I'm always interested,' he said. 'But we have a problem.'

'Ach,' he said, 'what's yir problem?'

'Well,' he said, 'it's the baby, young Alistair. Ever since Mary and me has been cuttin hay, a queer thing has come over him: he disna stop swingein and greetin. We canna have no peace, we're just put to the world's end with him – and we had the doctor up and everything, he says he cannae find no complaint!'

And the baby's lying in the cradle still swingein and greetin! When the postman went over to him the baby looked up.

The postman took a long look at him, pulled the blanket right back and stared at the baby . . . he had his own ideas about children. He looked at the baby's face and the blue eyes. But the thing that was interesting to the postman was the baby's skin – on its face the skin was as old as leather, old as leather! Mary and Alistair had never paid attention to this, but the postman thought it was kind of queer. 'I doubt,' he said to himself, '. . . something queer here.'

Alistair said, 'I would like to go to the market, postie, I wad love to go to the market, but there's no way in the world we can get going. Mary is needin to go to the village anyway, but what can we do? We cannae leave young Alistair here, he greets and swinges so often – there's nothing in the world I can do!'

The postie said, 'Well, tell ye the truth, I'm no very busy tomorra, the day o' the market. In fact, it's my day off, and if ye wad like tae go, you and Mary tae the market, I'll come up and take care o' the baby while you're gone.'

'Oh,' Alistair said, 'wad ye do that? It'd be just out of this world fir tae let us off tigether for one day! We've never had a day off for over a year and Mary wants to buy some things fir hersel, and I wad love to go tae the market. If you could take care o' the baby, we'd make it worth your while.'

The postman said, 'Luik, I'm no needin – you're my friends – I dinna need any money, I dinna want nothing. I'll take care o' the baby while you go to the market, I'll be up tomorra bright and early!'

But the swingein and the greetin still went on. Mary sat and sat and she rocked the cradle, she rocked the cradle till midnight! At last, when the old wag-at-the-wa clock[1] in the cottage struck twelve o'clock – quiet, peace for the night.

'Thank my God,' she said. 'Thank God at last fir peace!' So she put him to sleep, crawled in beside her husband, and the both of them fell asleep with exhaustion.

But in the morning, six o'clock, when the cocks on the farm crowed, the swingein started once more. Mary got out of her bed in her nightgown, ran down the stairs and she tried her best: bottle of hot milk, cuddled it, kissed it, broke its wind, did everything – no, the girnin and swingein still

1 wag-at-the-wa clock – pendulum wall clock

went on. But between the girnin and the greetin and Mary's shaking the cradle, Alistair had got up because he had to go to the market. The two of them were upset about what they were going to do.

She said, 'Dae ye think it's safe tae leave it with the old postman, dae ye think he can keep it quiet?'

'Well, Mary,' he said, 'we've had an awfu time o' it fir the last three weeks and fir a month and . . . luik, I hev tae get to the market and you hev tae get to the village for the things ye need. And if he's gaunna greet with hus, he's gaunna greet wi the auld postman tae, so what's the difference?'

They were sitting discussing it when a knock came to the door, here was the old postie with his old bike up from the village. 'Good morning, people, good morning! It's a nice bright morning,' the old postie said, 'a lovely day fir the market.'

'Oh,' Alistair said, 'it's a lovely day fir the market but it's no a very lovely day for us.'

'Well, tae tell ye the truth,' he said, 'I've cycled up the glen this morning tae see youse young people and I want yese tae take yir pony and yoke yir gig, gae doon to the village and enjoy the market! I'll take care o' the bairn! If it greets wi you, it'll greet wi me – I'll rock it tae sleep, I'll rock it,' said the old postie. The postie's name was old John.

Mary said to him, 'Luik, John, ye'll no need tae want for nothing, ye ken where the cupboard is and ye ken where the food is. If ye get hungry, help yoursel tae onything ye need!'

'This is my day off,' he said, 'and I want youse two tae enjoy yoursel,' because they were his friends and he loved the young couple very much. 'Dinna worry about the bairn!'

Now Alistair had cut his corn, a wee puckle oats he had and he'd built a corn stack out in front of the farm. After cutting the hay three months had passed by, now it was August. And Alistair always grew a wee field of corn to feed his beasts. He'd gathered it up and built a wee stack right in front of the farm on his stackyard, the hay and the corn were up. Now they had suffered the swingein and greetin for nearly four months but still they'd managed to get on with their work.

'Now I want youse two young people,' said the old postman, 'tae forget about young Alistair, forget about the farm, forget about me – I'll take care o' him.'

Mary says, 'You're sure ye'll be all right?'

Alistair says, 'I'm terrified tae go and leave ye.'

He says, 'Luik, get your pony and trap and get to the village!'

They were kind o' sweerin to go, but the old postman, old John, finally coaxed them to go to the market. Anyway, they were a wee bit relieved to get away for a wee while. Alistair yoked the pony, the garron horse, into the trap and he and Mary got in, bade 'good-bye' to old John. As he shook the horse on, Alistair shouted, 'Mind and take care o' the bairn!'

He said, 'Dinna worry – I'll be here aa day! So they had a big fire, it was all peats they burned. Old John pulled the cradle up beside the fire and he lay back. He stretched out his foot and began to rock the cradle. But the swingein and greetin is still going on in the cradle. Old John is sitting rocking the cradle, 'I wonder upon my sowl, what's makkin ye greet so much – there must be something wrong with you – you're in pain.'

But then all in a minute a head popped up! And the baby sat up, pulled the white shawl off its head – beautiful silver hair it had, blue eyes – but the skin was old and sallow-looking on its face. It said, 'John!'

'What, what—' John said, 'what, whit-whit – are ye talkin?'

'John,' he said, 'are they gone?' And the postman was amazed at this. He said, 'Are they gone, John?'

'Aye,' he said, 'are ye talkin aboot yir father and mother?'

'Aye,' he said. 'How long have they been gone?'

'Oh,' he said, 'they'll be well doon the glen by noo.'

'Well,' he said, 'I've got time noo, I can get oot o' this.'

And he got up out of the cradle! Nappy round his middle and the bare legs – he pulled the nappy back so he could walk – and the long silver hair hanging down his back: up out of the cradle, he walked across the floor. He was only about three feet high.

And old John stood up. He was shocked. 'Wh-wh-what am I gaunnae dae? What—'

'You dae nothing,' he said, 'listen, wheesht! Wheesht, you dinna ken nothing! You dinna ken a thing – you cam up here today tae take care o' me, luik – I'm gaunna take care o' you! But mak me one promise, ye never breathe a word o' what happens in this hoose!' Up he goes, with his baby-bowed legs, travels to the cupboard; out with the bottle of whisky, out with two glasses. Guggle, guggle, gugug, fills the glass. 'Noo, John,' he said, 'drink that up!' Guggle, guggle, guggle, fills a glass to himself, flings it back. 'Aye, they think,' he says, 'they're away tae the market today tae enjoy theirsel.'

The old postie's sitting, he's mesmerised, amazed, he doesn't know what to do! He doesn't know what to say – dumbfounded! But after he gets a glass of whisky down, the wee baby puts the bottle down on the floor and says, 'Look, this is for me and you, we're gaunnae finish this – me and you.'

'But,' John says, 'look, you're a baby?'

'Aye, they think I'm a baby! But,' he says, 'I'm no a baby ataa.'

'Ah,' old John says, 'no. You're no a baby, no, no way. You're no a baby, no way in this world!'

He says, 'Are ye fir another drink?'

'Aye,' says the old postie. Now the postie began to get a wee bit het up by this time.

Another glass to the old postie, one to himself. 'Aye,' he says, 'I bet ye they're enjoyin theirsel in the market noo. Oh, prob'ly he'll be buyin cattle and buyin sheep and aa these things, and she'll be spendin her money in the market. But, humph – they better enjoy theirsel because they're no gaunna enjoy theirsel tonight when they come hame!'

'But whit is it,' John said, 'what's the problem?'

He said, 'It's no my problem, it's their problem! They took me oot and left me in the hill, lying by my lane[1] while they cut the hay. I lay by mysel and they never gied me a thocht, and that's why they're gettin punished the day.'

But old John had his own ideas. He said to himself, 'That's nae, that's nae wean – they've nae idea.'

'But,' he said, 'that's no the start o' it . . . He's got a stack o' corn oot there. Go on and get me a corn strae!'

'Wean,' John said, 'Wean, what are ye gaun tae do?'

He said, 'Luik, are ye wantin something tae drink or are ye no wantin it?' And the old postie was well on now, the old postie would do anything. He said, 'Go oot and pick a big corn strae oot o' the stack. Pull a big ane!'

'But, Wean,' he said, 'what are ye gaun tae dae wi a corn straw?'

He said, 'You go and get me a corn strae oot o' the stack. it's only oot the door there, my faither's stack across the door – noo get a big corn strae!'

Poor old postie he was upset, he didn't know what to do. But to please this wean – he didn't know, was it a wean or what it was – and him being well on with drink, the best thing he could do was do what the wean told him. So he walked out and he walked round, all round the wee sheafs of corn on the stack till he saw a wide straw and he pulled the big straw out. It was half an inch wide, he pulled it in with the heads of corn on it. He came back in. It's sitting with its legs crossed at the fire and the bottle between its legs, the nappy round its bottom, the long silver hair hanging down its back, and the blue eyes and the old-fashioned skin on its face. Poor old John, he was so mesmerised he didn't know what to do.

'Did ye get it?' said the wean.

1 by my lane – without a companion

'Aye,' he said, 'I got it.'

'Well,' he said, 'gie it tae me!' He took a poker, rammed it in the fire, and made the poker red hot. He took the corn straw, measured about eight inches – the best bit of the straw – and he broke it off, flung the rest in the fire. He squeezed the top of it flat to make a reed. When the poker was hot, he took it out of the fire and bored six holes down the straw, turned it around and he bored a hole at the back. And old John's sitting watching him, the old poastman never saw anything in his life like this.

'Upon my sowl,' he said, 'and upon my God, this is nae wean! This is a fairy, this is a fairy,' the old postman said to himself. He never said it out loud! 'This is a taen-awa! Upon my sowl, a taen-awa!' (A 'taen-awa' means 'a baby that was taken away with the fairies'.)

Now he's sitting cross-legged with a bottle between his legs and he said to the old postie, 'How're ye feelin?'

The postie said, 'I'm feelin all right.'

'Well, come on,' he said, 'we'll finish the bottle, the're plenty mair in the cupboard,' and he gied the postie another glass. 'Drink that up, John! But we dinna hae much time tae waste because it'll no be long till they're back. But,' he said, 'afore they come back, I'm gaunna play ye a wee tune. Brother, I love music! I love music frae my hert!'

He got the corn straw in his hands with the seven holes bored into it, and he started to play – the jigs and reels and jigs and reels that you never heard in your life before. And the old postie was lost, he didn't know where he was, was he coming or going! Now the postie's half drunk. And the postie said, 'Go on, wean, go on, wean, go on, wean – play on!' The postie's drunk now. And the wean's playing the corn straw, the jigs and reels. The postie liked music himself. And he's playing all this music from the corn straw that you never heard before in your life. No way in the world did the postie ever hear music like this from a corn straw! And the time passed by. When all in a minute the music stopped.

He caught the corn straw and flung it in the fire, jumped back in the cradle, 'They're hame!' He lay back, pulled the blanket over him, put the cool[1] back on his head – 'Eh-hee, oo-hoo, u-hung.'

And then the door opened, in came Mary. She was carrying bundles and parcels and things in her oxter. 'Oh, John, I'm sorry,' she said, 'John.'

'Hay-heng,' it's lying greetin in the cradle.

She says, 'I'm sorry, John, to put wir troubles upon ye. I ken ye didnae hae much enjoyment.'

'Oh no,' he said, 'I didnae hae nae enjoyment!'

But by this time Alistair had loosened the pony out, taken off the harness, put the pony in its stable, and come in. He had a bottle of whisky in his hand. 'For bein so kind, John, I brought you a wee dram.' And there was the postie sitting well on with drink. 'Would you like a wee drink, John?' he said.

'Well, Alistair, tae tell ye the God's truth, no.' He said, 'Luik, I've had enough.'

'Oh, he said, 'you've been helpin yoursel.'

'No, I've no been helpin mysel, but,' he said, 'wait a minute . . . Can I talk tae ye a minute, you and your wife?'

And this thing's lying in the cradle and it's girnin, it's greetin and it's woein, greetin and girnin. And when it heard these voices it roared harder and harder and harder!

The postman said, 'Stop!'

She said, 'How did ye get on wi young Alistair?'

'Luik,' he said, 'let it greet. Come here, I want tae speak tae ye, let it greet – let it go on greetin for evermore. Come into the other room!'

But Alistair said, 'What's the trouble, what's the bother? Did it give ye so much trouble?'

'It gied me nae trouble,' he said, 'Alistair, it gied me nae

1 cool – cowl, close fitting cap

trouble:[1] it gied me a drink and it gied me the best music I ever heard in my life, frae a corn strae!'

Alistair said, 'John, you must be drunk.'

'No, I'm no drunk. Come intae the other room.' So the postie took them into the other room and he told them, 'Luik, Mary and Alistair, I want tae tell you something: I'm no drunk, but I've had a few drinks . . . that in your cradle is a taen-awa.'

And Alistair said, 'What's a "taen-awa"?'

And Mary said, 'What's a "taen-awa"?'

He said, 'When you took your baby oot to the hill tae cut the hay and put it on a knowe, the fairies took your wean and put that thing in his cradle. *That* played tae me like I never heard music before in my life, *that* sat and shared a bottle o' whisky wi me!'

And Alistair said, 'Ye're crazy, man!'

'I'm no crazy, Alistair, listen,' he said. 'That is no your wean, that is a *taen-awa* in yir cradle!' He finally convinced him that it was a *taen-awa*.

'But what're we gaunna do?' Alistair said. 'What are we gaunna do then?'

He said, 'I'll tell ye what ye're gaunna do: there's only one way that you're gaunna get rid o' that and get yir ain wean back. Kid on you don't know what I tell ye! Have you got a new shawl, Mary?'

'Aye,' she says, 'I bocht one today for to wrap it in.'

'Well,' he says, 'wrap it in the new shawl and pit its hands doon between its legs, wrap it up as ticht as ever ye can get it. But don't let its hands oot, no way in this world! And I'll come wi ye, and,' he said, 'Alistair, you come tae!'

'But,' Alistair says, 'what are ye gaun tae dae wi it?'

He says, 'A water clift! The clift – the waterfall is the only answer.' (There was a river running by the farm that was close by. A wee burn dropped about fifty feet over to a pool. The fish couldn't jump it because it was too steep. Alistair

1 It gied me nae trouble – did it give me trouble!

used to fish the pool in his own time for trout.) He says, 'Look, Mary, there's only one cure for it, if ye want tae get rid o' that thing that's in the cradle – that's nae wean, that's a fairy – a fairy took your wean's place! I'll stay wi ye the night and we'll take it to the clift. Wrap its hands ower very carefully because when you tak it there,' he says, 'if it gets a grip o' you and takes ye wi it, you'll never be seen again in a million years. If its hands even touches ye, you'll go wi it ower the clift – and you're the only one that can fling it ower the clift!'

'But God bless my sowl and body,' says Alistair, 'why should such thing happen tae the likes o' us?'

'Well,' says the old postman, 'this is no something new, this has happened tae many people, long ago.'

'But hoo,' says Alistair, 'in the world did you ken aboot this?'

He says, 'My granny tellt me: there's only one way tae get rid o' a taen-awa – fling it ower a clift wi its hands tied between its legs.'

'But,' Mary says, 'it's my baby, I dinna want tae fling it!'

He says, 'That's no yir baby, that's a greetin swinge that's in there. It played the pipes tae me and gied me whisky. Dinna ye believe me? It sat and drank a bottle o' whisky wi me, it played a corn strae tae me – that's nae wean! That's a fairy! So the old postman finally convinced them that it was a fairy. 'Noo,' he said, 'the night when the clock strikes twelve, we'll wrap it up in a new shawl and fling it over the clift.' He finally convinced Alistair and Mary it was really true.

So they sat and they talked. While they talked the swingein still went on. John said, 'Dinna shake it, dinna rock the cradle – forget about it, let it be, dinna even touch it, let it sit!' So time passed by. They sat and talked and they cracked till half past eleven. 'Now,' he says, 'Mary, go and get yir new shawl.'

'Ne-yeh, yen-gay, ae-yengh,' it's greetin. She took it and she wrapped it in the way the old postman told her, put its hands between its legs, wrapped it up in the new shawl as best she could.

'Noo,' says the old postman, 'you've got it done?'

'Right,' she said and packed it in the cradle.

He said, 'Come wi me!' So the old postman, Mary, and Alistair walked. They didn't have far to go to the wee burn.

But the burn made a waterfall . . . 'Noo,' says the old postman, 'you're the one that's got tae dae it. There's nae-body – we cannae help ye.' He says to Mary, 'You tak it, walk tae the top o' the fall, and fling it doon the waterfall!'

'But,' she says, 'I–I–I canna – I hate tae dae it, John, I might never see my wean again.'

He says, 'If ye want tae see yir wean again, ye dae what I'm tellin ye!' But the old postman had convinced her.

She took it to the waterfall and Alistair came with her and old John went with her right to the face of the cliff. She took it and she flung it over – it fell down the waterfall, and when it hit the pool it stopped, and the shawl opened. It came out, spun on the top of the water.

It looked up and shook its fist, 'Ye finally found the answer, but,' it said, 'many's the night when I lay in yir bosom and cuddled ye! I cuid have done terrible things to you – curse upon you! And curse upon your old postman!' Like that – he was gone. Gone, disappeared for evermore.

'Come on,' said the postman, 'that's it, that's it finished.' So they walked back to the cottage, opened the door, walked in.

There was the cradle, and John looked in, he said, 'Look, Mary, in your cradle!' And there lying in the cradle was the bonniest wee baby . . . his blue eyes . . . lying smiling up at his mammy. He said, 'There, Mary, there's your true baby.'

Alistair said, 'How in the world, John, did you ken these things?'

'Well, it's only grannies' cracks,' he said, 'and grannies' stories[1] . . . and if ye canna believe me and what I'm tellin you right noo, gang and get the bottle – let's hae a drink!' So Alistair and the old postman went and got the bottle. They sat and they drank, they finished the bottle. And that is the end of my wee story.

1 only grannies' cracks . . . and stories – old wives' tales, trivial stories, but inferring the opposite

JACK TALES

Jack and the Witch's Bellows

This was a story I heard from an old uncle of mine who used to come to Argyll . . . he's dead now, God rest his soul . . . I was only four years old and I walked down to see him one summer's evening. And he told me and my cousins so many stories that it was too late for me to go home, so I stayed the whole night with him till the morning and he told us stories all night. His name was Alexander Reid, he died a few years ago and he's buried in Helensburgh.

JACK and his old mother stayed in this wee house in the village. Jack had a job in a wee shop beside the house and he used to mend bellows for blowing up the fire. Oh, and he made some of the loveliest bellows you ever saw! He bought in his leather and he sorted[1] the bellows: he put new brass points on them, and he carved things on the handles . . . oh, he had a lovely trade! He kept himself and his old mother the best way he could. So his fame for sorting bellows spread all over the country.

But one day he was sitting in his wee shop, and was making two–three bellows when his mother shouted through to him, 'Come on, Jack, come on! You're working in there all day. Do you never think of stopping and coming through for a wee bit to eat?'

'I'll be with you in a minute, Mother,' he said. So, anyway, through he comes. And he and his old mother are sitting having a wee cup of tea when a knock comes to the door.

1 sorted – repaired

She says, 'Jack, that'll be somebody for you again. I'm pestered sick with so many folk coming to the door – I wish you would stop making so many bellows!'

'Well, if I stop making bellows you'll no have so much to eat,' he says, 'or be so well off!'

So she said, 'I'll go and see who it is while you finish your tea.' Out Jack's old mother goes to the door and she opens it.

Standing in the door is an old, old woman with a big, long, spiky hat on her head. She said, 'Is your son Jack in?'

'Aye,' she said.

'Is this where he sorts the bellows for blowing the fire?' the old woman said.

'Aye,' she said, 'he is in. What do you want of him?'

She said, 'I've got a set of bellows I want him to sort.'

'Well,' says Jack's mother, 'don't stand there, come on in! He's just having a wee mouthful of tea. Come on in, sit down a wee while and get a cup of tea!'

Now unknown to Jack and his old mother this was a witch, see! And she came from a place high up in the mountains called Blowaway Hill where the wind blew steadily day out and day in, where the wind was that strong you could hardly stand. And this old witch lived on Blowaway Hill where the wind always blew. In she comes. She sits down, and Jack's old mother gives her a wee cup of tea. And she opens this parcel she has with her and takes out a pair of bellows. She says, 'Jack, I think you could sort those for me!'

'Aye,' he said, 'I could sort them.' And Jack looked at them and he looked again. In all his days he had never seen a pair of bellows like these! They had a long, long brass point on the front, beautifully carved into the shape of a cat's head. And the two handles were two ducks' heads. They were made of solid brass. The leather in between them for gathering the air to blow the fire was completely finished. And Jack knew it was just the job for him, no bother at all!

She said, 'Do you think you could do anything with them?'

'Och,' he said, 'it's no bother to me to sort them.'

'But I'll tell you one thing,' she said, 'you'll have to be very, very careful because they belonged to my great-great-great-great-granny and I would like you to sort them and I'll make it worth your while.'

'All right,' says Jack. 'But where do you stay?'

She said, 'Have you ever heard of a place called Blowaway Hill?'

'I've heard my father speaking about it,' he said. 'It's a long road from here.'

'Well,' she says, 'I stay there. And if you sort the bellows and bring them up to me . . . I'm an old woman and I can't walk very far – it'll take me a long while to go home tonight – I'll have to be going home now, and thank your mother very much for the cup of tea . . . I'll make it worth your while.'

'Well, well, Granny,' he said, 'I'll bring them up to you when I'm finished.'

So the old woman went away. But she got around the corner – she looked round to see if anybody was watching – she jumped on her broomstick and off she goes through the sky! Home to Blowaway Hill! She landed at the door with her broomstick – into her own house and put the broomstick in at the back of the door.

Now Jack was left with his mother. Jack sat and took his tea. 'Mother,' he said, 'I've mended bellows many's the time and I've even mended bellows for the king, as you know. And never in my day, even when my father used to have the workshop here, have ever I seen a set of bellows look like that! That is the bonniest set of bellows that ever I have seen in my life! I wish one thing,' he says, 'God, that they were mine – I would never part with them!'

'Well,' said his mother, 'you'll have to sort them for the old woman, you can't keep them.'

'Oh no, I can't keep them!' he said. 'That's one thing I can't do, I can't keep them. I'll sort them,' because that was his trade.

So Jack takes them into his shop, loosens them down, cuts all the old rotten leather off the two sides of the bellows, picks out all the best wee nails he could get – all the lovely wee brass nails – cuts new leather, sets the bellows on, puts the new leather in them, puts the lovely wee nails in. And then he polished them. And he polished the brass. He polished the two ducks' heads and he polished the cat's head on the point (this was a big cat's head with its mouth open for the point of the bellows). And he fell in love with them when he saw them. He wished they were his own. 'I've never,' he said 'seen bellows like that in my life!' He was heart-sorry the next day when he had to roll them up in a wee parcel and take them back to Blow-away Hill, to the old witch's house on the mountain. Anyway, he got his breakfast and said 'good-bye' to his mother.

And his mother said, 'What time will you be home – will you be home late tonight, Jack? It's a long road to Blow-away Hill to where the old woman stays.' She said, 'I've heard of her – folk says she's a witch!'

'Tsst! Ach, Mother,' he says. 'Witch! You cry everybody a witch!'

'Well, I'll tell you one thing,' she said, 'she looks a civil enough old woman, but you never know about these old women, away on a hill staying in a big house away by herself up there. You never know what she's doing, working spells, one thing and another. I've heard many a bad story around the village about her.'

'Ah well, Mother, I'm away anyway,' he said. 'I'll see you tonight.'

Away goes Jack with the bellows in below his oxter wrapped in a bit of soft, chamois leather. His mother gave him a bit piece[1] to take with him. He travels and he travels, oh, he travels a long, long time. He must have travelled for nearly half a day till he came to this wood, and a hill, and

1 a bit piece – a sandwich

this path going up the hill right to the very top. A wee house was sitting on the top of the hill. And in the middle of the house was one chimney, and the wind was blowing on the chimney – the smoke around the chimney never went straight, it was always going zig-zag. Because there was always wind on the top of the hill where she stayed, they called it Blowaway Hill. So Jack buckles his coat round about him, gets the bellows in below his oxter, and he walks up the narrow path till he arrives . . . 'God,' he says, 'it's cold here! How does this old woman, this old cratur of a woman, bide up here in that cold wind? It's no half as cold down on the flat as it is up here.' But he knocked on the door and out came the old woman.

'Oh, it's you, son,' she said.

'Aye,' he said, 'it's me, Granny.'

'Come on in out of the cold wind!' she said. 'Ach, it's that North Wind – he's aye blowing in here. He never gives me peace. It's no long since he's been in here getting his tea, a minute ago, and he'll be back here again. I'm fed up with him blowing into the house. I never get peace with him – the door rattling, the windows rattling and blowing my wee bits of sticks all over the place. I wish he would go away for a while and leave me at peace!'

'Who are you talking about?' said Jack.

She said, 'It's the North Wind I'm talking about.'

'But, Granny,' he said, 'the North Wind can't bother anybody.'

'Ah, but he bothers me, he comes in and bothers me,' she said, 'comes in here and sits down and gets his tea.'

Jack said to himself, 'I doubt she's a wee bit away with the birds,'[1] he was thinking that when she took him in.

She said, 'Are you wanting something to eat?'

'Aye,' he said, 'I'll have something to eat,' and she made him a good tea.

1 I doubt she's a wee bit away with the birds – she's certainly gone mad

But the windows started to rattle and shake and the house started to shake. And the wind blew down the chimney . . . the fire went out. She says, 'Jack, did you get my bellows sorted?'

'Aye,' he says.

She says, 'Give me them!' He gave them to her. She caught them. She set them down at the side of the fire and she said, 'Blow, bellows, blow!' And the bellows started to blow by themselves. They puffed and they blew and they puffed and they blew, and up, down, and up, and down and up and down and out and in and up and down and up and down and . . . And Jack's sitting watching them – his two eyes are just sticking out of his head watching these bellows! The witch had put a spell on them: they were magic bellows! And he's watching – the fire kindled up in two minutes! She said, 'Stop, bellows, stop!' The bellows stopped – lay down.

Jack's heart began to beat fast. 'Dear, dear,' he said to himself, 'if I had that! What could I do with that, I could travel all over the country and show off to folk . . . take it to the king! And I would be made for life,' he's thinking to himself, you see!

But anyway, the windows start to rattle and the door starts to blow and the wind comes down the chimney, 'Bvizzzz!' the big heavy noise comes in. And in comes the North Wind! He sits down in the chair.

Jack has a look round about him. 'Who's that?' he says to the old witch.

'Ach, it's my friend,' she said, 'the cold North Wind. He's in for his tea.'

'Well,' he says, 'folk say you can see the wind but I never saw the wind before.'

'Well,' she said, 'you're seeing it now!' The North Wind's sitting with this big long beard, long hair and a big long coat, and his feet stretched out – sitting in the chair. The old witch gave him a cup of tea sitting next to Jack in the chair, so she told him, 'It's Jack from the village up sorting my bellows for me.'

The North Wind's sitting (it could speak to the witch), 'Oh aye,' he said, 'those bellows I gave you years ago.'

She says, 'You never gave them to me years ago, North Wind. You gave them to my great-great-great-great-granny years ago.'

He said to her, 'But I see they're still working.'

'Aye, they're still working. Well anyway,' she said, 'Jack, it's getting late and the North Wind and I have got a lot of things to talk about. It's time you were getting away home.'

'Aye,' he said, 'I'll soon have to go home.'

'But wait a minute,' she says, 'I'll have to pay you, I'll have to pay you for sorting my bellows.' She says, 'What would you like?'

Jack's sitting and he thought a wee while. He said, 'There's only one thing I would like from my heart – a pair of bellows like those ones.'

'Ah, Jack, Jack!' she says. 'I couldn't give you those bellows . . . they're magic bellows. You just say, "Blow!" and they blow the fire themselves. And say, "Stop!" and they stop themselves. But,' she says, 'if they ever get out of hand, if they get on their own, there's nothing but me can stop them.'

'Well,' he said, 'I don't care. I could do with a pair like that.'

'But wait a minute!' she says. 'I'll tell you what I'll do with you – I've an old set of bellows like that belonging to my auntie, my great-auntie, and, they're needing sorting. If you could sort them—'

'But,' he says, 'I like the ducks on the handles and I like the cat—'

'They're the same thing . . . they're mounted the same way,' she said, 'but they're a wee bittie bigger.'

'That would do,' says Jack. 'If they're a wee bit bigger they'd be all the better.' So, he took them. They were the same thing, looked the same but a wee bit different: instead of them being mounted with brass, they were common wood. But they had a long brass spout with a cat's head in the front and two ducks' heads for handles. The leather was finished inside them, but the rest was good. He looked at them, turned them all over. 'Aye,' he said, 'they're good enough bellows but they're not like yours – there's no magic in them.'

'Na, Jack, there's no magic in them,' she said, 'you'll have to blow the fire yourself with them.'

'But,' he said, 'could you no give me a wee spell, just a wee toy kind of a spell, a bit of one? I'm not wanting very much magic in them . . . you being a witch – as folk say you're a witch and . . . you're bound to be a witch when you can speak to the North Wind and bring him into the house. I had a long walk up here, you know, and I had a big job sorting them.'

'Well, Jack, you make my heart run away with my head and,' she said, 'as long as you look after them carefully, I'll put a wee spell on them for you and they'll blow themselves.'

'Good!' said Jack.

So she went in the back room, rumbled and rummaged with her hands, chanted words and things. She came out with the bellows in her hands. 'There you are, Jack!' she said.

'But wait a minute!' says the North Wind. 'Can you let me look at that wee spell before you give it to Jack – and I'll put it in the bellows for him?' (Ah, now the North Wind was wicked, you know. He wasn't bad – but he liked to play tricks on folk, see!) He said, 'I'll tell you what I'll do, seeing as I've met Jack here for the first time,' he said, 'let me put the spell into the bellows for him!'

'Well,' says the witch, 'I can't see any harm in that.'

So he caught the bellows from Jack, you see, and the North Wind said, 'I'll tell you what I'll do, I'll blow the spell in for you.' But in his own head he was thinking, 'I'll make it a wee bit stronger!' So he gave a hard blow into them and he says, 'We'll see the fun after this!' He put a big spell, a strong spell of wind, into the bellows. Poor Jack didn't know the difference!

Jack parcelled the bellows below his oxter, and he bade the witch 'good-bye' and he bade the North Wind 'good-bye'. He travelled away back home. Oh, it was near midnight when he got home to the house! His old mother was waiting up for him. In he went. She gave him his supper.

She said, 'You weren't a while away!'

'No wonder, Mother, I was a while away!' he said. 'I had miles to walk and after I got there . . . you weren't far wrong – thon definitely was a witch.'

'Oh, as low as my father,[1] she's a witch! She's a real witch,' she said.

'And to make things better,' he said, 'the North Wind was sitting in the house with her when I went up! Well, he wasn't there when I went up but he came in.'

'Tsst,' she said, 'laddie, have you been drinking?'

'Not me, Mother,' he said.

She said, 'What kind of drink did the witch give you?'

He said, 'The witch never gave me anything!'

'Well, she must have given you something,' she said, 'you're drunk – saying things like that.'

'No,' he said, 'Mother, I'm not drunk! I never had any drink of any kind.'

'North Wind!' she said. 'You know fine there's nobody can see the wind but a pig; a pig's the only one that can see the wind.'

Well, they argued about it anyway. 'But, I'll tell you one thing, Mother,' he says: 'I got a lovely set of bellows for my job.'

'Is that all she gave you?' said the mother. 'She must have given you a sixpence or something.'

'No,' he said, 'she never gave me a ha'penny. I wasn't wanting any money – I got the bellows . . . and they're magic!'

'You and your magic!' she said. 'You're always looking for something magic.'

1 as low as my father – as sure as the death of my father

'Well, Mother,' he said, 'I've got it this time.'

But anyway, Jack took them down. And these bellows, when he'd sorted them up, he started to polish them, and he polished them and he polished them and he made them that bonnie that they were ten times bonnier than the other ones. The more he polished them the bonnier they got! 'Look,' he said, 'Mother, did you ever see the likes of that? Those are the bonniest bellows in the world! Mother, they are fit for a king!'

'You're right, Jack, they are fit for a king,' she said. 'The best thing you can do now is go and take them to the king!'

'Oh, Mother,' he said, 'I couldn't.

'Look,' she says, 'Jack—'

'Mother, I couldn't give my bellows to the king,' he said, 'they're magic.'

'Magic,' she says, 'there's no magic in them. If they're magic, prove it!'

'No, no,' he said, 'no, no, I'm no wanting to prove it, no, no. They're magic for me,' he said.

But the old mother got him coaxed and she looked at him: she said, 'Jack, they are bonnie bellows right enough. They're the bonniest bellows that ever I've seen. Look at the cat's head in the front and look at those ducks' heads on the handles! Your father,' she said, 'God rest him, made hundreds of bellows and sorted many's the set in this shop years before – and your grandfather before you. But, never in my days have I seen a set of bellows like that! They are fit for a king! Jack, son, the best thing you can do is go to the royal gate, to the palace and hand them into the king. And I bet any money you'll get a good price for them.'

But they argued. He wasn't wanting to sell them, but anyway she got him talked into it. So the next day Jack packed the bellows below his oxter in a bit of skin and he set sail for the king's palace to show the king his bellows, see?

So he travelled on and travelled, he hadn't very far to go, through the village and away out to the end of the village there was the king's big palace and all the lovely big gardens round about. And he walked up the path leading up to the garden. At the same time who was in the garden but the queen!

And she was cutting roses in the garden. Jack came walking up . . . now he has these bellows wapped in a bit of leather, bonnie soft skin. He walks up the pad.

'Oh!' the queen said, 'Good – bonnie young man, are you the gardener?'

'No, no,' he said, 'I'm not the gardener; I want to see the king.'

'Well, I'll tell you what to do,' she said, 'he's sitting in the castle just now, the palace, and if you follow me, I'll lead you to him.' The queen was very nice to him. But she went to step out in front of Jack and she had a bunch of roses, flowers that she'd cut – and they fell on the ground.

And Jack being a good lad said, 'Wait, Your Majesty, and I'll lift the flowers!' He bent down to lift the flowers for the queen and didn't the bellows fall out of his oxter onto the ground!

'Oh, what a lovely set of bellows!' said the queen. 'It's the very thing I want, they're the very thing I want to blow my fire. I've always wanted a set of bellows in my bedroom to blow my fire, and I'll give you anything for them!'

'Well,' says Jack, 'I was hoping to take them, to show them to the king.' But he didn't tell her they were magic bellows!

So the queen couldn't wait till she got these bellows and she's admiring them. She says to Jack, 'You carry the flowers, and I'll carry the bellows!' In she goes to her bedroom.

Now Jack said to her, 'Look, there's a wee spell on those, on those bellows, and they work themselves. You don't need to pump them with your hands.'

'Oh, that's better,' she said. 'I'm delighted! I'll have to shout for His Majesty the King and shout for everybody in the castle to have them come and see these magic bellows. You'll get anything you want for them.'

So the queen caught her flowers and she stuck them into nice vases round about the room. She shouted for the king, the cook, the footman, the butler, for everybody to come in and see these magic bellows. And the fire, they had a great big fire. (Oh, the old-fashioned fires in the big castles were great big monster fires. And it was all sticks, they had no coal to burn in those days.) She said, 'How do they work?'

'Well,' he said, 'you just put them down at the fire and you say, "Blow, bellows, blow!"'

And the big, old, fat king – oh, he's dying to see this, you see! And the cook comes in, the butler comes in, the footman comes in, and the queen – she's standing close to the bellows. She said, 'Blow, bellows, blow!'

And the bellows started to blow, and they blew the fire clean up the chimney. And they started to blow – now, the North Wind had put a big spell in them, you see – and they blew the queen's hair right out straight, all that bonnie lovely yellow hair, blew the queen's hair all the way back. They blew the roses out of the vases. They blew the king up and he stuck to the chandeliers. And the bellows started to go around the room and around the room, and they blew on the footman; they blew up the clothes of the cook and she was battering them with a stew pot and she couldn't stop them!

They go out through the door and round the castle, round the palace, and are blowing all the flowers down, blowing the trees down . . . the king, he's shouting for somebody to come and help, for the footman to go and get a ladder to get him down. And the cook's after these bellows with a skillet, she's trying to skelp the bellows – but no, she can't stop them.

Now poor Jack didn't know what to do, he's dumbfounded. He's shouting, 'Stop, bellows! No!' The more he shouted the worse it got.

The queen's shouting for the bellows to stop, the whole castle is in an uproar with these bellows. They're blowing everything in the castle outside in, but no, they can't stop them!

Jack says, 'There's nothing for it! I'll never get them stopped in the world – there's only one cure, I'll have to go back for the witch – no other cure!' So it's off with his two boots. Jack rolled up his trousers and he set sail back, and he ran and he ran and he ran.

Now all this time he was away these bellows were still going, round the castle and round the castle and they blew every stick of furniture, everything, out of the castle. They blew all the trees down at the castle, blew everything out of the garden – these bellows. And they're going round in circles, puffing and blowing wherever they could get. Nobody could stop them. And the king! He's hiding away into a cupboard and he's got a hold of the queen with the fright of this thing, with the wind in these bellows. And he's shouting for Jack, but Jack's gone.

So Jack ran and he ran and he ran as fast as he could. He was out of breath as he ran to the top of the hill. And he told the witch, 'Oh—'

'What is it, Jack?' she said. 'Lord, what's wrong with you, laddie!'

'Look,' he says, 'I ran all the way . . .' and he told her the story.

'Oh, you did the wrong thing,' she said. 'But I put a spell in the bellows – I only gave it a spell to kindle your fire and no more . . . aye, Jack, I know who it was – it was the North Wind up to his tricks again! It was him, he blew into it and he made those bellows like that. God knows what'll happen now,' she said, 'with the disturbance it caused down at the palace, Jack!'

'I'm in trouble,' he said, 'because it was me who went with the bellows in the first place. I'll probably get my head cut off, the king will maybe put me to the dungeon!'

'No,' she says, 'I'll tell you what to do: you run away back and I'll be there as quickly as you. And I'll put a stop to the bellows,' says the old witch. 'See!' She went out the back door, jumped on her broomstick, got the broomstick between her legs and away she went, 'whist' through the air, and she landed in front of the castle just in minutes.

Here the bellows are still going – they're puffing and blowing around the castle and blowing the dust around, blowing in the windows. They had blown the queen's feather-bed till there was nothing left, they'd scattered the feathers all over the palace for miles. They'd blown every stitck of clothes off the cook and she's standing shivering at the back of the door. And the butler – he's worse!

Anyway, the witch landed – right in front of the bellows. And the bellows are circling, puffing and blowing and puffing round in circles. So the witch stops and she draws a big circle and she points to the bellows, 'Come here! Come you to me, bellows!' she said. And the bellows stopped. And they came round, came round and came back – when they came right into the middle of the circle the witch made a snap at them – and their power was gone. She pumped the bellows, pumped them, two–three times – no more wind. 'Right!' she said.

So everything quietened down at the castle and she went up to the king, and she told the king, 'Look, Your Majesty, it wasn't Jack . . .' and she told the king the story that I'm telling you. She said, 'It was the North Wind; Jack had nothing to do with it.'

'Well!' says the king. 'It'll take weeks, maybe months to put this castle back the way it was, but somebody has to pay for it.'

'Well,' says the witch, 'it wasn't Jack.'

'He was the one who came,' said the king.

'I'll tell you what I'll do;' she said, 'it was the North Wind that caused all the trouble, and I'll send him to you and you can make *him* pay for what he did.'

So Jack went in to the king and the king forgave Jack. And the queen looked at the bellows – oh, she was terrified! The witch says, 'No, no, Your Majesty the Queen, you're all right.' In one spell the witch had put everything back to normal, everything back the way it had been.

'Everything's back to normal,' the king said, 'but somebody has to suffer for what I suffered with those bellows!'

When the queen saw the bellows, she liked them but she was afraid to touch them. 'Go on!' said the witch. 'Go up to them, catch them, blow the fire with them!'

And the queen was kind of frightened, you know. She went up, she caught the bellows and she puff-puff-puff-puffed the fire. The fire blazed up beautifully . . . and the queen fell in love with the bellows. And she gave Jack a big bag of gold for the bellows and everybody was contented.

'But no,' said the king, 'there's one man who's got to come yet and be reckoned with. And that's the North Wind!'

'Well,' says the witch, 'I'll send him to you when I go back.' So the witch jumped on her broomstick and back she went to Blowaway Hill where her house was. And sitting on Blowaway Hill in her wee house was the North Wind.

And he's sitting and he's laughing, 'Ho-ho-ho-ho-ho!' Oh, he's laughing away to himself. He could see what was going on, you see!

'Aye,' said the witch, 'it was nothing to laugh about. You nearly got poor Jack in a lot of trouble with your carry-on.'

'Well, I didn't mean any harm, it was only for fun,' he said. 'I blew into the bellows and made the spell a wee bit stronger.'

'You nearly got Jack hanged,' she said. 'And if I hadn't got there in time and settled things,' she said, 'God knows what would have happened to the poor laddie! But anyway, all's well that ends well.'

'Ah well,' he said, 'that's it.'

'No, that's not it!' says the witch. 'You're wanted back at the palace – the king wants you!'

'What does he want me for?' asked the North Wind.

She said, 'He wants you for what you did!'

'Well, there hasn't been any wind around the palace for a long while . . . I'll have to go when His Majesty calls on me,' said the North Wind – 'I'll have to go!'

The king was lying back in his palace, he and the queen, when all in a minute the wind started round and round the castle, 'Whooo, whooo,' in through the window – right to the king's feet.

'Who are you?' said the king.

He said, 'I'm the North Wind.'

'Oh you are,' says the king, 'you're the North Wind, eh? You're the man that caused all the trouble with the bellows?'

'I am,' said the North Wind, 'and I've come to beg your pardon,'

'Well, look,' the king explained, 'I'm not in a bad mood now; but I was in a bad mood for a while and, you know, I'm not a bad king.'

'Well, I'm thankful for that!' says the North Wind.

'But one thing you'll have to do for me,' he said. 'I'm going to let you off on one condition: when there comes bonnie, warm warm days at my palace; when there's not a breath of wind round my palace, and everything is warm and hot and there's not a breeze to be seen, and the trees and everything are quiet, I want *you* to come and blow a cold breeze about me whenever I get hot.'

'Right!' said the North Wind. So he and the king shook hands onto it, and he bade the king 'farewell'.

And after that, the king had never any need to worry! Because when it was hot blazing sun and there wasn't a cloud in the sky, the king could lie back and enjoy a cool, cool breeze from the North Wind. And the witch was happy and Jack was happy and that's the last of my wee story.

Jack and the Devil's Purse

My father's cousin Willie Williamson of Carradale told me this story in Argyll when I was a boy. As a family we lived in a large handmade tent or barrikit in a forest near Loch Fyne. A river separated our part of the wood from another part, where my traveller relations, like Uncle Willie, would come along to camp in the summer and put up their low tents. We children would cross the river and go to the traveller camping places, sit there and listen.

A long time ago in the West Highlands of Scotland Jack lived with his old mother on a little croft. His father had died when he was very young and Jack barely remembered him. He spent most of his time with his mother. They had a few goats and a couple of sheep on their small croft. His mother kept a few hens and she sold a few eggs in the village. She took in washing and knitting and did everything else just to keep her and her son alive. But Jack grew up. He loved and respected his mother. And he tried to make the croft work, but things got very hard. The ground was too hard and stony, little crops could he grow. He always depended on the few shillings that his mother could bring in because he couldn't get very much off the land. And where they stayed was about two miles from the small village – there was a post office and a local store and a little inn. Jack used to walk there every week to get his mother's few groceries, or messages. And Jack had grown up to be a young man by this time.

So one day his mother called him, 'Jack, are you busy?'

'Well no, Mother,' he said, 'I'm no busy. I've cut the wee puckle hay and I've stacked it up, it's no much.'

She said, 'Would you like to go into the village an get something for me?'

'Of course, Mother,' he said, 'I always go, you know I always go.'

So she gave him a few shillings to walk into the village. And he went into the stores and bought these few groceries for his mother. He came walking across the little street, and lo and behold he was stopped by an old friend of his mother's who had never seen his mother for many years. But the friend knew him.

'Oh Jack!' he said, 'you're finally grown up to a big young handsome man.'

Jack said, 'Do I know you, sir?'

'Och laddie,' he said, 'ye ken ye know me, I'm a friend o' yer mother's.'

'Well,' Jack said, 'I've never remembered much about you.'

'Oh but your mother does! Tell her old Dugald was askin for her when ye go back!' He said, 'I was your mother's lover, you know!'

'Oh well,' Jack said, 'that's nothin to do with me.'

'Well, tell your mother I'll come out an see her first chance I get,' he said. 'I've been away travellin. But now I'm back and I'm settled here in the village, I'll prob'ly come out and see her sometime.'

'Okay,' says Jack, 'I'll have to hurry.'

'Oh no,' he said, 'laddie, ye're no goin awa like that! Come in wi me!'

Jack said, 'Where?'

He says, 'Into the inn.'

Jack says, 'The inn? Sir, I don't—'

'Dinna call me "sir",' he said, 'call me Dugald!'

He said, 'Sir, I never was in a inn in my life.'

'Oh laddie,' he said, 'you mean to tell me you never had a drink?'

'No me, Dugald,' he said, 'I never had a drink.'

'Well,' he said, 'you're gettin one now! Come wi me.'

Into the little inn. Jack had his mother's little groceries, he placed them beside the bar. 'Two glasses of whisky!' said old Dugald, who'd had a few glasses before that. 'Drink it up, laddie! It's good for ye. And I'm comin to see yer mother, mind and tell her!

Jack drank the glass of whisky for the first time in his life. Oh, he choked and coughed a little bit and it felt strange to him. He had never had a drink before in his life. But after a few seconds when the warm glow began to pass across his chest and his head began to get a little dizzy, Jack felt good!

And old Dugald said, 'Did you like that?'

Jack said, 'Of course, it was good.'

'Have another one,' he said. So he filled another glass for Jack and Jack had two full glasses of whisky for the first time in his life.

He said, 'Well now,' he was feeling a wee bit tipsy, 'I think I'd better go home wi my mother's groceries!'

'Okay laddie,' he said, 'mind my message now! Tell yer mother I'll come out to see her because she's an old girlfriend o' mine!' Old Dugald was well on with the drink.

Jack picked up his little bag and he walked back . . . two steps forward, three steps back. But he made his way to his mother.

When he walked in his mother was pleased to see him, she said, 'Your supper's on the table.'

'I'm no wantin any supper, Mother,' he said.

She said, 'Jack, have you been drinkin? You know, Jack, drink ruined yer father. It was drink that killed yer father.'

'Oh Mother,' he said, 'I had the best fun o' my life. In fact I met an old boyfriend o' yours!'

And she touched her hair and she pulled her apron down, you know! She smoothed her apron, she said, 'What did you say, laddie?'

He said, 'Mother, I met an old boyfriend o' yours!'

And she tidied her hair, pulled down her apron and said, 'What did you say?'

'I met an old boyfriend o' yours and he's comin to see ye!'

She said, 'A, my boyfriend? I have nae boyfriends, laddie.'

'Aye Mother,' he said, 'you've had a boyfriend – before you met my father.'

She said, 'What's his name?'

He said, 'Dugald.'

'Oh,' she said, 'young Dugald, young Dugald! God, laddie, I've never seen him for years.'

'Well Mother,' he said, 'he's comin to see you onyway.'

She was pleased about this. She'd forgot about Jack's drinking. So they sat and they talked and they discussed things. And things went on as usual. But Jack had the taste of drink.

Now every time he went to the village he would say, 'Mother, could I borrow a shilling fae ye?' or, 'two shillings' or, 'three shillings', every time for the sake of getting a drink. And Jack finally got hooked on drink. Till there was no money left, there was no money coming into the croft by his work or his mother had nothing to spare. She gave him what she could afford to buy the messages and that was all. 'Mother,' he said, 'gie us a shilling, or something!'

'No, son,' she says, 'I havena got it.'

'Anyway,' he says, 'I'll walk to the village.'

So on the road to the village there was a cross-roads, one road went to the left, one road went to the right. Jack was coming walking down, he said, 'God upon my soul, bless my body in Hell, and Devil . . .' he's cursing to himself. He said, 'What would I give for a shilling! My mother has nae money, she gien me everything she had. God, I could do with a drink! I could do, I could walk in an buy mysel a glass o' whisky and really enjoy it. *God Almighty, what's wrong with me*?'

No answer.

He said, 'The Devil o' Hell – will ye listen to me? '*I'd give my soul tonight to the Devil o' Hell if he would only give me a shilling for a drink*!' But lo and behold Jack walked on and there at the cross-roads stood a tall dark man.

Jack was about to pass him by when he heard, 'Aye, Jack, you're makin your way to the village.'

Jack looked up, he said, 'Sir, do you know me?'

'Ah, Jack, I ken you all right, you and your mother are up in that croft there.'

'But,' Jack said, 'I've never met you, sir.'

'No, Jack,' said the man, 'you've never met me. But I heard you muttering to yourself as you were comin down the road. And the things you were sayin I was interested in.'

Jack said, 'What do you think I was sayin?'

'Oh,' he said, 'ye talked about your God . . . and you mentioned my name.'

'Your name?' says Jack.

'Of course,' he said, 'you mentioned my name, Jack. I'm the Devil.'

'You're the Devil?' says Jack.

'I am the Devil, Jack,' he said. 'And you said "you would gie me your soul for a shilling for a drink".'

Jack said, 'Look, let you be the Devil of Hell or the Devil of Nowhere, I would give my soul to the Devil, *the real Devil,* tonight!'

He says, 'Jack, I am the real Devil!'

'Ah,' Jack says, 'I dinna believe ye.'

'Well,' he said, 'can you try me?'

Jack said, 'What do I try ye for? What hae ye got to gie me? Hae you got a shilling for me?'

The Devil says, 'I'll go one better.' Puts his hand under his cloak and he brings out a small leather purse. He says, 'Jack, look, you said "you would sell your soul to the Devil for a shilling for a drink".'

Jack says, 'Gladly, I would!'

'Well,' he says, 'look . . . I've got a purse here and in that purse is a shilling. But I'll go one better – every time you take a shilling out another one'll take its place – and you can drink to your heart's content. You'll never need to worry again. But on one condition.'

'And what's your condition?' says Jack.

He said, 'You said you would give me your soul!'

Jack said, 'If you're the Devil you can have my soul – it's no good to me – a drink I need!'

'Take my purse,' said the Devil, 'and spend to your heart's content, and I'll come for you in a year and a day!'

'Done,' says Jack, 'show me your purse!' The Devil gave Jack a little purse.

And he opened it up – a silver shilling in the purse. 'Right,' says Jack, 'it's a deal!' The Devil was gone, he vanished.

Jack walked to the village, spent his mother's two–three shillings to buy the things his mother needed, and he said, 'I've got a shilling in my purse.' And he walked across to the local inn. Took the shilling out, put it on the bar and called for a glass of whisky. Got his glass of whisky, drunk it up. Called for another one and drunk it up. 'Now,' he said, 'Devil, if you're telling the truth . . . .' And he opened the purse, lo and behold there was another one! He spent another one, and another one took its place. And Jack got really drunk. He walked home to his mother, purse in his hip pocket. 'Now at last,' he said, 'I can drink to my heart's content.' He gave his mother her messages.

'Where did you get the money to drink, Jack?' she says. 'You've been drinkin.'

'Och,' he says, 'I met a couple o' friends, Mother.' He never told her. But anyhow, Jack made every excuse he could get to go to the village. And every time he went he got drunk as usual. Day out and day in. Oh, he bought things for his mother forbyes.

But one night after three months had passed she said, 'Jack, you've been drinkin a terrible lot. Where are you gettin all this money?'

'Ach Mother,' he said, 'it's only friends I meet.' But she was pleased with that.

But after six months, after Jack had been drinking for another three months, she said, 'Jack, look, you'll have to tell me the truth. Where is this money coming from?

You've been drunk now for weeks on end. Not that I'm complainin . . . drink killed your father, it'll prob'ly kill you too. You're a young man and it's none o' my business.'

'Ach Mother,' he said, 'it's only money I've been gettin from my friends, they owed it to me.'

Another three months passed, and nine months had passed. Jack was still drinking to his heart's content. One night he came home very drunk.

She says, 'Jack, do you know what you're doin? That's nine month you've been drinkin every week. Laddie, ye ken you're workin with the Devil!'

He says, 'What, Mother?'

She says, 'Laddie, you're workin with the Devil, drink is Devil's work! It killed yer father and it'll kill you.'

'But Mother, what do you mean?'

'Well,' she says, 'I'm tellin you, laddie, *it's Devil's work*. Laddie, where are ye gettin the money?'

'Well,' he says, 'Mother, to tell ye the truth, I really met the Devil.'

'Ye met the Devil?' says his mother.'

'Aye, Mother,' he said, 'I met the Devil. And he's comin for me in a year's time.'

'But,' she said, 'what do ye mean?'

'Well,' he said, 'to tell you the truth, I coaxed you for a shilling and I begged you for money. I was cursin and swearin at the cross-roads and there I met a man. And he gave me a purse wi a shilling in it. And I sold my soul to him. And he tellt me he's comin for me in a year and a day.'

She said, 'Laddie, where is the purse?'

Jack took the purse from his pocket and the old woman looked. It was a queer looking purse, she had never seen nothing like this before. He said, 'Look in it, Mother, see what's in it.' And the mother looked in, there was a single shilling in it, silver shilling. He said, 'Mother, tak it out.' And the old mother took it out. She held it in her hand. 'Now,' he said, 'look in there, Mother!'

And she looked again, there was another one. She took

another, and another one took its place. Oh, she catcht it and she clashed it to the floor. She says, 'Laddie, that's *the Devil's purse* you've got!'

'But,' he says, 'Mother, what can I do with it?'

She says, 'Laddie, get rid of it. Ye ken the Devil's got ye!'

'But,' he says, 'Mother, I've tried. I'm beginnin to understand now that your words are true. I threw it in the fire when you werena lookin, but it jumped back out again. I throw it away, it comes back in my pocket again. Mother, what am I goin to do? I dinna want to go wi the Devil!' Now Jack began to get to his senses, he stopped drinking for a week, never had a drink. One shilling lay in the purse. He said, 'Mother, what can I do? He's comin for me!'

'Oh I ken, laddie, he's comin for ye! We ken that. You shouldna hae took it from him in the first place.'

'Mother,' he says, 'help me, please! I dinna want to go wi the Devil!'

'Well,' she says, 'look, Jack, there's only one thing I can tell ye. I have an old sister you've never met, your auntie and she lives a long way from here, Jack. And I was always askin ye to go and see her for a visit. She's an old hen-wife and people thinks that she's a bit of a witch, and if onybody can help you, she's the only one that can. Would you tak my word, Jack, forget about the purse! Tak it wi ye, show it to her and explain yer case to her.'

'But where does she bide, Mother?' He said. 'Ye never tellt me this afore.'

'Oh laddie,' she said, 'it's a long way fae here.'

'Well,' he said, 'Mother, if she can help me I'm goin to see her.'

So the old woman told Jack where her old sister stayed, and the next morning Jack went on his way to find his old auntie. And he travelled on for days and days and he finally came to his old auntie's little cottage. She had a cottage on the beach by the shoreside and she kept hens and ducks. He walked up and knocked at the door.

And a very old bended woman came out and said, 'Hello, young man! What do you want here?'

He said, 'Auntie, do ye no ken who I am?'

She says, 'What do ye mean, I'm no auntie of yours!'

He says, 'I'm Jack, I'm your sister's son.'

'Oh,' she said, 'my sister's son from the farthest point of Ireland![1] I never never thought you would ever come and see me. Come in, laddie, come in! I'm pleased to see ye. And how's my old sister?'

'Yer old sister's fine,' he said, 'but it's me I'm worried about.'

'And what's wrong wi you, laddie?' she said, after he'd had a wee bite to eat.

'Well look, Auntie, to tell ye the God's truth, I'm tooken over wi the Devil.'

'Oh dear me, laddie,' she says, 'sit down and tell me about it. So Jack told her the story I'm tellin you. She says, 'Laddie, show me the purse!'

And she took the purse, she opened it. There was one single shilling in it. She took the shilling out and she looked again – another one took its place. She took the shilling, she put it back in, and the other one vanished. She said, 'Laddie, you're really tooken over wi the Devil, that's the God's truth!' So she took the purse and she put it on the little table. She said, 'Jack, there's only one thing ye can do. But wait a minute . . . ye can stay here the night with me. But tomorrow morning you want to go up to the village and see the local blacksmith. Tell him to put the purse on the anvil in the smiddy and to heat a horseshoe in the fire, and *beat that purse like he's never beat anything before in his life*! But I have a wee present for ye and I'll gie it to you in the mornin.' So Jack spent a restless night with his old auntie.

But next morning after breakfast she came out. She had a wee small Bible that you could barely see, the smallest Bible

1 the farthest point of Ireland – the other side of the country

you could ever see! She said, 'Jack, put that in your pocket and don't part wi it for nobody under the sun!'

So Jack took the wee Bible and he put it in his pocket. He thanked his old auntie very much and told her he would go to the blacksmith and see him.

'Tell him I sent ye! Tell him old Isa sent ye up!'

So Jack bade 'farewell' to his auntie, walked up to the little village and came to the blacksmith's shop. The old blacksmith was busy over the fire with a bit leather apron round his waist. There weren't a horse in the smiddy or nothing. And Jack walked in, the old blacksmith was blowin up the fire.

He turned round, said, 'Hello, young man! What can I do for ye, ye got a horse with ye?'

'No,' Jack said, 'I've no horse, sir, I've no horse. I was down talkin to my auntie, old Isa.'

'Oh, old Isa,' said the blacksmith, 'oh, the old friend o' mine! Aye, what can I do for ye?'

'Well,' he says, 'I'm her nephew. And I want you to help me.'

'Oh,' he says, 'any friend of old Isa's is a friend o' mine. What can I do for ye?'

'Well,' he says, 'sir, look, it's this purse. It belongs to the Devil!'

'Oh, belongs to the Devil,' said the blacksmith, 'I see. And what am I supposed to do with it, throw it in the fire?'

'Oh no,' Jack said, 'you'll no throw it in the fire! I want ye to put it on the anvil and beat it, my auntie says to beat it with a horseshoe!'

'Well,' he said, 'your auntie cured me many times when I was sick. And what *she* says is bound to be true!' So the old blacksmith took the purse and he put it on the anvil. And he went in and got a big horseshoe, he put it on a pair o' clippers and held it in the fire. And he held it till the shoe was red hot. He took and he beat the purse. And every time he beat the purse a little imp jumped out! It stood on the floor, ugly little creature with its long nails and ugly-looking face. And the blacksmith beat the purse . . . another one and another one and another one came out. Till there were about fifteen or sixteen imps – all standing there looking up with their curled nails and their ugly little faces, eyes upside down and ears twisted – they were the most, the ugliest looking things you ever saw! The blacksmith and Jack paid no attention to them. And then the last beat – out jumped Himself, the Devil! And within minutes he was tall and dark.

He turns round to the blacksmith and to Jack, 'Aye Jack,' he says, 'heh-h, laddie, ye thought you could beat me didn't ye? You thought you could beat me by beatin this purse! But laddie, that maks nae difference, you only beat the imps out and they're mine. *And you're still belongin to me*!'

The old blacksmith stood in a shake, he was terrified. He said, 'I – I had nothing to do with it.'

Devil said, 'Look, nothing to do with you, old man, nothing to do with you. Tend to your fire. This young man is my problem.' He said, 'Jack, you thought you could beat me, didn't ye? I've come for you, Jack, you've got to come wi me!' And all the little imps are gathered round in a knot together and they are standing there, they're watching and they're hanging on to the Devil's legs. He says, 'Jack, you've got to come with me!'

But Jack says, 'I'm no dead yet.'

He says, 'That was no bargain – I never mentioned you being dead. You told me you'd sell me your soul, so you must come with me!'

'Well,' Jack says, 'if that's it, that's it!'

So the Devil walked out from the blacksmith's shop with the imps all behind him, and Jack and he went on his way. They travelled for days and weeks through thorns and brambles and forests and places, caverns and valleys till at last they came into Hell. And there in Hell was a great cavern with a great roaring fire and all these little cages full of imps. The Devil opened an empty one and he put all the little ones in, hushed them in and he closed the door. They stood with their nails against the cages, their ugly faces – some with faces of old women, faces of old men, ears upside down – the most ugly looking creatures you ever saw in your lifetime.

'Now,' says the Devil, 'I've got you!'

'Well,' Jack says, 'what are you goin to do with me?'

'Well, Jack,' he said, 'to tell ye the truth I don't know what I'm goin to do with you. You spent my money, ye know, and you enjoyed yourself.'

'That's true,' said Jack, 'I enjoyed myself.'

'And you tried to deceive me.'

'That's right,' said Jack, 'I did try.'

'But,' he says, 'I finally got ye. But I'll be lenient with you, Jack, if you'll do something for me!'

Jack said, 'Well?'

He said, 'I'm goin away for a long time, Jack. I must go on a journey, I have some people to see in a faraway country who are due a visit from me the Devil! And all I want you to do is to sit here by the fire and take care of the imps while I'm gone.'

'Oh,' Jack said, 'that's no problem, no problem at all.' So then there was a flash of light and the Devil was gone. Jack was left alone in Hell. Cages and cages all around him, a burning fire . . . all by himself.

So he sat for many hours wearied and wondering, how in the world was he going to get away back from Hell? Thinking about himself, thinking about everything else and then lo and behold, he put his hand in his pocket and he felt the little Bible that his auntie had given him. And he brought it forward. He looked at it and he opened the first page. And because he had nobody to talk to and the light was so bright by the fireside, and he was wearied, he thought to himself he would read – though he'd never read the Bible before in his life. He turned the pages and he got kind of interested. And he sat there reading and reading and reading . . . Quiet and still it was in Hell. He looked all around. All the little imps were up with their nails against the cages, and they were peaceful and quiet. They were not doing anything. Jack was reading away to himself.

And then he said to them, 'Would ye like a story?' They did not say a word. So Jack started and he read aloud from the Bible. And all the imps gathered round their cages with their hands round the steel bars, and they were sitting listening so intent. Jack read page after page from the Bible and they were so interested. Then Jack stopped.

And the moment he stopped they started the wildest carry-on, they were screaming, they were fighting and arguing with each other and biting each other, 'Aargh!' Jack opened the Bible again and then the screaming stopped.

'Aha,' said Jack, 'it's stories ye like isn't it?' He went round every cage in Hell and opened them all. He let them all out. And they gathered round him by the fireside. They sat on his legs, they climbed on his knees, they keeked into his ears, they sat on his head, they pulled on his ears and pulled his hair. And then Jack started reading aloud from the Bible. They sat quietly listening. And he read the Bible through and through and through for many many times. He must have read the Bible through a dozen times, and they enjoyed it. But the moment he stopped, they started arguing again and fighting! So to keep them quiet Jack kept reading the Bible. And the more he read the quieter they were. So Jack said, 'The only way that I'm going to get peace is to read the Bible to you!' So he read the Bible through a hundred times.

And then there was a flash of light! There stood the Devil with an old man on his back. And he came up and threw the old man in the fire. 'Right, imps,' he said, 'come on and get your spears, get this old man tortured!' But they all ran behind Jack, they curled behind his legs, they climbed behind his back. And they wouldn't look at the Devil. 'Come on, imps,' said the Devil, 'the're work to be done!' But the imps wouldn't look at the Devil in any way. Paid him no attention. The Devil said, 'Jack, what have you done to my imps?'

Jack said, 'I've done nothing to them, I read them a story.'

'A story!' says the Devil. 'Where did you read them a story?'

'From the Bible.'

'Take *that* from me,' said the Devil, 'take *that* from me, put *that* away from me!' He says, 'Jack, you're no good to me. No good to me, I'm sorry I ever even thought about you in the first place. Jack, you're too bad for Heaven and you're too good for Hell. Look, I'm goin to give you a chance. You take all these imps and go and start a place for yourself! I'll set you free. Now be on your way! And *that's* the road to take,' there was a space o' light. And Jack walked on.

'Good-bye, Devil,' he said, and he walked on through the space o' light and travelled on. Lo and behold all the little imps, one after each other followed him in a single file till he disappeared from the cavern o' Hell!

When the beautiful sun was shining he landed in a beautiful forest. And he sat down there, he wondered, 'Am I really free from Hell?' he said. 'Will the Devil ever bother me any more?' And all the little imps gathered round him. They sat on his knees, they sat beside him. And Jack said, 'Well, little fellas, we have a problem. You know I've led you from Hell. Now I canna take you back to my mother in any way. But look, this is a nice place for you to live. Go out in the forest and be good and kind and create in your own likeness, and enjoy yourselves. Make a home for yourselves here, you'll never need to go back to Hell again!' And then the little fellas vanished in the forest. Jack walked on to his mother's.

And his mother was pleased to see him. 'Did ye do what I told you, Jack?' she said.

'Aye, Mother, I did what you tellt me, and have I got a story to tell you!'

So the little imps lived in the forest and they spread out and they created in their likeness. And therefore began the legend of all the goblins and elves and gnomes in the land. And Jack lived happy with his mother. But he never took another drink, and that is the end of my story.

Death in a Nut

I've heard many different versions of this story, and this one particular version that I really like was told to me a long time ago by an old uncle of mine who was married to my mother's sister, old Sandy Reid, God rest his soul. This was one of his favourite stories because he was really good at it. And I'll try my best to tell it to you as close as possible to the natural way he told it to me.

JACK lived with his mother in a little cottage by the shoreside, and his mother kept some ducks and some hens. Jack could barely remember his father because his father had died long before he was born. And they had a small kind o' croft, Jack cut a little hay for his mother's goats. When there were no hay to collect, he spent most of his time along the shoreside as a beach-comber collecting everything that came in with the tide, whatever it would be – any old drums, any old cans, pieces of driftwood, something that was flung off a boat – Jack collected all these things and brought them in, put them beside his mother's cottage and said, 'Some day they might come in useful.' But the most useful thing that Jack ever collected for his mother was firewood. And Jack was very happy, he was just a young man, in his early teens, and he dearly loved his mother. Some days he used to take duck eggs to the village (his mother was famed for her duck eggs) and hen eggs to the village forbyes, they helped them survive, and his mother would take in a little sewing for the local people in the village; Jack and his mother lived quite happy. Till one particular day, it was around about the winter-time, about the month o' January.

Jack used to always get up early in the morning and make a cup o' tea, he always gave his mother a cup o' tea in bed every morning. And one particular morning he rose early because he wanted to catch the incoming tide to see what it would bring in for him. He brought a cup o' tea into his mother in her own little bed in a little room, it was only a two-room little cottage they had. He says, 'Mother, I've brought you a cup o' tea.'

She says, 'Son, I don't want any tea.'

'Mother,' he says, 'why? What's wrong, are you not feelin—'

She says, 'Son, I'm not feelin very well this morning, I'm not feelin very well. I don't think I cuid even drink a cup o' tea if ye gev it to me.'

'Oh, Mother,' he says, 'try an take a wee sip,' an he leaned over the bed, an held the cup to his mother's mouth.

She took two–three sips, 'That's enough, laddie,' she says, 'I don't feel very well.'

He says, 'What's wrong with you, Mother? Are you in pain or somethin?'

'Well, so an no so, Jack, I dinnae ken what's wrong wi me,' she says. 'I'm an ill woman, Jack, an ye're a young man an I cannae go on for ever.'

'But, Mother,' he says, 'you cannae dee an leave me masel! What am I gaunnae dae? I've nae freends, nae naebody in this worl but you, Mother! Ye cannae dee an lea me!'

'Well,' she says, 'Jack, I think I'm no long fir this worl. In fact, I think he'll be comin fir me some o' these days . . . soon.'

'Wha, Mother, ye talking about "comin fir me"?'

She says, 'Jack, ye ken wha he is, Jack. Between me an you, we dinna share nae secrets – I'm an auld woman an I'm gaunna dee – Death's gaunna come fir me, Jack, I can see it in ma mind.'

'Oh, Mother, no, Mother,' he says, an he held her hand.

'But,' she says, 'never mind, laddie, ye'll manage to take

care o' yirsel. Yir mother hes saved a few shillins fir ye an I'm sure some day ye'll meet a nice wee wife when I'm gone, ye'll prob'ly get on in the world.'

'No, Mother,' he says, 'I cuidna get on withoot you.'

She says, 'Laddie, leave me an I'll try an get a wee sleep.'

By this time it was daylight as the sun began to get up, and Jack walked up along the shoreway just in the grey-dark in the morning, getting clear. It must have been about half-past eight–nine o'clock (in the winter-time it took a long while to get clear in the mornings), when the tide was coming in. Jack walked along the shoreway and lo and behold, the first thing he saw coming a-walking the shoreway was an old man with a long grey beard, skinny legs and a ragged coat over his back and a scythe on his back. His two eyes were sunk into his head, sunk back into his skull, and he was the most ugliest-looking creature that Jack ever saw in his life. But he had on his back a brand new scythe and it was shining in the light from the morning. Now, his mother had always told Jack what like Death looked and Jack says to himself, 'That's Deith come fir my auld mother! He's come tae take the on'y thing that I love awa fae me, but,' he said, 'he's no gettin awa wi it! He's no gettin away wi it!'

So Jack steps out off the shoreside, and up he comes and meets this old man – bare feet, long ragged coat, long ragged beard, high cheek bones and his eyes sunk back in his head, two front teeth sticking out like that – and a shining scythe on his back, the morning sun was glittering on the blade – ready to cut the people's throats and take them away to the Land o' Death. Jack steps up, says, 'Good morning, Auld Man.'

'Oh,' he said, 'good morning, young man! Tell me, is it far tae the next cottage?'

Jack said, 'Ma mother lives i' the next cottage just along the shoreway a little bit.'

'Oh,' he says, 'that's her I want to visit.'

'Not this mornin,' says Jack, 'ye're not gaunna visit her! I know who you are – you're Death – an you've come tae take my aul mother, kill her an tak her awa an lea me masel.'

'Well,' Death says, 'it's natural. Yir mother, ye know, she's an auld wumman an she's reacht a certain age, I'll no be doin her any harm, I'll be jist do her a guid turn – she's sufferin in pain.'

'You're no takin my aul mither!' says Jack. And he ran forward, he snapped the scythe off the old man's back and he walked to a big stone, he smashed the scythe against a stone.

And the man got angrier and angrier and angrier and ugly-looking, 'My young man,' he says, 'you've done that – but that's not the end!'

'Well,' Jack says, 'it's the end fir you!' And Jack dived on top of him, Jack got a hold o' him and Jack picked a bit stick up from the shoreside, he beat him and he welted him and he welted him and he beat him and he welted him. He fought with Death and Death was as strong as what Jack was, but finally Jack conquered him! And Jack beat him with a bit stick, and lo and behold a funny thing happened: the more Jack beat him the wee-er he got, and Jack beat him and Jack beat him and Jack beat him – no blood came from him or nothing – Jack beat him with the stick till he got barely the size o' that! And Jack catcht him in his hand, 'Now,' he said, 'I got ye! Ye'll no get my aul mither!'

Now Jack thought in himself, 'What in the worl am I gaunna do wi him? I hev him here, I canna let him go, I beat him, I broke his scythe an I conquered him. But what in the world am I gaunna do wi him? I canna hide him bilow a stane because he'll creep oot an he'll come back tae his normal size again.' And Jack walked along the shore and he looked – coming in by the tide was a big hazelnut, that size! But the funny thing about this hazelnut, a squirrel had dug a hole in the nut because squirrels always dig holes in the nuts – they have sharp teeth – and he eats the kernel inside and leaves the empty case. And Jack picked up the hazel-nut, he looked, says, 'The very thing!' And Jack crushed

Death in through the wee hole, into the nut. And squeezed him in head first, and his wee feet, put him in there, shoved him in. And he walked about, he got a wee plug o' stick and he plugged the hole from the outside. 'Now,' he says, 'Death, you'll never get ma mither!' And he catcht him in his hand, he threw him out into the tide! And the heavy waves was whoosh-an-whoosh-an-whoosh-an, whoosh-an-whoosh-in in and back and forward. And Jack watched the wee nut, it went a-sailing, floating and back and forward away with the tide. 'That's it!' says Jack, that's the end o' Death. He'll never bother my mother again, or naebody else forbyes my mither.' Jack got two–three sticks under his arm and he walked back.

When he landed back he saw the reek was coming from the chimney, he says, 'My mother must be up, she must be feelin a wee bit better.' Lo and behold he walks in the house, there was his old mother up, her sleeves rolled up, her face full of flour, her apron on and she's busy making scones. He said, 'How ye feelin, Mother?'

She says, 'Jack, I'm feelin great, I never feelt better in ma life! Laddie, I dinna ken what happened to me, but I wis lyin there fir a minute in pain an torture, and all in a minute I feelt like someone hed come an rumbled all the pains an tuik everything oot o' my body, an made me . . . I feel like a lassie again, Jack! I made some scones fir yir breakfast.'

Jack never mentioned to his mother about Death, never said a word. His mother fasselt roun' the table, she's put up her hair Jack never saw his mother in better health in her life! Jack sat down by the fire, his mother made some scones. He had a wee bit scone, he says, 'Mother, is that all you've got tae eat?'

'Well,' she says, 'Jack, there's no much, jist a wee puckle flooer an I thocht I'd mak ye a wee scone fir yir breakfast. Go on oot tae the hen-house an get a couple eggs, I'll mak ye a couple eggs alang wi yir scone an that'll fill ye up, laddie.'

Jack walks out to the hen-house as usual, the wee shed

beside his mother's house. Oh, every nest is full o' eggs, hens' eggs, duck eggs, the nests are all full. Jack picks up four o' the big beautiful brown eggs out o' the nest, goes back in and, 'Here, Mother, there's four,' he said, 'two tae you, two to me.'

The old woman says, 'I'll no be a minute, Jack.' It was an open fire they had. The woman pulled the swey out, put the frying pan on, put a wee bit fat in the pan. She waited and she waited and she watched, but the wee bit fat wouldna melt. She poked the fire with the poker but the wee bit fat wadna melt. 'Jack,' she says, 'fire's no kindlin very guid, laddie, it'll no even melt that wee bit fat.'

'Well, pit some mair sticks on, Mother,' he said, 'pit some mair wee bits o' sticks on.' Jack put the best o' sticks on, but na! The wee bit o' fat sat in the middle o' the pan, but it wouldna melt, he says, 'Mother, never mind, pit the egg in an gie it a rummle roon, it'll dae me the way it is. Jis' pit it in the pan!'

His mother tried – crack – na. She hit the egg again – na. And suppose she could have taken a fifty-pound hammer and hit the egg, *that egg would not break*! She says, 'Jack, I cannae break these eggs.'

'An, Mother,' he said, 'I thought ye said ye were feelin weel an feelin guid, an you cannae break an egg! Gie me the egg, I'll break it!' Jack took the egg, went in his big hand, ye ken, Jack, big young laddie, catcht the egg in one hand – clank on the side o' the pan – na! Ye're as well to hit a stone on the side o' the pan, the egg would not break in no way in this world. 'Ah, Mother,' he says, 'I dinna ken what's wrong, I dinna ken whit's wrong, Mother, wi these eggs, I don't know. Prob'ly they're no richt eggs, I better go an get another two.'

He walked out to the shed again, he brought in two duck eggs. But he tried the same – na, they wouldna break, the eggs just would not break in any way in the world. 'Mother,' he says, 'pit them in a taste o' water an bring them a-boil!'

She says, 'That's right, Jack, I never thocht about that.' The old woman got a wee pan and the fire was going well by this time of bonnie shore sticks. She put the pan on and within seconds the water was boiling, she popped the two eggs in. And it bubbled and bubbled and bubbled and bubbled and bubbled, and bubbled, she said, 'They're ready noo, Jack.' She took them out – crack – na. Suppose they had tried for months, they couldna crack those two eggs.

'Ah, Mother,' he says, 'the're something wrong. Mither, the're something wrong, there's enchantment upon us, those eggs'll no cook. We're gaunna dee wi hunger.'

'Never mind, Jack,' she says, 'eat yir wee bit scone. I'll mak ye a wee drop soup, I'll mak ye a wee pot o' soup. Go oot tae the gairden, Jack, and get me a wee taste o' vegetables, leeks an a few carrots.'

Now Jack had a good garden, he passes all his time making a good garden to his mother. Out he goes, he pulls two carrots, a leek, bit parsley and a neep and he brings it to his mother. The old woman washes the pots, puts some water in, puts it on the fire. But she goes to the table with the knife, but na – every time she touches the carrot, the knife just skates off it. She touched the leek – it skates off it and all! The old woman tried her best, and Jack tried his best – there's no way in the world – Jack said, 'That knife's blunt, Mother.'

And Jack had a wee bit o' sharpening stone he'd found in the shoreside, he took the stone and he sharpened the knife, but no way in the world would it ever look at[1] the carrots or the neep or the wee bit parsley to make a wee pot o' soup. She says, 'Jack, the're somethin wrang wi my vegetables, Jack, they must be frozen solid.'

'But,' he said, 'Mother, the're been nae frost tae freeze them! Hoo in the world can this happen?'

1 look at – make any impression upon

'Well,' she says, 'Jack, luik, ye ken I've an awfa[1] cockerels this year, we have an awfa cockerels an we'll no need them aa, Jack. Wad ye gae oot to the shed an pull a cockerel's neck, and I'll pit it in the pot, boil it for wir supper?'

'Aye' says Jack. Now the old woman kept a lot o' hens. Jack went out and all in the shed there were dozens o' them sitting in a row, cockerels o' all description. Jack looked till he saw a big fat cockerel sitting on a perch, he put his hand up, catcht it and he felt it, it was fat. 'Oh,' he says, 'Mother'll be pleased wi this yin.' Jack pulled the neck – na! Pulled again – *no way*. He pulled it, he shook it, he swung it round his head three-five times. He took a stick and he battered it in the head, there's no way – he couldna touch the cockerel in any way! He put it below his oxter and he walks in to his mother.

She said, 'Ye get a cockerel, Jack?'

'Oh, Mother,' he said, 'I got a cockerel aa right, I got a cockerel. But, Mother, you may care!'[2]

She says, 'What do you mean, laddie!'

'You may care,' he says, 'I cannae kill hit.'

'Ah, Jack,' she says, 'ye cannae kill a cockerel! I ken, ye killt dozens tae me afore, the hens an ducks an aa.'

'Mother,' he said, 'I cannae kill this one – it'll no dee!'

She says, 'Gie me it ower here, gie me it over here!' And the old woman had a wee hatchet for splitting sticks, she kept it by the fire. She says, 'Gie it tae me, Jack, I'll show ye the way tae kill it richt!' She put it down the top o' the block and she hit it with the hatchet, chopped its head off. She hit it with the hatchet seventeen times, but no – every time the head jumped off – head jumped back on! 'Na, Jack,' she says, 'it's nae good. There's something wrang here, the're something terrible gaun a-wrong. Nethin seems tae be richt aboot the place. Here – go out to my purse, laddie, run up tae the village to the butcher! I'm savin this fir a rainy day,'

1 an awfa – a great many
2 you may care – it's hopeless

an she took a half-crown out o' her purse. 'Jack, gae up tae the butcher an get a wee bit o' meat fae the butcher, I'll mak ye a wee bite when ye come back.'

Now, it wasna far from the wee house to the village, about a quarter o' mile Jack had to walk. When Jack walked up the village, all the people were gathered in the middle o' the town square. They're all blethering and they're chatting and they're blethering and they're chatting, speaking to each other. One was saying, 'I've sprayed ma garden an it's over-run wi caterpillars! An I've tried tae spray it, it's no good.'

The butcher was out with his apron, he said, 'Three times I tried tae kill a bullock this mornin an three times I killed it, three times it jumpit back on its feet. I don't know what's wrong. The village has run out o' meat! I got a quota o' hens in this mornin, ducks, an every time I pull their necks their heads jumps back on. There's somethin terrible is happenin!'

Jack went up to the butcher's, he says, 'Gie me a wee bit o' meat fir ma mother.'

He says, 'Laddie, the're no a bit o' meat in the shop. Dae ye no ken what I'm tryin tae tell the people in the village: I've tried ma best this mornin to kill a young bullock tae supply the village an I cannae kill it!'

'Well,' Jack said, 'the same thing happen to me – I tried tae boil an egg an I cannae boil an egg, I tried tae kill a cockerel—'

'I tried tae kill ten cockerels,' says the butcher, 'but *they'll no dee*!'

'Oh dear-dear,' says Jack, 'we must be in some kin o' trouble. Is it happenin tae other places forbyes this?'

'Well, I jist hed word,' says the butcher, 'the next village up two mile awa an the same thing's happened tae them. Folk cannae even eat an apple – when they sink their teeth inta it, it'll no even bite. They cannae cook a vegetable, they cannae boil water, they cannae dae nothin! The hale worl's gaunna come tae a standstill, the're something gaen terrible wrong – *nothing seems to die anymore*.'

And then Jack thought in his head, he said, 'It's my fault, I'm the cause o't.' He walked back and he tellt his mother the same story I'm telling you. He says, 'Mother, there's nae butcher meat fir ye.'

She says, 'Why, laddie, why no?'

He says, 'Luik, the butcher cannae kill nae beef, because it'll no dee.'

'But, Jack,' she says, 'why no – it'll no dee? What's wrang with the country, what's wrang with the world?'

He says, 'Mother, it's all my fault!'

'Your fault,' she says, 'Jack?'

'Aye, Mither, it's my fault,' he says. 'Listen, Mother: this morning when you were no feeling very well, I walkit along the shore tae gather some sticks fir the fire an I met Death comin tae tak ye awa. An I took his scythe fae him an I broke his scythe, I gi'n him a beatin, Mither, an I put him in a nut! An I flung him in the tide an I plugged the nut so's he canna get oot, Mither. An God knows where he is noo. He's floatin in the sea, Mother, firever an ever an ever, an nothing'll dee – the worl is overrun with caterpillars an worms an everything – Mither, the're nothing can dee! But Mither, I wad rather die with starvation than lose you.'

'Jack, Jack, Jack, laddie,' she says, 'dae ye no ken what ye've done? Ye've destroyed the only thing that keeps the world alive.'

'What do you mean, Mother, "keeps the world alive"? Luik, if I hedna killed him, I hedna hae beat im, Mother, an pit him in that nut – you'd be dead bi this time!'

'I wad be dead, Jack,' she says, 'probably, but the other people would be gettin food, an the worl'd be gaun on – the way it shuid be – only fir you, laddie!'

'But, Mother,' he says, 'what am I gaunna dae?'

She says, 'Jack, there's only thing ye can dae . . . ye're a beach-comber like yir faither afore ye—'

'Aye, Mother,' he says, 'I'm a beach-comber.'

'Well, Jack,' she says, 'there's only thing I can say: ye better gae an get im back an set him free! Because if ye dinnae, ye're gaunna put the whole worl tae a standstill. *Without Death there is no life . . .* fir nobody.'

'But, Mother,' he says, 'if I set him free, he's gaunna come fir you.'

'Well, Jack, if he comes fir me,' she said, 'I'll be happy, and go inta another world an be peaceful! But you'll be alive an so will the rest o' the world.'

'But Mother,' he says, 'I cuidna live withoot ye.'

'But,' she says, 'Jack, if ye dinnae set him free, *both* o' us'll suffer, an I cannae stand tae see you suffer fir the want o' something to eat: because there's nothing in the world will die unless you set him free, because you cannae eat nothing until it's dead.'

Jack thought in his mind for a wee while. 'Aa right, Mother,' he says, 'if that's the way it shuid be, that's the way it shuid be. Prob'ly I wis wrong.'

'Of course, Jack,' she says, 'you were wrong.'

'But,' he says, 'Mother, I only done it fir yir sake.'

'Well,' she says, 'Jack, fir *my* sake, wad ye search fir that hazelnut an set him free?'

So the next morning true to his word, Jack walks the tide and walks the tide for miles and miles and miles, day out and day in for three days and for three days more. He had nothing to eat, he only had a drink o' water. They couldna cook anything, they couldna eat any eggs, they couldna fry anything in the pan if they had it, they couldna make any soup, they couldna get nothing. The caterpillars and the worms crawled out of the garden in thousands, and they ate every single vegetable that Jack had. And there's nothing in the world – Jack went out and tried to teem hot water on them but it was no good. When he teemed hot water on them it just was the same as he never poured nothing – no way. At last Jack said, 'I must go an find that nut!' So he walked and he walked, and he walked day and he walked night more miles than he ever walked before, but no way could Jack find this nut! Till Jack was completely exhusted and fed up and completely sick, and he couldna walk another mile. He sat down by the shoreside right in front o' his mother's house to rest, and wondered, he put his hand on his jaw and he said to his ownself, 'What have I done! I've ruint the world, I've destroyed the world. People disna know,' he said, 'what Death has so good, that Death is such a guid person. I wis wrong tae beat him an put him in a nut.'

And he's looking all over – and lo and behold he looked down – there at his feet he saw a wee nut, and a wee bit o' stick sticking out o' it. He lifted it up in his hand, and Jack was happy, happier than he'd ever been in his life before! And he pulled the plug and a wee head popped out. Jack held him in his two hands and Death spoke to him, 'Now, Jack,' he said, 'are ye happy?'

'No,' Jack said, 'I'm no happy.'

He said, 'You thought if you beat me an conquered me an killed me – because I'm jist Death – that that wad be the end, everything be all right. Well, Jack, ma laddie, ye've got a lot to learn, Jack. Without me,' he said, 'there's no life.' And Jack took him out. 'But,' he says, 'Jack, thank you fir settin me free,' and just like that after Jack opened the nut, he came out and like that, he came full strength again and stood before Jack – the same old man with the long ragged coat and the sunken eyes and the two teeth in the front and the bare feet. He says, 'Jack, ye broke my scythe.'

Jack said, 'I'll tell ye somethin, while I wis searchin fir you ma mother made me mend it. An I have it in the hoose fir ye, come wi me!' And Jack led him up to the house. Lo and behold sure enough, sitting on the front of the porch was the scythe that Jack broke. Jack had taken it and he'd mended it, sorted it and made it as good as ever.

Death came to the door and he ran his hand down the face o' the scythe, he sput on his thumb and he ran it up the face o' the scythe, and he says to Jack, 'I see you've sharpened it, Jack, and ye made a good job o' it. Well, I hev some people to see in the village, Jack. But remember, I'll come back fir yir mother someday, but seein you been guid to me I'll make it a wee while!' And Death walked away.

Jack and his mother lived happy till his mother was about a hundred years of age! And then one day Death came back to take his old mother away, but Jack never saw him. But Jack was happy for he knew *there is no life without Death*. And that is the end o' my story.

The Ugly Queen

My old granny came to live with us when she was very old, and she had a grip over us, because if she wanted something done we would do it for her; but she had to pay for it – no by money, money didn't mean anything to us – she had to tell us a story. Saying, 'C'mon, Granny, tell us a wee story an we'll go fir anything for ye,' go fir tobacco, get her a drink or sort her shoes . . . and old Granny. Macdonald would tell us a story. . . . If she had never told me a story, I wouldn't be sitting here with you today, nearly forty-five years later, telling you the same thing that was told to me? So I hope in the future that you will be able to tell your daughter a story that prob'ly she will tell her daughter maybe fifty or sixty years later!

JACK stayed with his mother in a little cottage in the forest. His father was a woodcutter and had died when Jack was very young. Jack's memory of his father was very faint, but the one thing Jack always remembered – because Jack's father was a very good man – 'Ye remember, Jack,' he'd said, 'there's only one thing at's gaunnae stead ye in life, son, when I'm gone: be honest an kind and truthful!' Jack used to go with his father by his hand to the wood when he was about three years old, and this is what the father told him, 'Be honest, be kind an be truthful!' That was the only memory Jack had of his father.

Now in this land where Jack lived there was a king and queen who ruled the kingdom. And the king had an accident, he fell off his horse and was killed. The whole country mourned for months and months about the king, because he was only a young man and he left behind him a young daughter only one year old. And the queen adored this daughter.

The king had had only one ambition in his life. In his kingdom in the sea was an island, and on this island was a giant fourteen feet high. He used to come across the mainland and take cattle, sheep, anything that he wanted, and there was nothing that the king could do. The king's only ambition was to get rid of this giant, but he never had a chance – he fell off his horse and was killed. Now this giant still remained in the island. And there's no one could touch him or no one could do anything to him, because he didn't have any heart. The king had sent for men, magicians of all description, and asked them 'how tae get rid o' the giant'. And they told him, 'There's no way that ye can get rid o' the giant.' Because the giant didn't have any heart, he was untouchable – no one knew where the giant's heart was. The only way to get rid of the giant was to find out where the heart was, and no one knew. So there was the queen left to rule the kingdom with a young baby a year old and this indestructible giant in the island.

She called all her wisemen together and all her hen-wives, says, 'There's only one thing I want in my ambition, as of my late husband, is tae get rid of this giant.' And no way could she find a way to get rid of him because he was indestructible. Till one morning.

It was a nice summer's morning and the queen put her little baby daughter who was coming up now near two years of age out in the front of the castle to play. She went back into the kitchen to do something. (The queen was just a woman; it was just a matter o' being the head of the clan or the head of the race, respected of course, but she had to do her part even in the kitchens.) She went back and left the child to play, and who came across from his island at that very moment – the giant – taking ten-league steps at a time! And the first thing he saw passing by the castle was the wee child, he picked it up in his oxters, in his bosom, and he set sail with the child through the sea back to the island. Because he wanted this child!

And the queen came back – the child was gone – and she cried, she asked everybody around the place what happened, 'where was the baby'? Nobody knew where the baby was, till somebody said, 'Oh, yes, Wir Majesty, the giant was here while you were gone. He took her an she's gone, the giant walkit across the sea with her in his arms back tae his island!'

And the queen was so upset, frantic, she didn't know what to do. She knew there was no way she was going to get the baby back. So she gathered all her courtiers and all her holy people around her, all these magicians and people, how was she to get the child back? Nobody could tell her. Till one day she was sitting in the front of the palace, when up comes an old woman with a basket on her arm, she's selling eggs.

She knocks at the door and one of the maids goes to the door, 'What do you want, auld wumman?'

She says, 'I'm selling eggs.'

'Eggs?'

'Yes,' she said, 'ask the good lady, would she buy some eggs?'

So the maid being a good lassie just walked up, said to the queen, 'Yir Majesty, there's an old lady at the door selling eggs.'

'Yes,' says the queen, 'bring the auld wumman in!' When the maid mentioned 'eggs', the queen knew the old woman must be a hen-wife. 'Bring the auld wumman in,' says the queen.

So the maid says, 'Would you come in?'

And the old granny with a basket laid full o' eggs said, 'Would you buy some eggs, good lady?'

'Yes,' says the queen, 'I'll buy some eggs. Who are you?'

'Oh,' she said, 'I'm jist an auld hen-wife who is selling eggs.'

She says, 'Dae ye know who I am?'

'No,' says the old woman, 'ye're jist a natural wumman of a big castle I sell my eggs tae.'

She says, 'I am the queen of the country.'

'Oh!' the old woman went down on her knees, 'I am sorry,' she said, 'Ir Majesty. I have dreamed all my life o' meetin the queen, but never in a million years hev ever I been here before!' And she went down on her knees and begged mercy from the queen.

So the queen says, 'well, it's all right, it's all right. We'll take yir eggs, we'll take the lot. But, eh, I wonder, could you help me?'

'Well,' says the old lady, 'A prob'ly cuid, if ye tell me what's ailin ye – ye ill?'

'No,' says the queen, 'I'm not ill; I'm ill in a way, an I'm vexed an broken-heartit.'

'Oh,' says the old woman, 'why should you be broken-heartit if ye're the queen?'

'Well,' she said, 'prob'ly ye've heard – I jist newly lost Ir Majesty the King.'

'I heard,' says the old woman, 'an I'm very grieved about it.'

'An,' she says, 'I have lost my baby.'

'Oh,' says the old woman, 'I'm very sorry that yir baby . . . is gone.'

'But,' the queen said, 'she's not dead.'

'I know,' says the old woman, 'she's not dead.'

'Then,' says the queen, 'you *know* she's not dead?'

'Yes,' says the old woman, 'yir child is not dead.'

So the queen says to the old hen-wife, 'Look, would ye tell me something if ye know that much – ye're gaunna tell me a little more?'

'Oh yes,' says the old wife, 'I can tell ye a little more . . . much more! Your child is in the hands of the Giant of the Island in the Sea.'

'Yes,' says the queen, 'that's true.'

'An,' she says, 'you would like tae get her back.'

'Yes,' says the queen, that's true, I would give my entire life to get her back!'

'But,' the old woman said, 'it's not as simple as that. I

know of the giant – in fact he is a relation of mine. An he is indestructible, there's no way in the world at you cuid do him any harm, or there's no way in the worl ye're gaunna get yir child back.'

The queen said, 'There must be something I cuid do.'

'Yes,' said the old woman, 'there's something ye can do: you must go an find a man who is truthful an kind an gentle, who'll tell ye the honest truth from his heart. But if you go as a queen, then you'll never find the truth. Luik, I'm gaunna do something for you, Our Majesty . . .'

And the queen says, 'You shall be repaid handsomely!'

And the old woman said, 'I want no payment. I'm going to do something for you, I'm gaunnae tell ye something, an if you do what I tell you you will get yir child!' She gropes in her basket and she takes out a little stone bottle, she says, 'Ir Majesty the Queen, I'll give you this: this is a potion an you must rub yirself wi this potion tonight at twelve o'clock. An by tomorrow morning you will be the ugliest person that ever walked on this earth. Now, to get your child, you must do this! If you think that yir child is not worth it, then don't do it.' And she takes another small bottle from the corner o' her basket, she says, 'After everything is gone, remember – and ye have done yir task an received yir child – the only way in the world tae get yirsel back tae normal is use the second one. But don't use the second one first!' So the old woman turned round to the queen and said, 'Remember, Ir Majesty, this is gaunnae make ye ugly, the most ugliest person in the world that ever walked, but through ugliness you're gaunna find *truth*! An you shall take with you a bag of gold, you shall give up yir entire reign as a queen an travel on through the country an find *truth*! You shall travel yirself as an ugly auld wumman with a bag of gold; sometimes along the way, for the greed, people will give you an tell ye this an tell ye that. *But you must find truth before ye can find happiness.* You'll ask anyone and offer em yir bag o' gold, tell them along the way that "you are beautiful," an if they agree with you then they are wrong – there is no truth in it –

because they are only doin it fir the greed of the gold. But remember, I'll not be here with you when you return!'

And the queen turned round and she was happy, 'But' she says, 'will that bring me my daughter?'

'Yes,' she said, 'it'll bring ye yir daughter for evermore; an tae tell ye something else, it will end the entire life of the giant who yir husband long bifore ye wanted to destroy. You do my biddin!'

'Where can I get in touch with ye, auld wumman?' says the queen.

She says, 'You can never get in touch with me anymore. All I want of you is to buy my eggs.'

'I'll take yir eggs,' says the queen, 'but how in the world can I reward you?'

'You can never reward me, Our Majesty,' says the old woman. 'You have rewarded me enough by buyin my eggs.' And like that the old woman left, she was gone.

Now the queen is left with these two bottles. 'Well,' says the queen, 'if I must get my daughter, I must!' and she knew what she must do. She took the last bottle, put it up in her bedroom and hid it. She took the first bottle, she went into her bathroom and scattered it around herself. She looked at herself in the mirror – and lo and behold she was sick – what she saw. She saw the ugliest old crone, warts on her face, nose as long as anything, chin hanging down, she was the ugliest thing that ever walked on this earth. And the queen was happy, she knew, 'I must do this for my daughter's sake.' She walked down the stairs, met her servants and her servants turned their heads. She walked into her bedroom, she packed a bag o' gold an turned round, tellt her servants, 'I'm on my way. I must find truth fir my daughter's sake.'

And the servants didn't know who the queen was, 'Ugly auld wumman,' they said, 'what are ye doing here?'

She says, 'The queen is gone on a visit an I must follow her, but she'll be back.' So she left the castle in charge of good hands. And then my story says the queen set off.

She travelled round the country with a bag o' gold, the ugliest old woman you ever saw in your life, she walked among the common people and she walked among the down-and-outs. She walked among woodcutters, farmers, and everywhere she came along she had her bag o' gold, everywhere she went she asked the same thing, 'Amint I the beautifules person you ever saw?' and she held the bag o' gold, jingled the gold.

And they said, 'Lady, you are beautiful! You are a wonderful woman!' because they heard the tinkle of her gold.

And she said, 'No, I am ugly!' and she walked on. She travelled and she travelled and she travelled on and . . . the same thing along the way. Till one night very late she came to a forest, she looked round and all the trees were cut and cleaned up. She walked on, saw a little light. It became late at night and she says, 'I must have somewhere to stay fir the night.' She walked to this little cottage, knocked at the door and out came this old woman. And the queen said, 'Excuse me, I am an auld woman on the road, would you give me shelter fir the night?'

'Yes,' says the old woman, 'come in, there's only nobody here but my son an I. Ye're welcome tae share what we hev.'

'Oh,' she said, 'I've got gold tae pay fir it.'

'Oh no, says the old woman, 'we dinna want yir gold. Jist come in an make yirsel at home.'

And the queen was amazed because the old woman had never even looked or paid any attention to how she looked. When the queen walked into the kitchen she looked: sitting on a chair, an old-fashioned chair by the peat fire, was the youngest, most handsome and best looking man she had ever seen in her life! Tall, blond, curly hair, blue eyes, the best looking man she had ever seen – it remembered her so much her husband – the queen was aghast to look at this young man sitting in the chair!

And the young man rose up, he took the old woman,

said, 'Sit down, my lady, an have my chair. Heat yirself by the fire an have something to eat.' And he never even looked or said 'ugly' or nothing, he never said nothing. So the queen sat down and she had something to eat, never giving a thought that she was in the most humble home that ever she could have met, the home of a woodcutter's son and his mother. But the secret was, *he* had known the truth – told to him by his father.

And after her meal the queen sat, she talked to the old woman, says, 'I'm jist an auld wumman.' And she turned round to the son, says, 'Are you working?'

'No, my auld wumman, I'm not working,' he said, 'I'm idle, I can't find a job. My father was a woodcutter, but wood is gettin very scarce, we're not allowed to cut more wood around here.'

'Well,' she said, 'I've got money, I cuid give you money.'

'My lady, I cuidna accept yir money,' he says, 'no way.'

She says, 'I'll give ye my money, my two bags of gold . . .'

And this was Jack who stayed with his mother in a little cottage that she had wandered into, and Jack said, 'Lady, I don't want yir gold. I have no need fir yir money or yir gold. I'm staying here with ma mother an we manage tae get by without yir gold. Poor old woman, you need it where you're goin.'

She says, 'Look, I'll give ye my full bag of gold if ye tell me one thing!'

'Yes,' he said, 'mother, I'll tell ye anything ye want – aye, there's only one thing I can tell ye – I hev tae tell ye the truth.'

She said, 'Am I not the most beautiful an handsomest woman ye hev ever saw in yir life – with my beautiful bags of gold? I can give you these bags o' gold an make you rich fir evermore!'

And Jack turned round, he said, 'Luik, no, my mother, auld woman, you are the most uglies creature that ever walked through my mother's door! An you could never give me any gold because I would never accept it. I'm not gaun to deceive you, how you get by in this world by bein so ugly and so stupid – why people has not tuik that from ye a long time ago I don't know. But try an give that to me, and ask me to say that you are beautiful, an try to bribe me – I wouldna accept one single coin from you!'

She says, 'I am a beautiful woman!'

He says, 'You are the uglies auld thing that ever walked through my mother's door!'

And the queen rose, she placed the two bags o' gold in front o' Jack. She put her arms round Jack's neck, 'John,' she said, 'dae ye know who I am?'

He says, 'You are still an ugly aul wumman!'

She says, 'I am Her Majesty the Queen!'

And John went down on his knees in front of her, he begged pardon for what he said and asked forgiveness. And she sat and told him the story, but she never told him that she had become ugly through the old hen-wife's bottle, she never mentioned that! But Jack accepted her tale and she told him that only he could save her daughter. She told Jack, 'In the island . . . I want you to do something fir me, Jack, my little daughter is a prisoner on the island.'

Jack said, 'Ir Majesty, why don't you send troops or men or something to re—'

She says, 'There's no way it can be done because the giant hesna got a heart, no way . . . hesna got a heart. Would ye do one thing fir me, would you rescue my daughter from the island an destroy that giant, take my daughter back, Jack? Because you survive on truth!'

'Well,' says Jack 'it disna look like a big job to me.'

She said 'I'll give ye everything under the sun. First you have got tae get to the island, an then you've got tae get to the home o' the giant and rescue my daughter.'

So Jack's mother came in, she sat down by the fire and the queen told her the whole tale. She says to Jack, 'I think you'd be better tae do whit the queen asks ye fir tae do.'

'Well,' Jack said, 'it's only a job fir me. In fact, I'm no doin very much at the moment, Mother. I'll do what the queen asks, I'll go and bring her daughter for her.'

So the queen turned round to Jack, 'You know what you've got to face?'

'Oh,' says Jack, 'I know what I've got to face: you told me, there's a giant that lives on the island an he has yir daughter a prisoner, it's very simple fir to take yir daughter from the giant, an bring her back to you is all you ask. Ir Majesty the Queen, I'll do that for you! But make me one promise.'

'What's that?' says the queen.

'That you'll be there – are ye tellin me the truth – that you'll be there whan I fetch yir daughter back!'

'Yes,' says the queen, 'I'll be there!'

So the next morning Jack bundled up a wee bag on his back. His mother made him a bannock and fried him a wee collop, and Jack set sail to do the job for the queen. He wanted no money, he wanted nothing, and he left the old queen with his mother, bade his mother 'goodbye'. He set sail along his way and he walked on, he walked on and he walked on and he made his way till he came to the sea, the shoreside. He thought to himself, 'I'll sit down here an rest fir a while.' And he took out his wee piece o' bannock that his mother had given him and his wee bit o' ham, and what came in beside him was a swan. And Jack naturally threw wee pieces of his meat to the swan. Though he was hungry himself he threw little pieces to the swan, and the swan came closer and closer and closer to him . . . and Jack threw pieces.

And the swan turned and spoke, 'Jack, you're good an truthful, an you fed me – I want to help you.'

Jack had never heard a swan speaking before and he was mesmerised, he said, 'Swan, are you talkin to me?'

'Yes, Jack,' he said, 'I'm talkin to you. Well, I know what ye're gaunna do, but remember one thing, you are goin into the island of the indestructible giant who has the queen's daughter a prisoner. But, Jack, you'll never do it because the giant has no heart.'

And Jack said, ' "The giant has no heart", I never heard a

thing in ma life – "the giant . . ." everybody's got a heart!' And Jack was young and strong, he thought himself fit enough to face the giant.

And the swan says, 'You could never do nothing to the giant! But remember, Jack, you fed me. You go inta the island, an in the island is my nest. In my nest is an egg an in that egg is the giant's heart. So you take that egg and squeeze it, take it in yir hand an squeeze it. Then ye'll have the power over the giant.' And like that the swan flew away!

Now Jack knows what he's got to do. Jack walks down and borrows a boat from an old fisherman, he says to the fisherman, 'I would like to borrow a boat.'

And the old fisherman said, 'Why do you want to borrow a boat?'

Jack says, 'I want to go out to the island.'

And the old fisherman said, 'Please, please, don't go out there! That is the home of the indestructible giant, you could never never . . .'

Jack said, 'I'm not asking you to take me, I jist want to borrow yir boat.'

The old fisherman said, 'Look, be it upon yir own head but you can have the boat, but I'll not go with ye.'

Jack said, 'let me have the boat!' So the old fisherman gave Jack the boat. Jack rowed and he rowed and he rowed out to sea, till he came to the island. He beached the boat, walked up and the first thing he saw when he landed in the island was a swan's nest. And inside the swan's nest was a large egg! Jack picked up the egg and he held it in his hand. He walked, he walked up this path and the first thing he saw was a great castle!

And when he walked up to the castle out came the giant – fourteen feet tall – 'What are you doin here, what do ye want?'

Jack said, 'I have come tae take the queen's daughter that you hev a prisoner here.'

The giant said, 'I shall never part with her! Fir years the king has destroyed his wrath upon me – he has tried tae destroy me fir years – an he has never succeedit. And now, by sheer bad luck the king is gone an I have got his daughter, and I am guanna keep her fir her entire life!'

And Jack said, 'You ain't guanna keep her, I'm gaunna have her!' an he started to squeeze and the giant put his hand on his heart, and Jack squeezed the egg.

He says, 'You can never destroy me!'

Jack said, 'I am gaun tae destroy you – I have the egg – an I am gaun to destroy you!'

'Where,' said the giant,' hev ever you discovered the power of my body?' And Jack squeezed the egg and the giant doubled in two, he said, 'Please, please don't do it!'

Jack said, 'I have you – it – and you are gaunnae tell it in truth!'

And he squeezed the egg and the giant said, 'What is it you want? What is it you want!'

And Jack said, 'You shall return the baby to the queen!'

The giant said, '*Please . . . please*, don't squeeze so hard, you're hurting me!'

Jack says, 'You shall take the baby in yir arms an you shall walk across the sea, and deliver the child back to the queen!'

And the giant said, 'Yes, I'll do that. But please don't squeeze it so hard, you're hurting my heart!'

The giant took the baby in his oxters and he walked across the sea, he delivered it to the queen. And the queen was there at the door, he put the baby in the queen's arms and the queen was as ugly as ever. She held the child and the child started to cry when she looked at her mother!

Jack is still in the island by this time, he could see across the water and he's standing watching the giant coming through the water. And he waited . . . till the giant was halfway in the sea, halfway through the water . . . he took the egg and he broke it on the floor. Naturally, as he broke the egg, down went the giant into the sea and the waves covered him!

Jack took his boat and he walked down, he rowed across

to the land, and he walked on. He came back to the castle where the queen was, and the first thing he saw was the ugly old woman with this baby in her oxters! He knew right away that she was the queen. There was a great meeting and everyone was carrying on, the queen's baby had come home and everybody was excited.

The queen said, 'Make way, make way, make way fir the man who has brung back my child!' And Jack was led up to the palace, they gave him the greatest reception in the world. And the queen said, 'We must have a great party, a great reception fir my child comin home. But we must give thanks to one person who has made it possible fir us to have wir child back, the princess; fir Jack – we must adore him an give him all that he asks for!'

And Jack was amazed, mesmerised, because he'd never been in this place before. Only one thing he wanted, was to get back to his mother.

The queen said, 'We mus have a great feast an Jack is gaunna be with us. Give him all the attention that we can give in this world because he has brought back my daughter to the kingdom.' So the great feast was held, the party was held and dancing and singing went on and everybody came, kissed the young princess because she had come home. And the giant was destroyed for ever and Jack was given a hero's welcome. But lo and behold Jack was so unhappy – he only wanted one thing – he wanted back to his mother. And the queen came in, ugly old queen she says to Jack, 'Won't you stay, Jack? Why don't you stay with me, why don't you stay with me fir ever?'

He says, 'I cuid never stay with you, you are . . .'

She says, 'Jack, tell me the truth – am I not the nicest person you ever saw?'

He says, 'I have done for you – got yir daughter back – and you are Er Majesty the Queen of this country. But you are still to me the most ugliest auld person that ever I saw in my life! An tomorrow morning I would like tae be gone from this place because I have got tae go to my mother.'

The queen walked up to her bedroom, she took the little bottle that the hen-wife gave her and she spread it around her face and her body, sprayed it around her. She looked in the mirror . . . and ye'll no believe it, it breaks my heart to tell ye . . . it was the most beautiful thing that ever walked on earth she became after she'd put this on her. She was younger, handsomer and more beautiful than ever she'd been in her life before! And she walked into her bedroom, she picked up two bags o' gold and she walked down the stairs. And there was Jack ready to take off to see his mother.

She walked down to Jack, said, 'Jack, here's yir reward.'

He says, 'Reward, fir what?'

She says, 'Fir bringin my—'

He said, '*Your* daughter? Who are you?'

She said, 'I am the queen!'

He said, 'You are no queen . . . you're the most beautiful person that ever walked in this earth!'

She says, 'Jack, I know.'

He says, 'Why do you know?'

'Because,' she said, 'you are tellin the *truth*.'

And Jack put his arms round the queen and kissed her; he says tae her, 'I don't want any gold, I want nothing.'

She says, 'What do you want, Jack?'

He says, 'I want *you* fir my wife!'

She says, 'I know, because you're telling the truth.' And Jack married the queen, and that is the end o' my story!

BARRIE MOOSKINS

The Coming of the Unicorn

This story was well known among the travelling people in my time when I used to walk among my people, because everyone loved it. It was told round the camp-fire as usual, same as the rest, and we were so interested, you know what I mean. Old Hector Kelby in Aberdeenshire was a great story-teller and he told me many tales – where the unicorn really began was one of his.

MANY many years ago, long long before your time and mine when this country was very young, there once lived a king. But this particular king was a great huntsman and he lived with his wife in this great castle. And the only thing that this king really loved to do was hunt, he hunted small animals, he hunted big animals, and in these bygone days the land was overrun with animals to hunt. He had his huntsmen and he had a beautiful wife, he had a beautiful palace, he had a beautiful kingdom and he was very happy. And he got pleasure from hunting. But the king only hunted to supply food for his own castle and for the villages around his kingdom. He used to collect all his huntsmen and go on hunts, maybe three–four times a year, to give his people enough food.

But one particular day this king gathered all his huntsmen together, said 'good-bye' to the womenfolk because they'd be gone for a couple days or maybe more, to bring back all these animals they would salt for the winter; bade 'good-bye' to his queen as usual and took all his huntsmen, they rode out. And they rode for many days in the forest, because in these bygone days it was mostly all forest, there weren't many townships or little villages along the way. The land was very desolate but was overrun with animals of all descriptions. Then the huntsmen always made sure that the king should get the best shot, anything that would come up before them.

So lo and behold what should stop before the king . . . it was all bows and arrows in these days and swords . . . who should they corner but a bear, a great brown bear. The huntsmen drew back and let the king have the first shot, because it was a big bear and they knew it carried a lot of weight, it would be a lot of food for the villagers. The king, who was a great archer, put his bow and arrow to his shoulder and he fired, he fired an arrow and he hit the bear, the arrow stuck in the bear's chest. And the bear stood up straight when the blood started to fall from its chest, it put its paw to its chest where the arrow had entered, it held it there for a few minutes. And the king was amazed: it stood straight there and it took its paw – it looked at the blood on its paw – and it looked at the king. And then it cowpled over, fell down dead. And the king was so sad at seeing this, he was so sad.

He told his huntsmen, 'Pick it up and carry it back. We will hunt no more today.' They carried the bear back to the palace, and the king said to his huntsmen, 'Take it and divide it among the villagers, but bring me its skin.'

So naturally the huntsmen divided the bear up, passed it around to all the people in the village and they brought the skin to the king. And the king gave orders for the skin to be dried, the skin was dried through time and brought into the palace and put upon the floor. But every time the king looked at the skin, he got sadder and sadder and sadder. And the sadder he got the less he thought about hunting.

Now the next hunt was coming up and the king didn't want to go, he didn't want to hunt. He went into his chamber and he felt so sad. The bugle was sounding for the next hunt, they called on their king, but lo and behold the king wouldn't go. And from that day on to the next months and the next months following and the next months following, the king never joined in – no more did the king join the hunt. His charger was waiting, his beautiful horses were in the stable, his bows and arrows were sharpened for him, but the king never went. The huntsmen hunted, but they couldn't coax their king in any way. The king was down-hearted and broken. The queen was upset, she was so troubled.

'Why,' she said, 'what happened to Ir Majesty the King, what's the trouble?'

The huntsmen told her, 'He has the bearskin.'

She says, 'Prob'ly if we take the bearskin away – it's prob'ly that that's upsettin him.' She removed the bearskin from the floor of the palace but it made no difference.

The king had his meals, he had his lunch but he had seemingly lost all interest in life in any way. He talked to the queen, he talked to everybody, but he just felt so upset that there's nothing in the world seemed to excite him. After him being a great hunter and a great huntsman nobody could excite him anymore.

Now the queen stood it for a few months but she couldn't stand it any longer. She could see her king was just fading away, he just wanted to sit in his parlour and be by himself. He was a great sportsman and a great swordsman, and he just seemed to have lost all interest in life for evermore! He didn't want to do anything, nothing in the world. The queen was very upset by this.

So one day she could stand it no more, she called the three palace magicians together, told them the story I'm telling you. 'Look,' she said, 'you must do something for the king. He doesna cuddle me, he doesn't make love tae me, he just sits there, he has his meals, he is completely lost! He's only a livin dead person. You must do something to excite him to bring him back to his own way – an make him a king once more! An his people are worried, he has never put in an appearance before his people. He disna join the huntsmen, he disna do nothing, he just sits there like a statue. He takes his meals . . . He disna even speak to me! He is lost, he's in another world! What has happened to our king?'

So the three wise men, the magicians of the palace, got their heads together and said, 'We know his trouble – it was the bear – the sadness of seein the blood fae the bear that made him so sad, he disna want to hunt anymore. But if we could between us construct something that would excite him an make him be a king again, then everything'd be all right.' So the three court magicians put their heads together. 'Well,' they said, 'what cuid we do to excite him?'

One said, 'We need tae construct something to raise Our Majesty's attention. What cuid we do?' They were very wise these men, very clever and they worked in magic in the king's court.

One said, 'If we could construct an animal, a special animal that . . . who would be swifter than the wind, fiercer than the lion an fiercer than a boar, that everyone was afraid of, an we'd beg the king to help us; then mebbe we cuid bring im back from his doldrums an make him a king once more.'

So the three magicians put their heads together and one said, 'Well, I could use ma power tae give it the body of a pony who will ride an fly swifter an the wind.'

And the second one said, 'I could give it the fierceness an the tusk of a boar.'

And the third one said, 'I could give it the power and the tail of a lion.'

So they put their heads together once more and said, 'What hev we constructed between us? We hev a horse that flies swifter than the wind, we have the tusk of a boar and the tail of a lion. Well, there's no problem: we'll give it the tail of a lion, we'll give it the tusk of a boar and we'll give it the body of a pony and we'll set it free! And we'll tell the king that there's a magic animal in his kingdom that no huntsman cuid ever catch – but we'll send it before the huntsmen.'

So lo and behold the three magicians constructed an animal between them: they gave it the beautiful slender body of the swiftest pony that ever rode on the earth, they gave it the tusk of a boar – but instead of putting it on its mouth – they put it on his forehead. They gave it the determination of a lion and the power of the lion – but instead of giving it the lion's body – they put the lion's tail on it. 'And what,' did they say, 'we're gaunnae call it?'

'Well,' one said, 'we universt between us[1] to construct it . . . we'll call it a "unicorn".' And there lo and behold became the birth of the unicorn, the most beautiful, the most wonderful, the most swift and the most fierce animal of all. These three wise men set it free to roam the kingdom – to interrupt every huntsman that ever went on their way.

So naturally, these huntsmen who had got tired of waiting for the king and tired waiting for food, knew that there's no way they could coax the king to go with them anymore, went on the hunt without the king! And they hunted. But whenever they went to hunt, up jumped before them this beautiful animal – white as white could be – a beautiful pony, the tail of a lion and the tusk of a boar straight from its forehead. And it ran before them and they hunted it and they searched for it. But it was fiercest and it attacked them, it threw them off their horses, but no way in the world could they hurt it, no way in the world could they catch it. So after many days hunting it, for weeks and months they finally rode back to the palace bedraggled and tired, with not one single thing because of the interest to catch this animal.

When one of the old court magicians walked out and he said to them, 'What is yir problem, men? Why hev you come home from the hunt so empty-handit?'

And they said, 'We have come home empty-handed because we cuid not catch nothin, because a animal that we hev never saw in wir life – with a horn in its forehead, with the swiftness of a pony, with the fierceness of a lion an

1 universt between us – united our efforts

the tail of lion – has come before us at every turn, an we tried tae fight it but it was impossible.'

'We must tell the king,' said the court magician, 'we must tell the king about this animal! Mebbe it will get him out of his doldrums.'

So they walked up, they told the king and they begged, 'Master, Master, Master, deares Huntsman, dearest King, Our Majesty, we hev failed in wir hunt an the people in the village are dyin with hunger because we've no food fir them.'

'Why,' said the king, 'yese are huntmen aren't ye? Hevna I taught yese tae hunt?'

'But, Majesty,' they said, 'it's a animal . . . this bein, this thing that we've never saw in wir lives – the swiftness of a pony an the horn on its head of a boar an the tail of a lion – who's as swift an so completely swift that drives before us, that we jist can't catch it.'

'There never was such a thing,' said the king, 'not in my kingdom!'

'Yes, Our Majesty,' they said, 'there is such a thing. He interrupts us an he interferes with our hunt, an every minute he disappears an then he's gone, we jist can't go on with the hunt an wir people are dyin with hunger. You mus help us!'

But then said the king, 'Is it true? Tell me, please, is there something that I've never seen in my kingdom?'

'Yes, Our Majesty,' they said, 'there's something you've never seen. This animal is bewitched!'

And at that the king woke up, he rubbed his eyes and the thought of the bear was gone from him for everymore. He said, 'If there's something that interrupts my people and interrupts my huntsmen, then I mus find the truth!' So the king calls for his horse, for his steed, he calls for his bows and he calls for his arrows, he blows the bugle and he calls for his huntsmen, 'Ride with me,' he says, 'tae the forest an show me this wonderful animal that upsets yese all! It won't upset me,' and the king was back again once more! And the people are happy, and they blow their bugles, everyone gathered in the court to see the king off once more after a year. And they rode out on the great hunt, 'Lead me,' says the king, 'tae where you saw this animal last!'

So they led him to the forest and the old wise men were sure that it was there. And *there* before him stood this magnificent animal – taller than any horse the king had ever rode, with a horn on its forehead and the tail of a lion, and the swiftness of the wind – and the king said, 'Leave it to me!' It stood there and looked at them, the king said, 'Leave it tae me!'

And the king had a great charger, he rode after it, and he rode for many many miles and he rode for many many miles, and the farther the king rode the farther it went. And the faster the king rode the faster it went – till it disappeared in the distance and then the king was lost. It was gone. Sadly and tiredly he returned to the sound of his trumpets of his huntsmen. But the king had never ever got close enough to fire an arrow at it! For days and weeks and months to pass by the king hunted and the king searched, the king searched for this beautiful animal, but it always disappeared in the distance; it always rose before him but he could never catch it. The king searched and the king became so obsessed with this animal – he became his ownself again. Gone was the thought of everything, he only had one thing in his mind, that he must catch this animal.

He called his great wise men together, he called his court together, he called everybody, his huntsmen together tried to explain what kind of animal was roaming his kingdom. 'Master,' said one of the great court magicians, 'it is a *unicorn*!'

'A unicorn?' said the king, 'how many unicorns are there on my land?'

And they said, 'Only one, Our Master, an it's up to you tae catch it.' But the king wasted his time, he searched for weeks and he searched for months, and he took his huntsmen and the people were dying for food. But the king could never ever catch the unicorn.

And then when the king became so sad and broken-hearted, he called his great men together, says, 'Luik, this is a magic animal – I'll never catch it in a million years!' He called his masons before him and he called the court sculptors before him, he said, 'Look, I know in my heart that I am a great huntsman. And I have searcht fir many months an I've done something that I should never hev done, I deprived all my people of food because we depend on the hunt. I have not killed a deer or killed a wolf or killed anything for months. But, 'he says, 'youse huntsmen, go out and hunt fir food fir the villagers and spread it among the people while I talk to my sculptors and my masons.' He said to these people, 'I know that I can never catch the animal they call a "unicorn". But there's nothing in the world I cuid love more than jist to hev a statue of him at my door where I cuid walk an see him.'

And they asked him, 'Master, we don't know what you want.'

'Well,' he said, 'I'll tell you what it's like and I want you tae make it for me.' So he explained to the sculptors and the masons, 'it was like a pony with a tail of a lion and a horn on his forehead and the swiftness o' the wind.'

So they carved him out of some stone, they carved from stone two things like the king had told them to be, and they put them straight in front of the king's castle. So that every morning when the king walked down, there stood before him the thing that he hunted for many many months which he had never captured – the unicorn. And the king loved to walk down, put his hand on his statues, two of them, one on each side of the door of his palace, put his hand on his statues that stood there before him – like a beautiful pony with a horn on his forehead and the tail of a lion – and he walked around them. And when all these people went on a hunt, he went with them. But he had his unicorn. From that day on he hunted with his friends and distributed all the food that he ever found – deer, bear, fox, wolf – he hunted the lot. But from that day, the day the sculptors built the unicorns in front of his door, he never saw his unicorn again.

But when the king passed on, for many many years still remained what the sculptors had made in front of his palace – and that's where your unicorn came from today. That is a true story and that is also the end of my tale!

The Giant with the Golden Hair of Knowledge

This is a well-known popular story in my time among the travelling folk. Some had different versions from others. This version is rather long, but it's one I liked most. Old Johnnie MacDonald told me . . . he says, 'You go fir tobacco tae me, I'll tell ye a story.' So I walked two miles into Coupar Angus for an ounce of tobacco, walked two miles back, and that's the story he told me . . . thirty years ago, easy. It took him two nights. Johnnie MacDonald was a cripple who looked after other travellers' children (and horses) while the parents were out working or hawking, in return for his keep.

MANY years ago in a faraway country there once lived a king. The king had married late in life, he had married a young princess from another country and they had a great wedding, it went on for many days and everyone was very happy for the king. But time passed by, and the king be getting up in years when he thought and wondered and worried why he wasn't going to have any children. He talked it over with his queen.

'Well,' she said, 'Ir Lordship, it would be lovely if we cuid hev a child,' So she prayed and she asked and she went to all the wise women round the country for advice, how to have a child. But a year passed by and sure enough she had a child, a little baby girl – and the king was highly delighted when he found out – he preferred to have a son but he was quite pleased to have a little girl.

He called all the wise women that the queen had visited round his kingdom to come to the christening of his baby daughter, and they all came, twelve o' them on the christening day. They had a great banquet and a great feast. Then lo and behold what the king had failed to remember – he had left one old woman whom the queen had visited out, completely forgot about her – she had never got an invitation to the christening of the king's baby daughter.

And she was very angry. The king had sent a coach to pick up the old women to bring them to the palace, but she had to walk. And the farther she walked the angrier she got, by the time she reached the palace . . . she walked in, everybody was busy feasting and dining. And lo and behold the king and queen remembered they had forgotten about her. But maids and footmen brought her forward, brought her in, sat her down at the table and they brought a plate before her full of lovely things to eat. The old woman looked, and all the other old women that the queen had visited, the wise women of the country, all were sitting with their food on golden plates, and she had only a common plate.

She stood up and she says, 'This is disgrace, Ir Majesty – why these auld friends of mine have golden plates and I jist have a common plate like a puir peasant – when you know that I am the most powerful woman among them all!' The king said nothing. He knew he had made a mistake.

He said, 'You were all called here today tae give my baby daughter yir blessings, youse bein the wise women of wir country.'

And everyone stood up and they gave blessing in turn, till they came to her, her turn. When she says, 'No, I won't give her no blessin, but will tell the truth: when your daughter comes eighteen years of age, she will marry the son of a poor fisherman! She will marry the son of a common fisherman who wis born the very same evening, the same evening an the same night under the same star as yir daughter!' And like that she was gone – she disappeared as quick as she came. Everybody was upset. The king was worried, so was the queen.

So after the banquet was finished and all the old women went on their way, the king drew his queen beside him and he said, 'That auld woman is very powerful, she's the most powerful wisest woman in the whole kingdom an I wouldna like tae go against her in ony way. Prob'ly she's jist angry because we left her out of the invitation. But,' the king said to his queen, 'just tae be on the safe side, we mus find this son of this fisherman an we must take im, destroy him so that he'll never mairry wir daughter – because I'm not havin my baby daughter marry the son of a poor fisherman!'

So he sent couriers all over the country searching and seeking there and searching here and seeking there, wherever they went asking about the new baby boy that was born the same time as the princess, on the same night under the same star. But they were gone for months and days and they returned haggard and hungry, but they never found the baby that was born on the same day as the princess.

The king said, 'It must be . . . the auld woman is too powerful tae tell any lies – we must find this boy! So, if youse can't do it, I'll jist hev to do it myself!' So the next day the king went on his way on horseback, dressed in common clothes. And he rode for days and he rode for weeks his ownself till he came hungry and tired one day to the seaside.

Beside the sea was a little cottage, a few hens scratching about, but there wasn't a soul about. And he looked down the shoreside, there was a fisherman casting his net in the water and the king could see that he was having very little success. Every time he threw his net in, he pulled it in, it was empty. (In these bygone days they just cast their net off the shoreside to see if they could bring in any fish.) So the king was kind of curious when he saw that the fisherman was casting the net so many times and getting nothing. He tied his horse to a tree, he walked down.

He said to the fisherman, 'You're not havin much luck!'

'No,' the fisherman said, 'I've had no luck for months. I've had no luck . . . five months ago was the last luck I had.'

King said, 'Five month ago? That seems a long time.'

'Well,' he said, 'the last luck I had was five month ago, an at this same spot: I cast ma net, it was full o' beautiful fish. An you believe me,' he says to the king, not knowing it was the king, 'it was a lucky night fir me in more ways an one – because whan I landed home wi as much fish as I cuid carry – sure enough, my wife had given birth tae a baby son!'

And then the king knew, this must be . . . the king calculated in his own head – he knew that his own little daughter was only five months old by this time. He says to the fisherman, 'I'm a traiveller on my way an I'm very hungry; if you could spare a drink or somethin tae eat I would pay you well for it.'

And the fisherman said, 'well, I have little tae spare, but, stranger, ye're welcome tae anything I hev.' So the fisherman gathered up his net, carried it on his back and walked up the shore till they came to the little cottage.

The king took his horse, led it round by the house and tied it once more to a tree, and he walked into the little cottage. Poor humble little cottage, just a fire, a table and a couple chairs, but sitting beside the fire was the most beautiful young woman this king had ever seen, even as pretty as his own queen but she was in rags. On her lap was a bonnie wee baby boy and she was sitting singing to him. She stood up, put the baby into an old-fashioned wooden cradle and it just lay there kicking its feet as happy as could be.

And the king looked down, he saw the most beautiful boy he'd ever seen in his life and he thought in his own mind, 'This must be it.'

'We have little to spare, stranger,' says the fisherman's wife, 'but we'll give ye half o' what we've got.' So she brought him some ale and some bread and cheese, she shared it with him.

And the king sat, he talked for a long long while and he said, 'Ye hev a lovely baby boy there.'

'Yes,' she said, 'we hev a lovely baby boy.'

'How old is he?' said the king.

She says, 'Five month.'

'When was he born?' said the king.

'Five months ago.' she said.

'Was it night or day-time?' said the king.

She said, 'He wis born at night, twelve o'clock at night – midnight.

'Oh,' said the king, 'I see. Well, you know, I'm a very rich man, and my wife and I has no children, I would love to have that baby boy. I would give ye anything ye want,' because the king had plenty money with him. His saddle-bags were full o' money, he carried them on his way. 'I wad give ye anything you want – I wad give ye as much gold that'll keep ye fir a lifetime, you can buy yirsel new nets, you can buy yirsel a boat – if ye'd only give me that baby boy. An I'll rear him up tae be my own son, when he's a grown man he'll come back an see ye.'

So the fisherman and his wife were very sad about this; they loved their little baby son but they were so poor . . . They thought about all the wonderful things they could do with all the money, and them being young themselves they knew they could maybe get another baby, but they would never get a chance like this to get as much money; so they finally consented to give the king the baby. The king walked out to his horse to his saddle-bags, he took two bags of gold and he put them on the table in front o' the fisherman and his wife – they had never seen as much money in their life. The fisherman's wife was kind o' crying and sad, but she rolled it in a shawl, she put it in the cradle and she gave the king the baby in the cradle.

He took the old wooden cradle and the baby, placed it on his saddle and bade the fisherman and his wife 'good-bye', went on his way. 'Now,' he said to himself, 'I have the baby an I'll make sure that this baby . . . who is born the same night wis foretold by one of my great women in my country, who is a great seer and the auldest even though the ugliest one, has always told truth. . . .' He rode on for many miles and he's wondering how, the best way to dispose of the baby, would he leave it in the forest to be destroyed by wild animals, or what would he – he could not have the heart to take a knife or a dagger and kill it . . . and as he's making up his mind the best way to dispose of the baby his horse was dandering on, and sure enough he came to a little lake surrounded by trees.

The king looked all around, there was not a soul to be seen – it was just a little lake in the hills and from the lake was a river floating down through the forest, and the king looked all around – he never saw a single huntsman or a soul. He says to himself, 'This is the very place tae get rid o' the baby.' So he took the cradle and the baby – as hard as he could swing – he flung it right out into the middle o' the little lake. He felt it kind o' sad, but he turned his back to the lake and he on his horse, he made on his way. 'At last,' he said, 'he is gone, he'll drown in the lake.'

But as the king made his way home to his own palace, little did he know that these old people who made these cradles of solid oak made them real, had made them good and they were watertight. And the cradle just floated like a little boat, round and round the lake it went and round and round the lake with the current, and the baby's still lying as dry as could be. The cradle floated on its way down the river, over rocks, down through bankings, down little streams, down it went, it travelled for over a mile and lo and behold – in it floated to a miller's dam!

This miller had a mill and he used the water coming from the river to turn his mill wheel, and behind the wheel was a dam which collected the water to give more force. And this particular day the miller was out with a long rake, a long pole, he's pulling leaves and bits o' sticks that come down the river from his wheel, big wooden wheel that drove the mill. When the first thing he sees coming floating down the dam was a cradle. The miller stood and he scratched his head, he knew it was a cradle and he saw there was something inside; and he rushed round, the cradle circled two or three times round the dam and he took his long pole, he pulled the cradle out. He lifted it up and he looked in – there lo and behold was the most beautiful little baby he'd ever seen in his life, a wee boy lying as quiet and content as if it was just in its mother's house.

The miller didn't know what to do, he's thunderstruck, 'Where in the world . . .' The miller knew that this led to a lake in the hills, he knew the river because he had followed it many times, 'but where in the world,' thought the miller, 'would this come from? Someone must have abandoned it, mebbe a coach overturned an it fell in the river.' He rushed back to his wife; they never had any children of their own. They weren't very old people, just middle-aged. And he said, 'Luik, wife, what I've got in the dam!'

'Oh dear,' said his wife, 'a baby! Where in the world did it come from?'

He said, 'It cam down the river from the lake an I caught it in the dam.'

The wife lifted it out and it started to giggle, she ran into the house with it and placed the cradle by the fire. 'Husband,' she says, 'ye better make yir way back up the river, because mebbe the're a coach overturned an the people are prob'ly hurt.'

The miller said, 'Yes, you take care o' the baby an I'll do the rest.' So the miller walked up the river as far as he could, for over nearly two miles till he came to the lake, and he searched round the lake, he searched all round – he looked for wheel tracks – but lo and behold he never saw a soul. All he saw was the mark of a horse's feet on the ground round the lake: he saw where the horse came in, he saw where the horse went out on the soft earth on the lake; he knew that someone then had thrown the baby in. He walked back to his wife and he told her.

'Well,' she says, 'if someone abandoned it, they must hae put it in the lake . . . it must be fir me and you, so we'll keep it.' And keep it they did. They kept the baby for eighteen long years, for eighteen long years they kept the baby. It grew up like their own son, a beautiful young man, handsome young man, tall and fair; and he worked from the day he was five years old with his daddy in the mill, he never knew who he was, he just called them his 'Daddy' and his 'Mammy'.

But lo and behold after eighteen years had passed, one day the same king who was getting up in his years now, was very old, had gone out with his huntsmen on a boar hunt. He'd hunted for many many days and for many many miles, and the king not being as able to keep up with the rest o' the huntsmen felt kind o' tired, he stopped for a rest. And the huntsmen left him and he got lost, he got lost and never knew what way the huntsmen went.

So he travelled on, he wandered on here and there trying to make his mind, find his huntsmen, when lo and behold the first thing he came to was a mill. He saw the mill-wheel go round and he saw the miller's dam. 'At last,' he said, 'I've found some habitation, someone must know here, there must be someone lives here.' So he rode his horse up to the front o' the mill, and the miller as usual was busy working in front o' the mill wheel, cleaning the leaves and sticks away from the dam to let the wheel turn round. The king slowly got off his horse, and the miller looked round. But now the king was dressed in his finery – the miller knew who it was!

The miller went down on his knees and he said, 'Ir Majesty, what can I do for ye?'

The king said, 'I'm lost. Have ye seen any of my couriers or my people or ma huntsmen?'

'No, Ir Majesty,' says the miller, 'My majesty the King, I have not seen anybody here fir days. Won't you come in an rest fir a while?' So he rushed the king into the kitchen into his little house, bade him 'sit doon bi the fire', called fir the woman to fetch the king something to drink. The king was really tired and hungry and weary. Then lo and behold in walks this young man.

And he turns round, the miller says to him, 'Go and take

care of the king's horse!' The young man bowed to the king and walked backwards out through the door.

And the king looked – he'd never seen a more handsome or beautiful young man in his life. Then the young man walked back into the house once more, he said, 'That is Ir Majesty's horse tooken care of, Father,' an he sat down by the fireside.

The king talked to the miller and the wife brought him something to eat, something to drink, and the king was quite pleased. 'I'll get your horse ready whenever you feel like it,' said the young man.

And the king said, 'That is a lovely young son you've got. I've never seen one look so clever an so intelligent.'

'Well, tae tell you the truth, Ir Majesty, I cannot lie to you,' he said, 'he's not wir son.'

The king said, 'Not yir son?'

'No,' said the miller, 'he's not wir son. Ir Majesty, many people we hev deceived along the way for eighteen years, but, Ir Majesty, we couldn't deceive you an tell you a lie because you are our king – he's not wir son.'

'Well, if he's not your son,' said the king, 'is he yir brother or yir relation o' some kind, or yir nephew?'

'No,' said the old miller, 'tae tell you the truth, Ir Majesty, it's a funny story – eighteen years ago I found him floatin in the dam in a cradle.' Then the king remembered! 'And that,' said the old man, 'is the same cradle by the fireside – we've never partit with it – that's his cradle.'

And the king looked and the king saw: this was the same cradle he got from the fisherman. The king was upset in a terrible way, he didn't know what to do! He knew now that the young man was alive and strong and good-looking, as beautiful a young man as he'd ever seen in his life. The king thought, he raked his head for a plan, how he was going to get rid of this young man he had no idea. He knew now that it was the fisherman's son he had thrown in the dam eighteen years before. Then he said to the miller, 'Has yir son ever rode on a horse?'

'No,' said the miller, 'my son has never had the pleasure of ridin a horse.'

'Well,' said the king, 'I'm very tired an I wondered if he'd take a message fir me to the palace – tae get somebody tae bring a coach because I'm not able to ride my horse back that long long distance? I wonder if you would ask him, would he take my horse – it's quite gentle – all he needs tae do is sit on its back, jist guide it, as it'll take him back tae the palace, there they'll find a coach to bring me home.'

Of course, Ir Majesty,' said the miller, 'my son will do that fir you!'

He called to his son and told him, 'You must take a message to the palace. And the king shall stay here at the mill with me till you return with a coach to bring him back, because he doesn't feel too good to ride his horse. Do you think ye could manage tae ride the king's horse to the palace?'

And the king said, 'Remember now, it's a long way from here, it's prob'ly two days' journey.'

And the young man said, 'I'm sure I'll manage, Ir Majesty, I've never been on a horse, but I've a good idea how to get there. I'll surely find my way.'

So the king calls for a paper and a quill and some ink; he writes her a letter, seals it and gives it to the young man, says, 'You take this to the queen! When you arrive there to the queen with it, you'll be well rewarded.'

The young man bids his father and mother, the old miller, 'Good-bye, good day', and he does the same to the king. He takes the king's horse, he rides on, and he rides and rides and rides for many hours, he came to the forest. He'd never been this way before and lo and behold – he got lost! He got lost in the forest and he didn't know in the world what direction to take to the palace or to the big town where the palace was, but he'd worked hard that morning and he was tired. He came to this little path, led the horse down, and sure enough in the middle o' the forest he came to a little cabin. He got off and tied up the horse. He walked to the cabin but there was not a soul to be seen – it was empty. There was a fireplace, a table and some chairs in the cabin, some sheepskins and some goatskins on the floor, plenty firewood by the fireside.

So the young man went out, he took the saddle off the horse, took the bridle off, got the reins and tied it round the horse's neck, and tied it to a tree, gave the horse enough room so's it couldn't escape to eat some grass, keep it alive. So after he saw that the horse was cared for and couldn't escape, could reach as much grass that would keep it for a few hours, the young man went in by the fireside, kindled up the fire; and he'd carried a few pieces o' meat and scones and things that his mother had given him to see him on his journey, he sat by the fireside and had a meal. Then wearied and tired he gathered some o' the skins, he lay down by the fireside and fell asleep.

Now, unknown to the young man this cabin in the forest was owned by many robbers, about five or six who robbed and stole and thieved all over the country, and they always disappeared into the forest, they stayed in this cabin. And lo and behold they were all away out thieving and stealing, then they came back one by one; when they came in one by one they came quietly, because they saw the horse tied up to the tree outside and they wondered who it was in their cabin. They came in very carefully, they all sat down round the table and they started to drink the wine they had stolen or bought, wherever they got it. And sure enough there by the fireside lay this beautiful young man.

The chief o' the robbers said, 'We've got an intruder in wir cabin and I don't know how we're gaunna get rid of him. If he wakes up an finds . . . this place, then this place'll be no good for us anymore.' So they're sitting talking and wondering what they're going to do, when the oldest one who was a family man himself, who'd remembered way back many years ago that he too had sons that he'd probably forgotten about and he'd wondered if they had ever forgot about him, looked once more – pulled back the sheepskins that the young man had himself happed up with – and he saw a letter stuck in his belt! 'I wonder,' says the old man (he could read even suppose he was a robber) – he pulled the letter from the young man's belt and he opened it, as carefully as he could. He read it aloud to the rest o' the robbers, some who couldn't read.

One was saying, 'What dis it say, what dis it say? Who is he, what dis it say? Is he a king's messenger, is he a king's son, is he a prince?'

'Not atall, not atall, not atall!' said the robber chief. 'Jist be quiet an I'll read it to ye . . . He's "a miller's son", an you know the miller as well as me – many times we passed by his place – he he's been guid to us, he's never interfered an never gien away wir secrets in any way . . . and he's on his way tae his death!'

'Tae his death?' said the rest o' the robbers.

'Yes,' he said, 'at the present moment the king is at the mill, an this letter says that "when this young man arrives at the palace he's got to be put to death immediately, because *this is the one*".'

'What in the name of creation,' said the robbers, 'what would a young man like that do to anybody to warran' his death?'

The old one went to his bag, and he was a scholar, he'd carried many books and papers even suppose he was a robber; he had in his bag some quills and some ink, because he used to leave messages for people along the wayside. He took the letter that the king had wrote and he threw it in the fire. Then he wrote in a hand as good as the king: 'When this young man arrives at the palace, *he is the one* that we want. And I want you to a-marry him immediately to my daughter the princess. (Signed) *The King*.' He folded it, put it back, stuck it in the young man's belt – and the young man's still sleeping on. The robbers sat, they had their drink and they quietly went their way into the forest. The young man had slept through all this, he'd never known a thing.

He woke up, rubbed his eyes, wondered for a wee while where he was and then he remembered. Got up, tidied up the rugs that he'd used, put them back where he found them, made sure the fire wouldn't do any harm (it was burned out by this time), walked out of the door, there was his horse standing quite contented full o' grass . . . the robbers were gone. He put the saddle on the horse, and the bridle, climbed up on the horse's back and made his way down through the forest. He hit the highway, the track going through the forest and he made his way on, he rode for miles. And sure enough at last he rode into the town where the palace was, the king's palace.

He landed up to the king's palace, the king's castle; and these castles in the old days were just made o' stone, a few hamlets and houses round about – they weren't like the big towns ye see nowadays – there was a few guards walking about. He walked to see the queen. They asked him why he had come, and he said he had a message from the king, that the king had sent a message that he must deliver to the queen immediately. And when he showed the message to the guards signed by the king's hand, they led him before the queen. He bowed to the queen, his horse was taken care of and he gave the letter to the queen.

And then the queen turned round, she smiled. She called for all the men and all the cooks and servants, says, 'We're gaunna have a great banquet. The king is off on a journey, he will be returning in a few days, but I have got strict orders that this young man has got to marry his daughter! Whatever he's done for it I don't know, but that's his orders.'

And then they all prepared for the wedding: sure enough the young man was led and he was dressed in the finest o' clothes, he met the princess, and the princess when she saw him just loved him immediately. They became good friends, they talked and they sat and they talked and they walked, and within two days they were married. And the banquet and the dancing went on for three days.

The king had waited and waited and waited for the return of the coach, but nothing turned up. But after three days the king got tired. Now, the miller had an old donkey and cart that he used for taking grain to the village, and the king finally made the miller yoke the donkey in the old cart; made him as comfortable as possible, and the miller and the king made their way on the journey. They travelled for two days. When they landed in the town at the palace all this great carry-on was going on. The king wondered what was the trouble. The miller wanted to go home, the miller wanted to return. People were singing, there were flags waving, everybody was happy, they were dancing in the street; the king wondered what was happening in the world! But they drove the old donkey and cart from the mill up to the palace, the king stepped out and the first person he met was the queen.

And the queen ran forward, she threw her arms round the king and welcomed him back. He said, 'Did ye get my letter?'

'Yes,' she said, 'I've got your letter.

'Have you done my orders,' he said, 'what I told ye to do?'

'Of course,' she said, 'Ir Majesty – an come and see them! Come an see them, don't they look handsome?'

'Look handsome?' said the king. 'What do ye mean?'

She says, 'Aren't they a handsome couple!' And there was the young miller's son walking in the garden, dressed in finery, his arm around the princess and they were the most beautiful couple you ever saw. The king was outraged at this.

He said, 'My letter said, "*This is the young man that was born under the same star as the princess – the son of a fisherman who was supposed to marry my daughter – which the old woman foretold eighteen years ago.*" An my orders was "to put him to death"!'

'Yir orders,' said the queen, 'was "to marry him immediately to the princess".'

'I wrote the letter,' says the king, 'I should know what I said!'

'Well, Ir Majesty, I don't know,' said the queen, 'but I've cairried yir orders to the hilt – there's nothing we can do about it now! He is mairried to the princess.'

And the king was upset! He went into his room, he stood by himself for hours and hours and hours, and he sat, he sat and he thought and he thought and he thought. And then at last he called the young man before him, shook hands with him – kindly and nice as if there were nothing wrong. He says, 'young man, you hev married my daughter.'

'Yes,' said the young man, 'I've married yir daughter, an such a lovely princess she is; I'm proud tae marry yir daughter, I love her dearly.'

'Well,' he said, 'if you love her so much as that, I'm her father . . .'

'I know,' says the young man, 'ye're her father, Ir Majesty the King, an I'm privileged to be married to your daughter, I'll do everything within my power tae see that I make her happy,' he said, 'an you and the queen as well. Anything ye ask of me – it shall be done.'

'Guid,' says the king, 'I'm proud of that. I'm a worried man,' said the king.

And the young fisherman, who was very intelligent, said, 'Why should you be worried, Ir Majesty, because you have everything under the sun, you've got a large kingdom an you've everything you need.'

He said, 'I don't have the knowledge of a king.'

'Of course, Your Majesty, you have the knowledge of a king!'

'But,' he said, 'I weary an I worry for something that I shall never have.'

'What is it?' said the young fisherman's son.

He said, 'Away, they tell me, in a faraway land miles from here is an island – I don't know if it's truth or fiction but I've never been there or none of my people's ever been there – but they tell me that in that island there lives a giant, a great giant who is very kind and tender but who has *the golden hair of wisdom*, an anyone who possesses the hairs of his head, event three of them or four of them or just one, will have the wisdom that he has. And I would give my life, everything I own, to have three hairs of that giant's head; if you would get them fir me, I would appreciate it very much.'

'Well,' says the young man, 'if it's possible, Ir Majesty, an it can be done . . . I'll do my best – when would you like me to start?'

'I would like you to start right away,' said the king. He called for the queen and he called for the princess, the three o' them sat together and the fisherman's son sat there beside them. And the king told them the same story I'm telling you. The princess was very sad, she didn't want her young man to go away on a long journey. But the king said, 'it's only fir a matter of time, my daughter, he'll return an then you'll have him fir life!'

The young fisherman's son wanted to please the king as much as possible, he said, 'I'll go, Ir Majesty, I'll start off – even tomorrow morning.' So he spent one more night with the princess; and in the morning the king gave him the best horse in the stable, as much money as he wanted, and set him on his journey. And before he left he promised the king he would never come back, unless he could bring back the three golden hairs of wisdom that the king required.

Now this made the king very happy, for he knew in his heart – he'd never wanted from the beginning for a fisherman's son to marry his daugher – he said to himself, 'At last I've got rid of him, he's gone for ever!' He walked back to his palace and he sat in his chamber. The princess his daughter came in, she looked very sad. And the queen came in, she sat down, she really loved the fisherman's son who was newly wed to her daughter the princess.

And the princess says, 'Daddy, my husband he is gone on a journey – where did you send him to?'

'Oh,' he said, 'my daughter, my baby, my lovely princess,

I've sent him on a journey, he's gone on to do something for me an he'll return to you, it won't be long before he comes back.' But deep in his mind the king thought, 'He is gone for ever, because I have heard there's no one who hed ever went out to search fir the three golden hairs from the head of the Giant of Wisdom has ever returned!'

So the fisherman's son left the palace that morning, bade 'good-bye' to his young wife the princess, the queen and the king, and he went on his way. And he rode and he rode and he rode and he rode for many, many miles, through forest and through towns and through villages for many many miles, for days and for days. The king had given him plenty money to carry him on his way. He's asking everyone along the way, woodsmen, foresters, old people, young people, have they ever heard of the Giant with the Golden Hairs of Wisdom? But lo and behold he never got a clue.

But he travelled for many many miles on horseback, his horse was weary and so was he. He came down this track, and lo and behold over the mountain he saw a little village before him. He said to himself, 'In that village there must be something to eat,' because he was hungry and tired.

And he rode into the village, it was small, and when he rode into the first o' the village he passed two–three houses and the houses seemed to be empty. He rode on to the centre, there was about twenty-five or thirty people all gathered round in the village green. And they were talking to each other, some were raising up their hands and they were speaking . . . when the young stranger rode up on horseback they all stopped and were quiet, never said a word. So the fisherman's son said, 'People, what's yir trouble?'

And one old man with a long white beard came up, he stood beside the young fisherman's son's horse and he put his hand on the side of the saddle, said, 'Stranger, where hev you come from?'

The fisherman's son said, 'I've come a long long way. Could you tell me something, are there any food in the village?'

'We have food,' said the old man, 'we hev drink, but we are sad.'

'Why are you sad?' said the fisherman's son. Everything seemed prosperous in the village. 'Why are you sad?'

'Well,' says the old man, 'look there before ye!'

And the fisherman's son looked – there was a tree right in the middle of the green – all the people were gathered round it. A tree and the leaves were hanging down, them all withered and the tree was dying. The fisherman's son thought this kind o' queer, and he said, 'Why is the tree so important?'

And the old man said, 'Luik, my son, you don't know, you have come from a faraway place, but this tree is so important to us. Where are you going? Where are ye bound for, stranger?'

And the young man said, 'I am going to seek three hairs from the head of the Golden-haired Giant of Knowledge.'

'Oh-dear-oh-dear,' said the old man, 'if only you could find im an tell us the truth!'

'What truth?' said the fisherman's son.

'Tell us why our tree, our favourite tree, has never borne fruit fir many years.'

What kind o' fruit?' said the fisherman's son.

He said, 'The Fruit of Health: this tree in our village, my son, has bore fruit fir many many years, an anyone who eats the fruit cuid live to be a hundred years old, never hev a headache, never have no trouble, never even have a hard day – but they would live fir evermore an feel well all their days! But suddenly the tree hes begun tae wither an the fruit is gone. Please, help us, stranger!'

'Well,' says the fisherman's son, 'I'm on my journey to seek the Giant with the Golden Hair of Knowledge, but if you would put me up fir the night an give me somethin to eat, I'll prob'ly tell ye – I'll prob'ly tell you on my way back when I return once more.' So all the villagers gathered round, they made the fisherman's son welcome. They gave him a place to stay, they gave him food. And he made a promise that when he returned he would find the truth of why their Tree of Health had never borne fruit.

So next morning, after a nice rest and some food and some breakfast, the young fisherman's son rode on once more. And he rode and he rode and he rode, he travelled for many many miles and he never came across a village. He travelled over hill and over dale for many's a day till he was hungry and weary and tired. At last, once more down a glen he comes, and lo and behold there once more is another village before him. He rides into the village, and lo and behold his horse was tired and weary and so was he. Once more when he lands in the village the little thatch cottages look empty, there's not a soul to be seen so he rides through. And then there in a little green in the village are all the villagers, they're gathered round a little stream that runs through the village. The young fisherman's son stops. And they saw there was a stranger among their midst. An old woman with long grey hair walks up.

She says, 'Where hev you come from, stranger?'

He said, 'I've come a long way from here.'

'Have you any news to tell us?'

'News?' said the fisherman's son, 'what kind of news do you require?'

'Please help us!' she said.

'Well,' said the fisherman's son, 'it's me that seeks help, not you! I am hungry an I'm tired an weary – cuid you help me?'

'If I help you,' she said, 'my son, wad ye help me?'

He said, 'I'm seekin for the Island of the Giant with the Golden Hair of Knowledge.'

'Oh,' she said, 'my son, I have heard many people talkin about him, but he lives in an island far away from here. But please, please, help us!'

'And what's yir problem?' said the fisherman's son.

'It's wir stream, my son,' she said, 'our stream – which used to run beautiful wine from our village – we enjoyed it an we drank from it, we enjoyed it and it never seemed to end, never seemed to stop. An we all gaithert here, we had wir sing-songs an we all enjoyed wir drink by the lovely Stream that Flowed Wine for evermore. But now hes it gone dry – no one knows what happened to our stream. Please, stranger, help us!'

And the fisherman's son said, 'If you help me, I'll help you.'

'What are you seekin, my son?' says the old woman.

'I'm seekin shelter, I'm seekin shelter fir the night, a place tae lie down an lay my head, because I'm weary,' said the fisherman's son; 'an I'm bound fir the place of the Giant with the Golden Hairs of Wisdom.' So they took him, they gave him a place to stay and they fed him; they made him promise in his return, they would pay him handsomely and reward him if he could find the secret – why their stream which had run with beautiful wine through the village had now dried up.

So next morning, true to his word, the fisherman's son got up, saddled his horse, bade 'good-bye' to the villagers and rode on his way after a nice rest. And he rode and he rode and he rode, and he travelled and he travelled; they had given him some food to carry him on his way and he travelled for many many miles, till at last he rode till he came to the open sea – there were no more land. He landed on the beach, he had come to Land's End. He rode around the beach for a while on horseback, jumped off his horse, led his horse looking for someone to talk to. But there was nobody there, not one single soul. So he led his horse who was tired and weary around the shoreside. And lo and behold the first thing he spied was an old man sitting in a boat, an old man with a long beard sitting in the boat.

He walked up to the old man, 'Excuse me, sir,' he said, 'cuid you tell me, where am I?'

And the old man said, 'My son, where have you come from?'

'I have come from many many miles away . . . I've been riding for months an days an weeks without end. I have passed through many towns, I have passed through many villages, but now I seem to be at ma end of my place, I can go no further.'

'Where are ye bound fir?' says the old man.

'I'm bound,' says the fisherman's son, 'to seek the Giant with the Golden Hair of Knowledge.'

The old man said, 'Luik, ye hev come tae the right place: I am the ferryman an there in the distance is yir island. An there in that island lives the Giant with the Golden Hair of Knowledge – but woe be tae ye, my son – it wouldna be safe for you to go there!'

'Please,' said the boy, said the fisherman's son, 'take me there! Take me there, I want to go!'

'Your life will not be worth nothing if you go there,' says the old man.

'I want to go, I must go,' said the fisherman's son, I mus go!'

'Well,' says the old boatman, 'I row across there sometimes an back an forward, but I don't take any passengers, but I'm stuck to this boat an I jist can't get out. I mus row tae the island, an row back an row forward two times a day, because I'm stuck here an I jist can't leave this boat in any way. I don't take any passengers – no one comes here anymore. But in that island lives the Giant an if you want tae go there, my son, I will take you; but before you go ye mus make me one promise!'

'What would you want me to promise?' says the young fisherman's son.

'Promise me one thing,' he said: 'find out fir me, why that I am stuck tae this boat an can never leave this row – that I mus row from the island back an forward, back an forward every day, every day non-stop – because I jist can't leave this boat! An no one seems to want tae go there because it's too dangerous for them.'

'Take me,' says the fisherman's son, 'an I will find the secret fir ye when I meet the Giant with the Golden Hairs of Knowledge!'

'I will take you,' said the old boatman, 'but ye must give me one promise.'

'I'll promise ye anything,' said the fisherman's son, 'when I find the Giant with the Golden Hair of Knowledge.'

'Ye mus tell me,' said the old boatman, 'why I must sit here and row the boat from here to the island, row it back again day out an day in, I'm confined tae this boat for evermore, that I must never leave this boat for one minute, that I must row for eternity!'

'I will tell you,' said the fisherman's son, 'in one condition – that you row me!'

'I will take ye there,' said the old man, 'but woe be tae ye, my son, what happens to ye – it'll not be my fault!'

Many many hundred miles back behind him in the palace of the king, the princess is worried. Now her young man has been gone for many many days, for many many months; and the king is happy and the king is pleased, and the queen is worried because the queen loved her daughter, and she loved any man – if her daughter was happy so was she. The king rubbed his hands in glee after two months had passed, the king rubbed his hands in glee after three months had passed, the king rubbed his hands in glee after four months had passed – no return of the fisherman's son! He said, 'He's gone fir evermore. I tried tae destroy him wonst, but the second time I have succeeded – he is gone for ever!' But the fisherman's son is not gone for ever.

He took his horse and he took this harness off it, he took the reins and he wrapped it around the horse's neck, he tethered it out on a nice piece of grass. He said to the old boatman, 'You will come fir me tomorrow.'

'I'll come fir ye tomorrow,' said the old boatman.

'I will spend one night in the Giant's castle,' he said.

'You'll never spend a lifetime in the Giant's castle,' says the old man, 'your life won't be worth nothing when you land there! But I'll take ye.'

So after he'd taken care of his horse, the young man got in the boat and the old man rowed him across from the end of the land to this little island that sat out in the middle of the sea. He rowed across and he rowed across and he rowed to the beach: 'There ye are, my young man,' he said, 'it's on yir own head what happens to ye frae now on. But I'll be here tomorrow morning at the same time, an if ye miss me ye'll have tae wait till I return again.'

The fisherman's son jumped off the boat on this island and he walked up the beach. This was a funny island; there were trees, there were flowers, there were birds, there were animals, everything; and he walked farther and farther and the more he walked it got more beautiful. At last he walked for about five or six hundred yards into the middle of this little island, he came to a castle, the most beautiful old stone castle he'd ever seen. He said, 'This is where I'm bound to go.' And he walked up three stone steps to the great oak door. He knocked hard on the door because he wasn't afraid, because he had come to do something for the king – and he made sure he was going to do it – suppose it cost him his life! He knocked again and then he heard footsteps coming.

Then lo and behold the door opened, out came a woman, a very old woman. But she was three times as big as the fisherman's son! She was tall and thin with long grey hair and a long flowing dress on her that swept the floor – the fisherman's son couldn't even see her feet. The old woman was surprised when she saw the young man standing at her door, she rubbed her eyes, said, 'My son, what are you doing here?'

He said, 'Mother' (he was very kindly this fisherman's son), 'mother, I hev come a long long way tae find you.'

'Well,' she says, 'ye found me now but peril fir you it might be!'

'Why?' said the fisherman's son. 'I've only come fir three things; please, help me!'

And the old woman never saw a human being for many many years, alone she lived there on the island with her son the Giant with the Golden Hair who was out hunting for deer in his forest, and no one had ever come near his place. She said, 'If my son finds you here, young man, your life won't be worth nothing.'

'Please, mother,' said the fisherman's son, 'please help me! I have come a long long way to find the truth.'

'What truth do ye want tae find?'

'I want to find three hairs of your son's head.'

She says, 'Hairs of my son's head is impossible tae get.'

'Please, mother,' he said, 'help me; I've come a long long way.'

'Well,' she says, 'come in.' So she took him in and she gave him something to eat. 'Now, sit down an tell me yir story.'

So the story he told the old woman is the same story I'm telling you, he said, 'I'm jist a fisherman's son an I married a young princess, her father sent me out tae seek three golden hairs from the Giant of Knowledge.

She said, 'That is my son, and the're nothing in the world that my son doesn't know – he knows everything! He is giftit with the golden hair of knowledge.'

'Mother,' he said, 'if ye cuid only get me three hairs from his head to bring back tae the king, I'd be happy to live with my bride the princess fir evermore.'

And the old woman felt sad for him, she says, 'My son will be home in very few minutes, he's out huntin. But what else dae ye seek?'

He said, 'I seek . . . as I rode on my way I came to a village, in that village there is a tree an that tree bore the Fruit of Life; an all its people were happy to eat the fruit, they lived happy ever after, no one tuik any trouble, no one tuik any disease an no one ever suffered from nothin. But now the tree is barren an grows nothing anymore – I want to know the reason why.'

'Oh,' says the old woman, 'I wouldn't know about that, but my son would know.'

'Then,' he said, 'I rode fir many many more miles an I came to another village; there in the village everyone was sad because they had a stream that beared pure wine, an everyone used to drink an enjoy the wine that ran through the stream – but now they are sad because the stream has gone dry.'

'Nice,' says the old woman, 'but my son would know about that better than me.'

'Then' he said, 'at the end of the land I came tae an auld boatman who took me here, who ferried me across. An he wonders why that he should be stuck in that boat, rows it back, foremost, back an foremos from the mainland tae the island with no passengers in it day out an day in?'

The old woman says, 'I don't know about that, but my son wad know.' But she was busy talking to him when they heard what was like a thunderclap, she said, 'He's comin home!' And the old woman was sitting in a high chair and her dress was hanging to the floor, 'Climb in below my chair, son,' she says, 'before he finds ye!'

And the fisherman's son, with the long dresses the old women wore in these days and the high chair which she's sitting on, he climbed in below the chair and she pulled her old dress over the top o' him. He sat there quite content, when who should walk in but a monstrous young giant with golden hair hanging down his back; but he never saw him, but he knew!

'Mother,' he said, 'hev you made something fir supper – I'm hungry!'

'Yes,' she said, 'my son, I've something fir supper for you, I've roastit . . .' And he had a deer on his back, he threw the deer down on the floor. 'Yes,' she said, 'son, I made ye supper.'

'What . . . any trouble or anything happen while I been gone?' he says. 'Things seems queer around this place . . . hev you hed any visitors while I was gone?'

'No, my son,' she said, 'no visitors. Only the aul boatman who has been . . .'

'Oh,' he said, 'him; he'll keep on rowin as long as . . . he'll go on rowin his wey till the end of time.'

She brought forth a haunch of deer, roasted haunch o' deer round the fire and she placed it before him, he ate it up. Then she brought a big flagon o' wine. She said, 'My son, you know you been gone fir a long time.'

'Yes, Mother,' he said, 'I had a long hunt today, but I might be luckier tomorrow.' And he sat by the fire after drinking three or four gallons o' wine.

She says, 'My son, you look tired and weary, come beside yir mother,' because this old woman loved this son like nothing in the world, and she took him beside her. He sat on the floor and she sat on a high stool. His head only came to her knee, he placed his head on, and being him hunting all day and after a feast and a drink o' wine, he fell sound asleep on his mother's knee. She began to run her fingers through his golden hair, which was long and beautiful. And then she wapped one of the golden hairs round her finger, and she pulled it. And the Giant wakened up!

He said, 'Mother, what hae ye been doin, you been pullin my hair!'

'Oh, my son, I'm sorry tae wake ye up, but I had a terrible dream.'

'Mother,' he says, 'what was yir dream?'

'I dreamt, my son,' she says, 'a long way from here in the mainland far from our island there is a village an in that village there is a tree an that tree bore beautiful fruit, the Fruit of Health, and all these people loved that Fruit of Health, they enjoyed it. But now they are so sad because their tree is withering an dying.'

'Ho, my Mother,' he said, 'if they only knew! If they only knew: there's a wicked, wicked wicked wizard had cast a spell on that tree an put a padlock an chain round the roots; if they only knew – jist tae dig up the root o' the tree an break the padlock – their tree would blossom for evermore. Please, let me sleep, Mother!' he said, an he placed his head on his mother's knee once more.

Now the old woman has one hair on her finger. She waited till the Giant fell asleep once more. She wrapped another hair round her finger and she pulled another hair from his head. The Giant woke up.

'Mother!' he said 'what are ye pullin my hair fir?'

'Oh, my son,' she said, 'while you were asleep I had another dream: I dreamt there's another village many miles from the first one; an through that village there runs a beautiful stream o' beautiful sweet wine, an now the stream has stopped the villagers are so upset – there's no more wine fir them an they're so sad! They would give anything in the world if their stream would run wine once more.'

'Ha,' says the Giant, 'it's quite simple! If they only knew: under the steppin stone in the well there is a frog an in that frog's throat is a crust o' bread thrown by a child in the well, stuck in the frog's throat. If they dig up the steppin stone that leads to the stream an takes the crust from the frog's throat – then their stream will run again for ever. But they'll never know an no one's gaun tae tell them!'

The wee laddie's sitting in below the old woman's dress and he's hearing everything. The Giant stretched his feet out again by the heat o' the fire and he laid his head upon his mother's lap once more, then he fell asleep. When the old woman gathered another hair round her finger once more, and she pulled – he woke up.

'Mother,' he says, 'stop pullin my hair!'

'Oh, my son,' she says, I had another wonderful dream.'

'Mother,' he said, 'ye've hed better dreams an me! What's your problem this time?'

'Well,' she said, 'son, I had another dream an I think I won't dream anymore tonight. But tell me: why is it that the auld boatman who rows across from our island tae the mainland back an forward, back an forward, although suppose he never takes you or takes me, he mus be confined tae that boat all his life an never can get a-free from it?'

'Ha-ha-ha,' said the Giant. 'I know, but he'll never know!'

'But what's the problem,' said the old woman, 'why has he got tae do this?'

'Well,' said the Giant, it's quite simple: there's no problem if he only knew, but he'll never know by me; if only he would give a shot o' the rows to the first person who comes in the boat, an give *them* a shot an let *them* row. When the boat leaves the beach – not in my island but on the mainland – an jump out, then the person who takes the oars will take his place, will be confined for evermore tae row back and forward till the end of eternity!' And the Giant fell asleep once more.

When the Giant was asleep, the woman beckoned to the wee fisherman's son – the Giant was asleep – 'Now,' she said, she took the three golden hairs from her finger – 'take them carefully, luik after them an bring them back to the king. But remember – did ye hear what I told ye?'

'I know,' said the son, 'I heard every word.' The fisherman's son rolled the hairs up in his hand, put them in his purse around his waist and he quietly stole away from the castle of the sleeping Giant with the Golden Hairs of Knowledge – for he knew he had done what he had set out to do. He walked for many miles till he came to the beach, by the time he reached the beach it was daylight.

There lo and behold was the old boatman waiting on the beach for him, the old boatman said, 'Tell me, my son, hev you found the secret fir me, why I row this boat back and forward from side to side fir eternity?'

And the young man said, 'Luik, auld boatman, after ye take me tae the mainland I'll tell ye!'

'Jump in, then,' says the old man, and the young fisherman's son jumped in the boat. The old man rowed back to the mainland and he jumped out. 'Now,' said the boatman, 'tell me why I'm confined tae this for evermore!'

And the fisherman's son said, 'The Giant of Golden Knowledge says: "You are confined fir only one reason – the first person who comes here to ask you to row them across to the island, tell em you're tired an give em a shot o' the oars – when it leaves the beach on this side, jump out an you'll be free for evermore! And the person who takes the oars will be confined tae the boat fir the rest o' their life." '

'Guid,' says the old boatman, 'guid.'

He bade the old boatman 'farewell', goes back to his horse and his horse had eaten all the grass around where it was tied to, but it was still there. He takes the saddle, saddles his horse, puts the bridle on it, jumps on his horse's back and rides back, because the old woman had given him a good meal in the Giant's palace, he rides back. Lo and behold when he landed in the same village he had come to, the second village, there was the people once more gathered round the stream. And they're all moaning and they're very upset, why this stream was dry.

Up comes the old woman once more with the long grey hair, 'Welcome back, stranger,' she said, 'did ye find your quest?'

'I have found my quest, mother,' he said.

'Please,' she said, 'tell us an we'll make you rich, we'll give ye a donkey with as much gold as you can carry, if ye will only tell us why wir stream doesn't run wine anymore!'

And the young man said, 'I have been with the Giant of Golden Hair of Knowledge an he says: "Under yir steppin stone there is a frog, an in that frog's throat is a crust o' bread thrown by a careless child an he cannae swalla it; but you must retrieve the frog an take the piece o' bread from his throat – wonst ye retrieve the bread yir stream will run again!" '

The old woman talked to some o' the men, within seconds they lifted the flagstone, and there lo and behold was the frog. Sure enough they took the frog, they relieved the frog of a crust o' bread in his throat and within seconds the stream was running most[1] wine once more! And everybody in the village ran into it, they were diving into it, they were sprinkling it on their faces, they were drinking it, they were playing – the kids were swimming in it – the most

1 most – entirely

beautiful wine of all! And the old woman said, 'Stop, we must help our young stranger who has found the secret.' She called once more for the donkey, loaded it with two bags of gold, she gave it to the young stranger, the fisherman's son, to go on his way.

He took the donkey behind his horse with two bags o' gold, he rode on and rode on for many days and many days and many days. At last he came to the first village, and lo and behold when he landed, sure enough there was the people gathered round the green once more. They're weeping, they're a-crying and the tree was getting withered, the leaves were falling off and it looked in a horrible state.

When he rode up the old man with the long white beard came, he said, 'Welcome back, stranger, where have you been?'

He said, 'I have been to the Island of the Giant with the Golden Hair of Knowledge.'

'Have you found our secret, stranger?' said the old man.

'Yes,' he said, 'old man, I have.'

'Why our tree doesn't nourish the most beautiful fruit?'

Said the young fisherman's son, 'Take a spade an dig under the tree an you will find a chain an padlock around the root of yir tree. Break the padlock of the chain – then once more yir tree will blossom in life with Fruit of Health!'

No sooner said than done, three men ran with spades, they dug up under the tree and lo and behold there was the truth: under the tree was a chain and a padlock; they broke the chain, threw the chain away, covered the roots up once more. And lo and behold the amazing thing happened – the tree was blossomed in minutes – it was hanging with fruit! And the people were running, the children were running, they're picking it off and they're eating them. They're happy and they're clapping their hands.

And then the old man said, 'Stop!' and they all stopped. 'We must thank our friend, the young stranger who has come here tae found the secret of our tree, we mus reward him handsomely.' And then once more they called for another donkey, it was given two large bags of gold. Once more the fisherman's son went on his way with two donkeys laden with four bags of gold.

He travelled on and he made his way back, all the way he had come, till at last after many days' travel he landed back in the palace. And there was the queen and there was the princess to welcome him home. His donkeys were taken care of, his horse was taken care of, the four bags of gold were carried up and placed before the king. And the fisherman's son walked up, from his purse he took out the three golden hairs of knowledge.

'You are back,' said the king.

'I am back,' said the fisherman's son, 'an I done yir quest: there is yir three golden hairs,' and he put them in the king's hand.

'Where in the world did you find em?' said the king.

'I found them at Land's End,' said the fisherman's son, 'an after the Land's End there's an island, there lives in that island the Giant with the Golden Hair of Knowledge.'

'But,' said the king, 'there's only three hairs – that will only give me a little knowledge – it won't give me all the Giant knows!'

'Well,' said the fisherman's son, 'if ye want any more knowledge, ye'll hev to go and find it yirself, because I cam home to spend the rest o' my life with my wife the princess.'

'Well,' says the king, 'you have deserved it. But I myself will go, I will find the Giant with the Golden Hair of Knowledge through your directions.'

'Go,' said the young fisherman's son, 'you are welcome,' and he told the king where to go. The princess was happy to see her young man back and she cuddled him and kissed him, and so was the queen. Now he had plenty gold.

The next day the king said he would go on his way, and himself, he was not content with three golden hairs, he wanted many many more. So he chose his best horse and he took as much gold that would carry him on his way. He left the queen and he left the young fisherman's son and the princess to take care of the kingdom till he came home, and he rode on his way. The king rode for many many miles, he rode through the first village, he never saw the Tree of Fruit; he rode through the second village, he never saw the Stream of Beautiful Wine; and he rode till the End of the Land, all he saw was an old man in a boat.

He looked out and there was the island, 'That,' says the king, 'is the place I want tae go to!' And he says to the old man, 'I leave my horse here if you will take me across there.'

'Willingly,' says the old boatman, 'I'll take ye across. But,' he said, 'I been rowin fir many many days an I'm tired; would ye do me one favour?'

'I'll do anything,' said the king who was an aged man by this time, but was still fit and strong.

'I been rowin all day,' said the old man; 'please, take a little shot of the oars an row us across tae the island!'

'Sure enough!' said the king and he spat on his hands. He jumped up in the front o' the boat and he took the oars in his hands. And the minute he took the oars in his hands, the old boatman jumped out and walked away, left the king. And the king was left there for evermore, he rowed back and he rowed forward and he rowed back and he rowed forward, but he could never, never never get his hands away from the oars or he could never leave the boat.

The young fisherman's son had his young queen, he became king after the queen had died, and he and his princess lived happy in their palace, they had many children. But the king still rowed on from time to time and of course, as the story says, he's still rowing yet! And that is the end o' my story.

The Thorn in the King's Foot

This is a story for a winter's evening, when you want to sit round and listen to a story. I heard it from my father when I was about five or six years old, and also from my mother's brother Duncan Townsley. But apart from the West Coast travellers and after I left Argyllshire at the age of fifteen, I never heard it. Knowledge of the disease 'King's Evil' was widespread among the travelling people, but this particular narrative was not.

MANY many years ago long before your time and mine, in a faraway country there once lived a king. He ruled his kingdom with a stern stern hand, he was a very strong king, very powerful. And he and his wife lived in this large palace, they had many farms and many people in their land. He said to his queen, 'These people – my bees – they have to wurk fir me, they're jist my bees; without bees you wouldna hev any honey, an they'll work hard. Whatever they do an whatever they make is half mine, because I am their king.' He was severe. The queen had to agree with him because he was her husband, but she knew that he had many faults in his life. And the one fault that she never forgave him for, they never had any children.

So many many late evenings he would go home when he would say to the queen, 'Isn't it wonderful we had a great harvest today! Tomorrow the horses'll come in, the donkeys'll come in, they'll bring hus all this harvest to my stores an we'll become richer an richer.'

And the queen turned round, she said, 'Husbant, all yir riches in the world you may fetch fir me'll never make me happy.'

And he said, 'Wumman, what is it you really want? What will make ye happy?'

She says, 'Husband, I know you enjoy riches. But the only riches that ever I'll enjoy is a baby, a baby son or a baby daughter fir me to love an cuddle an caress, an fir you – to follow after you an be the next king!'

'Oh,' he said, 'I am strong, a real man, I'll go on fir many many years!'

'Well,' she says, 'husbant, you go on yir hunt, you shoot an you fight, you go among yir people. But what's about me – I'm left all alone – husband, I want a baby.'

'Well,' he said, 'we've tried many times, but life hes been unkind to us. But prob'ly something will turn up.' And lo and behold something did happen, she had a baby.

And he was born, a little boy with a hump on his back, not a humped shoulder, but a hump right in the centre of his back! And he was beautiful but completely ugly, because his knees and his chin seemed to meet when he was born. The queen called for the king to come and see the new baby. And when the king saw the baby he was so upset, because he was a big strong powerful man himself. She said, 'Look, husband, we have a baby, a beautiful boy – isn't he lovely!'

And the king took him, he stretched his legs out, he looked at him, saw this hump right in the middle of his back, and the king got so upset, said, 'A baby prince – a humpy prince – who in the world is ever wantin a humpy prince! Wumman, you longed fir something . . . in yir life you been curst with this baby!'

'Oh,' she says, 'husband, I love him!'

'Well,' he said, 'you might, but I don't; I'm disgraced! That can't walk before me, down through the courtroom an walk among the people . . . show off my son who's gaunna be the next king – with a hump on his back! It wouldn't be bad if it was jist his shoulder at was out o' place, but it's right in the centre o' his back, he is a born hunchback – he'll never be my son in no way!'

The queen loved him like nothing on this earth because he was a beautiful little boy – long golden hair – the only thing that was wrong with him was the hump on his back. And the queen used to pet it, try and shove it down with her hand and . . . she was pleased that God had given her a baby, even suppose it was a hunchback! She didn't care, suppose it was like a gnome, suppose it was the ugliest thing in the world, she just wanted something to cuddle and kiss and talk to while the king was off on his own. Someone to be with her, someone she could love, something from her own body. But a year passed by and the boy grew up!

He grew up a nice wee boy and he started to walk, but he had a hump on his back. But other ways he was perfect – quite intelligent, quite happy, quite kind – and he loved his mother like nothing on the earth. But the king couldn't look at him. As far as the king's concerned he didn't exist, he was no good to the king in any way. Truth was, the king was ashamed of him: he wouldn't take him in his hand, wouldn't walk him through the courtroom, wouldn't take him down to a meeting or to anything. And everybody wanted to see the king's son. The king made many excuses, 'Oh, the queen is busy, an the queen's doing this, the queen's doin that, the queen's givin him a bath'; but he would never show him to the court.

Till the people got fed up with this and they all said, 'Where is the prince? Where is the prince, we want to see the prince!'

And this upset the king greatly, he said to the queen, 'I can't stand it anymore. I can't stand it, I can't go on like this. We hev tae tell em "the prince is dead"!'

'But,' she said, 'husbant, it's my baby, I love him! He's my child!'

He said, 'He has tae die! Because it's either him or me – I can't stand to go fore all my couriers an all my people, show off a hunchback son that will disgrace me in my kingdom.'

The queen was so upset, she cried, she cried and cried.

But the king finally made up his mind that the baby had to go. She says, 'Husbant, what are you gaunna do with him?'

He says, 'Look, I'll not kill him an make you sad.' Now he had the power to; he said, 'I'll take him into the forest, leave him fir the wild beasts tae get him an you'll never know if he lives or dies.'

And the queen was broken-hearted! She says, 'Please!' and she begged and she prayed, she begged for the world to the king *not* to take her baby from her. But no, the king was stubborn.

He said, 'Ye're not gaun to shame me, I'm the king!' And he was the head o' the court, the head of the land – his word was law – 'He must go! There's no way in the world I'm gaunna have a hunchback son walk . . . if he wasna a hunchback,' he said, 'I'd be proud to show him to the people. I would love him, I would carry him, show him to the people, I'd be happy. But I'm not takin a hunchback in any way before my people an before my court; neither are you! He has to go.'

So very quietly, after he'd settled with his wife, he talked to two of his finest huntsmen who were his dearest friends, told them, 'You must take this child to the forest an destroy it, but don't tell the queen! You must destroy it immediately. Take it to the forest as *far* away from the palace as possible, kill it, don't ever bring hit back before me! An then I will tell the whole world, we'll have a funeral, we'll bury his remains in a cask in the castle gardens and everyone'll come, they'll feel sorry for me. An once more I'll be the king an I'll feel very happy.' So true to his words the next evening very quietly he arranged with the queen who was very sad – they took the queen's baby who was only one year old – wrapped him in a shawl.

The huntsmen took him away and quietly slipped into the forest. And no one ever knew a thing. Now these two huntsmen went for many miles into the forest. They were family men of their own, and the baby was so beautiful a child, lovely little boy! Because he'd a hump on his back . . . and they talked about it.

One says, 'You kill him.'

The other says, 'No, I cuidna kill him, I've two babies o' my own. If I killed him, I cuidna go home then to my wife tonight. You kill him!'

'Well,' he said, 'look, I can't do it.'

The other one said, 'Aye, neither can I.'

'Well,' he said, 'luik, the're many animals roamin in the forest tonight, wolfs an foxes an bears! Why don't we jist place him against a tree, quietly fade away an go back, tell the king that we destroyed him. An the king'll never know any better. Now we've rode many many miles from the palace, and a little infant of a year auld won't last very long in the forest.' So they finally made up their mind, they would leave the baby beside a tree. None o' them had the heart to kill it, it was so beautiful.

And they took this little bundle, they placed it beside a tree and they blessed themselves. They walked away, they left it to the mercies of the earth. The baby lay beside the tree, and the owls called and the birds went to sleep, and he lay there all night . . . and fell asleep.

But lo and behold, unknown to them in the forest lived an old woman, a very very old woman who was suffering from a terrible disease known as 'King's Evil'. And her face was in a terrible mess, it's a cancer o' skin disease. People believed in these olden days . . . it was like a leper . . . it jist travelled in the skin an when one bit healed another bit startit over. And when the bit that healed – it left terrible holes, terrible places in their face. And she lived in the forest, she was ashamed to show her face before anybody. Always in the early morning when she knew no one was around she would go into the forest, gather sticks for her fire. And she had this little house in the forest, she never came in contact with a human soul. She was self-sufficient, she gathered berries, made her own food, kept a lot o' hens and things, lived herself in the forest and took care of herself. She didn't want contact with anybody because she was so deformed. Very very rarely she ever came to the town, and when she did come for any rations or any food she needed, she always kept her face covered with a veil.

So this particular morning – she always rose early – she needed sticks for her fire and she walked into the forest. And she's picking bits here, picking bits there in her apron . . . when lo and behold she came to this large oak tree, and there sitting below the oak tree was the little bundle. She stopped and she looked, when she saw this, 'Upon my soul,' she says, 'a baby, a beautiful little baby!' And she picked it up, it smiled in her face, didn't even cry. And she carried it back to her little cottage in the forest, she cuddled it to her bosom, says, 'I wonder where you came from, little one?' Now she kept some goats in her little place in the forest, she milked the goats and fed the baby goats' milk. The baby laughed and giggled, never cried a minute. She says, 'I wonder where you cam from, little one; someone must hae left you here, they couldn't take care of ye. But *I'm* going to take care o' ye and you'll never want fir nothing as long as you live!' Now the little child was with the old woman, and he was quite happy. She did everything for him under the sun, she loved him dearly from her heart and he was a gift to her because she was a lonely old person.

Now the queen back many many miles away in the large town in the palace was sad, and sadder and sadder. She lay in bed, wouldn't eat, wouldn't drink, she would do nothing, and she pined away and she pined away. The king went up and tried to coax her to eat, but no, it was no use.

He says, 'Please, have something to eat!'

She says, 'I don't want nothin to eat, I don't want nothing, I want my baby.'

'You know it's impossible,' he said, 'you can't have yir baby.'

'Well,' she said, 'if I can't have ma baby, life is no good to me anymore.' And she pined away and pined away till finally she died.

Now days before that the king had had a funeral for his

baby son, he'd made a mock coffin and buried it in the palace churchyard. They came from all over . . . the king's son had died, the baby prince had died. King made up his mind, he'd kid on he was being very sad, but in his own mind he wasn't sad at all, it was just a formality. But when the queen died, the king was really sad, he knew in his own heart that he was the cause of his own wife's death – his queen died because he had sent her little baby to his death. And he thought, took second thought, 'If only, if I could overcome the thought of having a hunchback son my wife wad be alive today.' He really loved his queen, he really did. But the queen was dead and there was nothing he could do about it. They had their funeral for the queen, the queen was buried in a little churchyard within the palace. And the king was very upset, very very upset! Very sad – now he'd lost his baby and he'd lost his queen – all through his own fault. So he thought to his ownself, 'The best thing I can do is tae walk down to the village, walk among ma people an talk to them. It'll keep the worry off ma mind.'

He walked down to the town and walked among the people, and everyone said, 'Ir Majesty . . . sorry' here and 'sorry' there. When lo and behold who should he see come walking up the street but an old woman – with a veil over her face and a hood on her head, carrying a basket. And she's hurrying on. She's walking along the pathway and when she came to the king she stopped. She stepped off when she saw the king, off the path leading to the village.

And she said, '*On your way, Your Majesty, curse upon you!*'

The king said, 'What did you say, auld wumman?' And the old woman never said anything, the old woman hurried on.

But the king was walking down towards the path and he thought it queer, he wondered to himself, 'What did that auld woman say?' He thought he'd heard her saying 'curse upon you' but he wasn't sure he ever heard a word atall. And he looked back – and all in a minute something jagged his foot – right there in the path something jagged his foot when he looked round after the old woman. He saw the old woman disappear in the distance. (In these days they wore shoes made of skin, and between the foot and the skin wasn't very much – like moccasins – and it was easy for a thorn or anything that was sharp on the ground to jag your foot!) And the king, it was his toe, his big toe was pierced with some kind o' thorn or something the king felt in his foot.

But he walked on to the village, talked among the people and everyone said how they were sad, how they were so sorry for the king. In their own minds they weren't really sorry, but they talked about this and talked about that. The king walked round to try and find some comfort among his people, but he could find no comfort. Deep in his mind he had this worry about his queen and his little son whom he'd destroyed, all because of his own fault. But the more he walked, the sorer his toe began to come. And it got sorer and sorer. By the time he'd walked through the little village where his pals were, by the time he got home he could barely move his foot, it was in such a sorry state. He came into his room, had his meal and went to his chamber to lie down. And he ordered for his people to come, to look at his foot.

Now in these days they didn't have any doctors; they had court magicians, and they came, took off the king's boot just made of skin. They washed his foot and bathed his foot, they anointed it with oil and did everything. But it was throb-throb-throb-throb-throb-throb, and the king was annoyed, he was in pain. He said, 'You must do something for this, it's terrible sore. Youse people who are learned people, I pay youse so much money, youse must do something, I'm in terrible pain!' But from that day on and days after and days after, the king's foot got worse and worse and worse.

All round the country, they came from all places to try and cure the king's foot, but no way, he never got any better! And the king got a rest for his foot, he got pillows under his foot and he stuck it out the window! Just lay beside the window and he stuck his foot out the window. But all the time the days were passing and the months were passing, the king was getting older, the thorn in his foot was getting bigger and bigger! And it grew and it grew till a branch came from it! They sent for couriers from all over, wise men from all over the country to come and cure the king's foot, but there was no way in the world – if they pulled the leaves off – the next morning they were back again. And the king was in agony. The thorn in the king's foot grew and grew, and nobody seemed to help him, no way. The king offered rewards, he offered everything, he was in agony. People came from different countries, wise men came and examined it, they cut the thorn off his foot, shaved it, bathed it, anointed it with oil – next day it was back as far as ever – there's no way in the world that the king could get any peace or any rest. He never slept, he never slept in any way.

By the first year the king was annoyed, by the second year the king was terrified, by the third year the king had made many promises and he'd suffered all this pain. And he promised anything to anybody that would come and rid him of this disease in his foot. But no way could the king get any peace, he had two–three cat-naps, but always this nagging pain in his toe! And the more they came and cut it, every time they cut it, it always came again. The king said he was 'curst fir evermore', and he knew that his life was fading away. And the only consolation the king had was to lie by the window, hold his foot out in the cold wind, and lo and behold the only time that the king got any peace – when the wind was blowing from the forest – when the wind changed and was blowing from the forest, it blew a cooler breeze on the king's foot, the king would go to sleep. But the minute the wind changed, the pain was so bad the king woke up once more!

Now, through the king's suffering for many many years, the little boy and the old woman lived in the forest all together. And she taught him everything, she learned him to hunt, learnt him to shoot, and she schooled him, learned him everything under the sun till he became the age o' fifteen years old. He never was away from the forest in his life, and he called her his 'mother'. And as she got older, she got uglier. When one piece of her face healed, the other piece got broken out, till her face was just a heap of marks like potwarts. But the young boy loved this old woman like nothing on the earth. And he went on loving her.

Always in the evening he used to love to come aside the old woman because he had known nobody else. As far as he believed it was the only mother and the only friend he had in his life. When the cold winter winds were howling round the little house in the forest, he used to come up beside his old mother's knee, he would put his head on her knee, and he loved her. Because even though she was the ugliest being that you and me would take to be ugly, to him she was just an angel, she gave him everything he wanted. And it wasn't all one-sided, he worked hard, he cut sticks and dug the garden, he did everything in the forest for her, tended the goats, tended the hens, whatever she needed – and they had just the greatest understanding between them. Till one particular night, the wind was blowing strong and it was a terrible storm.

She sat down, said, 'Robin,' (she called him Robin because he looked like a wee robin beside a tree when she'd found him) 'Robin, come beside me, son, I want tae tell you a wee story.'

He said, 'Mother, what is it you want to tell me? Are you gaun to tell me a story?'

She says, 'Yes, Robin, I'm gaunna tell you a story, a story about yir father.'

He said, 'My father?'

'Yes,' she said, 'about yir father. Do you know, Robin, I'm not yir mother.'

'But,' he said, 'you must be ma mother, I don't remember anyone else but you!'

She said, 'I found you in the forest many years ago, I took you here an brought ye up like ma own child.' This upset him a wee bit when he heard this fir the first time.

'Well, where is ma real mother, who is my real mother?'

She said, 'Robin, it's a sad sad story I'm about to tell ye. Your mother was the queen, the most loving an nices an gentle queen there ever was in this land – our queen, *my* queen.' Robin never said a word. He listened and she said, 'Yir father is the king of the country many miles from here, an he was ashamed of you when you were a baby!'

And he said, 'Why was he ashamed?'

She says, 'Robin, because of the hump on yir back.' Now, he had grown this boy by fifteen, but he still had the hump on his back right between his shoulder blades. He was a little crooked, a little bent, but otherwise he was the most perfect boy in this world, fifteen years old, and all these years had passed by. 'But,' she said, 'your father sent you into the forest to get killed, and the huntsmen who were family people wouldn't kill you, left you under a tree. I pickit you up fourteen year ago, I took you and I brought you up.'

'But, Mother,' he says, 'what has that got to do with me? If they didn't want me as a hunchback then, they don't want me now.'

'But,' she says, 'look, this is something you must know, your father is still the king and he is sufferin terrible because of me.'

'But why, Mother,' he said, 'what did you do to hurt him?'

She said, 'I hurt him to pay him back for what he'd done to yir mother and what he'd done to you!'

'But,' he said, 'what has that got to do with me?'

'I think the time has come,' she says, 'that you mus go an settle the problem between yir father, you an me. Look at my face – what do you see?'

And the boy looked at her face, he said, 'Mother, I don't see nothing.'

She says, 'Look at these scabs on my face. Luik at my face, it's destroyed with Evil!'

He said, 'I don't see nothing out o' the way in your face.'

She says, 'Luik, this is known as King's Evil.'

'But,' he said, 'why did the king do this on you?'

She said, 'Robin, the king never done it on me. This is a disease that comes to people, an it can only be cured by the touch of a king – *who must put his finger on this* – an make me better.'

'Well,' he said, 'if the king . . . I'll go and find the king an make him come to you, Mother!'

She says, 'Robin, before you go and find the king, you must hear the rest of the story. Your father the king he is sufferin from a terrible wound.'

'What kind o' wound?' says Robin.

She said, 'He hes got a thorn in his foot at was put there by me fourteen years ago, an no one can ever cure it – excepts you – you're the only one! He has tried, he has offered rewards, he has sent people. He's had quacks an wise magicians come all over the world to try an cure his foot. An he's in agony, he has little sleep except when the wind blows from the forest. But you must go an get his promise, that *if you cure him, he'll cure me.*'

'Mother,' he says, 'I'll do anything fir you, anything in the world. Tell me, please, what I must do!'

She said, 'Tomorrow morning, Robin, you mus make yir way to the palace an tell everyone who meets you along the way, if you're stoppit on the way, that you have come to cure the king's foot. But before you cure the king's foot, you must ask him fir two promises!'

'Yes, Mother,' he said, 'I'll do that, I'll do it, Mother, yes! What is the first promise?'

'The first promise is, you must ask him to come back and touch my face!'

'That's simple, said the boy. 'If I get to the king an can cure his foot, I'm sure he'll be willin to do this fir me, if he's suffering as what you say.'

'But wait a minute,' said the old woman, 'he mus make another promise: he must leave you to be king while he goes an walks among his people as a tramp, an works an labours an toils in the fields fir two hunderd days. An you must become king, take his place while he is gone.'

'But, Mother,' said the boy, 'there's no way in the world the king is gaunnae let *me*, a hunchback as I'm known to be, take his place an be king – *I'm* not qualified to be a king!'

She says, 'You're qualified to be a king – you are the king's *son* – and the sooner he knows it the better. But don't ever tell him who you are, you must promise me, you must never tell him who you are! Just tell him you hev come to cure his foot, an before you took the thorn from his foot he must make these two promises to you!'

'Right,' says the boy, 'it shall be done!'

So, he sat and had his lovely evening meal, and went to bed. But he lay and worried about this till morning. He hated to part from his old mother in the forest, he had never been away from her all his life. He hated to have a walk among strange people – oh, he had seen many hunters and he'd seen people, he'd been in the village with her two–three times, but he just hurried on – she'd done her little bit o' shopping and she'd hurried back to the forest with the little boy, the hunchback by her side. Nobody paid very much attention, nobody ever knew they were seeing the king's son, he was just another traveller going about their business. So the next morning he had a little breakfast and said 'good-bye' to his mother, the old woman in the forest.

And she said, 'Don't worry, my son, everythin'll work out the way it shall be.'

He bade her 'good-bye' and said, 'Luik, I am not leavin you fir long, I'll be back.'

She said, 'I know you will, I know you will!'

'I'll be back,' he said,' an when I come back I will fetch the king. If you're worried about that face of yours, I'm not worried; but if that makes ye happy, I'll bring back the king.' And he put his arms round her, cuddled her and walked away towards the village.

He travelled on for a long distance, it was maybe fifteen miles to the village over paths, through forests, over hills, right down till he came to the town and the palace. And he made his way through the town, he knew the way – but he'd never been back at the palace – he made his way. Everybody looked at the ragged youth with the humpback walking up towards the palace. When he came up he was stopped by the guards.

They said, 'Where you goin, ragged youth?'

He said, 'I want to see the king.'

They said, 'You can't see the king, he's in terrible agony.'

He said, 'I have come to cure the king and let me pass!'

People said, 'He's come to cure the king!' Everybody'd give their life if the king was cured of this terrible thing that happened to him, so word spread from one to the other, 'He's come to cure the king! This is ae young man who's come to cure the king, mebbe he knows something, mebbe this is hit, mebbe *he's* come!'

Before there was anything else could happen, he was rushed forward into the palace into the king's chamber. He walked into his great hall, his great bedroom, and there was the king lying with his foot up on a cushion through the window. And the young man walked up, he stood in front of the king – knowing he was looking at his father for the first time. And the king turned round, he looked very sad and his beard was long, his face was thin from many years o' suffering. But the boy felt no sorrow for him.

The king looked round, said, 'Who are you? They tell me you've come to cure my foot.'

And the boy said, 'Yes, I hev come to cure yir foot, Ir Majesty, I've come to cure yir foot.'

The king said, 'It's not possible. Many have tried it, there's nothing fir me, I must go on sufferin fir many many years.'

The boy said, 'No, that is wrong! You shall not go on sufferin fir many years. *I* will cure yir foot.'

King said, 'How can a youth like you, especially a hunchback . . .' But he ignored what the king said, he never said a word. 'A hunchback!' he said, 'have you any powers in medicine?'

'Oh,' the boy said, 'I've no powers in medicine.'

'Well, why do you come here an annoy me?' said the king.

He said, 'I have come to cure your foot.'

The king said, 'Well, please, I'm in terrible agony – don't torture me any longer – cure my foot!'

'Not yet,' said the boy, 'just a minute. First, you must gie me two promises!'

The king said, 'Luik, get on with it, I'm in pain, in agony, I can't talk! I'm in pain an agony.'

'First, you must give me two promises,' said the boy.

'Yes,' said the king, 'yes, please, I'll give ye two promises. What is it you want – money, gold, jewels, anything – please, please get on with what you're gaunna do! Get my foot – take this pain from my foot!'

And the boy said, 'Just take yir time, you've suffert fir many years an a little time longer is not gaunna make any difference.' And the king was in agony.

'What is it you want?' said the king.

He said, 'I want you, bifore I cure yir foot, tae give me two promises!'

The king said, 'Luik, get on with it; I'll make yir promises, what is it you want?'

He said, 'You'll come with me to the forest an see my auld mother, an touch her face!'

The king said, 'That's a . . . I'll go anywhere!'

'Next,' said the boy, 'you mus let me rule yir kingdom fir two hundred days!'

The king said, '*You* rule my kingdom fir two hundred days?'

'Yes,' said the boy, 'rule yir kingdom fir two hunderd days!'

'An what am I supposed to do,' he said, 'while you rule my kingdom?'

The boy said, 'You shall walk among the peasants in the village, among the peasants in the town, an you shall toil, you shall wurk, you shall help them an you shall see what like is to life among the puir!'

The king said, 'Look, it's not very much to do, but if you will take this pain from my foot, I'll swear I'll give you my promise!'

And the boy walked up, he walked up and he walked round the window. He lifted the king's foot up, he rubbed his hand around the king's foot and he did that – he catcht the thorn and he pulled it out – he threw it through the window. And he rubbed the king's foot with his hand like that, and lo and behold the king's foot . . . the pain was gone, the agony was gone from the king's foot! 'Now,' he said, 'Ir Majesty, stand up!'

The king stood up – no more pain, no more nothing – no thorn, no nothing. King was as free as if it never happened! The king stood up, excited that the pain was gone, he felt like he never felt before for years, said, 'Where in the world do you come from?'

The boy said, 'I came from the forest tae help you. An you made yir promise.'

The king said, 'I am the king an I gev you ma promise, I won't break my word. I'll come with you right away, lead the way!' And the king walked out – as free and fit and happy as ever he'd been in his life – he danced a wee jig with his foot to see was it really true! And there was no more pain, no more nothing, there was no thorn in the king's foot anymore. The king was just like a lark, happy as could be, and he was so excited he said to the boy, 'This is magic!'

The boy said, 'No, it's no magic, no magic in any way.'

'Lead on!' says the king. The king called for horses immediately. Everyone was happy, 'The king is better, the king is better, the king is better, the king's foot is healed! This magic youth has worked wonders.' They made way for the king. The king ordered for two horses – the young boy, one, the king got another – and they rode to the forest. They rode on and rode on till they came to the little cottage in the forest.

And lo and behold the boy said, 'Stop!' there at the little house.

'Where have you brought me,' said the king, 'what place is this?'

The boy said, 'There's someone here I want you to see, someone who's been good to me an took care of me fir a long long time.'

The king felt very humble because the boy had done so much for him, and he wanted to show his kindness towards the boy. He stepped off his horse, he said, 'Lead the way.' And the boy led the way into the little house, and there sitting in an old chair was the old woman. The king said to the boy, 'What is it you want me to do, *who* do you want me to see?'

And the boy said, 'My mother.'

And the king looked: her face had got ten times worse since the boy left, and the king looked, he said, 'What kind o' person is that you have fir a mother?'

The boy said, 'That's my mother who's been guid to me.'

And the king said, 'What do you want me to do?'

He said, 'I want you to go over an touch her face with yir finger, because you are the king an she is sufferin from King's Evil. The only thing that can cure her is the touch of the king.'

The king said, 'No!'

The boy said, 'Remember yir promise!'

And the king thought again, 'Well,' he said, 'you've done so much fir me, it's little that I cuid do fir you.' And he walked forward, he touched one o' the wicked scabs on the old woman's face with his finger. She stood there and looked straight into his eyes, and lo and behold after the king had touched . . . an amazing thing happened to the old woman. Her skin became wrinkled but beautiful, all the marks and everything were gone. And lo and behold, there was a beautiful old woman, old and wrinkled but beautiful, there wasn't a mark on her face or a mark on her skin. And the boy was happy, he ran forward, he put his arms round her neck and kissed her. And the king was so happy and pleased that he had done something worthwhile for the first time in his life. They sat and they had a lunch together.

And the king said, 'I mus be on ma way, I have tae go home to my people. I've done something . . .'

The boy said, 'Wait, you must fulfil yir second promise!'

And the king said, 'Yes.'

And the woman turned round to the king, she said, 'Ir Majesty, luik, I know it's a hard request to ask fir.'

He said, 'Woman, is this yir son?'

'Well,' she said, 'he's believed to be my son!'

'Well,' he said, 'he might be a hunchback, but he's a wonderful boy.'

The boy said, 'I'm gaun back with you because you made the promise to me.'

King said, 'Well, be it so.' They bade 'farewell' to the old woman, they got on their horses and they rode back to the palace. They rode back, the king ordered everything – meals, a room for the boy and everything in the palace.

'Now,' says the boy, 'tomorrow morning you make yir promise good to me an everything will be well.'

The king said, 'It is very hard for me, I've lived as a king fir so many years I don't know what to do.'

The boy said, 'Jist do it! Go on yir way, meet the people, walk among them, work among them.'

'But,' the king said, 'I can't go as a king.'

The boy said, 'You're not goin as a king, you're gaun as a tramp.' He called for the most dirty old coat and the most worn shoes in the palace that anyone could find, and told the king he must dress in the rags and go among the people.

The king said, 'Well, so be it! You've cleared me frae all my pain an I feel wonderful, I feel great.' And the king wanted to go among the people. He felt he should, because he wanted to see this: he had taxed them, he had taken half o' their grain, he'd taken half o' their cattle, taken everything and he thought he'd want to go among the people, but he felt kind o' queer . . . that, as if a great change was coming over him. He didn't want to tax them anymore, he didn't want nothing from them, he jist wanted to be among them and be with them, talk to them and work in the fields. The great change came over him, he felt so queer he couldn't wait to be gone!

And the boy said, 'Look, I'll be here, I'll see that nothing goes wrong in the palace till you come back. You give orders that I've to take your place while you go out among yir peasants an among your people as a tramp. But only tell it tae the people in the castle, not to the peasants in the land.'

So early next morning true to his word the king put on his old scruffy shoes, ragged coat, the old ragged hat, scarf round his neck and walked away from the palace. And no one seemed to recognise him. Before he had left he had given orders that all orders in the palace were to be passed through to the young hunchback who would rule while he was gone for two hundred days. Only the people in the palace knew the difference, that the king was gone. And the king walked away, just a beggar.

And he travelled on for many days, he viewed the land and saw the crops o' corn. He saw the people, he walked among the people until he got hungry. He had no money, he had nothing, and he walked up to this particular farm, he asked for a job. And the man gave him a job to work at the harvest, he worked at the harvest and lo and behold he enjoyed it. He carted the corn in, he stooked the corn, he helped scythe the corn, he cut it, he dined with the old farmer and his wife and he had such a lovely time till the harvest was stacked and put in the sheds. Then they paid him a little wage and he said he must move on. And the king carried on from place to place, from day to day on his way working here, working there, digging ditches, building dykes, cutting trees, working among the people, and he enjoyed every moment! And he learned more than he had ever learned before in his life as a king, by walking and working among the poor people on the land – who his own kingdom depended upon!

Now the young hunchback Robin is in the palace, and all these people came in and they told him things, they took men before courts; he'd done orders, he gave orders and people realised that this young man who had come over seemed to work things more wonderful than the king. The king is gone, the taxes were lowered, less grain was taken in, people were allowed to have more, people were allowed more freedom, and this became wonderful. Where is the king? The king is gone, but everybody would say, 'We don't worry if the king's gone or no; this young man who's tooken over the kingdom, who the king has left in charge, is a more wonderful person than the king. He's doin more wonderful things,' and the effects began to creep into the people, in the village, in the town.

And the same thing began to happen to the king: he walked among the people, he talked to the people, he sat with them, he slept with them, he ate with them, and the days began to pass . . . till at last the two hundred days were up. And the king felt sad and weary that he had to report once more back to the castle. He didn't want to go! Now the hunchback in the palace had changed everything that the king stood for, and the people were so happy. When the king walked into the village on his way to the palace, he saw smiling faces, happy people in all the way. And he wondered about this because every time he went to the village and the town before, he never saw . . . people were always sad and wandered about with their heads drooped, nobody was smiling, nobody was happy, nobody was singing. The king passed fires, ken, people are singing, people are working, happy at their work! The king wondered, 'What's gaun on here? A wonderful change has come over the place.' And then he thought, 'It's all because of that boy – all because of him! But when I go back, I'm gaunna make sure that he's gaunna be paid well fir it.' And the king was a different man, a changed man completely!

He walked home to the palace, had a wonderful bath, had a wonderful wash, had a wonderful supper. And lo and behold, he couldn't wait to call the young man before him, the young man was called before him and he said, 'Luik, young man, I don't know what you've done to me – you made me well, you made me happy – I'm happier than ever I was before in my life, since I lost my queen!'

'Well,' the young man said, 'I'm happy too, because my mother is happy in the forest.'

The king said, 'Luik, I'm not fit to be a king; before, when I walkit across the land there were no smilin faces. You have taught me wonderful things, young man, an you're a hunchback. You're jist a common hunchback, and I'm a king. You have taught me more than I ever knew existed. Ma people are happy, I'm happy, I've never been happier before.'

'Well' the young man said, 'I had come to cure your foot, because the only reason I wanted to cure yir foot – you cuid do somethin fir me.'

And the king said, 'Please, stay with me; please, stay with me! Be my prime minister, be anything, be anything you want! Be my second in command and run my country fir me, an be my friend!'

And the youth turned round, he said, 'Look, Father, you hev denied me wonst – and left me to perish in the forest.'

The king said, 'What?'

He said, 'Father, you have denied me wonst an left me to perish in the forest because I was a hunchback. But, a hunchback was no good to you as a son, why should a hunchback to you be good as a friend? I am your son, the person you abandont in the forest many years ago.'

And the king went down on his knees, he cried and he threw his arms around the hunchback, he said, 'Please,

please, please, you've come back to me after all these years. An I'm sorry, please stay with me!'

And the hunchback said, 'No, Father. Now you're happy and free. An so am I. If ye ever want to find me, you can find me with ma mother in the forest, the only person that ever was good an kind to me.' And the hunchback walked away back to the forest to his old mother, and left the king to his own thoughts, his own ideas. And that is the last o' my story.

Boy and the Blacksmith

This narrative is 'a bloody guid yin', says Big Willie, my close traveller friend from Perth. And when we all travelled with horses in the fifties Willie was famed for his skill as a smith. Sometimes the story is told as a dream, and sometimes the women's heads are the only parts of their bodies twisted backside-foremost. But the following version is the one preferred by the travellers.

MANY years ago there lived an auld blacksmith, and he had this wee smiddie by the side o' this wee village. He wis gettin up in years; he wis a good blacksmith when he was young, but he wis getting up in years. But one thing this blacksmith had was an auld naggin woman who wadna give him peace, and the only consolation he cuid get was tae escape tae the comfort o' the smiddie an enjoy hissel in peace an quietness. Even though she was a bad, narkin and aggravatin him, she always brung him in his cup o' tea every day at the same time. But times wis very hard fir im an he was very idle, he hedna got much work to dae one day.

'Ah but,' he says, 'well, ye never know who might come in – I'll build up the fire.'

So he bild up the fire, he blowed up the smiddie fire an he sat doon. Well, he sat by the fire fir a wee while, he's gazin intae the fire when a knock cam tae the door. An the auld man got up.

'Ah,' he said, 'prob'ly this is somebody fir me; but whoever they are, they dinnae hae nae horses cause I never heard nae horses' feet on the road.'

But he opened the smiddie door an in cam this boy, this

young man, the finest-luikin young man he'd ever saw in his life – fair hair, blue eyes – an he wis dressed in green. An he had a woman on his back.

'Good mornin,' said the blacksmith tae the young man.

'Good mornin,' he said.

He said, 'What can I do fir ye?'

He said, 'Are you the village blacksmith?'

He said, 'I am – well, what's left o' me.'

'You wouldna mind,' he said, 'if you would let me hev a shot of yir smiddie fire fir a few minutes?'

'Oh no,' the man said, 'I'm no wurkin very hard the day. If ye can – come in and help yirsel!' The old man thought he wis gaunnae use the fire, mebbe fir a heat or something.

So the young man cam in, an he took this bundle off his back, left it doon o' the floor. An the old man luikit, he wis amazed what he saw: it was a young woman – but she was the most ugliest-luikin woman he hed ever seen in his life – her legs wis backside-foremost, an her head was backside-foremost, back tae front! And her eyes wis closed – wis as still-l-l as whit cuid be.

Noo the young man turned roond tae the blacksmith an he said, 'Luik, old man, you sit doon there and let me hev yir fire. An luik, pay no attention tae me – what I'm gaunna do – whatever ye see, don't let it bother ye!'

The auld blacksmith said, 'Fair enough, son!'

So the young man rakit up the fire an he catcht the young woman, he put her right on the top o' the fire. And he covered her up wi the blazin coals. He went tae the bellows, an he blowed and he blowed an he blowed an he blowed an he blowed an he blowed! An he blowed her till he burnt her tae a cinder! There were nothing left, nothing but her bones. Then he gaithert all the bones and he put them the top o' the anvil; he says tae the auld man, 'You got a hammer on ye?'

The old man went o'er an he gied him one o' thon raisin hammers, two-sided hammer. An he tuik the bones, he tappit the bones inta dust – till he got a wee heap on the top of the anvil – every single bone, he tapped it in dust. An the auld man's sittin watchin him! He wis mesmerised, he didna ken what wis gaun on.

The young man never paid attention to the auld blacksmith, not one bit. Then, when he hed every single bone made intae dust, gathert all in a heap, he sput intae it, sput intae the dust. An he rumbled it wi his hands an he stude back fae it. Then the amazines thing ye ever seen happent . . . the dust begint tae swell an beginst tae rise – an it rose up on the top o' the anvil – it tuik into this form. An it tuik into the form o' the bonniest young wumman ye hed ever seen in yir life! The beautifules young wumman ye'd ever seen in yir life an she steppit aff the anvil. The young man smiled at her, she pit her airms roond the young man's neck an she kissed him, she wis laughin and cheery. And the auld man never seen the likes o' this afore in his life.

The young man pit his hand in his pocket, tuik oot seven gold sovereigns an he says tae the auld man, 'Here, you take that fir the shot o' yir fire.' And he tuik the young lassie's airm. But before he walked oot the door he turnt tae the auld man, said, 'Luik, remember something: *never you do what ye see another person doin*!' And away he goes, closed the door.

But the auld blacksmith, he sat an he sat, an he sat fir a lang while. He put the seven gold sovereigns in his pocket. Then he heard the door openin and in comes this aul cratur o' a woman.

'Are ye there, John?' she said.

'Aye,' he said, 'Margaret, I'm here.'

'Well,' she says, 'I brought ye a cup o' tea. Hev you no got any wurk tae do instead o' sittin there in yir chair? Are there nothing in the world you cuid find, cuid ye no get a job to do? You been sittin there noo fir the last two hours and ye've done nothing yet! How're we gaunna live? How're we gaunna survive? Here's yir tea!'

Auld John took the cup o' tea up an he drunk hit. An he luiks at her, he thinks, 'I've spent a long time wi her, an she's jist about past hit. Wouldna I be better if I hed somebody young,' he said, 'tae have aroond the place instead o' luikin at that auld wumman the rest o' ma life?' So he drinks the tea as fast as he cuid. He had made up his mind – an afore you could say 'Jack Robinson' – he snappit the auld woman!

She says, 'Let me go! What are ye doin, auld man?'

He says, 'Come here – I want ye!' He catches her an he bundles her – intae the fire wi her. And he haps her up. She's tryan tae get oot an he's haudin her doon wi a piece o' iron. He's pumpin wi one hand an holdin her doon wi the other hand. An he pumpit an he pumpit, he blew an he pumpit an he blew. And her shrieks – you cuidha heard her oot o' the smiddie – but fainter an fainter got her shrieks, ti he finally burned her tae an ash! There were nothing left o' her. The last wee bit o' clothes belangin tae her, he put them in wi the tongs on the top o' the fire . . . He burned her tae an ash. He's cleart back the ashes – an there wis the bones o' her auld legs an her hands an her heid an her skull lyin there – the way he placed her in the fire. He says, 'That's better!'

He gathert all the bones he cuid gather an he put them the top o' the anvil, he choppit em, he rakit em up and he choppit em. And the wee bits that he cuid see that were hard, he choppit em again and rakit em, gathert them up in a nice wee heap. He got her a-all ground intae a fine dust! Fine powder. There's a good heap on the top o' the anvil.

Then he stude back, says, 'This is the part I like the best.' So he sput in it an he rakit it wi his hands . . . Nothing happent. He sput again intae hit – nothing – he tried hit fir about five or six times, but nothing happent. So he sut an he scart't his heid. 'Well,' he said, 'that's it. I cannae dae—' and then he remembered whit the wee laddie tellt him. 'Now,' he said, 'she's gone now.' And he felt kin o' sad, ye ken, she wis gone. 'What am I gaunnae dae? I'm a murderer noo, whit am I gaunnae dae?'

So he finally rakit all her bits o' bones intae an auld tin aff the anvil. He dug a hole in among the coal dross, he pit the tin in an he covert hit up. He went inta the hoose, he collectit his wee bits o' belongings that he cuid get – what he thought he wad need – his razor an his things that he needit an his spare claes. He packit a wee bag, locked the smiddie door, lockit the wee hoose an off he goes – never tae show his face back the[1] smiddie again – in case somebody would find oot whit he'd done.

So, he traivellt on an he traivellt on, here and there an he's gettin wee bits o' jobs here an wee bits o' jobs there, but this wis always botherin his mind. He traivellt on an he traivellt on. Noo he's been on the road fir about a year, but things begint tae get bad wi him. His claes begint tae get torn, his boots begint tae get worn, he cuidna get a penny nowhere. But he landed in this toon. An he's walkin intae the toon, when he cam to an old man sittin on a summer seat wi a white beard. So he sat doon beside him, he asked the auld man fir a match tae light his pipe. (There were nothing in his pipe – just dross!) So he got tae crack wi the auld man.

The man said, 'Ye'll be gan doon tae the village tae the gala, tae the fair!'

He said, 'Are there a fair on in the toon?'

'Oh, there's a fair here every year,' he said, 'a great fair gaun on in the toon. They're comin from all over tae try their luck at the fair. What's yir trade?' the auld man said tae him.

He said, 'I'm a blacksmith.'

'Oh well,' he said, 'you shuid do well there. The're plenty jobs fir blacksmiths, they're needin plenty wurk. But, isn't it sad – hit'll no be the same fair as hit wis last year.'

'How's that?' said the auld smith.

'Well, ye ken, it's the king's daughter,' he said. 'The poor lassie she's paralysed, an she's the only daughter belonging tae the king. He adored her tae his heart, brother. She cannae walk – somethin cam ower her, she cannae walk an she's in a terrible state – her puir legs is twisted, her head is

1 back the – back at the

turned backside-foremost. An the king would give anythin in the worl if somebody cuid dae something for her! But they sent fir quacks an doctors all over the worl, but naebody can dae nothing for her. But,' he said, 'seein yir a blacksmith, could ye help me?' (He had this wee box of tools, ye see.) 'I have a wee job fir ye.'

The old smith says, 'Right!'

Go roond: an it wis a skillet the auld man had, he said, 'Cuid ye mend that tae me?'

'Aye,' he said.

Tuik him roond the hoose an he gi'n him somethin tae eat. The auld smith mended the skillet, and he gien him two shillins. This was the first two shillins he had fir a long long while. So the auld blacksmith made his wey doon tae the toon an the first place he cam tae wis a inn. He luikit, folk were gan oot an in an the fair wis goin – oh, it was a great gala day!

'Well,' he says, 'I canna help it, fair here or fair there I mus go in here!' So he went in. An drink i' these days wis very very cheap, by the time he drunk his two shillins he wis well on! Then he cam oot an he walkit doon the street. Och, what a place he cam tae! But then he thocht tae his ainsel, 'I'm silly, I'm moich – me, a learned blacksmith – I cuid be well aff!' He says tae this man, 'Whaur aboots is the king's palace?'

What'd the man say, 'Up in the hill,' he said, 'that big place up in the hill – that's the palace. Up that drive, follow the drive!'

So wi the drink in his heid, he walked up tae the palace, an he wants tae see the king. The first he met wis a guard, king's guards.

The guard says, 'Where are ye goin auld man?'

He said, 'I want to see the king.'

An the guard said, 'What di ye want tae see the king fir?'

'I come,' he said, 'tae cure the king's daughter.'

'O-oh,' the guard said, 'jist a minute! If you come tae cure the king's daughter . . . where dae ye come fae? Are ye a doctor?'

'No, I'm not a doctor,' he said, 'I'm a blacksmith, an I come tae cure the king's daughter.' Immediately he wis rushed intae the king's parlour an pit before the king and the queen. The auld blacksmith went down on the floor o' his knees an he tellt the king, 'I can cure yir daughter, Ir Majesty.'

'Well,' the king said, 'if you can cure my daughter, I'll make ye the richest man . . . ye a blacksmith?'

'Aye,' he said, 'I'm a blacksmith.'

'Well,' he said, 'I'll give ye a blacksmith's shop an everything ye require, and all the trade! I'll see that nobody else goes nowhere, excepts they comes to you – if you'd cure my lassie. Make her well is all I require! But,' he said, 'God help ye if anything waurse happens tae her!'

The auld smith said, 'Have you got a blacksmith shop?'

'Oh,' he said, 'they've got a blacksmith shop here; in fact, we've one fir wir own palace wurk an ye'll not be disturbed.'

'Well,' he said, 'hev ye plenty smiddie coal?'

'Come,' the king said, 'I'll show ye myself, I'll take ye myself tae the smiddie.' He went down, an all the smiths were at work in the palace smiddie. He said, 'Out, out, out, everyone out!' He locked the back door. He says, 'There – anvil, fire, everything tae yir heart's content.'

The auld smith kinneled up the fire, pumped it up – blowed it till it wis goin! He says tae the king, 'Bring yir daughter doon here an I don't want disturbed! I don't want disturbed.'

O-oh, jist within minutes the young lassie wis cairried doon o' the stretcher an placed i' the smiddie. The auld man says, 'Now, everybody out!' He closed the door. An the young lassie's lyin, legs twistit, head backside-foremost – the identical tae the young wumman that he had seen in the smiddie a long time ago! The smith said, 'If he can dae it, so can I!'

So he kinnelt up the fire an he placed her on the fire. He blowed, and he pumpit an he blowed an he blowed, an he blowed an he blowed an he blowed an he blowed. And he burnt her till there were no a thing left. (Noo, he had tellt the king tae come back in two hoors. 'Two hoors,' he tellt the king, 'yir daughter'll be as well as cuid be.')

So, efter he collectit all the bones oot the fire, he put them on the top o' the anvil. He got the hammer and he choppit an he choppit, he grint them all doon and he gathered them all up, put them on the top o' the anvil. An he sput in it. He waitit. He mixed hit again. An he sput an he waitit. But he sput an he waitit, he sput an he waitit, he sput an he waitit. But no, there was no answer, nothing wad happent. Then he heard a knock at the door.

He says, 'That's them comin fir me. Ach well – it's death fir me an the're nothin I can dae aboot it.' He opened the door, and in cam the young laddie, brother! In walked the young laddie an he looked at the blacksmith.

'*Didn't I tell you*,' he said, '*a long time ago, not tae dae whit ye see another body daein*!' And he drew his hand, he hut the backsmith a welt the side o' the heid and knockit him scatterin across the floor! 'Now,' he says, 'sit there an don't move!'

The young laddie gaithert the ashes that wis scattert on the top o' the anvil in his hands, an he sput in them. Then he mixt them up, an he waitit . . . a thing like reek cam oot o' the anvil aff o' the bones, a thing like reek cam oot. Then the thing took a form . . . the mos beautiful lassie ye ever seen – the king's daughter back – laughin and smilin like the're nothing happened!

And he said, 'You sit, don't move! Don't you move one move! Sit an wait till we're gone before you open that door!' He walked over an he pit his hand inta his pocket, 'But, I'm no gaun tae lea ye bare-handed—' he says, 'haud yir hand!' tae the auld blacksmith. 'Noo, remember again: *never never dae whit ye see another body daein*!' Another seven gold sovereigns in the auld blacksmith's hand. 'Noo,' he says, 'remember, *never let hit happen again as long as ye live*! And don't open that door till we're gone.' Jist like that the young laddie an lassie walkit oot.

An then there were a clappin o' hands an the music startit, and everything died away. The auld blacksmith sat an he sat and he sat . . . then he heard a knock at the door. He got up and he opened the door, in cam his auld wumman.

She said, 'Are ye there, John?'

'Aye,' he said, 'God bless ma soul an—'

She said, 'Dae ye never think o' doin any kin o' wurk atall, do ye sit an sleep all day? Nae wonder we're puir.' She said, 'Here's yir wee cup o' tea – drink it up – I see a man comin alang the road wi a horse, an you better get the fire kindled up!'

'Thank you, Maggie,' he said, 'thank God, Maggie, thank you, my doll, my darlin, thank you!' An he pit his airms roon her, he kisst her.

She says, 'Ach ye go, John, what dae ye think yir daein? It's no like you ataa! Were ye asleep, were ye dreamin?'

'Mebbe,' he said, 'I wis dreamin, Maggie, mebbe I wisna. I better kinnel the fire up.' He luikit doon: here's a man comin doon the road wi a pair o' Clydesdale horses.

He tuik the horses into the smiddie, the man pit the horses in the smiddie, an he said, 'John I want a set o' shoes.'

'Well,' he says, 'wait a minute, I hev tae go intae the hoose fir some nails. I keep em i' the hoose.'

Man says, 'I'll jist light ma pipe bi the smiddie fire ti ye come back.'

Aul Jock went roond the hoose. He ways to the aul woman . . .

She says, 'Ye've nae tobacca!'

He says, 'I want ma pipe an my tobacca.'

She says, 'We need tobacca – it's finished an ye'll hev tae wait till we get money – when ye get them horses shod. Ye ken we've got nae money fir tobacca.'

Shoves his hand i' his pocket, he said, 'We've nae money hev we?' Hand in his pocket, brother – seven gold sovereigns in his pocket – he says, 'Here, Maggie!'

She says, 'The name o' God, where you got that?'

He said, 'I made that while you thocht I wis sleepin.' An that's the last o' ma story. So ye can believe that – if it's true or a lie!

Afterword

Duncan Williamson was born in a tent on the shores of Loch Fyne, near the village of Furnace in Argyll, on 11 April 1928. he was the seventh of a family of sixteen. His father was Jock Williamson, born in 1892, a travelling basketmaker and tinsmith. Betsy Townsley, his mother, was born in 1895 in Muasdale, Kintyre. Duncan can recite the genealogy of his family back to his great-great-grandparents. Both Duncan's parents were illiterate, but his forebears on both sides were famed singers, pipers and storytellers, and had an enormous wealth of orally transmitted lore.

The King and the Lamp is dedicated to Duncan's mother's mother, old Bella Macdonald, who was a legend in Argyll – still is to this day. Duncan recalls her vividly: 'Nobody would turn Bella Macdonald from their door when she came hawking, because they thought it was bad luck to turn old Bella away. She was like a fairy! She was small and was so kind-hearted she had a pleasant word for everybody. I mean, if she went to somebody's door and they did turn her away, she would say, "God bless you, missus and thank you very much for your kindness," and walk away without spite.

'Her son, my Uncle Duncan, stayed with his mother all the days of his life. After travelling Perthshire and before the long cold winter months set in each year, he'd say, "Granny, I think the best thing we can do is mak wir way back to Furnace tae your dochter Betsy and Johnnie. At least we'll have a good place to stay, auld wumman, and you've got a bing o' friends in Argyllshire." Uncle Duncan could bring her back there and my father, being lonely, with about sixteen weans and just my mother to talk to, welcomed his brother-in-law. Father would say, "Okay, Dunkie, we'll just lift the side o' the barrikit, brother. I'll pit yir wee tent for you and Granny aside the barrikit". So he opened the main tent, which was as big as a large living room, drew a couple of sticks aside, and built Duncan's wee tent. It was just another room added to the kitchen. We used the same fire and Granny was happy to be back with her daughter Betsy; now she had her daughter, she had her son and all her grandbairns. She had her pipe and could sit by the fire and crack. My daddy always kept a big fire in the middle of the tent, just on the ground. But there was no drink, no, no drink. It was too hard to get food, never mind money for drink. When the dark winter nights came Uncle Duncan would tell stories past the common and Daddy would tell a story. My mother would tell a crack and then – "Come on, Granny, tell us a story!" There were fifteen or twenty of us in there, but we weren't strangers, we were all our own family and she felt happy – she was home. But anyway, that was the story, how much happiness we had. We were poor, really poor, we'd had hungry times. But you believe me, we had some good times too. It was really good – what we wanted in one thing we gained in another, see what I mean, we couldn't lose. We had our granny whom we loved so much, we had our uncle whom we loved so much, and we had our father and mother to tell us stories. Food isn't everything in the world; that's all we really looked for. We didn't pay any rent or need any electricity, we just bought a bottle of paraffin for the wee crusie lamp hanging inside the barrikit, which gave enough light for everybody.'

THE TRAVELLER'S WAY OF LIFE, 1914–55

Life was hard for the travellers, an outcast minority group, but the hardest time was at the beginning of World War I when fathers were called to the army and mothers were left alone to take care of the children. They needed their fathers because travellers were very very poor in these days, without the luxurious caravans, cars, lorries and televisions many have today.

In winter they stayed in one place in a barrikit, a three-part structure made from strong saplings bowed and tied, covered with canvas and other suitable materials, anchored to the ground with big ropes and rocks. The barrikit was dome-shaped, twelve feet high with a hole at the top for the fire-smoke and fifteen feet across, with room for seating up to twenty people. Kitchen tables were on one side, trunks and boxes on the other side for clothes, keepsakes, the man's pipes, tinmaking tools and so on. There was plenty of head-room for standing, hanging up rabbit skins and wet clothes. The floor was earthen with an open fire in the middle – 'if the fire wasnae shared you werenae welcome.' On either side of the dome were smaller bow tents made from young rowan, birch or hazel saplings bound together at a height of about five feet. These were the sleeping quarters separated by entrance covers from the main barrikit. One was for the children, one for the parents and possibly another for a family relative. A drain was dug around the whole structure to channel away rain and melting snow. Before the family started travelling again, the barrkit was burned and a new one made the following autumn.

But in the month of March, or April, when they moved off, every child would have to help carry something – a certain amount of clothes, canvas, sticks and string to tie the sticks for the bow tent, a hatchet for splitting logs, a saw for cutting firewood, the snotem [an iron crook for hanging pots over the open fire], the tea kettle, cooking utensils and basins for washing at the riverside. Travelling was really hard – I mean, you were tired and you wanted to sit down to rest but your father kept walking on.

No food was carried, the mother would have got their food as they went. She sold the father's handmade wares, baskets or tin items, at farmhouses or in villages. If she couldn't get money she traded them for food: she would prefer this, because shops were very far between. When the father came to a camping place he'd lay down his bundle and say, 'Children, we're staying here for the night.' The children took all they were carrying and left it down beside his bundle. He would say, 'Children, you know what you've got to do!' Right, some would go for sticks, some for water. While he put the bow tent up – one long enough to accommodate all the family asleep – and while the children brought firewood, the mother kindled the fire. There were no tables or chairs, spoons, knives or forks. The mother carried ten or twelve tin plates the father had made and one ladle for putting meat on the plates. No matter what the children got to eat, they ate it with their fingers. Then the mother would make the bed at the very back of the tent for the youngest ones, the two- to three-year-olds who were usually sleepy. The father would go for his bundle of sticks and packed them on the fire, right close to the tent outside the door. (The bow tents had no inside fires.)

The children all sat round the fire and as the night got darker they crept in closer! They got kind of frightened if they were in a strange place, but the father would always keep his big tools for making tin wares lying beside him in case he should need them for defence. Then they would say, 'Daddy, tell us a story.' He'd say, 'Well come on there, weans, gather round, I'll tell ye a story.' During the summer months it was likely that four or five travelling families would meet in the one camping place (until the mid-1950s when large numbers of the travellers' traditional camping sites – regularly used by certain families for centuries – were closed or destroyed by those in authority). If families were related to one another, their tents would be built in a circle around one fire; otherwise the tents were spaced wider apart with separate fires. At night-time after supper, the men would get together around the fire. They would start talking and telling 'cracks', short stories, to each other. One would say, 'I ken a story for the weans,' and they would come in close to the fire – suppose there had been a dozen you could have heard a pin drop. He might have told them a ghost story to make them quiet and stay close.

The most terrifying aspect of life for a traveller child would have been the encounters with schoolboard officials which sometimes resulted in a child being taken from their parents, brothers and sisters, and put away to home-schools.[1] The law required one hundred and twenty days in school annually for each child aged between five and fourteen. But some districts were stricter than others. Dumbarton, Greenock, Paisley, Glasgow (and for thirty miles around), Ayrshire and Stirling were areas where traveller children were taken to home-schools.[2] It didn't matter if the children were dressed like bene hantle [cant for 'gentry'] the police made the family stand in the road while the Cruelty Inspector said, 'Look, you and you never attended school (if there was no proof to the contrary, i.e. officially marked attendance cards) – right, get into the car – off to the home!' Many of the children of travelling families ended up there before and after World War I. But some districts didn't bother. In Perthshire, Angus, Fife, Argyll and Aberdeen the authorities maintained that the traveller children weren't suffering as long as they were along with their mummies and daddies.

Travellers often went up glens around Aberfeldy, Killin, Pitlochry and Perth and no one cared if the children weren't in school, for they were helping their fathers and mothers. That's all the education they needed – to learn how to survive. But the children who were interested in schooling got books and taught themselves if they wanted

1 home-schools: officially named 'industrial' or 'day industrial schools', these were not orphanages or boarding schools; but were certified institutions (thirty in Scotland at the time of World War I) operating until 1937 after the Day Industrial School Act, 1893, where tinker children would have been committed if their parents were found to be neglecting their education, in accordance with Section 118 of The Children Act, 1908.

2 See 'Report of the Departmental Committee on Tinkers in Scotland' (HMSO Edinburgh, 1918)

to. Traveller children were taught to work when they were five years old. The first job would have been thinning turnips on their hands and knees. From the age of three or four they experienced the labour by sitting on their mothers' backs and watching. Potato gathering was the most important contribution the young children made towards the family's maintenance – with all children chipping in, one week's pay might more than equal the total income of the previous half-year.

More valuable than learning how to read and write were the skills of the traditional trades traveller parents taught their children. Traveller women took their daughters with them everywhere, showing them every little quirk and corner of the hawking business. And hawking went on every day. If you didn't hawk, you didn't eat. The mother's main role was food supplier. If a young traveller lassie did not know how to sell, to beg or go to the houses, her future was doubtful: young traveller lads, potential husbands, might speak of her, 'Och, she's a bonnie lassie richt enough but what good is she? She's only fit for the country folk, no good enough for a traveller. What can she dae? She cannae beg or hawk or sell because her mother never trained her.'

Some traveller women didn't train their daughters to hawk round the houses because they wanted them to find other lines of work, get off the road and be something. Once I overheard my mother say, 'Lassie, if ye live the life that I live ye'll never be any better, all you'll end up wi is a bing o' weans and dae the things that I've done.' Some lassies didn't want to do it because they felt deeply ashamed, and in these cases the mothers never forced them: it was not uncommon for the village children to shout, 'Oh, look at the tinkies, look at the tinkies!' at a group of travellers hawking houses. But there were also young travellers who weren't bothered by the rude remarks of the country folk. A lassie who was not taught to be 'a real traveller woman' very likely remained single until the age of seventeen or eighteen, which was considered old to be single. The lassie who was as good as her mother at hawking would have been 'snapped up' by a traveller laddie at a very early age, perhaps fourteen.

For a traveller laddie there was no choice. It didn't matter what he could do, he was qualified to marry a traveller woman. The fathers taught their sons every single thing – poaching, basketmaking, tinsmithing. The sons were the favourites. They were interested in whatever their fathers did: they knew if they didn't watch and do the things their fathers did, they couldn't do it for themselves when it came to their turn.

Among the old travelling people marriage was a very serious ans strictly defined event. According to traveller law, a man and woman were married once they spean a night together out of sight of their parents. And travellers marry for life. A young man who has a young wife can come in to an encampment of travellers, crack and tell stories, sit and make baskets and feel free. As a married traveller man or woman you enjoy all the privileges of being in and joining the family circle. Birth is also a very important event – when news that a baby is born to a young couple reaches travellers, they will go and see – even if it means walking for miles, and bring what they can aford to the new baby. They do this because they believe that new baby. They do this because they believe that new baby might marry into their family, might become one of theirs, which naturally does happen among these people! All travellers are connected to each other in Scotland, connected to one extended kin group. Death is the most sacred event, when passage to the Other World is carefully prepared. As a traveller you are buried with a little cup, a piece of bread and a coin. Death is a beginning of time, when you really come to live. You need your jug and your wee piece of bread with you to carry you on your journey and your silver coin to pay your way into the Land of Eternity.

SOURCES; TRAVELLER BELIEFS

The King and the Lamp is a collection of stories drawn from books Duncan Williamson and I have already had published: the first, *Fireside Tales of the Traveller Children* (Canongate, 1983), was composed for a children's audience, to educate young people, travellers and non-travellers alike, about the wealth of heritage in traditional story-telling. The first part of *The King and the Lamp* includes four stories ('The Hunchback and the Swan', 'The Goat that told Lies', 'The King and the Lamp' and 'The Boy and the Boots') from *Fireside Tales.* 'The Cockerel and the Fox', 'The Fox and the Goat', 'Lion and the Four Bulls' and 'Boy and the Snake' were fist published in *The Genie and the Fisherman* (Cambridge University Press, 1991), fifteen Scottish traveller tales presented in a graduated collection for primary school children. Making up the balance, and at the core, of Fireside Tales of the Traveller Children (part one of *The King and the Lamp*) are four stories chosen from our Christmas collection, *Tell Me a Story for Christmas* (Canongate, 1987).

The first four stories of The Broonie, Selkies and Fairies (part two of *The King and the Lamp*) were published by Canongate (1985) in a book by the same title. 'Mary and the Seal' was originally published in *Fireside Tales*, and 'Selkie Painter' was the first of fourteen *Tales of the Seal People* (Canongate, 1992). These stories are based in the clan Williamson traveller territory, Argyllshire and Scotland's West Coast – from Kintyre north to Appin and inland from Campbeltown to Glen Fyne. All the stories here have a moral thrust and an 'Other World' theme.

Travellers believe seals are just folk, sea-people. Selkies (or 'silkies' a word derived from the softness of the skin of the seals) means the same to them as 'seal-folk' or 'seal-people. Not all seals are selkies, but some can take over the form of a human being, be a human, or take away a human to become a seal. This was taught down through the ages among the travelling folk. Where do the stories come from? Duncan Williamson got more selkie stories from the country folk than from the travellers. Most of the stories started with those Gaelic-speaking non-travellers who had wee crofts on the shore.

Another deep belief with the travellers about the Other World concerns the fairies. You see, travellers travel a lot during the summer months with their weans. Now, they don't like them to be cruel, no way in this world, and hurt wee animals and pull wee flowers. You know the contrivances of weans, they'll get into wicked things. Taking wee moths and pulling their wings off, or killing a butterfly in the summer-time, or pulling the heads off the wee flowers – that's evil, according to the tradition, that would bother the fairies. Traveller children are taught this; it is a kind of code, a discipline to keep them in hand. For example, you don't touch a moth – it could be a fairy in disguise. Moths and butterflies are associated with the fairies. You see, if the old travellers had got a curse put on them, they made a butterfly out of the tree bark. That was to break the curse. They cut a strip of bark and made a shape of a butterfly and kept it till the curse went off them. There are many cracks and tales about the fairies with the travellers. There's plenty of folk believe they have heard 'a fairy tune', music played on the fairy pipes or the fairy fiddle. And if anybody is a good piper, the travellers say he can 'play like a fairy', meaning he plays the right notes in the right manner. Fairies never teach people lessons, but they have 'gifted' people. If a traveller woman is really good at reading hands, telling fortunes truthfully, travellers say that woman has 'the gift fae the wee folk'. The gift was not made to her, but to her mother and her mother before her and her mother before her – you see, the gift passes on. And if a wean is clever – can stand at six months or walk at nine months – they say, 'Oh, that wean's gifted . . .'

In the summer-time if a wean is born to a fairy at the same time as a wee wean is born to a mortal, and the fairies know their baby is going to grow up to be a 'mongol' and is never going to be right, they won't keep it. The fairies only keep babies that are going to be healthy, strong, and clever. So, before they would destroy or kill a deficient baby, they will switch it over: they will go and take a mortal wean, and put in its place their one, and let the mortal folk look after it. In the story of the 'Taen-Awa', the fairy wean that comes is evil. It knows it isn't in its own dominion and that its own folk have put it away among strangers. That's why it cries so much – to return the fairies' wicked deed. But the travellers have a protection against the fairies, you see! My mother used to stick a needle in the wean's bonnet at night-time – the fairies can't take the wean as long as something made of steel is fastened to its clothes. The fairies steal babies during the three months of summer (May–July), and some travellers never get their weans back. Some are wee delinquent weans all the days of their lives. If there is a retarded person in the family, travellers believe this wean was given to them when their own one was 'taen awa'. But they love it just the same; even though it is bad and wicked, it is still loved.

The people of the Other World, the selkies and fairies, have the freedom, have the power, they are immune from persecution by the local public and can't be disturbed. People of the Other World are part of nature, and the traveller Williamsons believe most strongly in a spirit of nature called 'the Broonie'. Broonie stories are different from other kinds of story: they have no happy ending, they only have a lesson. That's why the Broonie couldn't come as a king or a prince, nor as a soldier or policeman or priest. If the Broonie came in the form of a minister, how was he going to walk up to a house and teach people a lesson? If a priest or a doctor or a lawyer came to a body's house, they would change completely; they wouldn't be theirsel but putting on a front to welcome a high person. No, the Bronnie always comes in the same form – the wee old tramp man, about five feet tall, with the wee white beard and the two blue eyes, the kindly old creature of a man who never insults, never hurts, is always looking for work and he's always hungry. His famous meal, he loves a bowl of porridge and milk, or a bowl of soup. (See 'The Broonie's Farewell'.) It's something that goes back many many years, long before your time and mine, long before Christianity . . . about the supernatural being who was cast down to take care of us, the humble folk. You see, the Broonie is a spirit that never dies. It isn't exactly the blueness of his eyes, it's their brightness and youth! The travellers believe dullness is a sign of old age; so as far as they believe the brightness of the blue eyes is to show that youth and the spirit are *in his eyes.*

Duncan Williamson's great repository of 'Jack tales' is the source of part three of *The King and the Lamp*. 'Jack and the Devil's Purse' was first published in our Canongate collection of devil stories *May the Devil Walk Behind Ye!* (1989). 'Jack and the Witch's Bellows' is here reprinted from *Fireside Tales*, and the other two, 'Death in a Nut' and 'The Ugly Queen' were published in our well received Penguin collection, *A Thorn in the King's Foot* (1987). The Jack tales were so popular, and time-honoured, that three collections were proposed for publication, after our first *Don't Look Back, Jack!* (Canongate, 1990). For further comment on the significance of this folktale genre see Barbara McDermitt's Introduction to this volume.

The final group in *The King and the Lamp* is a selection from the twenty-four stories, *A Thorn in the King's Foot* (Penguin, 1987 and Mondadori, 1990, an Italian translation). The travellers call these *barrie mooskins,* that is, very good stories (cant). After narrating 'The Thorn in the King's Foot' Duncan explained, 'It's what you call "a story for a winter's evening". As I told ye, it's no a story fir tellin i' schools, hit's a story fir when ye *want* tae sit round an listen tae a story.' Long winter tales involve the complicated, psychological development of a character, not unusually a king; in contrast to those simpler stories with a higher density of changing scenes, as in most Jack tales.

The telling of long stories was in circumstances where the narrator could break for intervals, to have a cup of tea or perhaps take up other activities. This was one sure way of building suspense, and the quality of attention shown by traveller listeners to their story-teller nurtured his art, sustained him. Duncan has explained, 'It wis whan all the children went to sleep and all the people who were fed up listenin tae this tales went away to bed, an some people who loved stories, mebbe two and three would sit round the fireside, they'd put on mair fire, make more tea and carry on with the story. And they all had to stop for a cup o' tea or a crack and a smoke, an then carry on the next bit. Noo that's the wey it wis taught to me, that's the wey hit went on.' 'The Giant with the Golden Hair of Knowledge' and 'The Thorn in the King's Foot' were each told in this way over a period of several hours, with breaks in the narration and intervals for refreshment.

The twenty-six stories making up *The King and the Lamp: Scottish Traveller Tales* I have written from my *verbatim* transcriptions of story-telling sessions, hundreds we recorded for the Sound Archives of the School of Scottish Studies, Edinburgh University from 1976 to 1986. Twenty-three of the tales have been anglicised, with their dialogues retaining as much of the narrator's spoken dialect as I have deemed possible – intended for a readership not necessarily Scottish and for folk who may never have heard Scots. But three stories, 'The Cockerel and the Fox' (opening the collection), 'Tatties from Chuckie-stanes' and 'Boy and the Blacksmith' (ending the work) are dialectal transcriptions, showing the rich tapestry of sound created by a narrator thoroughly engaged with his own most natural audience, close traveller friends and family members.

Linda Willamson
Edinburgh, June 2000

References

The Concise Scots Dictionary, ed. Mairi Robinson. 1985 Aberdeen: Aberdeen University Press.

Original recordings lodged in the main chronological series of tapes in the Sound-recording Archives of the School of Scottish Studies, University of Edinburgh. SA 1976/62 to 1986/4.

'Report of the Departmental Committee on Tinkers in Scotland'. 1918 Edinburgh: HMSO.

Tocher: Tales, Songs, Tradition, Selected from the Archives of the School of Scottish Studies; No. 33 (pp. 141–87). 1980 Edinburgh.

Williamson, D.

1983 *Fireside Tales of the Traveller Children*. Edinburgh: Canongate.

1985 *The Broonie, Selkies and Fairies*. Edinburgh: Canongate.

1987 *Tell Me a Story for Christmas*. Edinburgh: Canongate.

1989 *May the Devil Walk Behind Ye*! Edinburgh: Canongate.

1990 *Don't Look Back, Jack*! Edinburgh: Canongate.

1992 *Tales of the Seal People*. Edinburgh: Canongate.

Williamson, D. and L.

1987 *A Thorn in the King's Foot: Folktales of the Scottish Travelling People*. Middlesex: Penguin.

1991 *The Genie and the Fisherman: And Other Tales from the Travelling People*. Cambridge: Cambridge University Press.

1996 *Rabbit's Tail*. Cambridge: Cambridge University Press.

Glossary

ae	a certain (person)
afore, fore	before
ainsel	self
amines	most amazing
amint	am I not
an	than
ane	one
as low as	as sure as the death of
at	that
away with the birds	gone mad
awfa (e), an	a great many
ay(e)	always; yes, indeed
bachle	misbehaved man
back	back at
bairn	child
bannock	round flat oatmeal cakebarrie
bargued	wrangled
barrie mooskins	very good stories (cant)
barrikit	large dome-shaped traveller tent, winter quarters
beautifules	most beautiful
ben	further into
bene hantle	gentry
bide	stay
bild	built
bilow	below
bing, a	a great many
bit, a	a small piece of
bithout	without
blethering	trivial talking, babbling
bonnie	beautiful
bow tent	small summer structure built of saplings bowed and tied
Broonie, the	the spirit of nature, the last of a generation
burk	kill secretly and sell body for research; *from* Burke; body-snatcher
burn	stream
by my lane	without a companion
byre	cowshed
cam	came
canny	careful(ly)
carry-on	rowdy behaviour, mischief
catch	take

ceilidh	song and story get-together (Gaelic)
chuckie-stanes	white pebbles
clypes	lies, idle reports
collie	black and white sheepdog
collop	slice of meat
cool	cowl, close-fitting cap
country folk	non-travellers
couples	pairs of rafters
cowpled	overturned, over-balanced
crack	chat, news, gossip; short story
cratur	dear one (creature)
creel	deep basket for carrying fish, etc.
croft	Highland farm
crusie	open lamp with a rush wick
cry	call
dashit	damned
day, the	today
deith	death
destroyed	avenged
done	did
doubt	expect, believe
dram	small drink of whisky
drop, wee	small amount of (liquid)
efter	after
em	them
er	her
event	even
fae	from
fasselt	was busy; *from* fassen
feart	afraid
flyer	cleverer
forbyes	as well, besides
freends	friends
gang	go
garron pony	small, sturdy, Highland horse
gaun; -na(e)	going; going to
gets on to	attacks with words, accuses
gev	gave
gie; gied; gien	give; gave; given
girnin	grumbling, fretting peevishly
gloamin	twilight; dusky
grannies' tales	old wives' tales
greet; gret	cry; cried
guddle	catch fish with the hands
ha(e); hev	have
haet, a	nothing at all
ha'penny	halfpenny coin
haps	covers
heck	wooden press for holding hay so a cow can stand and chew
hen-wife	wise woman who deals in poultry
hes	has
het	heated
hissel	himself
hit	it (emphatic)

hoolits	owls
hummed and hawed	discussed, argued
hunderd	hundred
hunkers	haunches
hurl	pull, push, or whirl along
i', ind	in
im	him
ir	your
jeejament	cursed
jist	just
keek	peep
ken	know
kinneled	kindled
knowe	hillock
kye	cows
landed	arrived
lea	leave
learned	taught
look at	make any impression upon
mair; more	more; for what's left of
makkin	making
mavis	song thrush
mebbe	maybe
messages	groceries, shopping
moich	crazy
nattering	idly chatting
neep	turnip
never	not
night, the	tonight
noo, the	just now
nor	or
nothing	anything
o'; on(d)	of; on; about
o'er, ower	over
on'y	only
onything	anything
oxter	under part of upper arm; support with under-arm
pad	narrow leg of the path
peat	turf block used as fuel
piece	spread slice of bread, sandwich
puckle	small amount of
raiked	searched thoroughly through
reek	smoke
rummle	shake vigorously
run	ran
's	is
scart't	scratched
scraped an scratched	tried to get work
selkie	seal-person; *from* selch (seal)
set sail	set off travelling, walking
shaken	shook
shelfie	chaffinch
shot, a	a 'turn'
sing-songs	singing parties
sit, sut	sat

skelp	smack
smiddy, -ie	smithie
snotem	iron crook for hanging pots over the fire
sort	repair, fix up
speak to	trouble; attend to
sprachled	clambered
sput	spat
stone-dyking	dry-stone dyke building
strae	straw
sweerin	reluctant, unwilling
sweeties	candy
swey	movable iron bar over the fire
swinged	whined
taen-awa	baby taken over with the fairies
taste, a	a very small amount
tatties	potatoes
thae	those
theirsel	themselves
the're	there's
think	presume, expect
this	these
thon	that; those
tile hat	top hat
tin	articles of tin
tinker	nomadic tinsmith or metal worker; also, used contemptuously for one of the Scottish Travelling People (travellers)
tooken	taken
top, the	on the top
tottery	messy, unkempt
touch	harm, interfere with
traveller	one of the Scottish Travelling People
twa	two
two–three	a few
universt between us	united our efforts
wag-at-the-wa clock	pendulum wall clock
wapped	wrapped, folded
warran'	warrant
wean	wee one, young child
wearying	longing
well on	under the influence of alcohol
whar	where
wheesht	be quiet!
wi	with; by
wonst	once
yese, youse	you
yin	one
yon	those
you may care	it's hopeless